P9-DCY-594

Just Haven't Met You Yet

ALSO BY SOPHIE COUSENS

This Time Next Year

Just Haven't Met You Yet

SOPHIE COUSENS

G. P. PUTNAM'S SONS
NEW YORK

PUTNAM
— EST. 1838 —

G. P. PUTNAM'S SONS
Publishers Since 1838
An imprint of Penguin Random House LLC
penguinrandomhouse.com

Copyright © 2021 by Sophie Cousens
This edition published by arrangement with G. P. Putnam's Sons,
a division of Penguin Random House LLC.
First published in Great Britain by Arrow Books,
an imprint of Cornerstone. Cornerstone is part of the Penguin
Random House group of companies, 2021.

Penguin supports copyright. Copyright fuels creativity, encourages diverse voices, promotes free speech, and creates a vibrant culture. Thank you for buying an authorized edition of this book and for complying with copyright laws by not reproducing, scanning, or distributing any part of it in any form without permission. You are supporting writers and allowing Penguin to continue to publish books for every reader.

Library of Congress Cataloging-in-Publication Data

Names: Cousens, Sophie, author.
Title: Just haven't met you yet / Sophie Cousens.
Other titles: Just have not met you yet
Description: New York : G. P. Putnam's Sons, 2021. |
Identifiers: LCCN 2021034290 (print) | LCCN 2021034291 (ebook) |
ISBN 9780593331521 trade paperback | ISBN 9780593331538 (ebook)
Subjects: GSAFD: Love stories.
Classification: LCC PR6103.O933 J87 2021 (print) |
LCC PR6103.O933 (ebook) | DDC 823/.92—dc23
LC record available at https://lccn.loc.gov/2021034290
LC ebook record available at https://lccn.loc.gov/2021034291
p. cm.

Printed in the United States of America
1st Printing

Book design by Tiffany Estreicher

This is a work of fiction. Names, characters, places, and incidents either are the product of the author's imagination or are used fictitiously, and any resemblance to actual persons, living or dead, businesses, companies, events, or locales is entirely coincidental.

For Natalie, an exceptional friend
and a wonderful human

N
W
E
S
PLÉMONT HEADLAND
PLÉMONT BAY
GRÈVE DE LECQ
St. John
Maison D'Oie
L'Etacq
St. Mary
Surf here
Sans Ennui
St. Ouen
St. Peter
ST. OUEN'S BAY
St. Lawrence
ST. AUBINS BAY
St. Brelade
BEAUPORT
ST. BRELADE'S
PORTELET BAY

Jersey
I'm on top of the cheese!
BONNE NUIT
TRINITY
FETE
BOULEY BAY
ROZEL BAY
THE HUNGRY MAN
JAM
MILK
Trinity
St. Martin
ÉCRÉHOUS
Mill Manor
St. Saviour
St. Helier
THE WEIGHBRIDGE
Grouville
St. Clement
oysters here
LA ROCQUE HARBOUR

Just Haven't Met You Yet

The whole world is divided for me into two parts; one is she, and there is all happiness, hope, light; the other is where she is not, and there is dejection and darkness . . .

—Leo Tolstoy, *War and Peace*

Chapter 1

"Shall we begin?" I ask the couple on the sofa. "If you just tell me your story as naturally as possible, and remember to keep your eyeline to me rather than looking directly at the camera."

Sian and Paul both smile and nod. She is a redhead with neatly drawn makeup. He is a bodybuilder type with a jaw square enough to put him in a Marvel comic. While the cameraman, Dylan, makes a few final lighting adjustments, Paul whispers something in Sian's ear, gently stroking her knee with the back of his hand. In the small studio, I am close enough to see the skin on her leg rise into goose bumps. When was the last time another person's touch gave me goose bumps? *Seriously, when?* I literally can't think of a time, unless you count two weeks ago, when someone barged into me holding a frozen chicken in the freezer aisle at the supermarket.

"All set," Dylan says, and the light on his camera stops flashing and settles to a constant red.

"So, Paul, Sian, tell me—how did you meet?" I ask. It is the question I start all these interviews with.

"Well, it's a little embarrassing," says Sian, pressing her fingertips to her lips like a fifties pinup girl. "I was criminally drunk after a friend's hen do, and when I got back to my flat in the early hours, I had the silly idea of making popcorn on the stove. Of course, I then forgot all about it and passed out on my bed."

"We got a call from a flat across the road, saying someone's kitchen was on fire," says Paul. "I'm a firefighter, see."

"I think they can see that, honey." Sian smiles, framing his torso with her hands to show off the fireman's outfit I asked him to wear for the interview. I don't know how he isn't boiling alive under all those layers. The studio is tiny and windowless; it's a single-camera setup with just a couple of studio lights, our distinctive red sofa, and the Love Life logo prominent on the wall behind. The lights heat the room up fast, but Paul and Sian still look like freshly unboxed Barbie and Action Man. Maybe it's only me who's feeling hot and flustered.

"I was oblivious to any of this." Sian laughs.

"I had to kick the door down, put the fire out, and rescue the damsel in distress," Paul says, turning to give the camera a brooding pout.

"Only I didn't think I needed rescuing. I was still a little hazy after too many gin slings." She gives me a wink.

"I had to carry her out over my shoulder—"

"A proper fireman's lift—I was kicking and screaming all the way down the fire escape."

"I got bruises," he says, eyebrows knitting together in mock hurt.

"I'm sorry, honey." She kisses him on the cheek, he squeezes her knee, and they give each other a love-soaked look. I can practically hear the crackle of electricity between them.

If you put "hot fireman to get rescued by" into Google, I'm pretty sure a photo of Paul would come up. If I were to ever set my kitchen on fire, I guarantee, it would be a scary schoolmarm-type firewoman coming to save me. Someone who would give me a stern lecture on smoke alarm maintenance. As I look at Sian and Paul gazing into each other's eyes, I'm torn between being super happy that they found each other and just a tiny bit jealous that these situations never seem to happen to me.

"So, we sent Sian to hospital to get checked for smoke inhalation, standard procedure," Paul goes on, "and once my shift ended, I figured I'd go check how she was doing."

"Do you do that for everyone you rescue?" I ask, turning to give the camera my best knowing look.

"Well, she might have stuck in my memory more than most." He lifts his hand to stroke a tendril of her wavy, red hair. "This is one flame I never want to put out."

"Awww . . ." I say, feeling a genuine pang of emotion at their evident connection. Our viewers are going to love this guy—body of iron, heart of a marshmallow.

"He came to see me in the hospital," she says, fluttering her eyelashes, "but I'd sobered up by then. I was worried where my cat had got to in the fire, so I sneaked out before being properly discharged."

"We were in the same lift before I realized it was her." He's started caressing her leg again.

"Then the lift goes and breaks—would you believe it?" Sian sighs, nuzzling into his shoulder. "Forty-five minutes later, I was in love."

"It only took me ten minutes to know she was the girl I wanted to spend the rest of my life talking to."

How many times have I been in a lift in my lifetime? Probably four hundred. OK, that was a complete guess, I've got no idea how many times I've been in a lift. But it's a lot, and not once have I been in one that's broken down, and I've certainly never been trapped in one with a remotely eligible guy. Maybe the part of the universe that is in charge of meet-cutes also has jurisdiction over lift malfunctions.

"Sweetie," Sian whispers as she tilts her face toward him.

They kiss for the camera, and it's not a demure, other-people-are-in-the-room kind of kiss; it's a proper let's-race-home-and-rip-each-other's-clothes-off kiss. I bet she gets him to wear his fireman's outfit in bed. I shake my head, trying to stop my mind from wandering down these inappropriate thought alleys. But then I look back up and she's nibbling his earlobe.

Maybe it was easier to do these interviews when I wasn't single. My ex, David, and I weren't exactly having goose bumps–inducing sex, but clearly it was enough to stop me from feeling jealous when faced with crazily loved-up couples.

What if I never find a connection like these two have? The thought brings a lump to my throat. Everyone assumes single girls approaching thirty spend their time stressing about whether they'll ever get to have a wedding or a baby. But for me, I'm more concerned that I'll never know what it feels like to have that kind of life-altering connection with someone, and that I'll never get to experience sex like they have in the movies. I know,

I know, movie sex isn't real—it's all choreographed and everyone orgasms together, like a perfectly conducted orchestra, but surely *someone* must be having mind-blowing sex like they do in *The Notebook*. These guys, *these guys* are having sex like that.

"Don't try this at home, people," I say, turning to the camera with my most cheerful not-thinking-about-sex-voice. "We don't advise burning your house down to find your perfect partner. Ha-ha. If you've got a great story of how you met and would like to feature on *How Did You Meet?* please get in touch via the website. We love hearing your amazing real-life love stories! I'm Laura Le Quesne, reporting for Love Life—'Love what you buy, buy what you love.'"

I look over at Dylan to signal it's a cut, then jump up to open the door and let in some cooler air. We hire the studio and all the equipment by the hour, so I need to be mindful of the amount of takes we do.

"Guys, that was perfect, you were brilliant, adorable," I say, then scrunch my eyes closed in frustration. "Oh wait, I forgot to ask about the cat. Was the cat OK?"

Silence for a moment, and Sian lets go of Paul's hand.

"No, well . . ." She hugs her arms around herself. "It turned out Paul's fire truck ran Felicia over. She had to be put down."

Paul squeezes Sian's shoulder and shakes his head.

"Oh—I'm so sorry," I say, mirroring their sad body language. "Well, I think maybe it's best we leave that detail out—might be a bit of a buzzkill for our viewers."

Sian flinches ever so slightly. It looks like I've killed the sexy mood by mentioning the dead cat, and now they're not going to rush home and rip each other's clothes off. No sex for anyone! Woo-hoo!

What is wrong with me? I'm a horrible person.

I have three more interviews scheduled that morning: a couple from Liverpool who met sheltering from a lightning storm (they called their first child Light Ning Jones—seriously), a couple from North London born in the same hospital on the same day who reconnected and fell in love thirty years later (what are the chances?), and a couple from Nottingham who met as cancer patients on the same ward. Their oncology doctor was the maid of honor at their wedding.

By the end of the morning, I am emotionally drained. When the cancer woman says, "I might have lost all my hair in that hospital, but I found my heart," I let out a sob so loud I have to ask her to say it again two more times so we can get a clean take.

Don't get me wrong, I love these stories. "How did you meet?" is my all-time favorite question—the first thing I ask anyone in a relationship. I love hearing how people's paths have crossed in seemingly random ways, and how that chance encounter has affected the direction of their lives so profoundly. I'm your classic hopeless romantic. And yet recently, perhaps since losing Mum, I've been finding it harder to witness other people's "happily ever afters."

Maybe it was easier to be happy for other people when I felt my own soulmate might be just around the corner, but I keep turning corners, and no one is ever there.

Once we've wrapped filming, I walk through Soho on my way back to the office and pass the alleyway off Carnaby Street where Vera's Vintage, a grotto of secondhand clothes and jewelry, is tucked away. I haven't been inside a shop like this since Mum died, but today I find myself standing in front of the window, peering into the Aladdin's cave within.

When I was a child, Mum and I spent every weekend driving around the country in her worn-out Morris Minor, following a trail of flea markets and vintage fairs. She could scour a car-boot sale for treasure better than anyone; she had a magpie's eyes. Mum used to tell me that objects hold memories. That the more owners an object had had, the more meaning that object possessed. If what she said was true, her drawers and cupboards had been stuffed full of more meaning than anywhere else in the known universe.

She collected old jewelry to repurpose it, to give it new life. It started out as a hobby, but then she found people wanted to buy what she was making. Her jewelry was the one thing I didn't know what to do with when I packed up her house. I'm still paying forty pounds a month to keep the boxes in a storage locker in Wapping; a tax on deferred decisions. I press my hand against the shop window. Just looking at the treasures on display sends a skewer of pain into the everyday ache of missing her.

At the front of the shop window, near my hand, a ruby brooch—a beautiful stone in a weathered silver setting, the trace of writing just visible. I feel a flutter of excitement; is there anything more romantic than an old engraving? I imagine those scratched letters to be a clue, waiting for me to unravel the story they hold, just like the coin I've worn around my neck since I was fifteen. My hand reaches up to the pendant, the place my hand always goes to when I'm thinking about Mum. As I'm inventing a romantic backstory for the ruby brooch in the window, a man in a long camel coat leaves the shop. He drops something, a piece of paper, so I pick it up and call after him.

"Excuse me, you dropped this."

He turns around and looks me square in the eyes. He's in his thirties with salt-and-pepper hair, deep-set eyes, and a regal nose. He's attractive, in a Roman emperor sort of way. And for some reason, maybe it's the emotional morning I've had, or the fact that I'm thinking about Mum, but I just get a feeling that maybe this could be the beginning of *my* "How did you meet?" Sexy Caesar drops a receipt, I pick it up, we get to talking about vintage jewelry, stare into each other's eyes, and then *kablammo*, we just know: This is it; we've *finally* found each other.

"What?" he says.

"You dropped this." I reach out my hand to give him the piece of paper, tucking a strand of blond hair behind my ear and furnishing him with my warmest smile.

"I don't need it." He waves a dismissive hand at me and turns to go.

"Hey, wait," I call after him. "You can't just drop paper in the street."

The man stops, turns, and scowls at me, as though I'm a small dog that's just peed on his gray suede loafers.

"Who are you, the street police?" he asks, shaking his head as he turns to leave.

"If everyone dropped their receipts, then where would we be? We'd be ankle-deep in old receipts, that's where!" I call after him, still inexplicably waving the piece of paper in the air as though I've found one of Willy Wonka's golden tickets.

"Piss off, litter witch," he calls over his shoulder. I let out an indignant puff of air. OK, maybe that wasn't my "How did you meet?" after all. I've probably dodged a bullet, anyway. He might have been good-looking, but I wouldn't want the love of my life to be a litterbug.

Jersey Evening News—23 May 1991

FOUND: Half a ha' penny, with "Jersey, '37" just legible on the reverse. Inscribed on the face are the words: "the whole world is for me divided . . ." Seeking information about the origins of this coin. Are you or your family in possession of the other half? It may be inscribed with the words, ". . . into two parts." Any information, please contact Annie; Bristol PO BOX 1224.

Chapter 2

Pushing through the double doors on the third floor of the Beak Street building, I can see Suki already holding court in the glass-walled meeting room. A dozen of my colleagues sit in two neat rows listening with rapt attention. Editor in chief of Love Life, Suki Cavendish is a slim four foot eleven with a keen aversion to heels, yet she always manages to be the most prepossessing person in any room. Today she is dressed in a tailored cream jumpsuit with her black hair pulled into a taut chignon.

Carefully opening the glass door of the meeting room, I creep to the only free seat left, right at the front. The only thing Suki hates more than lateness is "freegans who shun consumer society." I'm only two minutes late, but Suki stops talking and everyone turns to look at me. My friend and flatmate, Vanya, shoots me a sympathetic look from the end of the row.

"Nice of you to join us, Laura," Suki says, one eyebrow darting up her forehead. "Since you're already standing, perhaps you can help me today?"

Oh great—I'm in the hot seat. Suki likes to punctuate her monthly roundups with a Q&A full of impossible rhetorical questions. It's like being on a game show that you can never win.

"What are we doing here, Laura?" Suki's lips pout in my direction, like a cannon preparing to fire.

"Having a meeting?"

Everyone laughs, which makes me even more nervous. I wasn't trying to be funny; Suki does not like funny.

"No, what are we *doing* here?" Suki glares at me, lifting her hand up to indicate I should stay standing while I'm in the hot seat.

Though Suki is short, she refuses to raise her eye level to look at people taller than her. I once heard her tell a male client that she didn't see why she should give herself a neck ache—if people want to look her in the eye, they can come down to her level. As a result, when you speak to her, you find yourself hovering in a crouch position. Vanya swears that she once saw Suki have a meeting with a particularly tall IT guy on his knees.

"Do we all show up at this office for fun?" Suki asks. "Are we here designing blueprints for atomic submarines? What are we *doing*, Laura?"

"Um, working for one of the top lifestyle platforms in the UK?" Yes! I remembered to call it a lifestyle platform. Suki doesn't like it being referred to as a website; she thinks it's reductive. Love Life started out as purely interiors but now covers everything from real life stories to beauty products and travel.

"We are selling a dream—that is what we are doing," says Suki, clapping her hands together. "We are showing people the life they want—the enviable love stories, the perfectly designed breakfast bar, the expensive mini break to Paris that might save their relationship. We suck people in with a dream, and we send them away with . . . Laura?"

"Hope?" I try. Suki stares at my chin unblinking. "Style tips? Um, a smile?" I crouch down a little lower. My glute muscles have gotten so much stronger in the four years I've been working here. "Hope?" Damn it, I think I said *hope* already.

Straight out of university, I worked for a music magazine. I'd have to wait backstage after gigs to try and bag interviews with bands. I learned how to thrust myself forward, find just the right question for musicians who had little time for me. I only lasted nine months before my editor tired of my "retro taste in music" and replaced me with a nineteen-year-old synth metal fan, but it was long enough to learn how to think on my feet and to swallow my nerves. Yet here, regardless of competence, something about Suki renders most of us incapable of forming intelligent sentences.

"We send them away with *stuff,* Laura. Suck them in with dreams, grab them with targeted ads, and send them away with stuff! Our followers might not have perfect lives, but they can have a new luxury mattress, a stylish holiday, the exact bronze light fitting that Kylie Minogue has in her Melbourne kitchen-cum-diner. With our help, they can buy a fragment of perfection."

I nod, holding my chin between thumb and forefinger, attempting to look as though I'm studiously digesting Suki's wisdom. Personally, I feel the world could do with a little less stuff, but no one's going to pay me to peddle my "reuse, recycle" philosophy in this room. I have a staff job here, which, as a journalist, is almost impossible to come by. So, I count myself lucky and try to keep my head and my eyeline down.

"And so, we find ourselves with a problem." Suki turns her attention back to the room and resumes pacing slowly as she talks. "In the current climate, no one wants to buy *stuff*. People are learning they can live with less. They can work less, earn less, buy less, do less, travel less—talk more, read more, enjoy the little things, the *free* things. Do they need another handbag, another outfit, another upgrade to their phone? Do they need sushi delivered at eleven p.m., Jazzercise classes, and BB cream for the cellulite no one ever sees? Do they, Laura?"

"Quite," I say, nodding solemnly. Ha! I can't be wrong if I say *quite*.

An invisible fishhook pulls at the edge of Suki's lip before she whips her face back around to face the room.

"So, where does that leave us, as purveyors of stuff?" Suki slaps the wall, rounding off her oratory frenzy. "What do people want when life gets tough?"

Her eyes dart back to me.

"Um, sex?"

Everyone laughs. I have sex on the brain today. I blame the hot fireman and feisty redhead.

"Love," Suki corrects me. "Love is what makes people feel good when the world outside feels bleak. Our *How Did You Meet?* and proposal pages are consistently the most clicked-on sections of the site. If we can lure in the numbers with love, we might just be able to keep the product partnerships paying all our wages."

Suki takes a pen from the table and starts scribbling on the white board behind her, the pen squeaking like a mouse being garroted. She writes, *Love = Views, Views = Sales, Sales = Jobs.*

"We need clicks. We need content that warms people's hearts." Her voice takes on a somber tone. "The reality is, if site traffic is down again this month, we won't be able to sustain a team of this size." Murmurs of concern circle the room; people glance at one another nervously. We already lost three colleagues in January. Suki's face softens, her eyes full of compassion as she holds out her hands to the room. "And you know you are all like family to me."

Her ability to flit from tyrannical to faux maternal in the space of a sentence is disturbing.

"So, what unmissable content have you got for me—Vanya?" Suki releases me from standing with a finger click, and my glute muscles sing in relief. Now it's Vanya's turn, and I know for a fact she was out on a Tinder date until three a.m. last night and that she has a killer hangover to show for it. Vee and I rent a place together near Queen's Park. I put in a good word for her here last year after the literary journal she worked for went under. There are only a few people I could embrace into both my home and my work life, but Vee is definitely one of them.

"Well, I had a couple of article ideas." Beads of sweat dot Vanya's upper lip, and her usually smooth black bob has sprung into frizz on one side. Suki clicks her fingers, indicating she should fire off her ideas. "Bed linen to save your marriage."

Suki shakes her head. "Kitchen appliances you didn't know you needed." Silence. "Working-from-home wardrobes of the rich and famous." Suki grimaces. Vanya's voice gets thinner; she pulls her arms up into her sleeves as though trying to hide inside her top. "Top ten lipstick shades to make your face look younger, happier . . . wiser?"

"Thank you, Vanya," Suki says in her "quiet, disappointed" voice. "Byron? Do you have anything substantial to share?"

"Well—I, er—I have a story that could work for Laura's *How Did You Meet?* segment," Byron says, pressing his gray mustache between thumb and forefinger as he stands up. "An elderly couple who met at a funeral home. They were both burying their other halves, and it's a funny story because—"

"There is nothing sexy about funeral homes, Byron—let's keep things young and lively, yes. No one likes reading about old people." Suki claps her hands.

"Laura, tell me you have something original. What happened to that *When Harry Met Sally . . .* story you pitched the other week?"

"Ah yes, the couple in America who met on a road trip who are genuinely called Harry and Sally."

"I liked the sound of that," Suki presses her hands together.

My throat suddenly feels painfully dry.

"I'm afraid when I looked into it in a bit more detail, well—Sally was trafficking drugs in that car, and she's now serving time. She and Harry are still together, though, so that's nice."

"No, no, no." Suki throws her hands in the air. "No old people, no felonies. And, Paula, before you tell us again about the hot cousin you met at a family barbecue, *no* incest. We need heartwarming, original content. Personal stories that no one else is covering."

I have nothing. My hand reaches for my pendant. Suki's voice softens again, her face an expression of pained pity. "Come on, darlings, help me here."

"There is one love story I could write." I start speaking before I can overthink it. "My parents' story."

Suki stares at me unblinking, so I take her silence as an invitation to elaborate and swallow the discomfort in my throat. I've never thought to pitch their story before. All our *How Did You Meet?*s usually take the form of an interview—but now, I wonder if that needs to be the case.

"My mother found half an old ha'penny at an antiques fair. The face had been smoothed flat, engraved with a quote, and then cut in two to make a love token—"

"How old is your mother?" Suki interrupts.

"She, um, she died, if you remember, two years ago . . . I took that time off." I clench my fingers into my palms, and Suki winds her finger in the air, as though fast-forwarding the tape of my explanation. I catch Vanya's eye across the room; she gives me a reassuring thumbs-up. "Anyway, she found this piece of coin and saw it had *Jersey* written on the back, so she placed an advert in the Jersey paper hoping she might track down the other half. My dad replied. He explained that his grandfather had engraved the coin with this quote, then split it in two before leaving for the war. He took one half with him and left the other half with his wife. Sadly, he never came home, and history doesn't relate how his half ended up in Bristol." I unfasten the coin from around my neck and pass it around the room for people to see. "My mum took the half she found to Jersey, reunited the pieces, met my dad, and the rest, as they say, is history. One coin, two love stories."

The room oohs and aahs in delight at my tale.

"It is so freakin' romantic," says Vanya loyally. "I can totally see it as a Hallmark movie."

I can't tell from Suki's face whether she loves the idea or hates it.

"Even though my parents aren't alive to interview, I know the story of how they fell in love as if it were my own. It's the most romantic *How Did You Meet?* I know—"

"Fine. Write the story," Suki says, waving a hand to stop me talking. "But you should go to Jersey. I want a personal angle, some scenic photos, interview this great-grandmother." I'm shocked. Suki never signs off on travel.

"I'm afraid she's no longer alive," I say with a grimace.

"Why is everyone in your family dead, Laura?"

I shrug. Suki makes so many tactless remarks, somehow the sting becomes diluted.

"Well, she would have been over a hundred if she was alive"—Suki's attention begins to drift, so I speak more quickly—"but the island itself is very much a character in their story. It's where they fell in love: the beautiful beaches, the romantic cliff-top walks—"

Suki raises a finger to the ceiling, like an insect sensing something with its antennae.

"You can bang out a travel piece while you're there, 'Reasons to Visit the Channel Islands' or something. We have a travel insurance firm looking to sponsor an article—and I'm sure you can find a hotel who'll put you up for a mention."

Suki clicks her fingers with satisfaction, then pauses before waving her arm across the room. "All of you, bring me fresh content ideas, otherwise, next time we're sitting here, there'll be fewer chairs in the room—and by that, I do not mean some of you will be sitting on the floor."

Despite the meeting ending on this threatening note, I leave the room feeling elated. I took a chance, pitched a story that means everything to me, and Suki actually went for it. If I'd had time to think it through, I'm not sure I would have had the courage to offer up something so personal. Now, I am going to Jersey, to the place my parents fell in love, where the idea of me was born, and I feel something bubble inside me I haven't felt in a while: excitement.

Chapter 3

Two days later, and my friend Dee has volunteered to drive me to the airport. She recently bought a car because she and her fiancé, Neil, are moving to Farnham and apparently you need a car if you live outside London. She says she needs the driving practice, and before we even get to the end of her road, it becomes very clear that she does.

Vanya is tagging along for the ride, mainly because she doesn't own a car and saw the opportunity to persuade Dee to drive back via the out-of-town IKEA. I'm worried what she's planning to buy for our tiny, already-full-of-unbuilt-furniture-from-her-last-visit flat.

"I can't believe Suki signed off on a three-day trip, you are so jammy," says Vanya from the backseat, thrusting an open bag of Haribo Giant Strawbs between Dee and me. It's less than an hour's drive to Gatwick Airport, but Vanya's come with enough car sweets to take us to Mexico.

"Only because she got a sponsor to pay for it," I say, taking a handful of sweets. "I wish you were both coming with me, it would be much more fun."

"You know, I have this weird intuition you're going to meet someone while you're away," says Vanya.

"Is this the same intuition that told you I wouldn't get a parking ticket if I pulled up on a double yellow line to drop you off outside Selfridges?" asks Dee, waving her left hand for someone to pass her a sweet.

"Yeah, well." Vanya clears her throat. "I'd say my intuition is more finely attuned to love than parking wardens."

"I wish you wouldn't perpetuate these ridiculous notions," Dee scoffs.

"What notions?" I ask.

"About love and relationships having anything to do with destiny."

I've known Dee since we were children; we met at age eleven, in the girls' bathroom on the first day of school. She had a long black fringe covering half her eyes and wore this serious expression. She grabbed me by the elbow as I was leaving the loo. I thought she was about to steal my lunch money, but she pulled me close and told me I had the back of my skirt tucked into my knickers. She saved me from humiliating myself in front of my new classmates, and she's had my back ever since.

Dee exhales loudly through her nose and shifts into fifth gear with a *clunk* as we merge onto the motorway.

"Look, I'm going to say something controversial now, OK?" she says.

"Brexit was a good idea? Brad Pitt hasn't aged well? You think we should all take up smoking again?" I give her a goofy smile as I try to think of what else might qualify as a controversial statement.

"No. I don't think you should have broken up with David."

I shake my head, and Vanya makes a *prrrrft* sound from the backseat.

"David wasn't the one, Dee. He was lovely, but you know—"

"No, I don't know. I don't know what it is you're holding out for. David was decent and kind." Dee glances across at me, her eyebrows knitted in concern. "I just want you to be happy, to have someone to share your life with."

"I have you guys!"

"Yeah, but Neil and I are leaving London in a few months." Dee sighs. "And Vanya. Well, Vanya is a bad influence."

"I'm not a bad influence—I'm the fun one!" Vanya says, raising her arms above her head to do a seat dance, as though this will illustrate just how fun she is. To be fair, Vanya is the fun one. On a night out, she will be the person to suggest getting shots at two a.m., but it will be Dee who holds your hair back when you're throwing up in the loo later.

"I worry with all the stuff you're doing for the website, seeking out these crazily romantic tales. Plus, with your parents' story"—Dee nods to my hand, which is toying with my pendant again—"it's made your expectations a little . . . unrealistic."

"Look, I wouldn't say I'm being especially picky. I know what I want and I don't feel like I should have to settle for less."

"And what exactly is it that you want?"

"I'll know it when I see it," I say. Dee raises a skeptical eyebrow. "Well, if you forced me to write a list, I'd want a man who is kind, charming, well dressed, well read, ideally musical, someone who likes the same things as me, no one too complicated. Is that really too much to ask?"

"On dating apps, it is," says Vanya.

Dee reaches a hand across the car to squeeze mine. "I think you have to start factoring in the statistics."

As teenagers, while I had posters of Busted and the Pussycat Dolls above my bed, Dee decorated her walls with the periodic table and a photo of Albert Einstein. She's the Monica to my Rachel, but it works and I've often been the beneficiary of her practical nature. When Mum died, Dee was the one who kept me upright when all I wanted to do was lie down and sink into grief. She ordered the funeral flowers because I couldn't get the words out over the phone; she moved in with me for a month because I didn't want to be alone. She was my Ariadne's thread, leading me out of a dark labyrinth. But now, two years later, I still catch her looking as me as though I might break at any moment. I yearn for our old dynamic, where we were equals and I wasn't the frailer half who needed parenting by a friend.

"Dee, I know I'm talking to a math teacher here, but not everything in life boils down to math," I say, with a smile.

"You have to believe in a little magic when it comes to matters of the heart," says Vanya.

Dee rolls her eyes.

"A: Everything does boil down to math, that's the beauty of math. And B: Not everyone gets some Hollywood-style meet-cute. I don't want to be the harbinger of doom, but the number of eligible guys over thirty is only going to get smaller. If you play the field for too long, only the divorcés and weirdos will be left."

"What about me? I'm single," says Vanya indignantly.

"You love the weirdos. You actively seek out the weirdos."

"That's true," says Vanya, pulling down her red beanie hat and drumming out a tune on the back of Dee's seat with her fingers.

"Look, all I know is, if I can't have a love story like my parents had—world stops turning, soulmate kind of love—then I'd rather be on my own." I pause, weighing my words, anxious not to offend my oldest friend. "And, you know, Dee, I'm not a baton you have to pass on. I'm not going to fall to pieces if I'm on my own for a bit."

"It's not that, Laura, of course it's not that. I didn't mean to suggest you need to have a man in your life. All I'm saying is, I thought David made you happy—*happier.*" Her lips twitch into a smile. "I just don't want you holding out for something that doesn't exist. These couples you interview for the site—you should go back and talk to them in six months when the oxytocin has worn off and they're arguing about how he leaves his sweaty running gear loose in the laundry bin and stinks out the whole damn bathroom."

"You're really selling married life to us, Dee," says Vanya.

Dee ignores her and shoots me a wide-eyed look, clearly worried she's caused offense.

"And you're not a baton I'm trying to palm off. Even if you met Prince bloody Charming and rode off into the sunset, I would never let go of this baton." She points a finger back and forth between us.

"I know. Me too," I say, feeling a gush of love for this woman.

"Right, anyway, I've said my piece." Dee blinks. "This conversation isn't passing the Bechdel test, so let's talk about something else."

Dee is obsessed with the Bechdel test. It's a checklist used to see whether women are being represented as well-rounded characters in fiction or film. Essentially, to pass the test, two female characters have to have a conversation about something other than men. On feminist principle, Dee won't watch or read anything that doesn't pass.

"Is us talking about the Bechdel test enough for us to pass the Bechdel test?" Vanya asks, pulling on her seatbelt strap and leaning forward between our seats.

"I don't know," Dee says, looking genuinely perplexed.

"Well, I have some non-man-themed news," Vanya says, pausing until she has our full attention. "I got my mortgage approved." She bites her lip and then squeals with excitement.

"That's wonderful," says Dee.

"Wow," I say, clapping my hands, but feeling my stomach churn. That means she's really moving out. "I'm so happy for you."

"Thank you. And don't worry, Laura, I won't be going anywhere until at least December, you'll have loads of time to find the new me."

Four months. Dee will be married and living in Surrey, and Vanya will own a flat in Hackney. Everyone is moving on, without me.

"Oh, and I have a present for your trip," Vanya says, handing me a paperback with an orange-and-black-striped cover.

"*Tiger Woman* by Bee Bee Graceful" is written in bold gold lettering across the front. "We're reading it for my book club. It's going to change your life."

She is always recommending me books that are going to "change my life."

"What kind of a name is 'Bee Bee Graceful'?" I ask.

"It must be a pseudonym. I don't think anyone knows who Tiger Woman really is, it's the biggest literary mystery since Elena Ferrante. Honestly, you need to read, it will help you re-harness your inner tigress, take control of your destiny."

Dee shakes her head but doesn't comment.

When we finally pull into departures at Gatwick, I feel a bit sick after Dee's swervy driving and all the Haribos I've eaten. Vanya and Dee both get out of the car to hug me good-bye.

"Don't forget to feed the fish," I tell Vanya, as I pull my black carry-on from the trunk. We don't have fish, it's just something we say to each other. "And thank you for driving me, Dee, I really appreciate it."

Dee takes hold of my hand and looks me straight in the eyes before saying, "I love you. Call me whenever you need to. I know this trip might be emotional for you."

I feel my throat tighten, but give her a grateful smile, then turn to walk toward the airport doors.

"And, Laura! Laura!" Vanya calls my name until I turn around. Then she presses a hand across her heart and yells, "Keep the faith. He's out there—you just haven't met him yet."

Chapter 4

Looking up at the departures board, I scan the place names and find my flight to Jersey. The word alone has so many connotations for me. I can't hear it without thinking of my parents' story, the prologue to my existence. Is it strange to feel nostalgia for a place I've never been? Mum used to say we'd go together one day, but she was always juggling so much and there was never a good time.

Now that I'm undistracted by my friends, I begin to worry how unprepared I am for this weekend. Suki insisted I go straightaway, so we could get the travel article up on the site next week. The sponsor liked the idea of promoting a "September sun getaway." I don't have a firm angle yet, though, and I haven't managed to map out what I need to make the coin story work, to make it "feel contemporary."

With everything being so rushed, I also haven't had time to dwell on how I feel about going on this trip. Will stepping into the footprint of my parents' story bring me closer to them, or am I just going to find it upsetting?

My mother is still so tangible to me. We shared a lifetime of memories, and my grief for her is still so ragged it gives her solid edges—I can conjure her voice in a quiet room. I can picture the way she would open her arms to hug me when I walked through the front door. When I pass the rooibos tea at the supermarket, I see her slim frame standing by the kettle, jiggling a tea bag up and down by the string.

With Dad it's different. He died when I was three, so I don't remember him. I only have a few things left that link him to me: the coin, of course, then there are several photos, his old watch that I never take off, a library of his favorite books, and his treasured LP collection. When I was sixteen, I spent all my pocket money on a record player so I could listen to his music just as he had. I'm probably the only twenty-nine-year-old in the world today whose favorite bands are Genesis and Dire Straits.

There is too much of Mum to ever be condensed into a box full of things, but all I have of Dad are secondhand memories and these objects he left me. If I let go of what he treasured, I worry his blurred edges will fade until there is nothing left of him at all.

A woman bumps into me, her apology breaks my reverie, and I realize I've been standing, staring at the departures board for a good ten minutes. Now I must run so as not to be late.

It is less than an hour-long flight to the small island off the north coast of France. I'm traveling with hand luggage, but at the gate a man tells me, "Madam, we're going to have to ask that you put your bag in the hold." I feel myself bristle. When had I become *Madam* rather than *Miss*?

"It's definitely regulation size," I protest. "I actually bought this case specifically because it adheres to the dimensions on your website . . ."

"I know, ma'am, but we have a very full flight today, so we're asking people to check wheeled cases into the hold. There's no charge; you'll get it back as soon as you land."

The man gives me an insincere grin that puckers his smooth, perma-tanned skin. Obediently, I shuffle out of the queue to open my case and extract what I need for the flight. I take out my mother's Jersey photo album—too precious to stow in the hold—and *Tiger Woman*, so I have something to read on the plane. Just as I'm trying to close my case, someone bumps me from behind, and my open toiletries bag flies into the air. A value pack of fifty non-applicator tampons hits the ground and explodes across the lounge in a spray of white bullets. My cheeks burn as I fall to my hands and knees to retrieve them. The man who bumped me bends down to help. Why did I bring so many tampons with me for one weekend away? I'm on my fourth day; I should have just decanted the amount I was going to need. *Always decant, woman!*

"I'm sorry, that was my fault," says the man.

I turn to look at him, glance away, and then look back, as I realize I'm looking at the most handsome man I think I've ever seen in real life. He has soft brown hair; green eyes; a tall, broad-shouldered physique; and the kind of well-sculpted face that commands attention. He is wearing blue suit trousers and a crisp white shirt unbuttoned at the collar. Our eyes meet, and he holds my gaze. His easy smile suggests someone who thinks the world a wonderful place, which no doubt it is when you look like him.

"I was in the way," I say, shaking my head and wiping my mouth with the back of my hand. Am I drooling? I think I genuinely just drooled. *Well done, Laura, Beethoven the slobbering Saint Bernard is a really sexy look.*

I try to retrieve the stray tampons as quickly as I can. Of all the things that had to fly out of my bag, it had to be the tampons, didn't it? The lounge must be on a slight slope, because the seemingly never-ending supply are now rolling down the aisle. I scurry around on my hands and knees, doing my best to fish the strays from beneath people's feet as they carry on reading their newspapers, too British to acknowledge that sanitary products are being flagrantly bandied about in public.

"Sorry, sorry," I mutter.

When I stand up again, I see the beautiful man standing with a fistful of tampons he has helped to retrieve.

"I think we got them all," he says with a dimpled grin.

Hardly daring to look at him, I take them and stuff them straight into my handbag. My forehead feels damp with sweat, my cheeks burn. Clocking my embarrassment, he says quietly, "Don't worry, I have sisters."

I give him a pained thumbs-up, too mortified to form words as I hurry back to the desk with my bag, hiding my face behind my passport. *All the cool, flirty body language I could have gone for, and I went for the thumbs-up.*

On the plane, I'm next to an empty aisle seat. If life worked like it did in films, this would be the perfect opportunity for a meet-cute. I wonder if people ever really meet that way. Maybe I should do a special edition of *How Did You Meet?* and interview couples who all met on planes. As I'm thinking this, a burly man with a sweaty face and a Day-Glo-orange money belt stops at the end of the row, indicating he is the person I have won in the seat-buddy lottery.

"Cheer up, love," he says, my face clearly betraying my profound disappointment with the seating plan. "It never hurts to smile."

I clench my teeth. He has uttered an expression that I loathe with a vengeance, and over the last two years I have heard it more times than I can count. It is an intrinsically sexist comment—if a man were looking contemplative or perplexed, would another man instruct him to cheer up and smile? No, he bloody well would not.

Money Belt Man attempts to talk to me throughout the flight. He asks me where I'm staying in Jersey and keeps "accidentally" brushing my leg with his hand. I curl into the corner of my seat, plug in my earphones to listen to *No Jacket Required*, my favorite Phil Collins album, and bury my face in my book.

Tiger Woman is full of exactly the kind of meaningless empowerment metaphors I imagined it would be. The first chapter is all about "reclaiming your roar." I quote:

> Do tigers worry about the volume of their roar? Do they play the pussycat so as not to offend? They do not. The patriarchy forces us to turn down the volume, but we must roar, and roar loudly, if we want to be heard.

It's the kind of language that makes me roll my eyes, but then I imagine turning to Money Belt Man and roaring at him to stop touching my leg, rather than cowering politely behind my headphones and a book. The thought brings a smile to my face.

All the optimism and excitement I felt as I packed my bag this morning has vanished, like air wheezing from a punctured tire. The news that Vanya will really be moving out has thrown me; I thought it might take her months, even years, to get organized with a mortgage. Everyone is moving on, growing up. Vee makes our flat a home; if a stranger moves in, it will just be a flat again. When I was twenty-five, I thought I would have achieved so much by the time I was almost thirty. But what have I got to show for the last four years? All that has changed is that the men who chat me up are now in their fifties and wear luminous money belts.

When we land, I dart off the plane as fast as I can, grab my black suitcase from the conveyor belt, jump into a taxi from the rank, and ask the driver to take me into town. All I want now is to be alone in my hotel, unpack, wash off the plane, and then order alcohol-based room service.

"Your first time in Jersey?" asks the cabdriver. He's wearing a plaid flatcap and has a wild brown beard flecked with gray.

"Yeah," I say quietly, all out of small talk. There should be some kind of code to politely convey to a cabbie that you'd rather not make conversation.

The driver's beard is quite extraordinary, and I find myself staring at it. It's nothing like a well-groomed hipster beard—more of a Tom Hanks in *Castaway* beard. This guy literally looks as if he washed up here a few years ago, has been sleeping in a hut, living off coconuts, and then today decided to start driving a cab. His car also smells distinctly castaway-like—there's a definite musk of wet, sandy towels.

He surveys me in the rearview mirror, and I'm slow to muster a smile.

"Cheer up, love," he says, in a soft, deep voice.

And that does it. Something inside me snaps, and before I can stop myself, I bite back.

"I am allowed to look grumpy if I want to. It is my face and my prerogative not to smile. You don't know what's going on in my life, and it is not my responsibility to make the world a prettier place for you, OK? So just keep your eyes on the road, please."

His dark eyes grow wide in surprise, and he dutifully returns them to the tarmac ahead. I know I should stop talking, rein it in, but it's like this bubble of rage has been sitting in my stomach for I don't know how long—but now that I've popped the cork, out it spews.

"And you know, maybe I don't want to look cheerful. Maybe I've got nothing to look cheerful about. Maybe I'm doing everything wrong and I'll have 'died with unrealistic expectations' engraved on my bargain basement headstone."

I sink back into the seat, having scared myself a bit. I'm not sure the author of *Tiger Woman* meant me to "unleash my inner roar" on a poor, unsuspecting stranger.

"You're over from London then," says the driver, shifting awkwardly in his seat.

Oh right, so now he thinks I'm some angry city cow. It's not city living that has made me angry. I cross my arms and turn to glare out of the window at the evening sky. We're driving along the seafront now, a huge expanse of dimpled, wet sand merging into a gray-blue sea. I try to catch my breath, taking a moment to absorb the sight.

The driver is watching the road, his shoulders relaxed, a finger tapping on the wheel, unflustered by my outburst. Obviously, I should apologize. I know I've overreacted and none of what I'm feeling is this cabdriver's fault. But if I try to be nice, I think I might cry, and I really don't want to cry on him—that would be even more awkward than him thinking me rude.

I'm booked into the Weighbridge, a hotel on a cobbled square in the center of St. Helier. It's got a spa, several restaurants, and a beautiful view over the harbor. Ridhima, one of the assistants at work, got me a great deal as long as I hashtag the hotel in social media posts. At first glance, it seems the ideal central location from which to explore the rest of the island.

As we arrive, I snap a quick photo out of the window for Instagram.

"Thank you," I say to the driver as he drops me off. Giving him a hefty tip, I mutter an apology.

"Good luck," he says, in a way that implies I'm going to need a great deal of it because I'm clearly bonkers. Fair enough really, given my earlier meltdown.

My hotel room is exactly what I need: clean and comfortingly neutral. I don't think I've ever stayed in a hotel alone before—only ever with a friend or boyfriend. Do I wish David were here? No, he'd only be calling the front desk to inquire about the duvet tog rating or checking if the TV has Sky Sports. I shall relish the luxury of having a king-size bed, a giant bathtub, and all this space just for me. I start running a bath and take a small tub of Pringles from the minibar. I know these things are a rip-off, but since my outburst in the cab, my hands won't stop shaking. I need to give them something to do.

Who was that person who exploded at that poor man? That wasn't me; I don't get angry like that. I didn't even know I was worried about any of that stuff. I know I've been a little all over the place since losing Mum, but deep down, I've always felt like an optimist. Maybe what Dee said in the car got under my skin, about needing to be realistic when it comes to love. Maybe I just need to accept I'll never be the happy-go-lucky person I was before Mum died.

I pour myself a strong gin and tonic and open the balcony window to look out at the cobbled square and the harbor full of boats beyond. The sound of people enjoying themselves in the bar below rises up to meet me. Walking back to the bathroom, I turn off the bath tap and splash my face with water. *Don't waste this weekend being melancholy, Laura—this should be a happy weekend, a celebration of what your parents had, an adventure discovering your Jersey heritage.*

Pulling my bag onto the bed to unpack, I notice it feels lighter than it should. Then I see the zip color is wrong; it's dark gray, rather than black. I frown as I open the case; on top is a man's white work shirt, a travel-size stick of men's deodorant . . .

For a moment, I can't comprehend what I'm seeing. These are not my things; this isn't my bag. As it dawns on me that I have picked up the wrong case, I close my eyes for a moment. This is all I need; now I'll have to go all the way back to the airport to retrieve mine.

As I stare down at the contents of the case, willing them to be different, I notice the paperback lying next to the pile of clothes: *To Kill a Mockingbird*, my lifelong favorite book, one of Dad's favorites too. I pick up the well-thumbed copy, an old edition just like the one Dad left me. Placing it on the bed, I find myself looking through the contents of the case. A strange sensation, like a cluster of clouds moving aside, comes over me, my irritation at having the wrong bag morphing into something new, something unexpected.

Beneath the book is one of those thick knit cream fisherman's jumpers. I love these sorts of jumpers on a man—the kind Chris Evans wears in *Knives Out*, or that Ryan Gosling might wear on a weekend away to a log cabin, where he'd chop wood and make gin martinis before asking if you're up for a game of Scrabble by the fire. Beneath the jumper is a book of piano music. I *love* men who can play the piano, it has to be one of the sexiest skills. I briefly dated a pianist when I worked at the music magazine, and his playing alone was *almost* enough to made me overlook the fact that he was a complete pig . . . and then I read the words on the book of music and slap a hand across my mouth—*Phil Collins' Greatest Hits*. OMG, what is this? This can't be a coincidence. I take everything out of the case in a frenzy, as though the man who owns this bag might be hidden at the bottom.

There are blue running trainers and a neatly tied clear plastic bag full of worn clothes and running gear (I draw the line at rummaging through that). At the bottom of the case, in a sealed duty-free plastic bag, is a perfume bottle—Yardley English Lavender, my mother's perfume. Seeing it sends goose bumps down my arm. I don't know anyone else who wears this scent. No doubt it is a present for someone, but it feels as though it is for me—a sign from Mum. I blink away the itch behind my eye.

Get it together, Laura—it's probably a gift for the guy's wife. Then, tucked against the side, I find an unsealed card in a blank envelope. Would it be terrible if I looked to see if it has been written in? *Best not to ask yourself these questions.*

Dearest Mum,
I know you wanted a beehive for your birthday—but I thought if you smelled of lavender, you'd have swarms of admirers . . .

Love J

PS Your real present is in the garden. I shall expect honey for Christmas.

Oh my, he sounds adorable. He bought his mother a beehive, I want a beehive! I feel bad for reading the card now, but also relived it wasn't for a wife. Oh, and his handwriting—there's something so appealing about good handwriting; it's so neat, but with these long, upright letters. He's a *J* . . . James? John? Jack? Jim? There are so many great *J* names. In fact, I can't think of a single *J* name that's not superhot—except maybe Jensen, but that's literally the only one I can think of.

I'm getting carried away, I know, but I can't help myself. This is too spooky, especially factoring in Vanya's intuition about this weekend. The final object of interest I find is a bunch of keys, hidden in a side pocket. They are tied to a piece of old sailing rope, and have a tag made from wood, with the words THE CABIN etched on. He has a cabin, wasn't I just daydreaming about cabins? His suitability is indisputable now.

I pick up the jumper and breathe it in. Amazing—like log fires and baked scones and the sweat from vigorously cutting wood.

Am I thinking like a crazy person? Probably. But there's something about this that feels so real. Everything about this man in this case, it all fits with my story. It is too perfect not to mean something, for it *not* to be a sign. This must be him, my Great Love, delivered to me in a black carry-on suitcase.

TIGER WOMAN ON DESTINY

Do tigers believe in destiny? They do not. Tigers think only of survival: hunt to kill, eat to live, sleep to recharge for the task ahead, which is always the same—survival. So stop looking at the stars for answers, press your paws to the dirt, and know there is only one guiding light in your life: you.

Chapter 5

Once I have caught my breath from the excitement of finding the man I am probably going to spend the rest of my life with, I start to worry about the whereabouts of my own suitcase. I don't have any clothes, and some of the research for my article is in my notebook. All I have with me is my laptop, the clothes I am wearing, my mother's photo album, *Tiger Woman*, and about one million tampons.

If I have Hot Suitcase Guy's case, that must mean he has mine. I could call the airport, get his number, and arrange a meeting to exchange bags—perhaps over dinner? Everything would fall into place. I imagine telling this story to my grandchildren. "Oh, how did I meet Grandpa? Well, it was a funny story—I picked up his bag by mistake and knew straightaway:

This was the man I was supposed to be with." OK, so maybe I need to dial it back, just a touch.

Pacing over to the window, I look out at the sea. I wonder if Jake/Jack/James has realized he has the wrong bag yet. Maybe he did the same thing as me, felt annoyed at first, then curious about the owner. I wonder what my possessions might say about me. I regret not packing my decent underwear now. With a jolt of anxiety, I realize that my diary is in that bag. The inner monologue of a grief-stricken twenty-nine-year-old woman might not be the best introduction to a potential soulmate. I shake my head. The book is clearly a diary; what kind of weirdo would go through someone else's personal possessions? I look back at the bed, where I have unpacked and inspected the entire contents of this man's case. *Oh.*

I find the number for Jersey Airport. The phone rings twice, then a recorded message tells me the airport is closed. What kind of airport closes at eight fifteen on a Thursday night? I suppose a small island airport where the last plane lands at seven p.m. I pace the room. This is a setback. It's Thursday today, and I'm leaving on Sunday, so I don't have long. I guess I can set up a meeting to exchange the cases tomorrow morning, but it would probably be better if the beginning-of-the-rest-of-my-life started tonight.

I do what I always do when I need advice; I call Dee.

"Dee—you'll never guess—something amazing has happened." I can hardly contain my excitement.

"You found out you're Jersey royalty? Queen Le Quesne of the Channel Islands? You get your own herd of cows and a lifetime's supply of potatoes."

I laugh, and then flop back onto the bed and tell her all

about the suitcase. Dee cuts me off. "Wait, what? You're telling me you lost your case and all your things, but you're excited because . . . some random guy has it?"

"Well, yes, it's logistically annoying, but all these signs, Dee, it can't be a coincidence, can it? How many bags in how many airports, in how many countries, would have my favorite book, my favorite music, *and* my mother's perfume in? Plus, my ideal man jumper and the—"

"Laura," Dee says firmly, "your life is not a film. People do not meet future partners by accidentally spilling coffee over each other, or getting stuck in lifts, or beneath trees while seeking shelter from freak lightning storms, or through some hilarious luggage-themed mix-up. People meet their partners at work, on dating sites, or through introductions from a mutual friend—I will send you the statistics."

I know Dee means well, but I'm starting to think I should have called Vanya instead. Vanya would be all over this.

"Well, the statistics can't always be right, can they?" I say defensively.

"Yes, they can, they absolutely can. Math never lies." Dee sounds exasperated.

"OK, look, math aside, how do I find this guy? The airport's closed—he has my bag. Whether he's my soulmate or not, I still need clean knickers tomorrow."

Dee sighs and I smile, imagining the torn expression on her face.

"Beyond the *J* in the card, there's no name or address tag on the luggage?"

"No, Einstein," I say, inspecting the bag again in case I've missed something.

"His name must be printed on the airline tag?" says Dee.

Why hadn't I thought of that? Vanya definitely wouldn't have thought of that. This is why I call Dee. I look beneath the barcode on the printed ticket.

"J. Le Maistre!" I cry.

Le Maistre. I immediately toy with the name in my head—he's a "Le" too, just like me, another thing we have in common. Ooh, if we got married, I could keep part of my name but double-barrel the "Le's" and be Laura Le Le Maistre. It sounds so French and chic, like someone who owns a patisserie and maybe a boulangerie too.

"I'm googling him now," says Dee, sounding excited despite herself, "John, James . . . John again . . . hmmm, seems like Le Maistre is a common name in Jersey, there are hundreds of them. Does it look like a tree surgeon's bag? Or a financial analyst's bag?"

"What would I be looking for? Bags of sawdust? A catalog of calculators?"

"Are there definitely no more clues—no membership cards, receipts?"

I lay everything out on the bed, looking for something I might have missed. "Dee, you'll be pleased to know this guy keeps his dirty clothes and running gear in a separate plastic bag away from the rest of his things."

"Marry him," Dee deadpans, and I laugh.

"Could we research beehive sales? Find out who's bought a beehive lately?"

"Oh yes, I'll just look up all the recent delivery addresses at Beehives.com," says Dee, and I can hear the eye roll. Oh wow, even his jeans are perfect. Worn, but not too worn, stylish, but not overly so . . . "Laura, online it says the airport doesn't close until nine?" Dee says, interrupting my thoughts about jeans.

"The phone went to answering machine."

"Try again, or maybe go back there if it's not far. Just because you picked up this guy's case doesn't mean he necessarily picked up yours. Yours could still be sitting there."

"OK, I'm on it, I'm going," I say, flinging Hot Suitcase Guy's possessions back into the case.

"And, Laura," says Dee, "don't be nuts about this. It's just a suitcase, you don't know anything about this person."

"Yeah, I know. Thanks, Dee."

Ha! Don't know anything about this person? I know *everything* about this person. I know he's reading my favorite book, and that he's learning to play music by my favorite musician. I know he has the perfect-color jeans, a sexy-smelling jumper, and a quaint little holiday cabin in the woods somewhere. Plus, he buys lovely thoughtful gifts for his mother. What else do I need to know?

I try the airport number again but get the same message. I'll have to go back. It's only a twenty-minute drive—worth a shot.

Outside, the sun has gone down, but there is a faint dusky light in the sky. There's a cab rank right next to the cobbled square. As I slip into the backseat of a car, I notice the driver giving me a strange look in the rearview mirror. Oh no, it's the same driver I had before: Beardy McCastaway.

"Oh, hi again," I say with a forced smile. "Is there only one cabdriver in Jersey then?"

"No," he says flatly. "I had a break, came back to the rank, and now here you are. Again."

"Right, yeah, no, I didn't mean . . ." The man's tone has wrong-footed me. "I need to go back to the airport, if that's OK."

"Seen enough of Jersey already?" he asks.

"Ha-ha, no. Just a bag issue." I shuffle forward in the seat as the car pulls away from the curb. "Listen, I'm sorry again that I shouted at you earlier. That was entirely uncalled for. I, um, I had a bad flight and, well, there's no excuse. I don't want you to think I'm some horrible person—especially if you *are* the only cabdriver on the island."

"That's OK," he says with a nod. Then after a pause, "You do know I'm *not* the only cabdriver, right?"

He says it as though I'm a small child with limited capacity for understanding.

"Yeah, sure—I was joking."

I sit back in my seat and pull out my phone. This is so awkward. I definitely prefer London-style cab apps where you know you'll never see your driver again.

"I picked up the wrong suitcase," I explain.

"Easily done," he says. "Everyone has the same bag."

OK, perhaps he doesn't hate me. He's just the quiet, unexpansive sort. Tom Hanks probably didn't have great chat either, after being marooned on an island for years. I decide to text Vanya, to get her view on the suitcase situation, but halfway through typing, my gran calls. Gran has become a bigger part of my life since Mum died, and we check in with each other at least once a week.

"Hi, Gran. Hey, you'll never guess where I am."

"Timbuktu?" she says. "The Science Museum?" Then after a pause, "Your flat?"

She's genuinely trying to guess; this could take a while.

"No, I'm in Jersey!"

I hear a familiar scrunching sound, and instantly picture Gran standing by her phone, sharpening her Sudoku pencils, which she keeps in an old Branston pickle jar on the hall table.

"I'm here to write about Mum and Dad's love story for the website. I think I'm going to use Mum's album to illustrate the piece—go to all the places they went that summer they fell in love and take photos of myself in the same locations, a sort of 'Jersey Then and Now.' If I could track down some pictures of my great-grandparents, I could show the journey of the coin passing through three generations."

The idea sounds even better now than when I first pitched it.

Gran makes a disapproving *tskkk* sound.

"I wouldn't go digging up the past, Laura. You shouldn't get nostalgic for someone else's memories."

"I want to find out about my Jersey family too," I say, ignoring her reservations. "I sent Aunt Monica a postcard, to ask if she'd meet me while I'm here."

My dad's "Mad Aunt Monica" is one of the few living relatives I'm aware of. I'm not in touch with anyone else in Dad's family, but Monica sends an illegible Christmas card every year. If she responds to my card in time, I'm hoping I can meet her. She might remember stories I haven't heard or have photos she could share.

"I should have come before," I tell Gran, "but you know how funny Mum always was about Dad's family."

"Your great-aunt Monica is mad as a bandicoot, I wouldn't rely on her to remember anything accurately," Gran says, clearing her throat.

"What about Bad Granny, do we even know if she's still

alive?" I ask, smiling at the nickname Mum had for her mother-in-law. Apparently, they had some "big falling-out" after Dad's funeral, and Dad's mum, Sue, cut off all contact.

"You shouldn't call her that," Gran says sternly. "She and your mother might not have seen eye-to-eye, but she buried her son and her mother within a few months of each other. That would take its toll on anyone." Gran goes quiet on the line. Then in a small, worried voice she says, "I wish you'd told me you were planning on going there, Laura. It was complicated, your mother's relationship with your father's family. Grief can make people behave in peculiar ways."

Gran's tone takes me by surprise. I thought she'd be excited to hear about my Jersey adventure, that she would be pleased I'm doing something positive.

"I didn't know I was coming myself until two days ago," I say defensively. "And I doubt I'll even get a chance to see Aunt Monica. She might not get my postcard in time, and I'm flying back on Sunday night. You don't have any contact details, do you, besides her address? I couldn't find a phone number or an email address."

"I'm afraid not. Well, you just try to enjoy having a change of scene," Gran says, her voice back to its normal volume. "Did you take David with you?"

"Oh. No." I should never have introduced David to Gran; we were only together for a total of four months, it was too soon. "David and I broke up." I've been avoiding telling her this for three weeks.

"Oh, Laura, no! Why? I liked David. He had such lovely clean nails."

Trust Gran to notice these things.

"Um. Yes, I liked him too." I glance at the driver, to see if he looks to be listening to my conversation; he doesn't. "It didn't feel like what Mum and Dad had. We didn't have enough in common. I don't think he was my person, Gran."

"Laura! This yardstick you're using . . ." She trails off. "I think your mother painted you a rather rosy picture of life with your father, but it was not perfect by any means. You shouldn't use her relationship as a benchmark for potential suitors."

I smile at Gran's old-fashioned idea of "suitors," as though there's a line of men wearing Regency fashion waiting to mark my dance card.

"Maybe she ruined my chance for happiness by setting the bar so high." I'm teasing her now, but Gran doesn't laugh.

"Look, I want to talk about all this properly, Laura, but Pam's just arrived with more wood glue so I'm going to have to call you back."

Gran and her friend Pam make miniature architectural models out of matchsticks. They spend months on each creation and, despite my concerns about it being a fire hazard, her bungalow is stuffed full of them.

"OK, happy gluing—love to Pam," I say, hanging up the call.

Gran has always kept herself busy, as though perpetual motion might help her elude feeling sad. We do talk about Mum, but Gran's of a generation who sees grief as a wound to be licked in private. One weekend when I wouldn't get out of bed, she accused me of being a "Wallowing Wendy." I called her a "Forget-About-It Fiona" and a "Move-Along Mandy," and then we both started laughing and crying at the same time. I got up and that was the end of the conversation. That's how it goes with Gran sometimes. Her own husband, a grandad I've never met, walked out when Mum was five, so I think Gran got used to taking care of herself.

My gaze drifts out of the window. Though it's getting dark, I can still see some kind of castle or fortress in the sea to my left. I glance back at the cabdriver, whose eyes are still firmly on the road. What a strange job being a cabbie must be, listening to hundreds of one-sided phone conversations, being privy to snapshots of people's unfiltered lives.

The airport is quiet, hardly any cars around and no planes in the sky.

"If you're just going in to swap your bag, do you want me to wait?" asks the driver. "There won't be any cabs on the rank now, so you'd need to call for one."

"Oh, if you don't mind waiting, that would be great. Thank you," I say, surprised at his thoughtfulness. Though perhaps it's less a case of him being thoughtful, and more of wanting to monetize his journey back into town. Either way, I'll take it. I grab the suitcase from the boot and hurry through to departures.

The terminal is deserted, except for a woman behind one of the airline desks. She has short bobbed black hair and fifties-style red-rimmed glasses.

"Hi." I beam at her. "I wonder if you can help me? Arrivals is closed, but I picked up the wrong bag when I came in from London earlier. Whoever's bag I have, I think they must have mine."

"Sure, you can leave it here with me," says the woman, holding out her hand.

"But what about mine?" I ask, making no move to give her the case. "Has it been handed in? If someone called, I'm happy to go and make the swap in person."

The woman wearily checks her watch, then picks up a telephone on her desk. She punches a few numbers into the keypad and gazes at me as she lets it ring.

"No one left anything in the baggage hall, and nothing's been reported to me," she says, hanging up the phone and shaking her head. "Best leave it here and call about your bag in the morning. Don't worry, it will turn up, they always do."

I grip the handle of the suitcase firmly.

"No, I'd rather swap the bags in person. Can't you look on the passenger list to see who owns this one? His name is here, J. Le Maistre—we could call him? He might not have realized the mistake yet."

"I don't have access to that information, madam." The woman holds out her hand for the bag again. "Just call in the morning when the lost luggage desk will be staffed, they can take all your details."

I hug both arms around the case.

"I'm not giving this bag back until I get mine."

I'm fully aware I might be coming across as a little persistent right now, but if I give up the bag, I might never find Hot Suitcase Guy, and I'm not sure how many chances the universe gives you in situations like this.

"You can't just take someone else's bag home." The woman shakes her head in bemusement.

"Surely you can find his phone number or his address? What if it was a matter of life and death?" I give the woman my best serious face, like maybe I've been injected with some kind of deadly serum, and the antidote is in my bag, but I can't tell her about it because there's a hit man watching my every move.

"Is it a matter of life and death?" the woman asks, narrowing her eyes. Clearly my "deadly serum" face is not being conveyed effectively.

I shift my eyes to the ceiling, trying to think of something more feasible.

"Look, if I was an undercover cop"—I give the woman a deliberate wink—"and my lost suitcase had important, urgent evidence in it, how would you go about getting it back? Who would you call? There must be someone who knows who J. Le Maistre is, and how I can track him down?" OK, that definitely sounded more stalkery than I'd planned.

The woman crosses her arms in front of her chest, peering at me over the top of her glasses.

"*Are* you an undercover police officer?"

"If I was, I wouldn't be able to tell you because of the sensitive nature of the case, so let's just say that I am not," I say, slowly nodding my head.

"Madam, if that is not your bag, I cannot let you take it." She stands up and holds out her hand for the bag. "Airline policy."

"OK. OK, fine—" I make as though to hand it over, then just as she's reaching for it, I hug the bag back to my chest, turn, and run.

"Madam, you can't take that bag! MADAM!" she calls after me.

Outside the terminal, I look left and right for my cab. For a moment, I panic that the driver's gone and Red Glasses is going to come out here and wrestle the bag away from me. Luckily, he's just pulled forward a bit. I run toward the car and jump into the backseat, the suitcase still clasped in my arms.

"Go, go, go!" I shout at the driver.

"What happened?" he asks.

"I stole this suitcase." I laugh, breathless. "Quick, you're my getaway driver. Floor it!"

Beardy McCastaway pulls the car away at a normal pace, making no effort to speed away from the crime scene with any kind of dramatic tire screech. Seriously, do Jersey people not watch *Law and Order?* Do they not have crime dramas? This definitely felt like it called for a tire-screech moment.

"That's not your bag then?" the driver asks, squinting at me in the mirror.

"No. They didn't have it, and I don't want to give this one back until I get mine."

The driver shakes his head.

"What are you going to do, wear this person's clothes until yours turn up?"

"It's a complicated situation," I say huffily, feeling deflated by my lackluster getaway.

The two of us travel in silence, out of the empty airport, left past the rugby club and the brightly lit showroom full of expensive, shiny cars. Little I've seen of Jersey so far makes me think of the idyllic island paradise my mum described. It feels modern and built-up, rather than rural and full of history. Perhaps a lot has changed in thirty years. I pull out my phone to check my work emails, shooting off a few quick responses as I scroll, hoping to see a message from Aunt Monica. I'm keen to plan out the next few days, but her phone number is ex-directory, and I'm not sure I want to turn up unannounced on the doorstep of someone Mum nicknamed Mad Aunt Monica.

"I wanted to, um, apologize about the comment I made earlier," says the cabdriver suddenly. He clears his throat and adjusts his flatcap.

"Which comment?" I ask.

"When I said, 'Cheer up, love.'" His eyes glance up at me in the mirror and then dart back to the road. "I don't know why I said that. I hate that expression." He shifts awkwardly in his seat. "I thought it was the kind of thing a cabdriver might say, I was trying it out. Which sounds ridiculous, sorry."

His voice is calm and deep, like the steady bass line in a song. I peer at the driver in the darkness of the car. I haven't properly registered much about his appearance beyond the beard and the flatcap. Looking at him now, I realize his dark brown eyes and thick lashes are probably those of a man in his forties rather than fifties.

"Are you just playing the part of a cabdriver in some *Truman Show* experiment?" I ask.

He lets out a deep, staccato laugh, and his dark eyes glint back at me in the rearview mirror.

"Something like that," he says.

"Well, I shouldn't have snapped at you. The guy I sat next to on the plane said the same thing, and I'm afraid you were on the receiving end of the anger I was feeling toward him."

"I will erase it from my cabdriver script notes," he says, his eyes smiling at me now.

We settle into silence again.

Maybe it's because he's being nice or the calm resonance of

his voice, maybe it's because I can talk to him without making eye contact, but I find myself saying, "Do you want to know why I held on to this case? It's a bit nuts."

"Sure," he says.

I lean forward to talk to him. "How much do you think you can tell about someone from what's in their suitcase?"

"Hmmm." He is quiet for a moment. "If the suitcase had a shovel, duct tape, a body bag, and some chloroform in it, I might not be inviting that person in for a nightcap."

"Yeah, OK," I say with a laugh. "But what about contents that make you think you're going to click with that person, that they might be someone you're supposed to be with?"

His eyes glint gold in the mirror, reflecting light from the headlamps of the car behind.

"You're serious?"

"Yes. This bag I picked up, the wrong case—everything in it makes me think this is the guy I'm meant to meet. He's got my favorite book—"

"What book?" the driver cuts in.

"*To Kill a Mockingbird*. It was one of my dad's favorite books too—he left me the exact same edition that this man has in his bag." Beardy McCastaway is frowning. "What? You don't like it?"

"Loads of people like that book. It's like saying your favorite band is the Rolling Stones."

"Well, my favorite band is not the Rolling Stones, and that brings me on to the next clue. This guy plays the piano—I mean, properly plays, there's some seriously difficult sheet music in here. I've always loved men who are musical, but not only that—the music is for *Phil Collins' Greatest Hits*. Phil

Collins is my favorite musician of all time. That's pretty freaky, no?"

The driver starts to laugh.

"What?" I say, pushing the bag onto the seat next to me and hugging my arms across my chest.

"OK, a Phil Collins–playing pianist who reads Harper Lee." His eyes in the rearview mirror flash with amusement. "What else?"

"He's bought the perfume *my* mum used to wear as a present for *his* mother."

Seeing his skeptical smile, I decide I don't want to tell him about the sexy jumper, the bees, the cabin keys, or the perfect jeans now.

"Clearly you think I'm being ridiculous. Look, it's a feeling more than any one specific object. I think fate brought me this bag so I could find the man it belongs to."

My eyes drift down to the steering wheel, and I notice a gold wedding band on the cabdriver's hand.

"How did you meet your partner? Didn't you have a moment where you just knew?"

The man's eyes dart back up to me in the mirror, clearly caught off guard. Then his eyes drop to the wheel and he twists the ring with his thumb.

"My wife," he says, as though testing the word. "We met through work, then we were friends for a long time."

"She's a cabdriver too?" I ask, confused.

He makes a short humming noise, like a laugh caught in his throat. "No, I didn't always drive a cab."

"Oh right, you said. Sorry." I lean forward between the

seats until the belt clicks, stopping me from going any further. "So, it was more of a slow build than a *kablammo* moment?"

"What's *kablammo*?"

"You know, KABLAMMO! Where you're just floored by how much you like someone. It's like a sucker punch to the heart—KABLAMMO!" I throw a punch into the space between the seats.

He lets out another deep, throaty laugh, and I feel surprisingly pleased. He doesn't look like someone who laughs a great deal.

"I guess it was like that for me, maybe not for her, not at first." He looks thoughtful for a moment. "She has this magnetic quality that draws people's attention wherever she goes." He thrums his hand on the wheel. "You really think you can get that feeling from a suitcase?"

The poetic way he talks about his wife makes me pause, then I shrug. "I don't make the rules. I guess you either believe in fate and serendipity or you don't. Listen, how big is Jersey? Maybe you know this guy?"

He frowns.

"I know you think I'm the only driver on the island, but a hundred thousand people live on this nine-by-five-mile rock. It's unlikely I'd know him." He pauses. "Though, come to think of it, there is this man—I've seen him at the library, very handsome, always has *To Kill a Mockingbird* under one arm. He plays the piano at Age Concern most weekends."

"Seriously!?" I say, before realizing he's winding me up. Then slowly, "Oh, ha-ha."

The driver gives a satisfied grin.

"Well, my mobile number is on my luggage. As soon as he realizes he's got the wrong bag he'll call, and then, well—"

"Kablammo?"

"Exactly," I say, spreading my arms as though to take a bow.

When we pull up at my hotel, I have a thought.

"You're local here, right?"

"I grew up here," he says.

"Can I show you some photos? You might be able to tell me where they were taken. You can keep the meter running if you like."

He gives me a single nod, turns the light above his head on and the meter off.

I take the brown photo album from my handbag and pass it to him.

"My mum met my dad here, in the summer of 1991. I'd like to try and find some of the places they went to together." He slowly opens the album to the first page. "They've both passed away, so this is all I have to go on."

He turns around, looking me straight in the eyes for the first time.

"I'm sorry to hear that."

His tone is so earnest that the words momentarily fluster me. I give the smallest nod of acknowledgment, then quickly lean forward to point at a picture in the album.

"Do you know where that is?"

"Hmm," he says, rubbing his beard. "I'd say from the look of the harbor wall in the background, it's Rozel Bay. This is your mother?"

"Yeah."

"She looks like you."

"Thanks, I'll take that as a compliment, but she was far prettier than I am, certainly more flexible."

In the picture Mum is balancing on a rock in a green swimsuit, her long brown hair covering her chest. She's holding a dance pose, one long, toned leg jutting out at a ninety-degree angle. I'm tall like her, my hair equally straight, but blond. We both have full lips and lightly freckled skin, but her nose is smaller, perter. In the picture she's younger than I am now. It's strange to think that by my age she was a widow—a single mum with a four-year-old child.

He turns the page of the album.

"This is Plémont headland, before they tore the holiday resort down. It looks completely different now." He flicks on through the pages to a picture of my mum standing in front of a hut by the sea. "This must be the Écréhous, these huts are still all there."

He tells me where each photo is taken. This is exactly the kind of intel I need if I'm to retrace their steps—take the same journey that the coin took my mother on.

"Listen, how would you feel about being my island tour guide tomorrow? I want to go to all the places in these photographs."

He shuts the album and hands it back to me.

"I'm afraid I only drive some evenings."

"Oh right, never mind. It was just a thought." I can't hide my disappointment. I guess there will be other cabdrivers who know the island just as well as Beardy McCastaway. "Can I just write down some of the names you said in my phone? How do you spell Play Mont?" I unlock my phone screen to make notes, my other hand reaching for my pendant, twisting the chain. When I look up, waiting for him to answer, he's looking right at me with those intense eyes of his.

He sighs. "I'll take you. You won't find half these places on your own."

"Are you sure? I don't want to put you to any trouble."

"It's not a problem. Shall we meet in the morning?" He pulls out a card from the glove box and hands it back to me. It has "Gerald Palmerston, St. Ouen's Cabs," and then a contact number printed on the front. "Wait, I'll write my mobile number on there." He takes the card back, finds a pen in the side door, and scribbles it down.

"You're Gerald then?" I ask, biting my lip. There shouldn't be anything funny about the name Gerald, but I wouldn't put Beardy McCastaway down as one.

"Gerry's my dad."

"Family business?"

"Something like that."

"Well, I'm Laura," I say.

"Ted," he replies. Yes, Ted, that suits him much better.

Back in my room, I order a club sandwich from room service and google J. Le Maistre to see if I can find a likely candidate or a phone number. When I have no success, I call Vanya.

"Hey, chick. How was the flight?"

"Fine—"

"Hey, I just remembered that literary potato peel pie film is set in Jersey, isn't it? Maybe you should join a book club, meet some hot farmers. Worked for Lily James."

"That was Guernsey, different Channel Island. Plus, that was set eighty years ago. Listen, Vanya, can I ask you something?"

"Always."

"If I told you I picked up the wrong suitcase from the airport, and the case's contents made me feel like they belong to the person I'm supposed to be with—would it be insane to try and track that person down?"

"I knew it! I knew something like this would happen. Didn't I tell you my Spidey senses were tingling? Oh, Laura, you would be insane *not* to track him down!" Her voice swoons through the phone.

"That's what I thought."

I can always rely on Vanya.

When my club sandwich arrives, I feel a sense of eager anticipation—mainly about the sandwich, because I'm ravenous, but also because somewhere on this small island is J. Le Maistre, my potential soulmate. And tomorrow I am going to find him, and the next chapter of my life can finally begin.

ꕥ

Jersey Evening News—23 June 1991

TWO HALVES OF A COIN,
REUNITED AFTER HALF A CENTURY

A local pensioner has been reunited with her late husband's love token, lost for half a century, after her grandson spotted an advertisement in the *Jersey Evening News*.

Yesterday, an emotional Margorie Blampied held the precious keepsake in her hand for the first time since June 1940. She said, "Holding the whole coin brought back the day William left as though it were yesterday. He was such a romantic man, and an exceptional craftsman. I will miss him until my last breath."

Chapter 6

I wake up confused as to where I am. The bed is too big, the room is too dark, and I'm surprised to find myself sleeping naked, until I remember why: I have no pajamas. There was a vivid dream about drowning—sailing in a suitcase boat, trying to get to an island where my parents were waving to me, but I didn't have a sail and the boat was sinking, because, well, it was a suitcase. My mother's face was still so clear and full of life in my dream. My father's was static—since I only remember his face from photos, I've always found it hard to imagine what he looks like in motion.

My phone is alive with messages and emails. It's only seven a.m. and I last checked my phone at ten. Dee has sent a link to an article from *Statistics Weekly* entitled, "Where People Meet

Their Partners—The Facts," and there are three emails from Suki. I click on the first one.

From: Suki@lovelife.com

To: Laura@lovelife.com

Laura,

Had a few list ideas, additional content you could pull together while you're away.

- Most Romantic Skinny-Dipping Locations. Get your body skinny for dipping. We have a weight-loss bar looking to sponsor an advertorial.
- Top Ten Attractive Men from the Channel Islands. Isn't Henry Cavill, the Superman actor, from there? Can you research? Ideally, get photos of Superman skinny-dipping. (People engage 20% more with articles that have a celeb angle.)
- Small Islands to Suit Your Mood. Feel silly in the Scilly Isles, flirty in Fetlar, merry in Mull . . . A hotel in the Outer Hebrides are keen to sponsor.

Her next email says,

We need your coin story for Tuesday. We're short on uplifting content, so it needs to deliver; heartwarming, life-affirming, etc. Try to find some long-lost relatives. Everyone likes stories about long-lost relatives.

Then finally,

And please plan to do an Insta live at twelve today. Somewhere beachy and beautiful to trail the mini-breaks piece.

Suki

I groan. It's Friday today, and I'm leaving on Sunday night. I'm not sure how Suki thinks I'm going to stumble upon nudes of Henry Cavill just because he has some connection to Jersey. But it's hard to push back on unreasonable requests with the pendulum of redundancy swinging over your head.

Dee often asks why I stay at Love Life, with the long hours and Suki's aggressive management style. But the truth is I enjoy my job—well, the part where I get to research and write stories. Yes, it has its frustrations, but no job can be perfect. Work has been one of the few constants in my life when so much was changing. I like being a part of the Love Life family because, besides Gran, it's the only family I have left. The thought of losing it makes my skin itch. So over breakfast, I get out my laptop and set about manically writing up notes for all of Suki's latest ideas.

Before meeting up with the cabdriver, I head out to find somewhere to buy a change of clothes and a few other essentials a luggage-less girl might need. The hotel was able to furnish me with a spare phone charger, toothpaste, and a toothbrush, but I can't bear to spend today in yesterday's plane clothes. Around the corner from my hotel, I find a department store that opens early, and in it a pale blue summer dress and some flip-flops on sale, both perfect for a warm September day. I prudently pick up a few bits of makeup too—when J. Le Maistre calls, I don't want to be caught looking anything less than my best.

The cabdriver, Ted, I remind myself, is waiting for me in the lay-by where he left me last night. The suitcase trundles along the cobbles behind me; I brought it so I can go straight out to meet Hot Suitcase Guy if he calls this morning.

"Morning!" I say to Ted as I climb into the backseat. He gives me a single nod in reply. He's wearing the same ugly plaid flatcap he was wearing yesterday, and his beard looks more Tom Hanksy than ever. "So, I'm ready for the grand tour. Where shall we begin?"

"You want to go to all the places in your album?" he asks, clearing his throat.

"Yes, please."

He holds out a hand. "Let me take a look at the photos again. I'll plan the best route. Oh, and we should agree on a flat rate for the day—it will cost you a fortune on the meter."

"Whatever you think is fair," I say gratefully.

Once he starts driving, I don't ask where we're headed but jump straight on my phone and start leaving messages for Le Maistres. The hotel receptionist kindly made me a copy of the Le Maistre page in the phone book. As keen as I am to track down my mystery man, I'm also now increasingly anxious to get my own bag back. It makes me wince to think about some of the things I've confessed to my journal, words not meant to see the light of day. There is simply too much in my bag I cannot contemplate losing: my research notes, my favorite jeans, my vintage silk blouse—one of the last presents Mum gave me, the L-shaped earrings she and I made together; all things I would not have checked into the hold if I'd had more than thirty seconds to think about it.

Gazing out of the window as I dial another number, I watch the suburban sprawl of houses, schools, and shops morph into more rural scenery. I notice how considerate all the drivers are to one another. Ted waits to let cars out from junctions, as though we have all the time in the world. It is a far cry from the aggressive London driving I am used to. The Le Maistre number I've called rings and rings, so I hang up.

The roads narrow into single-track, tree-lined lanes, and we pass dog walkers ambling along next to freshly plowed fields. Then, as the houses disappear entirely and we're surrounded by green, I see the distinctive face of a Jersey cow peering over a fence.

"Oh, a Jersey cow! Can we stop?" I ask. "Oh, will you look at them? They're so beautiful!"

"You want to stop to look at the cows?" Ted asks, as though I've just asked him to stop so that I can inspect the exciting tarmac on the road.

"If there's somewhere to pull in, do you mind? I'd love to get a photo."

He makes a nondescript grunt but pulls the car onto a grassy lay-by.

I get out of the car and walk around to tap on the driver's window, which he slowly winds down. Ted looks up at me and I see his full face for the first time in daylight. He has these dark, penetrating eyes with heavy lids that track my gaze—they're a little intense, unnervingly so. I glance away, then ask, "Would you like to come?" assuming he might want to stretch his legs.

"I'm good, thanks. I've seen cows before," he says, pulling a newspaper from the passenger seat and unfolding it in his lap. I suspect Beardy McCastaway lacks the rapport necessary to be a real tour guide.

Reaching the cow field fence, I take a long, deep breath. The early morning air is yet to be warmed by the sun, but the sky is a vast, vibrant blue, like a freshly unboxed day. Alongside the narrow road, ivy-covered oak trees sit behind a bosky bank of hawthorn bushes and wild grasses. It's so peaceful, I can hear the birds chirping in the trees, the low hum of a tractor several fields beyond, and the faint buzzing of flies as they flit around swishing cow tails. I step cautiously up the bank, fearful of spooking the herd, but the few cows standing near the fence simply eye me with idle curiosity.

I read about Jersey cows in the in-flight magazine—they're famous for producing amazing milk. They're basically the Kate Mosses of the cow world: elegant, angular frames, soft fawn, teddy-bear-colored bodies, and wide doe eyes. One with a dark brown face and long lashes blinks at me, flicking flies away with a twitch of her head.

There is a photo of my mother next to a cow just like this one, so I turn my phone around to try and take a similar shot.

"OK, buddy, don't move," I say quietly, shuffling myself into position. It's hard to get the angle right. Maybe if I just step up onto the fence rail, I'll be able to fit both of us in the frame. In fact, I could climb over into the field, just for a second, and the positioning would be so much better.

As I'm stepping down onto the grass, I feel a sharp jolt of pain and my leg suddenly buckles beneath me. I lose my footing and fall flat on my face, my phone flying from my hand. What the hell was that? I scramble to my feet. Turning around, I see a thin wire running alongside the wooden rail—an electric fence. Ten points to me for being a complete urban cliché and not noticing that. Brushing down my dress, I see a muddy mark near the hem. What an excellent start to the day; electrocuted and muddied before it's even ten a.m. Just as I'm thinking it can't get much worse, I feel a nudge from behind. One of the cows is pushing into me.

"Hey, back off."

When I look up, more cows are heading in my direction.

"Go away!" I plead. "Just shoo, will you?" I point a stern finger at the nudgy one.

"What are you doing?"

My head snaps back around to see Ted standing by the fence, watching me with a bemused expression. Nudgy is now looming over me, and I reach out my hand to push her away.

"They're not pets, you can't get in and stroke them," says Ted, looking at me like I'm completely clueless.

"I know that! I wasn't trying to *pet* them. I didn't know the fence was electric and— Hey, get off me!" The running cows are getting closer, and I feel a rising panic in my chest. People die from being trampled by cows, don't they? It always seemed a rather comical way to go, but now I'm staring death in the doe-eyed face, it doesn't seem funny at all. "Ahhhh!"

Ted jumps over the fence in one swift movement—he's surprisingly nimble. He walks purposefully toward the cows with an arm outstretched and says in a deep, stern voice, "Back you go now."

The cows obediently scatter.

My heart still pounding, I look at Ted, impressed. He's like a cow whisperer.

"They're only young heifers, they won't hurt you."

"Thanks," I say. "I didn't mean to get in here, I'm not a complete idiot."

His lips twitch, like he's about to smile, and now I feel embarrassed that I freaked out about the admittedly rather small cows.

"Did you get the photo you wanted?"

"No, I dropped my phone when I fell," I say feebly.

Ted shakes his head, takes off his cap and runs a hand through his hair before replacing it. Unlike his beard, his hair isn't flecked with gray; it's thick and brown. In fact, he's got surprisingly good hair beneath the ridiculous cap.

The ringtone of my phone punctures the air. Ted and I search the long grass by the fence for the source of the sound. Ted gets to it first, but by the time he's handed it to me the ringing has stopped. Unknown caller. Damn, it might have been J. Le Maistre.

"I'm sure they'll call back. Do you want me to take a photo for you?" Ted asks, distracting me from my disappointment.

"Well, they've all gone now," I say, waving a forlorn hand toward the retreating gang of cattle. "And I think I might have gone off cows."

He laughs, a proper chesty laugh, and I can't help feeling like I want him to take his cap off again, so I can see what his eyes look like when he laughs like that.

"Come on, Lady Muck."

He reaches out to take my phone, holding it up to take a photo. I feel self-conscious beneath his gaze. Then he hands it back and wordlessly holds out his arm to help me climb back over the fence. It's a gentlemanly thing to do, and his forearm feels firm and steady beneath my hand. At the car, he opens the side door and points to the seat.

"Just sit there a minute," he instructs me.

Perching on the edge of the seat, I watch as he walks around to the boot. He returns with a bottle of water and some wet wipes. "My dad always keeps these in the car just in case."

Bending one knee to the ground, he takes my hem in one hand and starts cleaning the mud from my dress. It's a strangely intimate gesture, and I fiddle with my hands in my lap, not sure where to put them.

"I see—I really am Lady Muck."

I should say "I'll do it" and take the wipes from him, but I don't. There is something calming in watching him; he's gentle, yet his hands have a surgical precision.

"Not perfect, I'm afraid," he says, standing up to return the water and wipes to the boot. He has done his best, but there is still a residual pale brown stain. Why did I buy such an impractical dress?

"Well, that was beyond the call of duty. Thank you." I turn to watch Ted close the boot, dusting his hands off on his jacket. "Would you mind if I sat up in front, so I can see out more? I was starting to feel a bit carsick in the back with all these windy roads."

"Of course."

He hurries over to open the passenger door and doffs his cap. He's mocking me, but in a sweet way, so I don't mind.

"Thank you, kind sir," I say, with playful formality.

As he gets into the driver's seat, he throws his cap onto the backseat, then runs both hands through his hair, almost self-consciously.

"Your wish is my command, Lady Muck."

TIGER WOMAN ON DOMESTICATION

Tigers hunt when they are hungry, sleep when they are tired, and growl when they are angry. We have been domesticated into cats—told when to eat, told when to sleep, told never to growl only to purr, told to play quietly in the corner with a ball of string, then roll over and have ours tummies rubbed. Remember: You are not a cat. You are NOT a cat. You are a wild animal.

Chapter 7

As Ted is driving, I check the photo he took of me. It's perfect, there's a cow in the background looking right at the camera, and I look happy, not like someone who stared death in the face just moments before. I post it on the Love Life Instagram feed alongside a snap of my mother's photo. "Jersey Cow: Then and Now. My island adventure begins."

Ted drives to a village harbor on the northeast coast called Rozel. He parks the car next to some white railings by the beach, and I instantly recognize the cove from the album. My phone pings with a text from Vanya:

Have you found him yet?

She has attached a succession of photos with half-naked men all holding suitcases—I can only imagine they are the result of a Google image search for "sexy suitcase man."

I bite my lip to stop myself from snorting with laughter.

The narrow road hugs the bay, along the top of the harbor covering one side of the cove. At the far end is a bright blue kiosk with a red-and-white awning. Some boys jump off the harbor wall, squealing with delight before hitting the glassy water below. On the sand-and-pebble beach, I can see a woman climbing over rocks with two toddlers, collecting shells and other treasures in bright pink buckets. The children's skirts are tucked into their knickers to stop them getting wet. *This* is the Jersey I imagined.

"What a beautiful place," I say, half whispering. "It's like a postcard."

"Your photo—it's taken at low tide over there," says Ted, nodding toward the rock pools. "And the Hungry Man kiosk up there does the best hot chocolate on the island."

"Would you like a drink?" I ask. "Call it a thank-you for rescuing me from death by cow."

"That isn't necessary." He shakes his head.

"It would be my pleasure."

He looks across at me, scratches his beard, and then slowly moves to unbuckle his seatbelt.

At the kiosk, I order a hot chocolate for myself, on his recommendation, and a black coffee for Ted. We take a seat across from each other on one of the wooden bench tables. Ted looks about as comfortable as a cat stuck up a washing line, as though he's never been out to coffee with anyone in his life. He was right about the hot chocolate—it's spectacular; piled high with cream and decorated with marshmallows and Maltesers.

"So, what's the best local cuisine, besides this hot chocolate?" I say, hugging my elbows toward me and clapping my hands together. "What else have I got to try while I'm here?"

Ted's eyes crease into a smile, he looks amused by my enthusiasm.

"Black butter, I suppose—it's a sort of apple jam—oysters fresh from the tide, Jersey wonders—my mother used to make them, they're like doughnuts. You're only supposed to fry them when the tide is going out."

"Ooh, I love traditions like that," I say, leaning toward him.

Ted catches my eye for a moment before quickly turning his attention to picking at a splinter of wood on the table. I start telling him about my job, the article I'm writing about my parents, the coin, and my great-grandfather who started it all. Ted listens attentively, as though he is genuinely interested.

"These photos in the album are of that first summer they spent together, falling in love. By September, they were engaged." I feel myself beaming as I tell the story that is so familiar, it feels like my own. "When I was fifteen Mum gave the coin to me"—I show Ted the pendant around my neck—"so that I would always have their story close to me. I've always believed it must possess talismanic qualities—to have led my mother to the love of her life."

Ted is watching me now, his face entirely still.

"Your dad took all these photos of her then?" he asks.

"Yes. Dad was a chef, she was a dance teacher. They worked together at the Pontins holiday resort. Mum managed to get a summer job there at the last minute, so she could stay on the island and be with him. On their evenings off, he would cook for her, and she taught him to dance beneath the stars. She tried to teach me when I was young, she'd get me dancing around the washing line as she hung up clothes, but I'm about as graceful as a panda. She always said Dad was a better student than me." I feel myself grin. I love telling people their story. "You see this picture of her in a cave?" I say, showing Ted a photo in the album. "This is where my dad proposed. It's at the bottom of a blowhole. Everything you say in the cave travels right up to the cliff path above. Mum said he asked her there, so that the blowhole would broadcast her saying 'yes' to the entire island."

Ted's eyes drop back to the coffee spoon and I shake my head, aware I've gotten carried away as usual. I reach for my phone to occupy my hands.

"Look, your cow photo already has a hundred and forty-six likes," I say, showing him the Instagram post. He frowns in incomprehension. "So, how about you?" I ask, changing the subject. "How did you meet your wife, was it here in Jersey?"

"No, in London," he says, glancing up at me. Perhaps he glimpses my disappointment that he hasn't offered more, because after slowly shaking his head from side to side he adds, "I don't live here anymore. I grew up here, but I'm only back to help my dad with something."

"What a place to spend your childhood," I say, nodding toward the boys still jumping from the harbor wall. "Do you have a favorite memory, of growing up here?"

It's a trite question, perhaps too personal, but Ted looks to be considering it seriously. He gazes out across the cove, tapping a finger against his mug.

"When I was younger, I used to drive around with Dad in his cab when my mum was working. Passengers didn't seem to mind. I loved hearing him talk to people; he always knew the right thing to say. He could tell when someone wanted to talk, when they didn't. People always left his cab happier than they got in. Even those having a bad day, it was as though he drove them away from whatever had upset them. All these years later, if ever I'm stressed, all I want to do is drive . . ."

He trails off.

"It's a happy association for you," I offer. He nods.

Taking a swig of coffee, he stands up, turns to lean both hands on the white railing, and looks down into the sea below.

I walk over to stand next to him, keen to keep the conversation going.

"I think objects can be powerful conduits for memories." I hold out my arm to show him my wristwatch. "This was my dad's. He died when I was three. I've worn it ever since my wrists were thick enough to hold it. I had to have an extra hole put into the strap so it would fit. I know it's big and ugly, but it's all I have left of him." I stroke my finger across the face of the watch. "I often think how the leather is ingrained with his sweat. I like to imagine how many times he must have glanced at the face, just as I do. Maybe something of him is still in there."

When I look up, Ted is watching me almost reverently. Then his eyes quickly fall to his wedding ring, and he turns it around and around between his finger and thumb.

"That's a beautiful way to think of it. I . . ."

"Ted? Ted Palmerston?" comes a voice from behind us. We both turn to see a thickset, muscular man with a shock of ginger hair and a tattoo of the Jersey flag, a white rectangle with a diagonal red cross, on his arm. He has his hand outstretched toward Ted, a huge grin on his face. "While I live and breathe, Palmerston returns." He laughs.

Ted's eyes seem to grow larger as he holds up a palm in greeting.

"Hey, Danny," he says.

Danny looks at me, waiting for an introduction he doesn't get.

"I'm sorry to hear about your dad," he says, turning back to Ted. "I always poke my nose into his porch whenever I pass L'Étacq. You know, check he's OK."

"That's decent of you, Danny."

I look back and forth between the two men.

"And I . . . I heard about your, er, situation. I'm sorry, that's got to be tough."

Ted nods, and Danny eyes me curiously.

"Hi, I'm Laura," I say, giving him a wave. "I'm a passenger of Ted's."

Danny glances down at the cups on our table and at Ted's awkward expression. He's rubbing his beard again, as though if he rubs it hard enough, a conversation genie might spring out. Maybe it's not just me he gets all monosyllabic around.

"I see." Danny looks back and forth between us with a sly smirk. "Well, you ever want to go for a beer and set the world to rights, you just let me know, mate. Though maybe you're all set."

Danny gives him a wink and then rejoins the woman and boy waiting for him over by the kiosk awning. They start talking, looking back in our direction.

Now I have so many questions: What is wrong with Ted's dad? What's his "situation"? Is he in trouble with the law? Has he entered a beard-growing competition for money and now doesn't know how to get out of it? By the look on Ted's face, now isn't the time to ask.

"Excuse me, I need to make a phone call. Thanks for the coffee, take whatever time you need to explore the beach," he says gruffly, then strides off back the way we came, shoulders hunched up around his ears.

Now I'm worried he felt interrogated. Dee tells me I have a habit of asking too many questions when I first meet people. She says, "People don't want to be bitten into like an apple, Laura—to show you their core in one conversation. Sometimes you have to peel the skin away slowly." It made me think of the game my mother used to play when I was a child—where she'd try and peel an apple all in one go. You had to be gentle with the knife, create an even ribbon of peel, so it came away in one piece. I've never been able to do it—I don't have the patience or the sleight of hand.

I check my phone again. Why hasn't this guy called yet? My number is right there on the baggage tag. Picking up my hot chocolate, I take a final swig but misjudge it and slosh the dregs down the front of my dress. *CRAP!* I desperately blot at the brown stain with a napkin, but it's useless. What is wrong with me today? Now I'll definitely need to find something else to wear before the suitcase exchange.

Climbing down to the beach via a ladder on the harbor wall, I try to shake off my irritation. The woman and her two children are still on the beach, and I ask her to take a picture of me on the rocks, in the same place my mother was standing. Checking the old photo for reference, we line up the harbor wall in the background to make it match. I tilt my body away from the camera then turn my head back around, in an effort to hide the hot chocolate stain. The tide is different, and the light is wrong, but the woman is kind and patient, and I'm satisfied with the image she takes.

Her children are wide-eyed girls with blond hair, sun cream–streaked faces, and sand-dappled legs. They show me what they've been collecting in their buckets.

"Beach tweasure," says one, handing me a shiny green rock the size of a coin. "For you."

The sweetness of the child and the kindness of the gesture sends a stab of something through me, and I clasp the rock to my chest as though it really is treasure. Heat rises behind my eyes as I say good-bye to the family and head back to the car. All those hours my mother must have spent doing childish activities for my benefit: collecting shells at Portishead beach, making papier-mâché crowns to paint and decorate, endless treasure hunts in the garden to find buried coins made of kitchen foil. All that time she invested in my childhood happiness. I wish now I had held on to just one of those papier-mâché crowns.

Back at the car, Ted has put his cap back on, pulled low over his brow. He looks at my chocolate-covered dress as I climb into the passenger seat.

"What happened?"

"Clumsy-itis. Does it look terrible?"

Ted pauses and then shrugs. "As long as you're not trying to impress anyone." His eyes flash me a sly look.

He knows that is exactly what I am trying to do—as soon as I can *find* the person I am trying to impress.

"Look, I got a present," I say, showing him the green rock.

"Sea glass," he says.

"Sea glass?"

"It's all over these beaches. It's old glass—rubbish, worn down, and tumbled smooth by the sea," he says, looking at the piece in my hand. "My mother used to collect it. She'd say the sea was trying to give us back something beautiful from the ugly things we throw away."

"I like that." I stow the sea glass in a zipped pocket of my handbag. After biting my lip for a moment, I can't help asking, "So, is that guy Danny an old friend of yours?"

Translation: Tell me about your dad and your "situation."

"Everyone knows everyone else's business in Jersey. It's part of the reason I left." He turns back to the road. "Ready to go?"

Like I said, I don't have the patience or the sleight of hand to peel an apple slowly.

TIGER WOMAN ON SOCIAL MEDIA

Tigers do not seek "likes." They do not need the validation of other tigers; their success is self-evident—they are alive. YOU are alive, you beat the odds to even exist, you have got yourself this far in life's journey. Take a moment to "like" that.

Chapter 8

We drive in silence for ten minutes or so. I'm not offended. If Ted doesn't want to tell me what that guy Danny was talking about, that's fine. I've got other things on my mind—like, how am I going to track down Hot Suitcase Guy if he doesn't get in touch with me soon?

My phone repeatedly pings with text messages, and Ted glances across at me.

Suki: Can you tie your article in with some photos of Lily James in that Potato Peel Pie film?

Seriously, is that film the only cultural reference anyone has for the Channel Islands? I tap out a reply.

Me: Great idea, Suki! That was Guernsey rather than Jersey though.

Suki: ☹ Any headway on Henry Cavill skinny-dipping photos?

I shake my head—Suki appears to have lost focus on the purpose of this trip.

Vanya has created a new WhatsApp group with Dee and me, called "Hot Suitcase Guy," with a group icon of yet another naked man, holding a suitcase in front of his groin.

Vanya: I thought we needed a chat group so you can send us both updates. If you haven't found him yet, do you want me to get someone I know to hack the airline database to get his deets? Vx

Dee: Vanya, do you know how illegal that is?! Fact: the place you are statistically least likely to meet your life partner—prison.

Gran: Please call me when you can, Laura. Not urgent, but there are a few things I'd like to discuss. Also, could you bring me back some black butter if it's easy? Annie used to eat it on crackers—the taste makes me think of her.

Gran rarely volunteers memories of Mum like that, and I savor this tiny nugget of new information.

"You know you're missing the view," says Ted, distracting me from replying.

"I'm sure you think I'm glued to my phone, but I am here to work."

"And find your soulmate," he says, flashing me that teasing look again.

I tilt my head sideways at him.

"That will be a bonus. If I don't do the work, I won't have a job to go home to."

As though reading my mind, another text from Suki pings through.

I trust you will come up with something marvelous for the mini-break piece—I have every faith in you. #LoveLife4Ever

I am used to Suki's oscillations. One minute she is cold and critical, the next she is praising you, claiming you as family. It's effective, because just as you give up hope of ever pleasing her, she drops a breadcrumb, and you would do anything to keep the warmth of her approval shining in your direction. No one is immune, not even Vanya.

I thank Suki for her confidence in me, quickly respond to some work emails, and then call the airport, asking to be put through to the lost luggage desk.

"Hi, yes, my name is Laura, last name spelled L-E-Q-U-E-S-N-E. I picked up the wrong bag after a flight yesterday. I wanted to know if mine had been returned, or if the man who has it called?"

"Ah, Ms. Le Cane," comes the nasal reply, "my colleague tells me you left with another passenger's suitcase last night."

Damn it, Zany Specs dobbed me in.

"Er, yes, that's not exactly what happened. And it's *Ques-ne*, rhymes with *Chesney*." Ted clears his throat beside me. "I just thought it would be easier if I deliver the bag directly. If you could give me the man's details, we could work it out ourselves. The airline doesn't appear to be doing a great job of retrieving my luggage for me."

Maybe I can scare this woman into giving me his number if I get all "customer complaintsy" on her.

"Miss Le Ques-ne," she imitates the way I said my name. She doesn't sound at all scared of me. "It isn't airline policy to release customers' private details. Be assured we are trying our best to get in touch with the passenger whose bag you have. Please could you give me the code on the baggage receipt for your missing luggage?"

With a sigh, I read out the number on the receipt stuck to the back of my wallet.

Then she says, "We will do our best to locate your missing item. Now, if you let us know where you are staying, we'll send someone to pick up the bag you have taken"—she pauses—"*in error*."

"Hang on . . . my reception is going," I lie. "Just, er, call me if he calls! Bye!"

I hang up and then look in trepidation at the screen, as though the woman I was talking to might leap out of my phone. How crazy am I acting, on a scale of one to Amy Dunne in *Gone Girl*? Probably still only a three or a four, right? People do crazy things for love all the time.

"What's your plan then," asks Ted, "with this case?"

"I'm not sure. He's bound to call, though, right? How can this guy not have realized he has the wrong bag by now? It has my mobile number written on the tag."

"Remind me why you are so intent on meeting this man?" Ted says, drumming the steering wheel with his fingers. "What was the book that makes him so irresistible?"

"I don't need your mockery, thank you very much."

"I'm not mocking you. Maybe I could help search the bag for clues."

"I don't know. I should probably just wait for him to call." I turn to see if Ted looks serious. "What qualifies you to help anyway?"

He pauses for a moment, stroking his beard with one hand, as though genuinely contemplating his skill set.

"Hmm, I have a Boy Scout badge for signs, signals, and codes?"

"Well, in that case . . ."

The car turns out of a lane boxed in by low granite walls, and we emerge again on the coast. The island is small, so nowhere is much farther than a fifteen-minute drive, but the place is a maze of lanes I am glad that I don't need to navigate myself. Ted pulls into a gravel car park overlooking the sea and drives right to the edge of the cliff. It is a very different scene to the bay where we have just been: Instead of low by the shore, we are now high above the sea, gray-blue water stretching to the horizon in every direction. On either side of the car park, narrow footpaths follow the undulating shape of the land's edge, the slope covered by a blanket of green and brown. Down below, waves turn white where the rock meets the sea—a wild swell pulsing against the dark granite edge of the island. I think of pirates trying to land here centuries before, how impossible it would have been to get ashore.

Ted and I both get out of the car. I stretch my arms above my head, exhilarated by the blustery cliff-top breeze.

"This place isn't in my album."

"No, but you wanted me to look in the bag, and it's a good place to stop."

"I didn't know Jersey had all these cliffs," I say, snapping a photo of the scene.

"The island slopes down like a block of cheese. The north is like this, the south is flat, beaches."

"So, I'm on top of the cheese right now?"

He smiles. "You are."

"I'M ON TOP OF THE CHEEEEESE!" I shout at the sea.

He laughs and then screws up his face as though he thinks I am silly. I can't help smiling at his reaction, and then I keep smiling from gratitude that he's shown me this beautiful view. The air here feels so unlike London, like breathing new air that no one has ever breathed before. Ted's gaze meets mine, and I notice his eyes are calm, like a boat with a deep, even keel.

"Are you always like this?" he asks.

"What am I like?" I ask, curious as to what he might say.

"Joyful," he says, and it is the last word I expected.

"Not always," I say, trying to cover the surprise in my reaction. "All right then, Boy Scout, let's see if you deserved that badge of yours."

His eyes smile then, and the moment passes, but the word "joyful" reverberates in my head like the name of a long-forgotten friend.

As we walk around to the boot of the car, Ted says, "You do realize this suitcase is the McGuffin in your story?"

"What's a McGuffin?"

"Not a Hitchcock fan then?" Ted shakes his head, takes his cap off and flings it into the boot. As he runs his hands through his thick hair, I'm struck again by how much younger he is than I first assumed. He is certainly not making the best of himself. I wonder how his wife handles kissing that beard. There's just so much of it, it would be like kissing someone through a hedge. *Why am I imagining other people's kissing predicaments? Inappropriate, Laura.*

"A McGuffin is an object or event that motivates a character in the story but is ultimately unimportant or irrelevant, like the Holy Grail in Arthurian legend, the ring in *The Lord of the Rings*, Rosebud in *Citizen Kane*."

"Oh jeez, you're one of those weird movie geeks, aren't you?" I say, pretending to yawn as I unzip the bag in the boot.

"Anyway, by that logic, this suitcase isn't the McGuffin, it's the suitcase *owner.* I already have the suitcase."

He thinks for a moment, and then looks almost impressed. "Lady Muck, I do believe you are right."

"Not that this little lecture in movie geekology isn't fascinating, but are you going to look for clues or what?"

Ted's lips twitch into a smile, then he turns his attention to the case and starts lifting clothes out, carefully laying them out on the back shelf of the boot.

"Well, he's a got a thirty-four leg and thirty-two-inch waist, so you know he's tall and lean. Expensive work shirt, must earn a bit . . ."

He picks up *To Kill a Mockingbird* and skims through the pages.

"Let me guess, you wanted a father like Atticus Finch."

Am I that much of a cliché? Who wouldn't want a father like Atticus, with his strong moral compass and sage advice? But I don't feel like admitting to Ted that when I read the book, I imagine Atticus with my father's face.

"I just like the book," I say, taking it back from him.

Ted peers into the plastic bag of worn running kit and wrinkles his nose.

"Well, your Mr. McGuffin may be well read, but his sweat still stinks."

"He exercises and looks after himself, I like that in a man," I say, feeling myself prickle. I don't like Ted being rude about Hot Suitcase Guy's things. It feels like a strange betrayal that I'm letting him look through the bag at all.

Ted picks up one of the expensive-looking trainers and looks at the tab inside.

"Size eleven—well, they do say you can tell a lot about a man from the size of his feet." Ted raises an eyebrow at me.

"Give me that," I say, reaching out to grab the shoe. I pull the trainer a bit too hard, and then watch in horror as it flies out of my hand and sails over the side of the cliff. We both stand in silence for a moment, our eyes watching its long route, bouncing down the cliffs toward the sea below—there's no way we're getting that back.

"Oops," says Ted.

"How the hell am going to explain that?" I cry.

Then we look at each other, and Ted starts to laugh.

"It's not funny!" I say, pushing a hand against his chest.

"He won't mind about the trainers once he's met you," says Ted, and the compliment sends a warm pulse up my neck. "A small price to pay for meeting your soulmate." His tone is back to teasing. "Come on, there's got to be something more to go on in here."

He pulls a worn running top from the plastic bag and holds it out in front of him. "Bingo," he says, turning it around to show me.

On the back of the top, it reads: JERSEY RELAY MARATHON—"THE BEE TEAM," RAISING MONEY FOR JBCS.

"What's that?" I ask.

"The Jersey Bee Conservation Society. If he raised money for them, they might know who he is, and I happen to know that they have a stall at the Trinity Community Fete this morning—we could go ask them."

I high-five Ted, and he looks genuinely delighted at having found a lead.

"When we find him, I'm telling him you threw his shoe off a cliff in a jealous rage that he has bigger feet than you," I say.

"He doesn't. Mine are eleven and a half."

We get back in the car, a strange giddy feeling in my stomach, and my cheeks feel flushed. Maybe I'm still feeling a bit carsick. I should probably stop looking at my phone on all these windy roads. Resting my cheek against the cool glass of the side window, I try to think of a good excuse for losing a shoe; what I will say when I finally track down Hot Suitcase Guy.

ꝏ

Jersey Evening News—24 August 1991

A LOVE TOKEN RETURNED
SPARKS LOVE FOR THE NEXT GENERATION

The chance discovery of a lost wartime love token has kindled a new romance fifty years later. In June of this year, Bristol resident Annie Carter visited Jersey to return half of an engraved coin belonging to Alex Le Quesne's late grandfather, William Blampied.

"I came to Jersey to reunite the two halves of the coin," said Miss Carter. "Then I met Alex, and couldn't bring myself to leave. It felt as though the coin had led me to him—like a fairy tale." It would seem that half a century on, romance still follows this coin around.

Chapter 9

The Trinity Community Fete turns out to be a small affair; in fact, just a few trestle tables are set up in the car park next to the parish hall. The Women's Institute is selling tea and coffee in disposable cups, a woman dressed in colorful knitwear sits behind a tower of homemade jam, someone is selling goat's cheese, and a local author is hawking copies of her book next to a dreary tombola. Several charities have set up tables full of leaflets, and there is even someone dressed in a dog costume collecting money for guide dogs. It all looks decidedly underwhelming as far as country fetes go. I was imagining a field full of bunting, beautiful cream teas, merry-go-rounds, and maybe some kind of quaint "who's grown the biggest carrot" competition.

As we survey the scene from the parked car, Ted says, "OK,

what's our strategy?" He nods toward the man sitting behind the JBCS table, a stout-looking gentleman with a bald scalp, haloed by tufts of white hair. "That guy looks like the keeper of the contact details. We could kidnap him and smother him in honey until he gives up a name."

I let out a snort and cover my mouth in embarrassment.

"I think I'll just go and talk to him, no kidnapping required."

As we approach, the author and the jam lady eye us eagerly. Then the woman in a wax jacket behind the coffee urn at the WI table calls to Ted.

"Ted Palmerston, is that you under there?" she asks. "What's all that hair? You shouldn't hide your lovely face, boy. What would your mother have said?"

I smile at the fact someone seems to know Ted everywhere we go. As he walks over to talk to the woman, I make a beeline for the JBCS stall, where I find honey for sale, leaflets about bee conservation, and even a beekeeper's hat to try on.

"Hi!" I beam. "I'm Laura, I wonder if you could help me?"

"You're interested in supporting the bees?" asks the man, glancing down at my chocolate-stained dress.

"Oh yes, big bee fan." I grin.

"I'm Keith, Chairman of the JBCS. Can I give you a leaflet about membership?"

"I would love a leaflet, Keith, and some honey. Hook me up with some of the sweet stuff, ha-ha!" I'm babbling. "But where you could really help me, Keith, is I'm trying to track down some people who may be members already. Do you know the Le Maistre family? I think Mr. Le Maistre might have raised money for you running the marathon, and his mother has a particular interest in beehives?" I look at the man hopefully. Now I've said it out loud it doesn't feel like a lot to go on. I can't imagine an episode of *Luther* starting with a lead like this.

"Maude Le Maistre. I've just finished building a beehive for her birthday tomorrow," says Keith, pronouncing it "Le May-tch," a broad smile creasing his round, ruddy cheeks.

Yes! He knows her! He's not looking at me like I'm a crazy stalker. I clench my fists in excitement. Then, just as I'm about to ask Keith for more details, an alarm goes off on my phone. Two minutes to twelve—what did I set that for? What does "IL" mean? Then, as it dawns on me, my throat starts to feel as though I've swallowed a pint of wet cement—in two minutes, I'm supposed to be doing an Instagram live from a beautiful, scenic Jersey location.

"Oh, Ted! You've got to help me," I call over to him. The WI woman is examining his beard from every angle, with a distinct look of disapproval. Ted looks grateful for the opportunity to escape. "I need to do a live broadcast for work, right now. Please, could you just hold the camera for me?" I ask, searching for a remotely scenic backdrop, but it's literally a choice of the recycling bins or the road. "Just frame out the background as much as possible."

I quickly log on to the work account. Suki will kill me if I miss this.

"What about your top?" Ted nods toward the chocolate stain on my dress.

He's right; I can't represent Love Life looking like this. I search frantically for something to cover me. All I can see is the beekeeping hat, perhaps I could make a kooky feature out of it?

"Keith, would you mind if I borrowed this hat, just for two minutes? Lovely, thanks."

He nods slowly, but his wispy eyebrows dip into a suspicious *V*.

I quickly pull the large mesh sheath down over my head; it covers the top of my dress perfectly. Hopefully the hat part looks like a cool, wide-brimmed sun hat, the kind Audrey Hepburn might wear on a holiday to Rome. I try to own the look, taking the advice of Vanya's book and channeling my inner tigress. Handing the phone to Ted, I flap my hands for him to point it at me and then press the button to go live.

"Hello—I'm Laura Le Quesne from Love Life, and I'm coming to you live from Jersey—the land of milk and honey! Ha-ha. There are beaches galore and much to explore—" *What is coming out of my mouth? It's like a poem made up by a six-year-old.* "And I'm here visiting some of the most romantic places on the island. It's a personal story for me, as my parents met here—so I wouldn't even exist if it weren't for the island's aphro-aphrodesy . . ." memory blank, memory blank! *What's the word?* "Ecclesiastical properties." *Damn, no, that's churches.* "I mean aphrodisiastical qualities—SEXY QUALITIES, nothing religious, ah! Though I'm sure some people here are religious."

I usually pride myself on my ability to wing interviews or presentations, but I'm not used to being center stage. The focus is usually on the people I'm interviewing, and Ted's sympathetic eyes and grimacing mouth are not instilling me with confidence. I turn frantically to Keith.

"Keith—tell us, what is romantic about bees? Jersey is famous for its delicious honey, isn't it?"

Ted swings the camera around to Keith, who looks nonplussed.

"Not really. I wouldn't say it was famous for honey. Milk and potatoes, yes. Honey no."

"Well, I don't bee-lieve you, Keith—he's being modest. So, what got you into bees? You just love those little black-and-yellow buggers, hey?"

Keith frowns, then looks back and forth between me and the camera phone with such a perplexed expression, you'd think I'd just asked him to yodel me the square root of eighty-seven.

"I am interested in conservation and I have an experimental breeding program that I devised with a specially constructed hive—"

Oh wow, Keith is not helping me at all, he's speaking at the pace of an asthmatic snail. I'm going to have to cut him off. "Oh, that sounds so romantic, Keith." Seeing he's wearing a ring, I think on my feet; I need to divert this conversation away from bloody bees. "I see you're married. How did you meet your partner?"

Keith now looks at me as though I've propositioned him for sex. He frowns suspiciously, then says, "I met my wife through a mutual acquaintance. We had a shared interest in ordnance survey maps."

Possibly the most boring How Did You Meet? *I've ever heard.*

"So, she found the map to your heart, aw!"

Ted winces. Keith looks as though he's watching some kind of pagan goat sacrifice take place on his trestle table. I imagine the comments full of question marks flashing up on the screen. I need to save this somehow. *Think, Laura, THINK!*

"Now, you might have been expecting to see me at a gorgeous beachside location, but at Love Life, we're all about supporting local business, that's why I thought I'd come to the community village fete and discover genuine Jersey." I walk over to the jam lady, a woman in her fifties, who is sitting behind a cardboard sign that reads JENNY'S JAM. She's wearing a pale green cloche hat, with an eye-catching gold-and-green dragonfly hatpin. Ted follows me with the camera.

"What are you selling here, Jenny?"

"Homemade jam, all berries from my own garden. Farmhouse black butter too," she says, pointing to a small dark brown pot, tied with a red ribbon.

"Ah, my grandmother asked me to get her some of this, but I wasn't sure what it was."

"It's a medieval recipe for applesauce, made from cider apples. Delicious on a bit of cheese," Jenny explains.

"Well, I will take three!" I say, filling my arms with jars. "How many customers have you had today, Jenny?"

"Just two," she says mournfully. "Including you."

"Just two! Look at this stuff. Come on, Jersey—if you're watching, come out and support local produce at the Trinity Community Fete. Love Life believes in the charm and importance of local businesses, so come and buy something from someone with a name—you'll make their day. From Jenny—" I wave to the woman behind the goat's cheese stall. "From . . ."

"From Lou," says the cheese lady cheerily.

"From Sophie," says the author.

"Aaron," says the man dressed as a guide dog.

Ted gives me a thumbs-up, and I try to wrap things up.

"Well, there's a *hive* of reasons to visit! Ciao for now."

Ciao for now? I do a little pirouette, and Ted stops recording as I yank off the beekeeper's bonnet. Wow, it was hot as a witch's armpit under there.

"How bad was that?" I ask Ted, whose face looks both genuinely impressed and bewildered at the same time.

"I think you rescued it," he says.

I'm not sure Suki is going to think so. Right on cue, my phone starts to rings.

"Suki, hi!" I say with forced excitement.

"What was that, Laura? Why are you standing next to some bins, dressed as a lunatic, talking to some senile old man about bees and fucking jam?" She's shouting loud enough for Keith to hear, and he looks suitably offended. I back away, out of his earshot.

"Well, I was going for something experimental," I say, the cement now set dry in my throat. "People love bees, they're very on trend."

"I do not like bees, Laura, and we do not support local business, we support *big* business who have budgets for advertising. What the hell are you trying to pull here? I was expecting you in a bikini, on a beach, eating oysters—SEXY! ASPIRATIONAL! HOLIDAY! Not bee feces in a car park."

"Honey isn't actually bee feces, Suki. They make it from—"

"Thin ice, Laura—skinny Frappuccino thin."

She hangs up on me. My chest flutters with panic as I feel Suki's faith in me vanishing like a rapidly retreating tide.

"FUCK! Fuckity fuck, fuck pants," I scream at the phone.

Then I turn to see everyone at the sad little fete watching me. Ted's WI friend has a hand pressed to her mouth in horror. I swallow my work-related terror. I just need to finish the conversation with Keith, get the Le Maistres' address, and get the hell out of here. I'll worry about Suki later.

"So, Keith, sorry about that. Um, as you'd started to say, Maude Le Maistre—any chance you could give us her son's full name and contact details?"

Keith is now looking at me as though I've admitted to being a serial killer who's trying to hunt these people down in order to stuff both their decapitated corpses into one of his home-made beehives.

"Maybe I should give your number to Maude, let her know you're trying to get in touch with her son." His voice comes out at rather a high-pitched squeak. "The bee club takes data protection very seriously."

Ted tries to reason with him, we explain all about the suitcase, but Keith isn't budging and then the guy dressed up for the guide dogs asks Keith "if these people are bothering him." I end up leaving with a promise from Keith that he'll call Maude with my number as soon as he gets home. Then I dole out the last of my cash on black butter and goat's cheese, and compliment the author on the bluebell-shaped earrings she's wearing, all in an attempt to make amends for my sweary outburst.

Back in the car, Ted is biting his lip, trying not to laugh.

"What?" I snap. I am nowhere close to laughing about this yet. Interviewing people is the one thing I thought I was good at. I don't understand how that went so badly wrong. "Sorry," I say. Ted is the last person I should be angry with.

"We just don't see a lot of 'fuckity fuck fuck pants' at the community parish fetes."

"Gah! And we were so close. He was about to offer up Maude on a plate before I cocked it up."

I close my eyes, wondering why the universe is intent on making this so difficult. If I am destined to meet J. Le Maistre this weekend, it could just have been a very simple suitcase exchange.

"Look, don't worry. We have a name. She'll be easy to find now," says Ted.

He reaches out to put a consoling hand on my shoulder. Now we're looking at each other face-to-face, I can better see Ted's eyes again, his facial features beyond the beard. His honey-brown irises contain flecks of gold and maybe it's because the rest of his face is hidden, but his eyes radiate real warmth. When his hand drops from my shoulder, I feel a strange coldness, like taking off a cozy coat in a cold foyer.

"For the record, I thought your broadcast was excellent."

A phone starts to ring. I'm so used to it being mine, I start to root in my bag, but it's Ted's phone that's ringing. His eyes flash with concern as he sees the caller ID.

"Dad, what's happened?" he asks, answering the phone with one hand, the other gripping the steering wheel. I watch him as he listens, then says, "OK, stay there, I'm on my way."

TIGER WOMAN ON FAILURE

Tigers are expert hunters, yet only roughly one in twenty hunts ends in a kill. After an unsuccessful hunt, do tigers go home and lament how bad they are at hunting? Do they call their friends and wonder how they'll ever eat again, because they are clearly such failures? They do not. They get back out there and try again.

Chapter 10

"Is everything OK?" I ask Ted.

"My dad had a fall." His face has clouded over, all levity from the fete gone. He pulls the car into gear with two sharp thrusts of his elbow.

"I'm so sorry. Drop me anywhere, I don't want to be in the way if you need to go to him."

"The neighbor is with him, but I should go." Ted clears his throat, then says quietly, "Dad has Parkinson's."

We're driving fast now, out of the village, onto another tree-lined country road.

"Have you been looking after him?" I ask, tentatively picking up the apple peel.

"I came back to Jersey to help him move into assisted

living," Ted says, his eyes on the road. "He can't manage on his own anymore. I'm packing up his house."

"I'm sorry, that must be hard." I pause before adding, "I had to pack up my mother's house after she died and— Well, I know how difficult it can be."

"My father isn't dead," Ted says sharply, then glancing across at me he shakes his head, as though shaking off his reaction. "I'm sorry. You were close to your mother."

It sounds like a statement rather than a question, but I reply with a single nod.

"She was my best friend." I am surprised at myself, that I have willingly brought Mum into this conversation. I would usually be too wary of the torrent of emotion, which I know flows so close beneath the surface.

"How long ago was that?" Ted asks.

"Two years," I manage to say.

"We lost my mother to breast cancer four years ago. Dad's managed alone since then, but now he needs more support," says Ted.

"I'm sorry." I can't think of any different words to say. I'm sorry. I'm sorry. How many times have those words been said to me? Maybe we don't have enough words to express sympathy. We have fifty ways to describe a cup of coffee, but I can only think of one way to say, "I'm sorry for your loss."

"I don't think he minds going," Ted says with a rueful smile. "He already has a girlfriend lined up at the place he's chosen."

I look across at Ted and see the muddle of emotion dancing behind his eyes as he tries to make light of something dark.

"He knows it's time. Packing up the house is the part I'm finding difficult. My dad was born in that house, and Mum didn't like to throw anything away. She was a hoarder, I suppose. Is it bad that I just want to bonfire the lot of it?"

Ted gazes ahead, talking as though to himself.

"Tough to do it alone. You don't have any siblings?"

"A sister in the UK. My nephew has special needs—it's not easy for her to leave."

"I wouldn't throw everything away. Keep the things that have meaning."

"Everything in the house just reminds me of how things used to be, a different life. Nothing I keep can bring that back." Ted massages his chin through his beard, his eyes still intently focused on the road. His voice is full of pain when he says, "Dad goes to bed early because he's up half the night with his restless legs, and there's something about being left alone at night with a task I don't know how to start—picking through the rubble of my parents' lives. That's why I started driving the cab again."

I can see Ted's eyes are welling up, and he puffs out his cheeks to take a slow exhale. I reach out to squeeze his arm.

"Sorry, you don't need to hear all this." He rubs his eyes with his sleeve and clears his throat. "I'm deviating from my cabdriver script again, aren't I?" he says with a lopsided smile. "Plémont headland is on the way. I'll drop you there, and you can see where the Pontins used to be, where you said your parents worked that summer, and there's the cave on the beach where your dad proposed. I can come back for you in an hour or so." His words are now brisk, as though he's embarrassed to have shared as much as he did.

"Please don't worry about coming back for me, just throw me out anywhere," I say, still watching Ted's face. I never see a man get emotional. Perhaps, growing up without a dad, I am not close enough to any men to be allowed to see. Maybe the ones I have dated have not been particularly emotional men.

We drive in silence for a minute, and then Ted says, "I feel like I'm ruining this romantic comedy you're in."

"What?" I say, blinking at him.

"Your hunt for Mr. McGuffin. It feels like a romantic comedy to me: love in a suitcase, shoes falling off cliffs, a bee-themed treasure hunt." He grins. "Now I've muddied the tone by talking of dying parents and depressing house clearances. Your audience will be asking for their money back."

I laugh. It's one of those laughs where you've been about to cry, and then someone says something, and their words tack your boat into the wind and take you in a new direction—there's a thrill in the snap change of emotion as your sail billows out on the other side of the mast.

"I don't know," I say with a smile, "real life can't be all bee-themed treasure hunts, can it?"

Ted's phone rings again and he pulls into a lay-by to take the call. He talks to someone called Sandy, who I assume must be the neighbor. He sounds reassured and when he hangs up his face visibly relaxes.

"Good news?" I ask.

"My neighbor. She says Dad's OK. He was mainly confused—just a cut on his arm, it looked worse than it was." Ted pulls the car onto the road again and rubs his shoulder with the opposite hand. "The headland is just up here."

Around the next corner the coastline reappears. Ted parks

the car next to a field full of wild gorse with a footpath leading up to the cliff edge. He picks up my photo album from the armrest between our seats and flicks through to the pictures of the holiday resort as it looked in 1991.

"The resort that was here went derelict," Ted explains. "They pulled it down a while back and put the headland back to nature."

A photo of Mum and Dad dancing together in a hall is one of the few photos I have of them together. I don't even have one of them on their wedding day because the budget photographer they used overexposed the film. In this shot, Mum's wearing a blue dress with puffball sleeves, while my dad is rocking sideburns and wears a pale denim shirt and white jeans. The vibe is so eighties, it could be a still from the film *Footloose*. Though it's a grainy picture, it captures a look in both their eyes, as though they only see each other, completely unaware of whoever took the photo.

"This must have been taken here," I say, pointing to the picture. "This is Mum teaching Dad to dance. They used the hall to practice once all the guests had gone to bed. Usually to Phil Collins, Dad's favorite." I smile at the memory of Mum telling me the story. Then I tap the photo and say wistfully, "I doubt I'll ever have a moment as romantic as this."

I turn to see Ted looking at me with an almost tender expression. I didn't mean it to sound that way, I don't want him to pity me. It's this photo, the look between my parents—it weaves a strange spell on me.

"It's hard to imagine a huge holiday resort standing in this wild place. Soon, no one will remember it was even here. All the stories that happened here will be lost to posterity." I glance back down at the photo. "Where do you think the love goes, when no one's left to tell the story?"

Ted looks thoughtful for a moment, then he says, "Someone once told me that growing up feeling loved allows you to go on to love other people. Maybe love is simply a huge chain letter, passed down through the generations. The details of the stories begin not to matter."

The sentiment of his words surprises me. I've never heard a man talk about love so plainly, with so little coyness. I wonder if all the men I've known have actually been boys.

"That's a lovely way to look at it," I say with a smile, then reach forward to drum a hand on the dashboard. "Sorry, Ted, I'm holding you up."

"It's fine. Your cave—" Ted reaches across to turn the page to the picture of my mother standing in a cave in a red bikini—the place where they got engaged. "Follow the footpath around the cliff and you'll get down to the beach. This cave is at the far end, right around to the left." Ted looks at his watch. "Don't hang around there after one forty-five. The sea comes in quickly at Plémont, and you can get cut off fast. There's a café at the top of the steps, I'll meet you there at two."

I'm pleased he wants to come back, but I scribble my mobile number on one of the cards in the glove box, just in case he needs to change the plan.

"I hope your dad is OK."

As I get out of the car, I shiver. The sun has gone in and I'm only wearing a strappy sundress. I don't want to be cold, especially if I'm going to be out here for an hour and a half. In the absence of anything else to wear, I grab the cream fisherman's jumper from the suitcase in the boot. Putting it on, I inhale the smell of it again, then I catch Ted watching me in the rearview mirror. Something tells me he doesn't approve of me borrowing it.

"What did I say about the cave, Lady Muck?" he shouts after me as I start walking away up the footpath.

"Don't stay there too long, or I'll get washed up the blowhole, gotcha!"

I turn to wave as he drives away, and he gives a salute, which makes me smile, then I hug my arms around myself as I set off up the dirt footpath.

I try calling Gran back, but she doesn't answer, so I leave a message saying I've bought her some black butter. I'm surprised how downbeat she sounded about me being in Jersey, but then Gran has never been one to get sentimental about the past. "Fiercely practical," Mum called her.

The headland feels truly wild with its tangle of ferns and sun-bleached grass overlooking the wind-whipped sea. The only stark reminder of a human footprint is the remnants of an old concrete bunker, left behind from the wartime occupation. I take photos of the headland, a selfie to contrast then and now, then spend some time trying to work out from the pictures where the holiday resort would have stood; my mother's apartment, where Dad's kitchen might have been, the hall where they danced. It's impossible. Nature has taken the headland back so entirely—there isn't even a trace of the resort's foundation.

From the footpath that hugs the cliff, a powerful swell is visible, pulsing toward the island, then churning white over craggy brown rocks as it reaches land. To my left, the sharp coast softens to sand and Plémont bay comes into view below me—an enormous sandy cove, guarded on every side by steep rock. There is something hypnotic about watching waves break on sand. They are so reliable in their behavior; not one breaks rank, refusing to adhere to the ebb and flow.

My phone interrupts me from being mesmerized by the sea. It's Vanya.

"Hey, I was just calling to check you were OK after that Insta live?"

"It was bad," I say with a wince.

"Personally, I loved it, super kitsch, but Suki dropped a few f bombs in the office. How's the stalking going?"

"Not well. The airport thinks I've stolen this guy's bag, I've managed to accidentally throw one of his shoes off a cliff, oh, and now I am wearing the guy's clothes because my only dress is covered in mud and chocolate, like I'm a five-year-old in an advert for washing powder. On the plus side, I have found out that his mother's name is Maude and that her birthday is tomorrow."

"Well, that's a start. Forget the Insta live. Suki loves your coin story, everyone does, it's exactly the feel-good romantic content the website needs right now. Don't get thrown off your stride, just get what you need to write the best article you can." I'm not used to Vanya giving me serious pep talks like this, maybe she's been talking to Dee. "How far have you got with *Tiger Woman*?"

"I've started it," I say evasively.

The truth is these kinds of books scare me. They make me feel inadequate for not being the self-possessed, fiercely independent woman I know I should be, or at least should aspire to be.

"Laura, it's going to change your whole outlook," Vanya says. "It talks about this idea of being roar, like raw—R-A-W—but spelled the tiger way, it's about following your instincts rather than the narrow path society has presented us with."

"Do you think it's possible to be a romantic and also a feminist?" I ask, my eyes drawn back toward the foaming waves.

"Of course it is."

"Because sometimes I feel conflicted; like I want to stand up to the patriarchy and everything, but I'd also quite like to be in love and have a boyfriend."

"Look," Vanya says with a sigh, "Michelle Obama is queen of modern feminism, but she's still a wife and mother and she still has great hair. It's about having the right to choose—you can choose to put on a pinny and be a fifties housewife if you want, you can choose to travel to Peru and join a commune or enlist in the space program and be the first woman on Mars. You can live how you like; but the point is we should have the chance to choose, not get railroaded into a role society dictates for us."

She is right. Vanya surprises me sometimes. She is this dichotomy of Tinder and hangovers and looking for love in all the wrong places, but she is also self-possessed and self-aware and radiates this inner strength I sometimes fear I have lost. I feel surer of myself when I am around her, and that is a valuable attribute for a friend to have.

"Like, this search for Hot Suitcase Guy," I say. "Do you think even believing in fate or destiny feels dated now somehow? Like, it's a little nineties Meg Ryan, rather than twenty-first-century 'take control of your own destiny.'" I screw up my face, unsure what my point is, my mind fizzing with unformulated philosophies.

"If you want to be nineties Meg Ryan, I am so here for that," says Vanya firmly. "People have believed in fate for longer than they've believed the world is round—it will never go out of fashion."

The conversation with Vanya reassures me; I'm not crazy, I'm just a romantic. Once we've said good-bye, I look up Maude Le Maistre on my phone while muttering under my breath, "If I want to be Meg Ryan, I can be Meg sodding Ryan." I find an address and a phone number. YES! Screw you and your "data protection," Keith, I found her anyway, ha!

I try her number and it clicks straight to an answering machine. She has one of those messages older people use, where they just give their phone number rather than their name. I leave my details, explaining about her son's bag. The trail finally feels as though it's getting warmer.

It's her birthday tomorrow, he has a gift for her in his suitcase—surely, he has to notice he has the wrong bag before then? What if he lost his phone, or he's been in an accident? What if he's in the hospital now, with my suitcase, and he's lost all power of speech, but he's desperately trying to communicate with the doctors about needing to get the case back to its rightful owner? Maybe I should call the hospital, just in case.

As my mind darts down unlikely alleys, I open Google Maps to see where Maude lives in relation to where I am. Then I see a street name I recognize from yearly Christmas cards: Rue du Val Bach. Only a few minutes' walk from where I'm standing—Mad Aunt Monica's house.

ecee

4 December 1995

Annie,
I am sorry it has come to this, but with all that's happened, I think it best we cease communicating. Losing my son and my mother this year has been upsetting enough, without the added distress you have contributed to our lives. Clearly, you and I are never going to see eye to eye on what is right, and what belongs to whom. I don't want to be reminded of it every time you get in touch, so it would be better if you are not.

You will not receive another penny from our family. Anything else pertaining to Alexander's estate, please contact my lawyer, details enclosed.

Love and best wishes to your daughter,
Sue Le Quesne

Chapter 11

If I'm going to get a firsthand account of Mum and Dad's story from anyone, it will be from great-aunt Monica. There are only a few houses on the road, so her place is easy to find. As soon as I see the front garden, I know it must be hers. Ceramic ornaments litter the lawn and patio. They are all hedgehog figurines carrying out various hobbies—a ballerina hedgehog, a hedgehog in waders with a fishing rod, and two ceramic hedgehogs on a miniature tandem bicycle. Now I come to think about it, most of the Christmas cards I've received were hedgehog-themed: hedgehogs in Christmas hats or poking out of stockings, hedgehogs on ice skates or encased in snow to make spiky snowballs.

I ring the bell tentatively, not sure what or whom I might be about to meet. I have a vision of the door being opened by a life-size Mrs. Tiggy-Winkle.

"Hello?" says a gray-haired woman as she opens the door, thankfully no spikes in sight. She looks like a normal seventy-something-year-old woman, with a bob of straight hair, spectacles on a chain around her neck, a green floral blouse, and—oh, bright purple galoshes on her feet.

"I'm so sorry to knock on your door like this, but—"

She puts her glasses on and peers at me, then cuts me off. "Laura?"

"Yes." I feel myself beam. Either she recognizes me, or she received my postcard.

"I got your card this morning"—she grins—"and now here you are! My, my, don't you look like your father."

No one's ever said that to me before, and I eagerly tuck away her words as though she's given me back a piece of him. Monica beckons me in, pointing to a brush mat in the shape of a hedgehog where I can wipe my feet.

"Sorry to turn up unannounced like this, I was nearby and—"

"I should have been most offended if you had not turned up," she says staunchly, marching back into the house and throwing both hands into the air. Her voice is posh and clipped, like a drill sergeant Julie Andrews. "Kitty would have been particularly upset, wouldn't you, Kitty?"

As I follow her through to the kitchen, I look around for a cat or some other pet who might answer to the name.

We walk through to an open-plan kitchen-living area, a haven of chintzy furniture and net curtains. There are two mustard-colored armchairs in the living area and an orange rug covered in geometric patterns. The kitchen Aga is lined with tea towels. One has the words, *I may be prickly, but I don't bite*, next to a cartoon hedgehog with a maniacal smile.

"Kitty Kettle," says Monica, holding a kettle aloft like an Olympic flame, "she loves to make a brew for two!"

I laugh nervously, unsure whether this is a joke.

"Tea would be lovely, thank you."

"Don't thank me," Monica says, leaning toward me with two unblinking eyes. "Kitty does all the hard work."

Well, it seems Mum was right; Monica is mad as a handbag full of hedgehogs.

"As I mentioned in my card, I was hoping I could ask you a few questions about my parents' story, Aunt Monica. I write for a website and I'm putting together an article about the coin and how it brought my parents together." I reach a hand instinctively to my pendant.

"Such a shame, Al and Annie, such a shame, the whole business," Monica says, making a tutting noise as she leans in to get a better look at the coin around my neck. "Well, I'm glad you still have my mother's coin safe." Then with a sigh she says, "Good match for each other, your parents were, if only Alex hadn't been such a terrible bounder."

I'm not sure what she means by the word "bounder." Dad was killed in a motorcycle accident in Morocco—perhaps she means he was adventurous, he didn't like to sit still. I nod in any case.

"All I really know about him is what Mum told me."

"Well, I wouldn't believe all of it. He wasn't all bad," Monica says as she pours out tea and hands me a cup. "I assume milk and no sugar unless someone says otherwise."

"That's perfect."

"Thank you, Kitty," she says, patting the kettle. Then she looks at me expectantly, so I follow suit, offering a mumble of thanks to an inanimate kitchen appliance.

Monica leads me through to the living room area, which is full of dark mahogany furniture. Every surface is covered in little ceramic hedgehogs, and framed cross-stitches line the walls, mainly of hedgehogs, but there are various maps of the Channel Islands too.

"You like hedgehogs then?" I say.

Monica takes a seat in one of the mustard-colored armchairs and waves me to the one opposite.

"Who doesn't like hedgehogs?" she asks, as though I've commented on the fact that she likes air and breathing. "Harmless, adorable little things. Show me a person who doesn't like hedgehogs, and I will show you a psychopath. Lock them all up, I would."

I'm not convinced this is the universal test for assessing psychopaths, or whether people should be put in jail, but I nod politely and take a sip of my tea, which is, in fact, ninety-eight percent milk.

"I volunteer for Hedgehog Rescue," Aunt Monica explains. "Always scooping them out of drains and ditches, we are. I like to be prepared, hence—" She points down to her feet.

"The galoshes," I say.

"Now, Laura, I must tell you how sorry I was to hear about your mother passing. To lose both your parents too soon, well, that's a raw straw as they say."

"Thank you." I nod, clasping my mug with both hands.

"Despite all the upset, I never had a word to say against

your mother. I thought she was a ray of sunshine—Alex was a fool to let her go." Monica shakes her head, lost in recollection. "And then to waste his last years on this earth in arguing."

"What do you mean, 'let her go'?" I ask, shuffling forward in my chair and putting the tepid milk down on a side table.

"Well, he should have made a go of it, shouldn't he? I shouldn't speak ill of the dead, but he was a prize chump, my nephew, bounded about from woman to woman. Didn't have the sense to see when he should stop dillydallying and settle down—especially with you on the way."

"But—" I feel myself squinting in confusion. Aunt Monica must be mistaken or thinking of someone else. "They did settle down. They got married."

Monica makes a face, then laughs.

"They—they got engaged on the beach down there . . ." I trail off, thrusting my arm in the direction of the sea. Monica clasps her hands together, resting them against her chin.

"Who told you this then?" she asks.

"Mum did." I feel myself frown.

"Laura, your parents never married, and if they were engaged then your father certainly never told any of us. I'm sure they had a merry time of it that summer while it lasted, but— I don't know why she would have told you that." She pauses, picking up a hedgehog pincushion from the side and starting to redistribute the pins more evenly. "Maybe Annie was old-fashioned, didn't want you to feel 'illegitimate.'" Monica whispers the word. "Though I thought nobody worried about that kind of thing these days."

"Of course they got married," I say, standing up and pacing the room. "Why would Mum make something like that up?"

Monica shrugs and carries on rearranging pins.

"The way I saw it, they had a gorgeous fling, got their story in the paper, then Alex got the jitters and broke it off. He'd never had a girl last more than a few months before. I'm not sure he knew how to be in love, especially with all the attention, and they were both so young. Annie flew back to Bristol and found out you were on the way." Monica sighs. "In my day, they'd have been hauled up the aisle before the bump got too big."

I sit down again and cross and recross my legs, then clasp my hands on my lap, unable to compute what she's telling me. None of this makes any sense.

"Of course all your mother's phobias didn't make life easy for anyone. Not that Al wasn't sympathetic, but I'm sure that took its toll."

"What phobias? Mum didn't have phobias!" Clearly Monica has no idea who or what she's talking about.

"Oh, she was terrified of the dark, of storms, of seagulls. I remember Alex saying they had to sleep with the lights on—quite exhausting."

"She didn't have anything like that."

"Really?" Monica taps her lip thoughtfully. "I'm sure it was her who had a whole catalog of phobias."

The telephone rings, and Monica springs across the room to answer it.

"Yes, Hedgehog Rescue . . . Yes. You think it's alive? Don't get too close, you'll scare her. Address? . . . Don't try to pick her up. I'll be there with a box in a jiffy."

She scribbles a note on a pad and then hurries to put her coat on.

"Sorry, Laura, duty calls. Prickler in distress." She pulls a pair of pink washing-up gloves from an inside coat pocket. "Look, I'm sure your mother thought it was for the best. Such a shame she fell out with everyone, though. I always liked her, and, of course, we all wanted to know you. Now, you must come for tea when I'm not on call. I've got photos to show you—your father as a boy, and I want to hear all about your life, about this website you write for. Do you have pets? Any health conditions? What day starts the week for you? It's a Wednesday for me, which I know is unusual." She starts hustling me out of the door and picks up a purple flatcap to match her galoshes. Then she pauses for a moment, holding both my hands with her pink gloves, "You know, it's rather disconcerting to see his good looks on a woman."

"That's kind, Aunt. I'll try and come back. It's just I've got a lot to fit in before I head home on Sunday." I try to hide the disappointment in my voice. Clearly Mad Aunt Monica is not going to be a reliable source for my article.

We walk together down her drive, and Monica climbs into a heavily dented green Škoda. As she's about to drive off, she rolls down the window and asks, "Do you need a lift anywhere?"

"No, I'm fine, thank you."

"I'm visiting my sister, Sue, your grandmother, tomorrow. All that unpleasantness between her and Annie was a long time ago. Now that you're here, I'm sure she'd want to see you, patch things up."

Patch things up, with Bad Granny? Mum told me they fell out over Dad's will. I found a letter from her saying as much when I packed up Mum's house. I wonder if the Jersey family convinced themselves Mum and Dad were never married so they could rationalize cutting Mum off.

"I've got your number now, you wrote it in the card, we'll make a plan for Sunday," Monica shouts as she reverses down the drive. "I'll make us a Swiss log, everyone likes Swiss log—except for psychopaths. You're not a psychopath, are you, Laura?"

"I don't think so."

"Excellent."

Then the green Škoda, hedgehog stickers lining the rear window, shoots off up the road. The whole encounter leaves me feeling completely bemused. I don't know what I'd expected Aunt Monica to be like, what I'd expected her to say, but it wasn't that. I'm not having much success on any fronts today. There's still no word from J. Le Maistre, and Maude hasn't called me back.

I check my phone again, hopeful for a message, but the screen is blank, the battery gone. Oh no, what if they've tried to call? My watch says it's five past two—and I realize I'm now late to meet Ted. Running back down the road to the car park, I see his cab, but he's not inside. I rush down to the Plémont beach café, looking to see if he's waiting for me, but there's no sign of him. Maybe he nipped to the loo, he can't have gone far. While I'm waiting for him to appear, I walk around the café to the top of the steep steps that lead down onto the beach. The stairs look as though they've been rebuilt many times over the years, a constant battle to stave off the destructive power of the sea. I can see why Ted warned me about the tides now—the waves are lapping against the bottom of the steps and they are the only way off this beach.

As I'm watching the shallow water dance against the rocks, a figure emerges from the sea and strides up the small strip of sand that's still accessible. As I blink in confusion at what this sea creature might be, I realize it is a fully dressed Ted. What on earth? Has he gone for a spontaneous swim in his clothes? He looks like some kind of plane crash survivor, with his wild hair and wet clothes clinging to him, his dark blue jeans and maroon T-shirt slick against his body. He looks up and sees me at the top of the steps, and I wave—his face looks relieved to see me and then furious.

"Where have you been?" he shouts up to me.

"Here! Sorry, I got caught up visiting my great-aunt," I yell back down.

He charges up the rest of the stairs and is breathing heavily by the time he gets to me.

"I was worried you'd stayed too long in the cave—that you'd got stuck," he says, glaring down at me.

I slap a hand over my mouth.

"Oh no, you didn't go in the sea looking for *me*?"

"I thought you might have hurt yourself, or you couldn't get back."

He closes his eyes. I'm touched he was so concerned about me, but I was only fifteen minutes late—it feels like a slight overreaction.

"I didn't even make it to the cave in the end."

"And I tried calling you."

"My phone died. Ted, I—" I can't help laughing. I know I shouldn't, but I can't get over the image of him leaping in the sea to look for me like some kind of primordial David Hasselhoff.

When he sees me laughing, he charges past me, back to the car. I hurry after him. "Ted, I'm sorry, but I was only fifteen minutes late. I didn't know you'd launch a one-man, fully clothed rescue mission."

He doesn't turn around until we get to the car. Wordlessly, he opens the boot and pulls off his sopping-wet shirt. I can't help but look at his bare chest as he wraps a towel around himself—he has an incredible physique for a middle-aged man. He's got these defined pectoral muscles and a slim, toned stomach, tanned with a light smattering of brown hair. He catches me looking at his body, and I quickly avert my eyes. I was only staring because I'm surprised he looks like that—I didn't have Beardy McCastaway down as the gym-bod type.

"You don't mess around with the tides here, Laura," Ted says tersely. "People get into trouble on this beach all the time. You have to respect the sea."

"I do, I do respect the sea," I say, composing my face. "Do you want to borrow some dry clothes from the suitcase?"

"I do not want to wear your stolen clothes. Besides, you seem to be wearing half of them already." His voice is now a quiet growl.

He walks around to the driver's seat, takes the towel from around his shoulders, and folds it into a square to sit on. Now he's sitting there topless, his hair still dripping wet and his jeans clinging tightly to his firm thigh muscles.

"I'll need to go back to my place to get some clothes."

"Is your dad all right?" I ask gently, willing him not to be cross with me.

He blinks his eyes closed, exhaling slowly. "Yes."

"I'm sorry that I was late, Ted."

"It's fine. You just have no idea how fast the tide comes in here—I wouldn't want to be responsible for anything happening to you." His voice has a serious, earnest quality.

"I really appreciate you looking out for me," I say, reaching out to touch his arm. His skin is surprisingly warm considering he's been in the cold water. He looks down at my fingers, and I take back my hand—conscious the gesture feels overly familiar when the man is sitting there half naked. My eyes drop to his hand, to his wedding ring.

"Your wife will be wondering why you're flinging yourself in the sea after strange women." I say it with wide eyes. I mean it as a joke, something to break the tension, but Ted doesn't smile.

"No, she won't," he says flatly. I feel stupid then, as though I've implied there's something between us and he's telling me, in no uncertain terms, that there is not.

Chapter 12

We drive in silence. The tips of Ted's ears have turned red, and then I hear myself start to babble, "Ted, I hope you don't think I was being inappropriate back there—I wasn't trying to—I mean, obviously, even if you weren't married, you wouldn't be—" I swallow nervously, apparently unable to finish a single sentence. "Just so long as it's clear, that—well—"

Ted rescues me from tying myself in verbal knots.

"Laura, it's fine. I didn't mean it to sound like that." He exhales again. "My wife and I are separated. I haven't seen her in two years. That's why I said she wouldn't care."

"Oh," I say, genuinely surprised. Then without thinking, "What happened?" When Ted doesn't answer immediately, I add, "You don't have to tell me. Sorry, I'm being nosy."

"It's fine," he says, clearing his throat. "I don't mind telling you. She just left the house one day, said she was going to get her hair cut. When I went downstairs, I found a note, her wedding ring, and her mobile phone on the kitchen table."

He goes quiet again, but I wait, trying not to fill the space, to allow Ted room to say more, the art of the apple peel. "She took a suitcase of clothes and that was it. Left me with the house, all our stuff from nine years together, all our friends to explain it to."

"Just like that?" I can't keep the surprise from my voice.

"Just like that," he says.

"What did her note say?" I ask.

Ted flexes his hands on the steering wheel.

"It was complicated, we didn't want the same things in the end."

He doesn't want to tell me the details, but I'm beginning to understand his *Castaway* vibe.

"Did you look for her?" I ask.

"Yes." Ted's eyes have turned glassy. "But she cut off all contact. Her note said she was going to Nebraska, it was this joke between us. When one of us had a bad day at work, the other would say, 'What are you gonna do, move to Nebraska?' It was from some show we'd watched, about Nebraska being in the middle of nowhere. It wasn't a particularly funny joke." Ted bites his lip, rubbing his jaw with one hand.

"So, you've got no way of getting in touch with her, you don't even know what country she's in? That's nuts."

Ted flexes his fingers on the wheel. "I don't know why I'm telling you all this, sorry."

"Don't be sorry. I asked." I pause, watching his face. "Besides, you know all about my crazy suitcase chase. Rule of the cab—it's a safe space."

He smiles at me then. There must be something about sitting next to someone, both your eyes on the road, that allows you to express what you might not say face-to-face.

I find myself hoping we don't arrive at our destination too quickly; I want to hear more.

"You know, two years on, I still wear my ring, even though she left hers behind."

I can't believe someone would just walk out of their life like that. *How could you do that to someone you had loved?*

"Do you miss her?" I ask, then clench my jaw, worrying it's too personal a question.

"She was a part of me," he says softly, the pain palpable in his voice. "When you are with someone for a long time, you grow into each other, like adjoining trees with tangled roots. It's hard to extricate yourself and find the part that's left—who you were before."

"Especially when she hacks her tree down and runs off with it," I say, indignant on his behalf. This makes him smile. His shoulders fall, and he rubs his neck with the heel of his palm as though releasing tension.

I pull the fisherman's jumper, which is too big for me, down over my hands. Then I find myself pressing the soft wool to my nose and breathing in the smell. I wonder if the owner of this jumper really is the person my tree roots might grow into like that.

"I haven't talked about it much with anyone," he says, looking sideways at me without turning his head.

"Well, people do say I'm very easy to talk to," I say, in a singsong, jokey voice.

"You are," he says, earnestly, and I feel the warmth of the compliment fill the car.

Ted turns down an avenue lined with trees and pink and purple hydrangea bushes. As we emerge from the tunnel of foliage, the sea comes into view again, and I have the sensation of being at the top of a roller coaster. This must be the west coast; there's a huge sweep of golden sand, miles long, almost the length of the island.

"Is this St. Ouen's?" I ask.

"Yes, it's pronounced *St. Ones*, Jersey has some strange spelling," Ted says. "My dad's place is just around the corner. I'll grab some clothes and then we'll head to the next place in your album. You won't be able to go back to the cave until low tide now."

As we drive down toward the sea, the road fenced in by steep fields and a few old granite houses, I think about what Ted has told me, about his runaway wife. I can't imagine what that would feel like, to have found your person and then have them abandon you. I think of Mum losing Dad when I was only three, how hard that must have been for her. Then I think about the strange version of events Monica told me and wonder again how she could have it so wrong. What would I do if someone left me the way Ted's wife had? I don't think I would be able to move on until I knew where they had gone.

Ted pulls the car into a driveway in the middle of a line of houses all facing the sea. It's a detached granite house with a forked roof. It has a modern-looking porch at the side but otherwise looks as if it's been here for hundreds of years. There's a sloped garden running down to a tiny white cottage, not much bigger than a garden shed, then a plowed field, before the beach and the wild expanse of sea beyond. To our left, the rocky escarpment of L'Étacq headland rises up, as though standing sentry over the long bay. There's something timeless about the scene—neither the view nor the houses here can have changed much in centuries.

"What a place to live." I sigh.

"Do you want to come in?" Ted says. "Have you eaten?"

His whole demeanor has changed. He pulls his back straight, perhaps aware he's been hunching over the wheel, and gives me a bright-eyed grin. It's as though he's turned the page on our conversation about his wife and wants to get back to more cheerful ground.

"You don't need to feed me as well as everything else you're doing."

I follow him past the yellow skip in the driveway, in through the porch. The place is a mess of boxes and belongings. I see marks on the floor where furniture must have stood, a bureau and a chest of drawers in the middle of the room and labeled plastic boxes stacked high against the walls. I ask Ted if I can charge my phone, and as I'm plugging it in, a small, wiry white dog darts in and jumps up at my dress.

"Oh, hello, little guy!" I say, bending down to pet him.

"Scamp, down. Sorry," says Ted. "He's a bit feral."

"Hi, Scamp."

Scamp is a terrier cross of some kind, with one ear in the air and the other flopping over his friendly little face. I notice he's left dirty little paw prints on my dress. Someone calls Ted's name from the garden, and we walk through the narrow, box-cluttered kitchen out of some French windows onto a gravel terrace overlooking the steep garden and the sea beyond. A woman in her early forties with a cheerful round face and short peroxide hair is sitting at a table with a whippet-thin, elderly man who is nursing a bandaged arm.

"Ah, sorry, you got Scamped before I could tie him up," says the woman, jumping up and trying to catch the dog. Then she notices Ted is topless. "Why are you half naked, man?"

"Long story. I'm going to get changed. Dad, Sandy, this is Laura, Laura—Sandy and my dad, Gerry. Do you like crab, Laura?"

I hold up a hand in greeting to Gerry and Sandy.

"I adore crab," I say, grinning at Ted as he retreats inside. I turn to catch Sandy's eyes shifting between us. Her gaze settles back on me, and she enthusiastically offers me a chair.

"Sit, sit! Oh no, look, Scamp ruined your lovely dress!" Sandy covers her mouth in horror.

"Oh, don't worry, it was already ruined."

The sun is beating down on the patio, and I'm now too hot in Hot Suitcase Guy's jumper, so I take it off and hang it on the back of my chair. "Look," I say, pointing to the chocolate stain with a smile, "testament to a disastrous day." I turn to Ted's father. "I'm sorry to intrude like this, Gerry. Ted went in the sea looking for me, so it's my fault he got soaked."

"You're this Laura then," says Gerry. His voice is quiet, lacking resonance. I can see a shadow of Ted about his features, but Gerry's face is softer, less expressive. Both his hands shake with an obvious tremor. "I'm pleased you persuaded him to take you around the island and have a break from all these boxes."

Looking at the state of the house, and Gerry's fragile frame, I feel guilty for persuading Ted to drive me around today.

"He's been an excellent tour guide. I only hope I haven't deprived you of his help."

"Good for him to get out. Terrible job, having to babysit your old dad and do his packing for him," Gerry says with a warm smile. "Though one benefit of my vision going is that I can't see what he's throwing away. 'Make sure you keep the good china.' 'Yes, Dad. Sure, Dad. That breaking sound? Oh no, that was the stuff you didn't like.'" He chuckles.

We chat away; Gerry and Sandy ask me lots of questions about my visit. They are both so friendly, I feel myself relax, bask in the warmth of their easy company. When Ted reappears in a clean blue linen shirt and dark jeans, holding two plates of crab salad, Sandy says, "Ted, why don't we let Laura stay in the cottage for a few nights? I've no bookings in this week, and it will be nicer than staying in town."

"Oh, I'm sure I'm fine where I am—" I say, embarrassed to have Ted put on the spot. "This crab looks wonderful, you really didn't have to feed me."

"Always looking after everyone but himself," says Sandy. Then she points to the tiny white cottage, just before the garden wall. "Laura, wouldn't you rather wake up to this view? Best spot on the island—it might be small, but it sure is cozy. I've taken over the running of the place for Gerry. You can stay for free in exchange for a five-star review," she says with a wink.

I imagine the stark beauty of this wild bay, with rocks jutting out from the sea and the long sweep of sand stretching for miles down the coast, is exactly the kind of scene Love Life subscribers would like to see.

"It is a stunning view, you're so lucky to live here, Gerry." I realize too late what I've said and feel the skin on my neck prickle with embarrassment. "I mean, to have lived here. Sorry."

Gerry gives me a reassuring smile, then reaches out to briefly press a shaking hand over mine.

"Best view in the world. I was born in this house, so it's etched on my eyeballs—though, with the changing tide and sky, it never looks the same one hour to the next."

"So, what do you say, Laura?" Sandy asks. "Get some sea air into those London lungs? It's a shame to have it there sitting empty."

Looking down at the little cottage, I'm suddenly overwhelmed by a desire to stay here. This place, this beach, this view all feels much closer to the Jersey my mother described than the glass office blocks of St. Helier. I glance up at Ted, anxious that it isn't him who's inviting me to stay in his garden. I can't read his expression as he hands me cutlery.

"It is tempting, I've never slept so close to the sea before."

"Yes!" Sandy claps her hands together.

"But I insist on paying. I'm on a work trip, so they'll cover the cost."

Sandy flaps a hand in the air at me, as though to say, "We'll work all that out later."

"Then you can come to my party this evening," says Gerry, "we'll give you a proper Jersey welcome. I'm having a bit of a do on the beach later. Though I'll have to start walking down there early, it takes me so long to get anywhere these days. In fact, if the party starts in four hours, I might start walking now." He opens his mouth into a wide, silent laugh.

"Oh, Gerry, what nonsense. You're faster than me, you old goose," says Sandy.

I tell them I wouldn't want to gate-crash, but Gerry insists. Sandy says I can meet the locals and quiz them on stories about the island for my article. Ted stays quiet, removed from the conversation.

"I would love to stay, as long as Ted doesn't mind me invading his life like this?"

Sandy gives Ted a long look, but he won't meet her gaze.

"Oh, I think Ted's probably very happy about you invading his life—"

A blush creeps up my neck, embarrassed that they might have got the wrong idea.

"Tell Sandy all about your suitcase man, Laura," says Ted abruptly. "It's her kind of story."

Sandy frowns, then looks at me expectantly. I explain about the suitcase, about the objects inside and the clues we've been following. As I talk, I see her face take on an expression of disbelief. When I first told Ted about the case, I thought I was having an anonymous conversation with a driver whose name I'd never know and who'd never know mine—I didn't care what he thought of me. Now, looking across the table at Sandy and Gerry, I find I do care what they think, very much.

"Of course, it only makes sense if you believe in fate and serendipity," I say, flustered by Sandy's skeptical expression. "Ted thinks it's a wild-goose chase."

Sandy looks to Ted for a reaction, but he is intent on his food.

"Well, even more reason to hang around then, Laura," says Gerry brightly. "You can invite your mystery man to my party too if you track him down before tonight."

"Well, I don't know if I've bought enough sausages to feed the entire island," says Sandy.

"What are you talking about, woman? I've never seen a fridge so stuffed full of food," says Gerry.

"Ted, this really is delicious, thank you," I say, keen to change the subject. Then I lean in to quietly add, "Would you mind me staying? I wouldn't want to intrude."

"I don't mind at all," he says, while inspecting a knot of wood in the table. I notice the tips of his ears have turned red again.

"You'll stay, it's settled," says Sandy. "I'm going to go and get you the key and open the windows, let some air in."

Sandy gets up and moves to hug Gerry around his shoulders before she leaves, then she glances sideways into the house.

"Oh no!" she cries, running through the French windows. "Scamp, bad dog! Oh, Scamp, you haven't— Laura, I'm so sorry."

She comes out holding the tangled remains of the fisherman's jumper in her hands. One arm looks to have been ripped to pieces, and the bottom is starting to unravel. I clasp both hands to my mouth.

"I don't know what's got into him! Gerry, he's just pinched Laura's jumper and taken it off to maul it to pieces. He's a wild animal!" cries Sandy.

"Sorry, Laura, he wouldn't usually do that, especially not to a woman," says Gerry.

"Look, Ilídio's going to change his mind about taking this dog on," says Sandy, still inspecting the damp lump of wool in her hands.

I look up at Ted, who is trying not to laugh.

"It's not funny, Ted," I say, my hands clenched onto the edge of the table.

"It's not Laura's jumper," Ted explains, unable to stifle his mirth. "She borrowed it from her mystery suitcase man."

"That explains it," says Gerry. "Scamp probably smelled a rival male in the house, loyal little bugger he is."

"Scamp is Dad's dog," Ted says, "but Sandy and her husband, Ilídio, are taking him in once Dad moves."

"No dogs allowed in Alcatraz," Gerry says, in a voice of mock horror.

"Dad, it's assisted living, not Alcatraz." Ted gives his father a disapproving look.

"We're going to need to go back to puppy school," Sandy says, shaking a finger at Scamp's nose.

I don't want to make a fuss and make Sandy feel worse than she already does, but that's now two things in the case I've lost or damaged, and I can't help but feel my good mood punctured. What am I going to say to J. Le Maistre when I find him? "Hi, I think you're my soulmate, sorry I destroyed all your possessions." I take the mauled jumper back from Sandy and lament the tragic end of my Ryan Gosling sweater fantasy.

"I'm going to lock him in our kitchen, it's the only way he'll learn," says Sandy, picking up Scamp and carrying him over the low garden wall with her.

"He can sense change in the air, I'm afraid," says Gerry, pressing a shaking hand onto his bandaged arm.

"Please don't give it another thought," I say, trying to compose my face so that no one but me feels bad about this.

"Laura, if I take you back to town to check out of your hotel, we could go via Maude Le Maistre's place," Ted suggests. "I looked up where she lives, it's on the way."

"Ted, I would never have asked you to ferry me around all day if I'd known you had so much going on here. I'll happily find a bus—"

"Oh, let him drive you, Laura, maybe some of your sparkle will rub off on that dour face of his," Gerry says, looking as though he's struggling to stand. "He's been so—"

Ted cuts Gerry off before he can say any more. "Dad, let me help you, do you need to go inside?" He takes Gerry's arm and helps him to his feet.

"I'm not totally decrepit yet," Gerry says to me. "It's just chairs I can't get on with, or out of."

Sandy returns with the key to the cottage and takes me for a tour of the pocket-size house. Inside it has the feel of a well-kept ship's cabin. There's one main room, with a window looking out to sea, a tiny en suite, and a kitchenette with a washer dryer. The place has been decorated beautifully, with nautical curtains and sky-blue bed linen.

"You could wash your dress here, get the Scamp out of it," says Sandy, pointing to the washer dryer. "I'm so sorry again, about the jumper."

I wave away her apology, then open the suitcase on the bed to see if there is anything else that I can borrow, just while I put my dress through a quick spin cycle. It crosses my mind I could ask Sandy for a change of clothes, but I have only just met her, it feels too much to ask. There's the white work shirt and belt in the bag—I could probably fashion that into a dress, just to take me to town and back. Sandy has positioned herself on the bed, and I'm not sure I know her well enough to strip down to my underwear in front of her, so I nip through to the bathroom to change.

"Lucky you climbed into Ted's cab then, hey?" she says through the door.

"He's been so helpful. I didn't realize he wasn't a proper cabdriver—well, not that he's not proper—just that he only does it here and there." I'm babbling.

Looking at my makeshift shirtdress in the narrow mirror, I'm pleasantly surprised—it looks good. I don't feel too guilty about borrowing it; he's the one holding my case and all my clothes hostage. Though I do feel guilty about the trainer and the jumper.

"Did he tell you he's a doctor in his other life?" Sandy asks, interrupting my thoughts about clothes.

"A doctor? Who?" I come out of the bathroom and do a little twirl.

"Nice. I like what you've done with it. Jeez, if I had legs like those, I'd just walk around in my knickers all day," Sandy says with a sigh.

I laugh, surprised by the compliment.

"Well, I might be forced to walk around in my underwear if I don't get my suitcase back soon."

Sandy draws her eyes back to my face and blinks.

"What were we talking about before your ridiculously long

legs? Ah yes, Ted being a doctor. He's training to be a surgeon, you know." Her voice lilts into a sigh. "He's had a bit of an unusual career path, worked in conservation in his twenties, traveled all over; he was a right hippie. Then he had this epiphany about being a doctor, cut his long hair and enrolled in medical school. I have a lot of respect for anyone who goes back to studying in their thirties."

A surgeon, wow. I feel strangely indignant Ted hasn't told me any of this himself. But then I don't know why he should have. Plus, we've covered quite a lot of other topics in the short time we've known each other. With his calm demeanor, I can see him as a doctor, but in another sense, I can't—not with that beard.

As though reading my mind, Sandy says, "He hasn't always been so scruffy. He's just having a little"—she pauses, searching for the right word—"time-out. Trust me, underneath it all, Ted's a real looker. Once upon a time, every girl in Jersey was in love with Ted Palmerston." She watches my face for a reaction.

"Not you, though?" I ask, looking into the small mirror, shaped like a ship's porthole, and pulling my hair up into a scruffy bun.

"Nah, he's like a brother to me. You can't fancy someone when you've seen them play air guitar with their winkle at the age of eight."

I choke on my laugh and Sandy stands up to pat me on the back.

"Well, he's clearly a man of many talents," I say, keen to steer the tilt of this conversation elsewhere. "He's been very helpful in the search for my lost suitcase."

Sandy shakes her head and sits back on the bed. "I'm not convinced by this tale of yours, about the suitcase man."

"You don't believe in serendipity?" I hold a bobby pin in my mouth, before using it to pin down some flyaway strands of hair. "How did you meet your partner?"

Sandy gives a slow smile as she conjures the memory. I know that face, the face of someone who has a tale to tell, so I sit back down beside her to listen.

"It's a silly story," she says. "There was a mix-up at the license plate office—Ilídio had been sent mine, and I'd been sent his, along with all the wrong paperwork. It had his phone number printed on it, so I called him up and rather than send them both back, we met up to swap 'em over. Nothing's far in Jersey."

I clap my hands in excitement. "And then?"

Sandy nudges me with her shoulder.

"And then, a few days later he asked me out. It's hardly Romeo and bleedin' Juliet."

"Oh no, but it is! It's a great story. The universe sent you the wrong plates, just like it sent me the wrong suitcase. My story could turn out just like yours."

"It wasn't the universe; it was some lass called Sheila on her first day at the job," Sandy says, scrunching up her nose. "First thing I noticed about him when we met up were these huge white teeth he has. He's just one big smile, Ilídio is." She grins fondly. "If he'd been bog ugly, I would have told the universe to bugger off." I laugh, and Sandy prods my shoulder with a finger. "Your suitcase man could have a face like curdled custard for all you know."

"Love is blind," I say dreamily, a palm to my chest.

"It isn't, and people aren't akin to their possessions. If they are, God help me, because I've just adopted that devil dog."

When we head back outside, I see the trace of a smirk on Ted's face when he sees what I'm wearing.

"You don't think I can pull off a shirtdress?" I ask as I wave good-bye to the others and climb back into Ted's car.

"I didn't say anything," says Ted.

"It's just for an hour while I put my dress through the wash. I don't have anything else."

"I didn't say anything," Ted repeats, his eyes growing wide in mock offense, but there's the hint of a smile. "How are you going to explain the jumper then?"

I raise an eyebrow at him. "I will blame you, of course. You went mad and threw his shoe off a cliff and set your dog on his jumper."

Ted laughs that deep, chesty laugh that makes his whole body move. I like seeing it. It's like watching a drawing of a person come to life right in front of you.

"Scamp's not my dog." He turns his eyes to meet mine, a flicker of mischief in them.

"I found something in the house," he says, reaching into his bag and handing me a CD—*Phil Collins . . .Hits*. "From my mum's old collection."

I open the case to slot the CD into the car's dated music system.

"Do all your passengers get a curated playlist?"

"Just you. Mum clearly shared your terrible taste in music." He pauses, his mouth twitching. "While Scamp shares your terrible taste in men's jumpers."

"Funny." I reach out my hand, playfully hitting his thigh with the base of my fist.

Am I flirting with Ted? Is Ted flirting with me? No, I shake off the thought. That would be weird. We just know each other a little better now, well enough to make jokes.

But my hand feels hot where I've touched his thigh. I look up into his face, and he catches my embarrassment before I whip my head back around to face the window, hugging the tingling skin on my fist into my other palm.

Chapter 13

While we are driving, listening to Phil Collins, Ted pretending to wince at every new song that comes on, I text Suki:

Article's coming together well. I'm moving to the beach to get a more local angle on the travel article. It's stunning here, our followers will love it!

Then I send her a picture of the view from Gerry's patio.

She sends back a photo of a skinny Frappuccino, I assume referring to the fact that I am still on thin ice. The Love Life Instagram account has hundreds of notifications, and I open it to see photos of people at the community fete who have tagged #LoveLife, #ShopLocal, and #GenuineJersey. There's a beaming photo of Jenny behind an empty trestle table.

"Oh, look, Ted, people must have gone to the fete after I posted about it. Jenny sold out of jam!"

"That's because your broadcast was so inspiring," he says. I glance across at him, looking for the sarcasm, but there is none.

While I have a moment, I also text Gran and have a painfully slow back-and-forth with her over WhatsApp.

Laura: Is now a good time to talk, Gran?

Gran: Just heading to the dump. Mike Johnson from five down agreed to help me take my Amazon boxes. We're getting a pasty on the way. Did I tell you about the new pasty shop on Grave's End Road?

Laura: No. Silly question, but Mum didn't have phobias, did she? Of the dark and seagulls?

Gran: No. Where did you get that idea?

Laura: I thought not. Don't worry, we'll chat later.

As we drive, Ted points things out to me, the honesty boxes at the side of the road where you can leave your money in exchange for freshly grown fruit and veg; Elizabeth Castle, the fortress in the sea I noticed yesterday. Ted tells me you can walk to the castle at low tide, but once the sea comes up, it can only be reached by boat. I love hearing these details about the island, and it seems too soon that we arrive at our destination—a large granite farmhouse on the outskirts of town.

MILL MANOR is engraved on the stone gatepost, the lettering painted in gold. Through the gate, a circular drive winds around an old stone cider press, filled with orange dahlias. The house itself has wisteria and white roses covering half of the front wall.

"Right, this is Maude's place. Maybe you'll get some answers from her," says Ted, nodding toward the house. "There's a car in the drive and the front door is open, so someone must be home. Are you impressed with my detective work?"

"So impressed, Ted," I say, biting back a grin. "I did leave her a message, but she hasn't called me back. Maybe I had the wrong number, maybe these Le Maistres all have some kind of phone aversion."

"Well, this way you can at least ask to see some photos of her son—see if this treasure hunt of yours is going to be worth the effort," says Ted, a mischievous glint in his eye.

"Ha-ha, I do need to get my case back, you know. This isn't all about him being a potential—"

"Kablammo."

I wish I hadn't told Ted about the kablammo.

"It's not all about the kablammo either," I say, rolling my eyes at him.

"Sure." Ted nods slowly.

"It's not!" I push him on the arm. "Do you want to come?"

"I think I'll leave you to dazzle your prospective mother-in-law. I need to pick up some things for Dad's party tonight. You can walk into town from here—just take this road down the hill and you'll end up at the harbor. Shall I meet you outside your hotel in an hour?"

"OK, thank you so much, Ted."

Our eyes meet again. He was so quiet at the house, but now, back in the car, on our own, he's different again, a new energy to him. There's suddenly so much I want to ask him; about being a doctor, why his wife left, if he'd take her back tomorrow if she came home. I like hearing him talk. No doubt it's the journalist in me, always keen to get "the story." I have to stop myself trying to bite into the core of Ted's tale.

I get out on the drive and watch him drive away, then I walk toward the house, the case trundling along the gravel behind me.

"Hello," I call from the front step. The door opens onto a large open hallway, with several doors off each side. "Hello?" I call again.

There's no answer, so after a few minutes I decide to walk around the side of the house—maybe Maude is in the garden and can't hear me. The lawn to the side stretches around to a beautifully kept garden, split onto terraces, flowerbeds laden with white roses and giant purple daisies.

"Hello? Mrs. Le Maistre? Is anyone home?"

I see the garden door is open too—she must be here. I head back to the front, put the case down next to the porch, between a stone pillar and a small triangular shrub, then take a tentative step across the threshold of the house. There is a loud noise coming from somewhere, a whirring clattering sound.

"Mrs. Le Maistre?" I call into the hall, while knocking again on the open front door.

Behind me, I hear a car trundle into the driveway. It suddenly feels intrusive that I've stepped into this woman's hallway, and without thinking, I duck farther inside the house, scooting behind Maude's front door. I realize too late: This is the worst thing I could have done. Now I am stuck here. Peeking out through the window, I hope it might be a delivery driver who leaves quickly. But it is not a delivery driver; the man getting out of the car is Keith—Bee Man Keith from the community fete.

"Shit!" I mutter under my breath. Keith already thinks I'm a weirdo stalker. What if he's here to warn Maude that some lunatic woman is trying to get hold of her, and then they both find me crouched behind the front door? That would not look good. In a panic, my eyes dart around for somewhere better to hide, and I duck down from the window.

Keith walks up to the front door and calls out just as I did. He pauses, then I hear a voice call out from above my head and I try to flatten myself against the wall like a salamander.

"Oh, it's you hollering, is it?" comes a female voice from upstairs. "I had the dryer on, it makes a right old racket. Go on through, I'll meet you in the garden."

Cold sweat prickles my skin, my mouth is dry. How have I got myself into this situation? I feel like a cat burglar, a really rubbish cat burglar who doesn't want to steal anything. I worry Keith is going to see the case sitting next to the porch, but he's walked past it and now he's standing in the hallway too. I slowly lower myself to the floor.

"Do you need a hand up there, Maude?" Keith calls up the stairs. I hold my breath, worried he is going to hear me breathing. If he closes the door, he will see me, lying on the floor like a human draft excluder. There are footsteps above us.

"No, I'll come down. Give me one minute," comes the voice, which must be Maude. I can only see one more secure place to hide, an alcove full of coats in the hall, just a few yards away from me. Keith is facing the stairs, and the dryer noise is still rumbling through the floorboards; this might be my one chance to move. Holding my breath, I get to my feet and tiptoe across to the alcove, then quietly push myself backwards into the forest of coats, pulling a brown Barbour jacket around me, as I hear footsteps on the stairs and a "There you are," from Keith. Then the clunk of the front door closing—*SHIT!*

Peering out from behind the coat, I see a woman in her sixties, with a gray bun and plaid skirt, standing by the door next to Keith.

"Well, this is a nice surprise," says Maude. "The sun's out, we should sit in the garden." *Yes, sit in the garden, then I can sneak back out of the front door undetected.* "I just need to get my specs."

"Someone was looking for you at the fete this morning," Keith says, following Maude into one of the rooms off the hall. I should dart out now, sprint out of the back door while they're out of sight, but I want to hear what he's going to say about me, so I stay put. "This girl who said she mistakenly picked up Jasper's suitcase from the airport. She's under the impression he must have hers."

Jasper! Jasper! At last, I know his name. I *love* the name Jasper! It's perfect. Laura and Jasper, Jasper and Laura; that certainly has a nice ring to it.

"I didn't want to be responsible for giving her your details, you know. She was a bit . . . odd."

Odd? Bloody Keith, dissing me, especially when my broadcast brought his fete some much needed customers.

"Oh yes," says Maude. "I got a rather garbled message from someone, but I couldn't make out the number to call her back, the line was so crackly." They both come out of the other room and walk back across the hall—I've missed my chance to escape through the garden now. "Jasper rang me to say he'd left his personal mobile at the London flat, so she'll be having no luck getting hold of him. He went straight out on a lifeboat training exercise to Seymour Tower last night, so I suspect he's completely incommunicado."

"He'll be back for your birthday tomorrow, won't he?"

"Oh yes, I think he's back tonight. So, he picked up the wrong luggage, did he? Oh dear. Do you have the girl's number to hand? I should call her and explain. What made you think she was so odd?"

"She was rather foulmouthed, and she had wild, hysterical sort of eyes," says Keith.

FOULMOUTHED! WILD EYES? Literally, Keith heard the one time I've ever sworn in public.

They are out of sight now, at the other end of the hall, but I hear paper rustling, and then the clunk of a handset being lifted from its cradle. A cold bead of sweat trickles down my neck as I realize what's about to happen—she's dialing my number and the phone in my handbag is not on silent. It's going to start ringing, and they will freak out when they hear it coming from inside the house. It will be like a horror film; Keith might murder me with a fire poker, and he wouldn't even go to jail because I'm the intruder hiding behind a brown Barbour jacket in Maude's coat alcove.

Scrambling about in my handbag, pinching my lips closed to suppress a scream, I manage to flick the phone onto silent just as the screen lights up with the call. From farther down the hallway, I hear Maude leaving me a message explaining Jasper's lost his phone and he's off on a training exercise all day, but that she'll get him to call me about the bag as soon as he returns.

With the phone-ringing/death-by-poker emergency averted, I have a few moments to digest the fact that Jasper is a volunteer; the guy just gets better and better the more I hear about him. He has a flat in London—great for a potential relationship with me, since, well, I live there. He's called Jasper—such a hot name *and* he rescues people from the sea. He must have quite muscular upper arms if he hauls people out of the water all day. An image of Ted's arms springs unbidden to my mind, as he stripped off his sea-soaked T-shirt, that understated, muscular definition, strong but lean—

Through my musing about the sexiness of upper arms, I hear Keith's and Maude's footsteps across the hall again and tuck myself farther back behind the coats. This really is a very deep coat alcove; you could fit a short bowling alley in here.

"So, when am I giving you your birthday present?" Keith asks Maude.

I feel briefly indignant on Jasper's behalf—he better not be about to give Maude the beehive. *It's supposed to be a surprise, Keith.*

"Oh, you are a mischief," says Maude, with a chuckle. "I thought there was a reason you came over today when you knew I'd be here on my own."

"Mrs. Le Maistre, I'm shocked you would suspect me of such base motivations. I am purely here as a messenger—though if you would like a little something—you know I'm always happy to oblige." Keith's voice breaks into a little purr.

Then they stop talking, and I hear what sounds like kissing sounds. No! Maude and Keith? I did not see that plot twist coming. They must be in their late sixties—no one kisses like that in their sixties, do they?

"My queen bee," says Keith, "undress for me."

What? No! I can't believe what I'm hearing. I dare to peep out from behind the Barbour jacket, and sure enough Maude drops her plaid knee-length skirt to the polished wooden floor. Keith stands watching, his bushy white eyebrows jumping up and down like caterpillars on a trampoline. Surely this isn't happening, not here in the hallway. They could at least go upstairs!

"Come on then. I've got the gardener coming over at four thirty, so you'll need to be quick about it," says Maude.

"The chaise," Keith purrs, and I hear more kissing sounds.

My eyes dart around the hall and to my horror I see a green chaise longue directly opposite my hiding place. Please no, just say no, Maude, I'm sure you'd rather have a nice comfy bed, not a quickie in the hallway.

"You only like the chaise so you can hold on to the antlers," Maude says with a girlish giggle. Sure enough, above the chaise, I see two huge antlers protruding from the mounted skull of a stag, "If Frank only knew what his hideous family heirloom was being used for."

Ooh, who's Frank? Husband? Hang on, isn't Keith married? Yes, I asked him how he met his wife at the fete—the plot thickens. *Am I witnessing a clandestine affair?*

"Well, my balance isn't what it was," cackles Keith, and I hear the sound of trousers being unzipped.

Closing my eyes, I hear my heartbeat thrumming in my ears. Should I make myself known now? It might be better to be arrested for trespassing than to witness what's about to happen. But it's too late. Daring to peek again, I see Maude is now sitting on the chaise, and Keith is unbuttoning her cardigan, bending down to kiss her neck. I retract my head, like a horrified tortoise. If I'm going to have to listen, I certainly shouldn't watch.

The furniture starts squeaking, and I pull out my phone for distraction. What if Keith wrenches those antlers off the wall? What if they fall down, skewering them both like some horrific sex kebab, and I have to jump out and call an ambulance? I'm also worried about the chaise. It looked like more of an ornamental piece than something built for serious action.

If there's any silver lining to finding myself in this horrific situation, I can't help but be comforted that two people in their late sixties are still having some pretty satisfying-sounding sex. It gives me hope that I've got another thirty years to find my movie sex.

I open the "Hot Suitcase Guy" WhatsApp group and send a message to Vanya and Dee:

Laura: So, I accidentally walked into HSG's mum's house, and now I'm listening to her have sex with the MARRIED chairman of the bee society—in her hallway. 😱 🐝 🍆

Vanya: WHAT?!!

Laura: No joke. It is happening now. I'm hiding in her coat alcove.

Dee: What's a coat alcove?

Laura: Kind of like a cupboard without a door. Nice easy access to coats on your way out of the house. I think I'd like one in my forever home.

As I'm typing, a message comes through from Gran.

Gran: Laura. Sorry we keep missing each other. Trip to the dump was great success. I can talk now? At Stitch 'n' Bitch Club tonight. Attached—picture of our latest building project. Can you guess what it's supposed to be?

Attached is a photo of an angular building made from matchsticks, with a large tower protruding from the middle.

Dee: Send me a photo. I don't believe you.

Laura: Of what? The live sex show or the coat alcove?

The noises beyond the coats escalate, and I prop my phone between my knees to put my fingers in my ears. Of course I'm not going to take a photo; I wouldn't think of invading their privacy, well, any more than I already am. My phone lights up with another message.

Gran: It is not a sex show, Laura, it's supposed to be the Tate Modern!

Confused, I scroll back, realizing I sent the message meant for Dee to Gran. Whoops, the darkness of the coat alcove and all the horrifying noises are making it difficult to WhatsApp effectively.

Laura: Sorry, Gran, glitch with my phone, I didn't mean to send you that. I can clearly see it's the Tate, well done! Can we chat tomorrow? Bit tied up with something just now. Xx

I do want to tell Gran about all the crazy things Aunt Monica said, but I don't think it's a conversation to be had over WhatsApp. Turning the phone around, I take a photo of myself in the alcove. With the flash off, the picture comes out looking a bit Blair Witch, with the whites of my eyes shiny luminous against a backdrop of tweed coats and wax jackets. I send it to Dee and Vanya.

Dee: Why are you in her house, Laura?!

Laura: Long story. Does witnessing this rule her out as a potential mother-in-law?

Vanya: Not if she's good at sex, maybe it's hereditary.

Dee: Bee man definitely isn't her husband?

I don't think so. He doesn't live here. Plus, I don't think married couples have sex in hallways. What if Jasper doesn't know about their affair, then when I meet him, I'll have this secret on my conscience? Why does my perfect meet-cute have to be so bloody convoluted?

Muffled voices, and then—I release my fingers—silence, blissful silence.

"Oh, my queen," Keith purrs.

"You are incorrigible." Maude laughs.

"I prefer the blue sofa in your sitting room, softer cushion," says Keith.

These two are clearly at it like rabbits, doing it in every room of the house. Most of the relationships I've been in have involved sex very much in bed, under the sheets, with the lights dimmed to "mood." Apart from Australian Shayne, who couldn't have horizontal sex on account of his back and had a preference for the stairs, but that was just a bit bumpy and uncomfortable. *Oh wow, am I actually jealous of Maude's sex life?*

"Shall we have some Earl Grey in the garden? I made those buttery biscuits you like," says Maude.

I *am* jealous. Especially now they're having postcoital biscuits—those are the best kind of biscuits. Another message from Gran lights up my screen.

Gran: I agree, the Tate Tower is rather phallic. I told Pam we should have done the OXO Tower—far more distinctive. Where's the Coat Alcove, maybe we'll tackle that landmark next?

It takes a while for Keith and Maude to get dressed, and then, chatting away, they walk to a room off the hall, which I assume to be the kitchen. This is my best chance to escape. It's like *Shawshank Redemption*, I've just got to hold my nose and wade through the sewer of fear to freedom. Taking a deep breath, I dart, gazelle-like, through the hall—it would be too noisy to try and open the large oak front door, but the garden door is still wide open. I run past the kitchen, pause for a split second to glance at a picture on the wall, sprint around the house, pick up the bag from behind the pillar on the porch, and then I'm off down the driveway faster than I've ever run in my life.

As I'm sprinting, in flip-flops, my heart pounds against my chest: with adrenaline, with the fear of being caught, but also with excitement, because the picture I glimpsed on the wall on the way out told me something: Jasper Le Maistre is the beautiful man from the airport.

Hot Suitcase Guy *is* Hot Tampon Man!

Though I must not him call him that.

Jasper, he is now just Jasper.

ꝏ

4 September 1991

Dearest Al,

I can't believe the summer is over. I yearn for the sound of the sea. I miss Jersey and I miss you like a limb. Do you have to start the Greece job so soon? It will mean I only see you twice before Christmas. Phone calls and letters are no substitute for your company, your touch, your face.

I have a confession to make. I took the coin back with me to Bristol. I wanted it to be a surprise but now worry you might notice it gone and think it lost. I am going to make a setting for it, a glass-fronted locket, so it can be worn as a necklace, the two halves set together as one. I hope it will be ready for next weekend and you can take it back to your grandmother. Won't she be thrilled, Al? Don't give away the secret before I have it made.

Miserably missing you,
Annie

Chapter 14

Having started to walk down Trinity Hill, I manage to intercept a bus to take me the rest of the way into town, so I'm back at the Weighbridge in ten minutes. Strangely, they don't seem to have bus stops here—they just write BUS at intervals along the road where the bus is going to stop.

"Any luck with the manhunt?" Ted asks when I meet up with him outside the hotel.

"Not really," I say. I don't want to tell Ted what I witnessed at Maude's house; I'm too embarrassed to admit I walked into the woman's home like that. I do tell him I found out that Jasper is due back from a lifeboat training exercise this evening, so I expect to get my suitcase back soon. He must have dumped the case before leaving and not even realized the mistake yet.

"I bought you something," says Ted, handing me a brown paper bag on his lap, which I open with a curious frown.

"Jersey wonders," he says. "You wanted to try the local cuisine. I know this lady who still makes them the old-fashioned way, only fries them while the tide is going out."

Inside the bag are a dozen small knots of baked dough. I take one out and bite into it, then offer them back to Ted. They are soft and sweet and still warm, and I let out an appreciative moan.

"Oh, those are good," I say, covering my mouth with a hand. Ted gives a small nod.

"They remind me of— Have you ever been to New Orleans?" I ask and he nods.

"Beignets?"

"Yes!" I grin, amazed he knows what I'm talking about. "Beignets are the best."

The summer we were twenty-six, Dee and I did a road trip across the States. It was one of the most exciting holidays I've ever been on; we felt like Thelma and Louise, but without the sad ending. "When were you in New Orleans?" I ask.

Ted pauses and his face changes. The laughter lines around his eyes fade.

"My wife, Belinda, she loved traveling," he says softly, and I'm worried I've unsettled the clear water of our conversation by reminding him of his wife.

"Not you?" I ask.

"I used to," he says, eyes straight ahead. "When we met, we were fueled by wanderlust. We both worked in conservation, took jobs in far-off places and lived out of backpacks. We were boundless." Ted sniffs. "I was the one who changed, I guess, decided that I was going to retrain as a doctor. I had to root myself in order to study, and then I found I'd outgrown the wanderlust."

"But she hadn't?" I ask gently.

"She said she was happy to stay still for a while, but I always sensed this restlessness in her. I think she associated standing still with having a conventional life. In the note she left, she said she didn't want a life full of gas bills or school-gate mums, washing the car, picking up milk, trips to the hairdresser."

"But you wanted all that?" I ask.

"Trips to the hairdresser?" Ted says with a rueful smile and pats his beard in a way that makes me smile. "Well, yes, maybe the rest of it." He shrugs. "Though mainly I just wanted her."

Looking at Ted, I imagine this is what heartbreak looks like, and I wonder for a moment if true love really is worth the risk. My mother said she never fell in love again after Dad died. If she'd had the choice, I wonder if she would she have swapped those four intense years with Dad for a lifetime with someone else, even if the intensity had to be diluted.

As I watch the emotion on Ted's face, it makes me feel strangely powerless. If you believe in fate leading you to love, do you also have to believe it is fate that leads love away? Are we all just floating in the sea, completely dependent on the tide and the universe to steer us to a happy harbor, or do we have oars? Do we have a chance to steer ourselves to shore?

"Thank you, Ted, for the doughnuts, that was thoughtful of you," I say, moving the conversation away from heartbreak and back to food.

"You're welcome. I've got to give you a proper taste of the island," and as he says it, the smile returns to his eyes.

When we arrive back at St. Ouen's at around five, Sandy is folding napkins and stacking them onto paper plates on the table in Gerry's garden. She introduces me to her husband, Ilídio, who is scraping down a greasy-looking barbecue to take down to the beach. He is short, with dark stubble, tousled black hair, and bright white teeth I assume must be veneers. I ask if I can help them get ready for the party, but they insist they have everything under control, so I take the opportunity to have a shower and wash my hair. I now have yesterday's clothes back from the hotel, but Sandy has kindly left me an emerald-green wrap dress to borrow. It's too big for me, but it's clean, and if I wrap the cord around my waist twice, it just about works.

I look at my laptop and feel guilty at how little work I have achieved today. I need an angle for the mini-break piece, reasons to visit Jersey outside the summer season. Suki wants something original, and I thought being here would inspire me. Then I think of Ted's Jersey wonders, the story of only making them when the tide is right, the community fete with all the homemade produce, all the potato fields and the cows. Food does feel like a big part of the island's identity. Could I tell the island's story through food—"A Taste of Jersey," perhaps?

As an idea begins to form, my phone buzzes.

Vanya: Did you escape the sex dungeon? Been thinking about what you said, about whether you can be a feminist and a romantic. Love this quote from the singer Eartha Kitt: "I fall in

love with myself, and I want someone to share it with me. I want someone to share me with me." That's how I feel. V

I love that Vanya has kept thinking about our conversation. How many nights have we stayed up late with a glass of wine, talking about *Schitt's Creek* one minute and Dostoyevsky the next? I will never find a flatmate who can replace her.

Outside, I hear voices and poke my head through the doorway to see a group of people gathering on the beach beyond the fields. Ted is fixing balloons to a wall that follows a narrow footpath down to the sea, and I walk down to join him.

"How's your puff?" Ted asks, handing me two uninflated balloons.

"Excellent," I say, reaching for one.

Ted looks at me, pausing his gaze on my smile.

"You look pleased with yourself?"

"Your Jersey wonders, they gave me an idea for my article."

"'Around the World in Eighty Doughnuts'?" he suggests.

"Something like that."

"Has your suitcase man called yet?"

"Not yet, but he will," I say, pushing my tongue into my cheek, and Ted gives me an unreadable smile.

"Ted, Laura, get on down here, will you!" Sandy's voice travels up from the beach. "Ilídio's going to burn the sausages to a crisp if someone doesn't stop him."

"We've been caught slacking," Ted says, securing the balloons to the wall with a rock.

The whole village of L'Étacq has turned out for Gerry's leaving do. It's a perfect warm evening for a beach party, and people have brought their own camping chairs to sit on around the campfire. There are about thirty of us in all, a collection of Gerry's friends from all over the island. Half a dozen of Ilídio's extended family are here. He tells me his parents moved over from Madeira when he was a baby. His mother fell in love with Jersey, so she persuaded all her sisters to move here too.

Sitting between Sandy and Ilídio's sister Teresa, they ask about my Jersey connection. I explain my father's family are from here.

"What are their names?" Sandy asks.

"Well, I'm a Le Quesne, like my dad's family, but my grandmother was a Blampied before she married."

"Proper Jersey names," says Teresa.

"Sorry, Ques-ne?" Sandy asks with a frown. "Q-U-E-S-N-E?"

I nod my head. I'm used to having to spell out my surname.

"Um, I think you'll find that's pronounced *Le Cane*," Sandy says, collapsing into laughter.

"What? No, it isn't . . ." I trail off. Sandy is doubled over, snorting like a warthog.

"Trust me, it's a common Jersey name, with a *French* pronunciation—you don't say *Ques-ne*."

My mind starts doing backflips. That's how the woman from the airport pronounced it. Now I think about it, people have said my name like that before. I just assumed they didn't know how to anglicize it. Why would Mum have taught me my name wrong?

"But no one speaks French here!" I say indignantly. "You have all these French names for things but then pronounce them in English."

When Sandy finally stops cackling about the fact that I've been mispronouncing my own name my entire life, she says,

"The island was originally French, before William the Conqueror got involved."

"It was part of Normandy until 1204, and the traditional island language, Jèrriais, is a form of Norman French," chips in the man sitting next to Sandy. He is in his sixties, dressed entirely in brown, and has long gray hair tied back in a ponytail.

"This is Raymond, he's a bit of an island expert," says Sandy, shooting me wide eyes.

"All the original road names were French," Raymond explains. "Some get pronounced the original way, some have been mangled into English, which can get confusing, but people's names stay as they always were, pretty much."

Am I going to have to change the way I say my name? I wonder, as Raymond shifts his chair around to better join our conversation. Then he says, "Jersey history goes back more than two hundred and fifty thousand years. It's only been an island for six thousand."

Sandy is still looking at me with wide, unblinking eyes. She must be worried that Raymond is about to dispense quite a significant volume of history to me, because she quickly changes the subject, pointing out how good the surf is this evening. Then she tells me about what a good surfer Ted is, how he used to sneak out surfing at night if he knew there was a big swell coming in, then go to school with seaweed in his hair.

Ted catches my eye from across the circle. He shakes his head, but his eyes are smiling and, with a beer in his hand and his friends around him, he looks more relaxed than I've seen him all day. I can't believe how at home I feel among these people I've only just met. It crosses my mind that I can't think of the last time I made a new friend back in London.

Ilídio walks over and nestles down in the sand at Sandy's feet, reaching up to hold her hand, smiling up at her with his huge white teeth. The affection between them appears so easy, so delightfully unfiltered. The thought prompts me to check my phone, waiting for Jasper to call. Surely, he'll phone this evening.

Picking up a jug from the camping table, which is doubling as a bar, I help top up people's drinks around the circle. When I reach Gerry, he beckons me to sit down in the empty chair beside him.

"Is everyone making you feel welcome, Laura?" he asks. I shuffle the chair closer so I can hear him better.

"Oh yes." I nod. "Incredibly so."

"What a night for it, hey." He nods toward the fading light on the horizon, the warm red of the clouds as the sun disappears behind them. Gerry's face is remarkably free of worry lines; he looks cheerful, even though he is about to say goodbye to the only home he has known. I watch his limbs vibrate in constant motion, and I imagine how exhausting his condition must be.

"Can I ask you a personal question, Gerry?" I ask, the glasses of sangria I've consumed loosening my curiosity about him.

"Of course—the best kind of question." He smiles and widens his eyes.

"How do you stay so positive? Do you worry what's around the corner?" He pauses, and I'm worried I have offended him. "Sorry, that's a big question to ask."

"It's a good question," he says, putting his drink down in the camping chair's cup holder. "The thing is, with a degenerative condition like mine, if I look back at everything I could do before, the things I used to love—sailing, woodwork, playing the guitar—it can only depress me. Equally, if I look ahead to tomorrow, no doubt I'll only be able to do less than I can today. The tremors and my eyesight may be worse, my step less steady. This is not something that gets better," Gerry says with a calm smile. "So, if I can't look back, and I can't look forward, I'm forced to live here, right now. Today I can sit around a campfire and talk to my friends. Today I can watch the sunset, even if the outline is getting hazy. Today I have made a new friend and I'm enjoying her company and her vibrant conversation." He makes a single, slow nod in my direction. "The Roman poet Horace said: 'Don't hope or fear, but seize today, you must! And in tomorrow put complete mistrust.' All any of us have is today."

Calm washes over me as I listen to Gerry talk. His words feel like a parent stroking my hair, and there is something in his outlook that reminds me of Mum. It makes me wonder at how petty my own concerns are by comparison, how much time I spend dwelling on the past and fretting about the future. How many times have I asked, "Why me?" Why did I have to lose both my parents before the age of twenty-seven? Why haven't I found love yet? I look at Gerry, at what he's lost, and I doubt he has once asked, "Why me?"

Across the circle, Ted stands up and clinks two bottles together to garner people's attention. Sandy walks around the circle and tops up my glass on her way past.

"Everyone here knows I'm not one for speeches," Ted says, and there are some jeers from the group, "but I just wanted to say a few words about the man we're all here to celebrate. I'm sure he'll have a few words to say himself."

Gerry raises his glass with his unbandaged arm and says, "Always," and everyone laughs.

"Firstly, this is not a good-bye party. Dad's going to be just around the corner at Acrebrooke, and I know you will all be visiting him. If you don't, he'll be calling you all endlessly, persuading you to come— Oh, and while you're about it, will you bring him those cheese biscuits he likes." People laugh, and Gerry bites his lip and nods. "But, while it's not a good-bye, Dad moving is the end of an era. Our family have lived at Sans Ennui for over two hundred years, and this house has seen happy memories, as well as some sad ones. So, I'd like to raise a toast to Sans Ennui—this beautiful house that has been a home to Palmerstons past and present. May whoever takes it on be as happy here as we have been."

Everyone raises a glass, and I hear mutters of "To Sans Ennui."

"And Dad, whose life has been changed so much over the last few years, I just wanted to say that I've never known anyone who's borne the hand they're dealt with more unbridled positivity. I think we'd all be happier if we woke up in the morning and tried to be a little more Gerry."

I swallow a lump in my throat, and looking around I see it isn't just me who's been moved by Ted's words. He sits down as people clap, then Gerry is helped to his feet by his friend Raymond.

"All seems a lot of fuss for a shaky old codger like me," he says, directing a wink in his friend Ruth's direction. "But I appreciate all the effort, and Ted's not wrong about the cheese biscuits. Oh, and sloe gin, if you please." People laugh while

Ruth smiles and shakes her head. "I don't have much to say. 'There's a change,' you're thinking. But one thing I have learned in this life, as a wise woman once said to me, 'Tide and time wait for no man.' So get on your surfboard and catch that wave, even if you're shaking like a rattle all the way in, because I'm yet to be reliably informed if there's decent surf in heaven."

Everyone cheers, Ilídio whoops, and Gerry slowly presses his hands together in thanks, before carefully lowering himself back into his chair.

"There'd better be surf in heaven or I'm not going," Ted calls across to Gerry.

The words make me well up, and I bite down on the inside of my cheek to try and cauterize the feeling. It doesn't feel appropriate that I should be the one getting so emotional—I only met the man this afternoon.

The party proves to be great fun. I chat with Gerry's friends, help Ilídio with the barbecue, and run around giving everyone sausage baps in napkins. Sandy keeps topping up my glass with her "secret recipe sangria," which puts a glow in my cheeks and then a stagger in my step. Gerry laughs with everyone, beckoning people to come and sit next to him, making sure he has made time to speak to everyone individually.

"You know, Gerry is one of the best cabinetmakers you will ever meet," Ilídio tells me, as he tops up my drink. "He taught me everything I know, but I'll still only ever be half as good as he was."

"He did that alongside driving the cab?" I ask.

"He spent so much time perfecting each piece, he didn't always make much of a living out of it. Cabs put money on the table, but working with wood was always his passion," says Ilídio, cracking his knuckles. "It's tough to watch all the talent in his brain unable to come out through his fingers anymore."

His words make me think of Mum, all her talent for jewelry making gone with her.

"But you do it anyway, even if you think you'll never be as good as he was?" I ask Ilídio. He shrugs and takes a slug of his beer.

"Most of us will never be the best at anything we do. It isn't a reason not to do it."

"We need some music, it isn't a party without music!" yells a tall South African man called Ian. He picks up a guitar and passes it around the circle. "Send it around to Ted."

Ted shakes his head and waves the guitar away.

"Come on!" says Sandy, fluffing up the back of her short blond hair with one hand, and sloshing a bit of her sangria onto the sand with the other. "Give us a tune."

People start clapping a rhythmic encouragement. Ted takes the guitar but carries on passing it around the circle, reluctant to be left holding it.

"Edward Palmerston," says Gerry firmly, and everyone stops talking so that Gerry's quiet voice can be heard, "indulge your old man on his last night of freedom, will you? If I could play for my friends, I would."

"You know, you can't play the Parkinson's card every time, Dad," Ted says, taking back the guitar and giving Gerry a friendly scowl across the fire. "He tried to tell me he was entitled to the toast I was about to eat yesterday, because it was such an effort to butter his own."

Gerry makes a comical shrug, and a few people laugh. I'm

sitting a few places around the circle from Ted, but I can see his face in the firelight. From what I know of him, I can't imagine he'd enjoy performing to a crowd.

"Any requests?" Ted asks, his eyes flitting around the circle and then landing on me.

"'Shake It Off' by Taylor Swift," says Gerry, waving his cane in the air.

"'Hippy, Hippy Shake,'" shouts Raymond.

"'Shake Your Body,'" says Ruth.

"'Shake, Rattle and Roll,'" says Sandy, laughing.

"I'm seeing a theme here," says Ted, tilting his head in amused disapproval.

People fall silent as he strums a chord, and then launches into a simplified version of "Shake It Off." His voice is not perfect, but there's something about his performance—it's full of soul and I cannot take my eyes off him.

Sandy whispers in my ear, "Didn't I tell you he was talented? More sangria?"

Gerry and his friend Ruth are now standing in the sand, dancing hand in hand. Gerry looks like he's having a wonderful time. I glance back at Ted, who's looking across at me, his eyes glinting gold in the firelight. He comes to the end of the song, and I put my cup in the sand so I can clap properly. Ted spends the next twenty minutes taking requests, and I drink and dance and bask in the warmth of the occasion.

"OK, last song," says Ted, in a mock croaky voice, "or I won't be able to speak tomorrow."

"That was my plan," says Gerry.

"Can I make a request?" I ask, moving around the circle to squeeze in next to Ted.

"Let me guess, your friend Phil?" he says in a low voice.

I nod eagerly, and then stop because my head is beginning to spin.

"I don't know the words to any of his horrible songs," says Ted, with a challenging look.

"He's lying," says Sandy, who's eavesdropping.

Ted sighs in mock resignation, looks down at the guitar, and plays a chord. I know straightaway what it is. He plays "You Can't Hurry Love," and he knows plenty of the words. More people stand up to dance, but I suddenly feel too drunk to stand so I just stay seated and sway gently to the music. The song makes me think of my dad, of all those Phil Collins LPs he kept for me. It makes me think of all the times in my life this music has brought me back to myself. I think of the sheet music in the suitcase and feel more certain than ever that it must mean something; there is a Phil Collins–shaped trail of breadcrumbs leading me out of the woods toward something important.

Then out of nowhere, I feel a flood of emotions rising up behind my eyelids and I realize I'm about to burst into tears. Where did that come from? Oh no, I'm going to drunk cry. Drunk crying is the worst because you don't even really know why you're crying, and everyone assumes you must be upset about something, when really, you're just drunk and all the alcohol pushes unexplained emotions out of your eyes. I quickly turn away from the group, pretending to look for my drink, then quietly take myself away up the beach.

I bite the inside of my cheek again, trying to suppress that morose part of myself, which always rears its head at the worst moments. I turn to look at the water and take a few long inhales of sea air. Part of me just wants to walk into the waves and wash off the curdling brain fog. I haven't drunk much in the last few years, partly for fear of finding myself vulnerable, without the mental agility to steer myself back.

"Are you OK?"

Turning around, I see Ted walking toward me and quickly wipe my fingertips beneath my eyes. He must have followed me along the beach.

"Yes, just had a little too much to drink, I think." I smile. "Needed to walk it off."

"I thought you might be about to launch into a nighttime swim," he says, his eyes searching out mine.

"No, well, maybe." I stagger, losing my footing, and he reaches out a hand to hold me upright. "I liked your singing."

Ted looks down at his feet.

"Dad was the one with the musical talent, not me."

"Well, I enjoyed it."

Then our eyes meet again, bright beacons in the half-light, and I want to fall into his arms, partly because I'm finding it hard to stand up straight, and partly because I just want to feel what it would be like to have a strong pair of arms close around me, to lean myself against the inviting warmth of his broad chest.

"Whydoyouhavethisbeard?" I ask, the words merging into one another. I reach out to touch it, and the hair is surprisingly soft. "I think you'd look so much better without it."

Ted reaches up to remove my hand from his beard, but he keeps hold of it, and a tingle of electricity pulses up my arm.

"You think so?" he says, in an amused, gruff tone.

I'm suddenly overwhelmed by a desire to press my whole face right against his beard, to feel what it would be like to nestle into this warm, comforting nest, like a baby bird coming home.

"I mean, you're actually pretty all right, Ted, underneath your disguise of scruffy clothes and that horrible old cap you wear. I see you in there—Beardy McHottington."

I swipe my other hand at his chest, and he catches it, before I stumble, so he's now holding on to both my hands. His eyes are drilling into me in a way that makes my brain feel suddenly sober, and my feet even less steady on the sand. Then I lean forward to kiss him, all logic washed away by this wave of need. I see in Ted's eyes that he's not going to stop me.

Ring, ring.

My head darts left and right, looking for the source of the strange chirruping. It's my phone. I pull my hands away from his, searching my handbag with fumbling fingers. Shit, how did I get this drunk? Bloody Sandy and her "special recipe sangria"!

"Laura, ignore it, just once," Ted says, his voice imploring.

I can't not get it; it might be about work, or my suitcase. *Was I really just about to kiss Ted?* I finally clasp the phone and accept the call before it stops ringing. Glancing back at Ted, I see the heat in his eyes dampen.

"Hello, Laura speaking," I say, biting my lip to make myself sound less drunk.

"Hi, Laura, this is Jasper Le Maistre—I believe we may have each other's suitcases."

TIGER WOMAN ON ALCOHOL

Tiger Women do not need alcohol. It poisons the brain and pollutes the soul. People use it to escape, to find confidence, to soften the edges of reality. Do not soften your reality—keep your senses sharp. You must be present to catch your prey. Drink water. Eat power. Be roar.

Chapter 15

"Jasper! Hi!" I say, swinging away from Ted. There is a sobering chill in the wind, and I rub my arm with my free hand.

"I must apologize for not being in touch sooner, I hope it hasn't been a huge inconvenience." His voice, it is him, it's Hot Tampon Man! *No, don't call him that.*

"It's fine, though I'm afraid I did get cold and borrow one of your jumpers, hic." I slap a hand across my lips. *Did I just hiccup into the phone?* I hear Ted make an amused sound next to me.

"Well, you'll be pleased to hear I haven't needed to wear any of your clothes," Jasper says, his voice as smooth as I remember it. "Where are you? I can bring you your bag straightaway."

My stomach swirls, and I clasp my hand tighter around my

mouth, swallowing down an involuntary gag. I don't want Jasper to come here—he'd just drop the bag and leave. Plus, I'm far too drunk to make a good impression—I need some water, or coffee, or a time machine to go back in time and drink less sangria—anything that might sober me up.

I look back up at Ted. Did he know I was about to kiss him? What was I thinking? Ted is technically married, way too old for me. There might be elements of hot mess about him, but no. *Why am I even thinking about this?* Jasper is the one I want to kiss; Jasper is the man I've been looking for.

"I'm just at a party with some friends." I cough, suppressing another hiccup. "But if it's not too late, maybe I could come to you to swap the bags in half an hour or so?"

I feel my stomach lurch again. Jasper says that's fine—in fact, he sounds keener on that idea. I shove the phone in Ted's direction and mouth "address" with pleading eyes, before sinking to my knees to try to make the world stop spinning. Wow, I really do need some water.

"Yes, I'm her friend," I hear Ted say, clearing his throat. "I'm local, you can tell me the address."

He's my friend, that's nice. Would Ted pass one of those quizzes they have in teenage magazine, "How Good a Friend Are You?" He bought me Jersey wonders today and found me a Phil Collins CD. He's a really good listener. Now he's getting Hot Suitcase Guy's address for me. So, yes, I'd say he'd score pretty highly on a friends quiz.

"Are you all right, Laura?" Ted asks once he's hung up.

I sink into a starfish shape on the dry sand.

"Sorry, I'm not used to drinking so much," I say feebly. "I just need some water."

"Maybe it would be better if you collected the bag tomorrow?"

"No, I'll be fine." I wave him away, trying to get up, but then after two steps, I find myself lying facedown on the sand again. What is it with sand? It's so wobbly to walk on; I'm not sure how anyone does it. It's like a moving, shifting carpet. Even if I was sober, I'm not sure how I'd manage to walk on it.

Without saying anything, Ted reaches an arm around me, props me up, and walks me steadily back toward the footpath up from the beach. I don't protest. When we get back to the cottage, Ted is still holding me up.

"Zorry, Ted." I hear myself slur. "I'm zo embarrassed, that zangria really hit me."

"Come on, I'll make you a sobering brew."

We go inside, and Ted sits me on the bed, then fetches me a large glass of water.

"Thank you," I say, gulping it down gratefully, as he goes back through to the kitchenette to put the kettle on. How did I go from fine to jelly brain in—I check my watch, the party started at six and now it's eight. OK . . . and I haven't really eaten anything since the Jersey wonders. No wonder I'm wasted. I stumble through to the bathroom, realizing I'm going to be sick, and manage to shut the door behind me just in time. This is mortifying. I don't think I've been sick from alcohol since I was a teenager. *Did Ted hear me throwing up?* Cold shower—that's the answer. I need to change anyway; my dress is damp from lying in the sand. There's nothing as sobering as—

"ARRGGGGHHHH!"

"What's wrong?" Ted knocks sharply on the bathroom door.

"Nothing, just in the shower and it's cold! Out in a jiffy joff!"

Jiffy joff? Who says that? I gulp down some of the water as it flows over my face, then grab my toothbrush and brush my teeth in the shower. The only good thing about being sick is that now it's only a matter of time until I feel sober. It's like turning your phone on and off again when it gets all glitchy. The shower helps, and I emerge in my towel feeling considerably clearer headed.

Ted is waiting for me in the bedroom, holding two cups of tea. When he sees I'm wearing only a towel, he averts his gaze, mumbling that he'll wait outside. I've noticed his ears go red when he's embarrassed. I love that Ted's this strong, manly-looking guy, who at times can seem so sure of himself, but then something innocuous like a woman in a towel can get him all befuddled. Through the window, I see him take a seat on one of the cottage's patio chairs. He shifts uncomfortably—it is too small for him—and I find myself smiling, grateful that he is here.

Now, what am I going to wear? I have my clothes back from the hotel, the ones I wore yesterday, or the pale blue dress, now laundered and dry in the machine. I go for the dress. Whoever invented dresses was a genius—nice, easily put-onable dresses with no fiddly bits or leg holes.

"Thank you," I say to Ted, coming outside, picking up the mug of tea and sitting down next to him.

The first sip begins to calm my stomach. "I'm so sorry about this, taking you away from the party."

Ted gives a single nod, his face devoid of judgment.

"Are you still thinking you'll try and get your case tonight?

I'll go and get it for you if you want, if you aren't feeling great," Ted offers.

"If you swap the cases, then I won't have any reason to meet him, will I?" I put the tea down and cross my arms tight against my chest. This feels awkward, the fact we just had a weird moment on the beach and now we're talking about me wanting to go and meet my suitcase guy.

"Look, obviously I don't know you very well, Laura, but I remember what you said when you first got into my cab—about having unrealistic expectations."

"I'm embarrassed I said that," I say, studiously focusing on the handle of my mug.

"Just because a guy likes the book your dad read and buys the perfume your mum wore—it doesn't mean he's going to fill the hole in your life that they left."

His words are gentle, but they feel like a punch to my fragile stomach.

"I don't think you're qualified to dabble in pop psychology, Ted—you're a walking example of how not to process loss. Clearly, you haven't been looking after yourself since your wife left. Is growing a beard some kind of penance until she comes back? Because it doesn't sound like she *is* coming back."

I regret the words as soon as they are out, scratches from a cat feeling cornered. I see hurt flash in his eyes and almost leap out of my chair to beg back my cruel words. Instead, I freeze.

Ted gives me a tight smile and stands up. "I shouldn't have said anything. It's none of my business."

As he starts walking back toward the beach, I call after him, "Wait, Ted, the address?"

He calls back without turning around, "In the notes on your phone."

"Any chance you could drive me?"

"Don't push your luck, Laura. I'm not a bloody saint."

I don't know why I asked that. I think I just wanted him to stay a moment until I could find the words to apologize properly. My mind hums with discomfort over my behavior, and hurt by Ted's words, but I push those feelings down. I just need to focus on meeting Jasper now, on seeing if my instincts about the case were right.

I order a cab from a different taxi firm, reapply my makeup, and then pack the contents of Jasper's bag so they look less interfered with. I still haven't quite worked out how I'm going to explain the mangled jumper and the missing shoe.

When the cab arrives, I stand for a moment in the driveway. Watching the party in full swing down on the beach, I feel a tug of remorse—an urge to stay, to rejoin the party, and to make peace with Ted. On the grass, where the footpath meets the sand, I see Sandy—wildly waving at me to come back—but I just wave in reply. I look down at the case in my hands—my mind running over the contents again. It has to mean something. It *has* to.

It feels strange to be sitting in the backseat of a cab again—like I've been demoted. It's only a ten-minute drive before we pull up to a large granite house called Maison D'Oie, north of St. Ouen's village. These Le Maistres certainly live in fancy houses. This place is a similar size pile to Maude's, large enough to be the setting for some kind of murder mystery with a billiard room, a scullery, and a house party full of suspects.

As I give my reflection a final check in my compact, blending a little nude eye shadow across my lids to ease my post-sangria pallor, the driver says, "Don't worry, you look gorgeous, love."

I give him a tight smile.

Standing on the doorstep, I feel my heart in my throat. I'm definitely feeling more sober now, but for a moment I wish just enough of my drunker self back, to muffle the overthinking. I put the suitcase down on the doorstep, press my palms together, and hear my own heartbeat, loud and fast, in the quiet of the evening. This is it. I'm finally going to meet him; the person the universe has led me to, my destiny. I ring the doorbell.

Chapter 16

Jasper opens the door, and I feel a wave of relief when I see his warm, handsome face. He is wearing a light gray cashmere jumper and dark jeans that look similar to the ones in his case. He brushes a hand through his thick, foppish brown hair and there is a look of recognition in his eyes. Then he gives me a smile that lights him up.

"You," he says.

"Me."

And we just stare at each other like idiots for a minute.

"Will you come in?" he says, holding the door open wide.

Now I really hope I brushed my teeth properly. As I walk ahead of him, I discreetly breathe into my palm just to check. I doubt the heroines in Richard Curtis films ever had to worry about their breath smelling.

Jasper leads me to a spacious farmhouse kitchen, all sleek pale granite work surfaces and a few tastefully retained period features—large oak beams and stone slab flooring. This is good; if I'm noticing the stone flooring, I must be sober. Jasper pulls out a leather-topped bar stool for me.

"I owe you an apology, Laura—carelessly picking up the wrong bag, and then revealing myself to be so slovenly as to not even have unpacked or noticed for twenty-four hours." He looks across the kitchen island at me, and his cheeks crease into dimples. Wow, he really is incredibly attractive. Though a little younger than I remember from the airport. His face has a boyish quality, but he's probably late twenties like I am.

"Well, you have a decent excuse—lifeboat training, your mother mentioned," I say, daring to glance down at his hand—no ring. *Cha-ching.*

He nods.

"I'm only a part-time volunteer, but it's still a big commitment training wise."

Though he has a lean build, he has broad, manly hands, perfect for pulling people from the water, or kneading dough, or playing the piano, or putting one on either side of my naked hips and— *OK, inappropriate.*

"Will you stay for a drink? Whatever you feel like, I have a fully stocked bar."

"I shouldn't have anything alcoholic, I've already had a few this evening," I say, giving him my most demure smile. "Maybe just a tea?"

Jasper starts pulling down cups and saucers from a shelf. "I have Darjeeling, Assam, oolong?"

"Any of the above." I shrug, I know nothing about tea except I like it with milk, no sugar.

"Let's have oolong for a change then," Jasper says, tapping a glass jar and taking it down from the shelf. "I have to say it feels fortuitous, us picking up each other's cases," he says, spooning loose leaf tea into a small gray earthenware teapot.

"It does?"

"This might be speaking out of turn, but when we ran into each other in the airport, I—" He turns back toward me, shaking his head in feigned embarrassment.

"What?" I say with a girlish giggle that doesn't sound at all like me.

"Well." He closes his eyes briefly. "I wanted to ask you out. I know we barely said a word to each other, but, well, I've never scrabbled around the floor to retrieve"—he pauses, his lips twitching briefly as he searches for the right word—"the toiletries of someone so beautiful before."

I clench every muscle in my body. *Did he just say I was beautiful?*

"Hardly," I say, feeling a playful scowl crease my forehead.

"You're stunning, Laura, as I'm sure you know, but—I don't think we British folk know how to ask someone out in the middle of an airport." Jasper wrinkles his nose. I can't stop watching the muscles in his face move. *Is this really happening, or is this a fantasy?* Maybe I passed out drunk in the sea and this is some kind of drowning hallucination.

"I would have felt sleazy asking if I could have your number in front of a concourse full of people. Plus, you probably have a boyfriend or a husband or a . . ." He lets the sentence hang, and I look up to meet his eye with a deliciously laden look.

"None of the above."

"When I got the message about a woman having my case, I— It sounds ridiculous, but I hoped it might be you."

This could literally not be going any better.

"Can I tell you something even stranger?" I say, leaning forward to take the cup of tea and saucer he hands me. "When I opened your bag—before I knew it wasn't mine—some of the things inside, they made me feel that I was meant to find you."

"Really, like what?"

He walks around to my side of the kitchen island, pulling out the bar stool next to me, and I feel flustered by his proximity. *Don't tell him* everything, *Laura, you'll freak him out. Apple peel, apple peel.*

"*To Kill a Mockingbird* is my favorite book."

"No," he says, eyes wide with surprise, "I've only read it about fifteen times."

"You haven't!" I gasp.

"I even went to law school because I wanted to be Atticus Finch," he says, rolling his eyes. "Though I soon realized being a lawyer wasn't all about getting to be the good guy; often you're forced to be the bad guy too. Thus, my career in the legal profession turned out to be short-lived." He shakes his head, as though not wanting to get too far off topic. "What else was in my bag? You have me well and truly intrigued now."

"Phil Collins." I let the name hang between us.

"Only the greatest musician ever born!" says Jasper, slapping his hand on the counter.

"You had the piano music in your bag, and, well, to say I'm

a massive Phil fan would be a huge understatement." I feel myself grinning—everything he is telling me is confirming my instincts about the case.

Jasper shakes his head, smiles, then starts talking to the ceiling, "Alexa, play 'I Wish It Would Rain Down." The walls begin to sing. "I found that sheet music in an obscure music store in London; I thought playing more music I actually like might encourage me to practice more."

The chorus kicks in, and we both start singing along. He knows every word, just like me. It's cheesy, but delightfully so. We're both nodding our heads to the beat. Jasper rolls up the sleeves of his jumper, picks up two wooden spoons from a pot and pretends to play the drums on some saucepan lids; it makes me laugh.

My mind starts getting ahead of itself: Maybe our suitcase story will be made into a musical one day. Reese Witherspoon could buy the movie rights and turn it into something like *La La Land* or *Les Misérables*. Ooh, it could be like *Mamma Mia* but full of Phil Collins songs.

"I don't know anyone else who truly appreciates Phil's genius. I mean, who else can combine up-tempo pop with that kind of musical dexterity and lyrical complexity?" says Jasper.

"Right! Exactly," I say, throwing both hands in the air. "I've loved him since I was a girl. I inherited my dad's old LP collection, and all the Phil records are scratched from overuse—"

"You listen to LPs?" Jasper grins. "I have a whole library of LPs upstairs. OK. Favorite song, on the count of three. One, two, three . . ." And then we both say, "'Sussudio,'" at the same time. He holds my gaze, and I feel that warm glow that comes from knowing someone likes you.

"Well, well." He smiles at me. "I think we should make a toast." He pauses, contemplating what to toast to, and then says, "To lost luggage."

"To lost luggage."

Looking at Jasper take a sip of his tea, it's as though someone has found the list in my head filed under "perfect man" and made him flesh. I ask Jasper where the loo is, just to give myself a time-out from all the delicious eye contact, and he points me down the corridor.

There are all sorts of interesting prints and vintage maps adorning the wall; they don't look like the kind of art someone our age would choose. I must have walked farther than he instructed, because when I open the door, I find, not a bathroom, but another kitchen. Unlike the kitchen we were in, this one is cream and white, and all the units gleam as though brand-new and unused. I shut the door, confused. Why would anyone need two kitchens? Maybe this is some kind of granny annex or a lodger lives here.

Following the corridor around, I pause to inspect a line of butterflies in wall-mounted cabinets. They're both beautiful and strangely morbid. The next door I come to is open a crack. I reach out for the handle, inexplicably nervous about what I might find behind it. As I push the door slowly open, I find—another kitchen.

What the hell? I am Alice in Kitchenland, and it's slightly freaky. This kitchen is stylistically entirely different from the first two, dark charcoal surfaces and deep mahogany cupboards, with a large steel extractor unit in the center of the room. I back out, my heart racing.

Bugger, I knew he was too good to be true. It's not as

though I've opened doors to find a string of corpses or a coffin with my name on it—but I still feel unnerved. Is Jasper *obsessed* with kitchens? How many more kitchens are there? Why do guys that tick every other box always have to have a weird "thing"? Why can't I just meet a normal, unmarried man who likes Phil Collins and has a regular number of kitchens in his house?

"So, um, I think I went too far down the corridor and— You have two kitchens?" I say as nonchalantly as possible, once I'm back in the first kitchen with Jasper. Best to just ask him. I genuinely can't think of anything other than "kitchen murderer" right now, like he has a fetish for killing people in a culinary environment, but he likes to mix it up with different backdrops. I won't let on I've seen all three; he might conclude that if I've seen three, I've seen too much, and he'll have to murder me right here with a bread knife.

"Five actually," he says with a grin.

I swallow nervously. There is a touch of the Patrick Bateman about Jasper, now that I look at him with fresh eyes. Not in personality, but he does looks like Christian Bale. Oh God, what if this is my last night on earth? I haven't even seen the latest Bond film yet—I'll die not knowing if Phoebe Waller-Bridge managed to revive the franchise.

"Sorry, I should have warned you," says Jasper. "You're probably thinking I've got a bizarre kitchen obsession now."

"Ha-ha, no." I let out a high-pitched laugh.

Please don't kill me. Please don't kill me.

"It's my job—I sell kitchens," he explains. "We needed a showroom, and I inherited this house, which is far bigger than

I need." He shrugs. "When people want to see the kitchen fixtures they're buying, they come here. There are three in the main house, two more in the outbuilding. I host a lot of culinary and lifestyle photo shoots too."

My throat stops constricting, my shoulders relax, the rising tide of Christian Bale–related panic recedes. OK, that is definitely a more logical explanation than that he's a serial killer who likes to murder people in different styles of kitchen. Maybe I do watch too many true crime shows.

"Let me give you the full tour," he offers, jumping to his feet.

Jasper tells me that his company is called Contessa Kitchens, and that all his kitchen designs are named after women he admires. The kitchen we are in is the Michelle (as in Obama). There's the Maude (after his mother)—a modern take on a rustic farmhouse theme. The chic cream design I'd stumbled into is the Diana (as in the princess). The dark charcoal fixtures make up the Emmeline. And then, finally, there's a more traditional oak-framed kitchen called—wait for it—the Malala.

As Jasper gives me the tour, he gears into "salesman mode," and I hear a lot of words I don't know the meaning of, like *compact laminate* and *polymer resin*. He explains all the Contessa styles can be adapted to a U-shape, an L-shape, a peninsula, or islands, but he might as well be speaking Danish for all the kitchen-speak I understand.

I nod along, impressed by his enthusiasm.

"You're regretting asking about the kitchens now, aren't you?" he asks as his gaze settles on my perplexed face.

"No, not at all." I quickly change whatever expression my

face was displaying. "So, *all* the kitchens are named after women?" I ask, leaning against the dark mahogany island of the Emmeline. "Isn't that slightly, I don't know, sexist?"

Jasper looks wounded.

"Oh no. It's a tribute to some of the people throughout history I most admire, just as you might name a ship in someone's honor." He pauses. "I have four older sisters. I was a feminist before I could walk."

I'm not convinced any of these women would be thrilled about having a kitchen named after them, but he appears so earnest about it, it must be well intended.

"And is there enough demand for new kitchens on an island this size?" I ask.

"Oh yes. It's the first thing people change when they buy a new house. People like to make the heart of the home their own." Jasper leans an elbow against the wall, then ruffles his hair with the other hand. "There's a manor in St. Lawrence that's had three of my kitchens in about as many years—the chap keeps getting divorced and each new wife insists on ripping their predecessor's kitchen out."

The story amuses him, so I smile along, but the thought of such waste casts a bleak image in my mind.

Jasper suggests we move to the living room, almost as though he wants to reassure me that there are some rooms in his house that aren't kitchens. He holds the door open before following me through. The living room has an old-fashioned feel: green velvet sofas, wooden side tables with protective glass tops peppered with ornaments, and a well-polished grand piano in the corner.

"This was my uncle's house—he didn't have children, so he left it to me. This décor needs redoing, but I'm putting it off because, well, I'm only good at kitchens," he says, with a charming, self-deprecating shrug.

Walking over to the piano, I lay my fingers on the lid.

"What a glorious piano," I say. "You play then?"

Jasper walks over and takes a seat on the sofa. "I was in a quartet at university, but I haven't played much since. My sisters are always nagging me to keep it up—saying it's a waste to let it slide. They also tell me women love men who are musical." He winces at the admission, and I raise my eyebrows in surprise, as though this is the first I've ever heard of such a thing.

Stepping away from the piano, I look around at the pictures of his family on the wall.

On the mantelpiece, I notice a photo of four naked men on a beach, their bottoms on display, all turning their heads to face the camera. One is clearly Jasper, and the man next to him almost looks like—

"Wait, is that Henry Cavill, the Superman actor?"

"It is—I was at school with his brother. Skinny-dipping on a stag do is par for the course here."

I can't help smiling, imagining what Suki would do if she were here: She'd probably be stuffing the photo into her handbag. Next to the naked men is a picture I presume to be Jasper as a boy, standing by a house on stilts on a small rocky beach, next to four girls of varying heights.

"Oh, is this the Écréhous?" I ask, pointing to the picture.

"Yes, my family have a cabin there."

"A cabin?" I think of the keys in his bag.

"When I was a child, we used to go out there for most of the summer to fish and swim." He pauses, a wistful look in his eyes. "I'd love to take a son of my own there one day, teach him to sail, how to catch mackerel."

Wants a family, tick. Hunter-gatherer type who can catch food in emergencies, tick. Access to cabin for cabin-themed fantasy, tick, tick, tick.

"It sounds idyllic," I say.

"I'll take you there," Jasper says eagerly, crossing the room to stand beside me.

"What, now?" I tease.

"No, no, it's too dark now," he replies earnestly, "but tomorrow. I could take you there for lunch—on a date." He looks shy all of a sudden, which is sweet.

"I—" I feel myself grinning. "I would love that."

We move back to the sofa and share stories about our lives and our families. I tell him what I'm doing in Jersey: the travel article I'm writing, my parents' story. I show him the coin around my neck, my mother's album. I have told this story so many times I can recite it as though on autopilot.

"That all sounds incredibly romantic," Jasper says, his sea-green eyes attentive to my tale. "You've got to believe in destiny when you hear a story like that."

Believes in destiny, tick, tick, tickity, tick.

Telling the story prompts a flutter of panic about my looming deadline and doubt over whether the photos and my perspective on the story are going to be enough. Monica's strange version of events replays in my mind. Maybe I should try and meet Bad Granny before I leave? Even if there had been bad blood between my mother and her, she might remember what happened more clearly than Monica, she might have something to contribute.

My mind is drifting, and I force my concentration back into the room, asking Jasper to tell me more about his family. He tells me his sisters are all fiercely protective of him, that part of the reason he set up the kitchen business was to prove he could do something on his own.

"My entire family told me law was the right fit for me: I had the right degree, the right contacts, the right work ethic. But I just always loved kitchens. In some ways, it felt like a calling, the way you hear priests talk about their jobs." This comparison makes me smile.

"You should talk to my mother for the travel piece you're writing. There's nothing she won't be able to tell you about this island or its recipes."

"Oh?" It comes out as a strangled-sounding *oh*, as the image of Maude Le Maistre prostrate on the chaise longue forces its way to the forefront of my optic nerve.

"She will love the fact we met through a suitcase. We'll be the talk of her pétanque club."

"Um, speaking of which, I'm afraid I have a confession to make, Jasper," I say, pulling my lower lip between my teeth.

"This doesn't sound good." He frowns. "Is there a boyfriend after all? You only have four months to live? An allergy to kitchens?" He raises his eyebrows in a comical expression.

"No," I say with a mirthful sigh. "It's about your case. I'm afraid some of the things inside—well—there's this dog where I'm staying, Scamp, and I stupidly left your case slightly open, and your jumper and one of your trainers came to a rather sticky end. I will replace them, of course." I feel slightly guilty about blaming everything on Scamp, but he did maul the jumper; it's only a slight fudge.

Jasper pauses for dramatic effect, and then says, "I think a jumper and a shoe are a small price to pay to have met you." He holds eye contact for a moment, and then his eyes dart down to my lips and back. It's a tiny movement, but it makes me suspect he might be thinking about kissing me. I cannot believe how well this is going. Most men this attractive might be arrogant or conceited, but Jasper is neither; he is earnest and charming—everything I had hoped he would be. If only everything could freeze right here, then I wouldn't be able to do anything to ruin it.

"You know, I still haven't actually been to the loo," I say, springing up and clasping my hands together. "Sorry, I got distracted by the kitchens before."

The bathroom is covered in what looks like very expensive wallpaper, decorated in geometric gold shapes. There are framed articles from magazines, photo shoots of kitchens I assume must be Jasper's, and a certificate for his grade eight piano, which makes me smile. I stare at myself in the mirror. Why am I running away to the loo, when everything is going so well?

I reach for my phone, feeling the need to hear a familiar voice, to speak to someone who will tell me straight why I am acting weirdly. I FaceTime Dee. It's past ten, but she never goes to bed before eleven.

"Hey, can you talk?" I whisper into the screen when she answers.

"Yes, Neil is out with his running club friends, I'm Marie Kondoing my wardrobe, rather than packing a load of clothes I never wear." Dee shifts the screen so I can see the piles of clothes on her bed. "Why do I even own a single pair of heels? Have you ever seen me wear heels?"

"Never." I shake my head.

"So, have you found Suitcase Man?" Dee asks, sitting down on the bed and giving me her full attention.

"Yes, I'm in his bathroom," I say quietly.

"It must be going well then." She mirrors my quiet voice.

"It is," I hiss. "He's amazing, like, dream-man-with-a-cherry-on-top amazing."

"So why are you calling me? And why are we whispering?"

"I don't know. It's almost disconcerting how well it's going. He's good-looking, intelligent, and charming, he plays the piano, he ticks *all* the boxes. Plus, I think he likes me." I pause, "He has five kitchens, though—"

"Five kitchens?"

"He's a kitchen salesman. His house doubles as a showroom."

Dee pauses for a moment, "Unconventional, but not a deal breaker."

"It's not. It's actually kind of geeky and sweet."

"So . . ." Dee says, clearly still wondering why I have called her.

"I met this crazy aunt today, she told me my parents were never married."

"What?" Dee's face creases with concern.

"She's nuts, she also told me Mum had a phobia of seagulls

and the dark. She must have their story confused with someone else."

"Seagulls?"

"I think I would have known if Mum had any phobias. Then Suki's mad at me for messing up this Instagram Live today, and then there's this cabdriver, Ted, the one I shouted at, he's been driving me around today, and we've been talking a lot . . ." I trail off, not sure why I mentioned Ted.

"Laura, have you been drinking?" Dee asks.

"Yes," I say with a grimace.

"Right, well. It sounds like you've had a pretty full day. Maybe you should rain-check Suitcase Guy, see him tomorrow when you have a clearer head. If he's really so perfect, you don't need to rush anything."

"Maybe you're right. He's already asked me out on a day date tomorrow."

"Great. Everyone loves a day date. Look, don't put yourself under too much pressure. It feels like you're set on writing the perfect article about the perfect story, all while trying to meet the perfect guy—it's a lot to put on one weekend away."

"Hmmm," I say, screwing up my face at the screen, tucking a wisp of flyaway hair behind my ear.

"You look tired, Laura. Have a good night's sleep, pick things up with him tomorrow." I give her a grateful grin. I'm sure it's good advice. "And next time we talk, we need to have a conversation about the state of the nation or politics or something," Dee says, opening her eyes wide and bringing them right up to the screen. "I refuse to be the 'best-friend sounding board,' constantly playing second fiddle to the primary, male-focused story line."

"OK, you've got a deal," I say, bringing my eyes right up to the screen too. "Look, I'd better go. And, Dee—thank you."

Jasper is sitting at the piano when I come back. The sheet music from his bag is on the stand, and he starts playing "Against All Odds" as I walk across the room. His fingers move organically across the keys in a rapid flurry of notes; he's clearly talented. I tilt my head to the beat as I sit down on the window seat near him. Unbidden, my mind drifts back to the beach, to the warmth of Ted's voice, and I realize that this is the second piece of live Phil Collins music I've enjoyed this evening.

"Didn't I say I wouldn't be able to do it justice?" Jasper says as he closes the lid.

"You're amazing. I could listen to you play all night long," I say, bringing my mind back into the room, then I bite my lip, worried that sounded suggestive. "But listen, if we're going boating tomorrow, I might call it a night. It's been a long day for me."

Jasper's eyes flash disappointment, but he quickly hides it with a smile. I offer to call a cab, but he insists he will drive me home.

We're about to leave when Jasper says, "Your case!"

He presses a palm to each cheek, and we both laugh at the fact we might have forgotten. Opening a hall cupboard, he pulls out my suitcase. When he hands it over, I hug it to my chest—relieved to finally have it back. I'll have so many choices of what to wear tomorrow, my good mascara, my silk pajamas, my diary, and the shampoo that makes my hair smell like a spa in a citrus farm. I didn't know these objects were so important to me, but clearly they are.

There are two cars in Jasper's driveway, a black SUV and a red sports car. He takes me to the Land Rover, which he opens with two beeps of a key fob. Were these expensive cars inherited from his uncle too, I wonder, or are kitchens a lucrative business? When we reach Ted's road in L'Étacq, I tell Jasper he can drop me on the road—I don't want to disturb anyone by driving in so late—but Jasper insists on seeing me to the bottom of the drive. The beach is dark; no sign of the party, but inside Gerry's house the living room light is on.

I start to open the car door, but Jasper says, "No! Wait. Stay there." He leaps out of his side and runs around to mine, opening my door and taking a little bow. He has rather sweet, old-fashioned manners, or perhaps he's simply trying to impress me. If he is, it's working.

"Why, thank you," I say, with a little curtsy. Then I lean forward to kiss him on the cheek, but he's leaning in to kiss my other side and we end up bumping foreheads. We both clutch our heads and laugh. Jasper blushes at his own clumsiness and then feigns leaning in again, knocking his head on the car door, and falling down on the ground, flat on his back on the gravel. His clowning makes me burst out laughing, and I reach out my hand to help him up.

"That wasn't very suave of me," he says. "I was trying to be suave."

As his eyes meet mine, I see a flash of nerves and I'm surprised a man who looks like Jasper could be nervous. Standing opposite him, I feel a warm glow of validation; I was right about the suitcase. Everyone thought I was being nuts, but look, here he is, exactly what I sensed from his luggage he might be.

"I'm looking forward to seeing more of this suaveness tomorrow," I say with a grin.

"Another day in paradise," he says.

"Well, if leaving me is easy."

"You'll be in my heart." He smiles, pressing a hand to his chest.

"Are we actually doing this? Are we having a conversation with Phil Collins' song titles?"

"Oh, I could keep going all night," Jasper says with a dramatic sigh, and I feel my cheeks begin to ache with smiling.

"I'll see you tomorrow," I say, turning toward the garden.

"Laura," he calls after me, and I turn to look back at him. "I can't wait."

The words send a hum of contentment through me, and I raise my eyes to the sky, silently thanking the stars for their part in all this.

ꓫ

12 September 1991

Alex,
I'm so disappointed you aren't coming this weekend, when it's our last opportunity to see each other before you go to Greece. Surely you could find the money for the flight. Would your mum not lend it to you?

I can't understand why you were so cross with me on the phone. I only borrowed the coin to make a way for it be to worn—otherwise, it will only sit in a drawer. I know you don't believe me, but I feel its memories when I hold it, it shouldn't be hidden away. I thought you would be taking it back to her after your visit this weekend. You will be so pleased when you see how it looks.

Let's be friends again, please? Maybe I can find a way to come and see you in Greece once my dance classes break for half-term. I miss you every day, and the days you do not call are hardly days to me at all.

All my love,
Annie

Chapter 17

Once Jasper has driven away, I glance furtively back at the house. I'll have to walk past the kitchen window to get to my cottage but don't want to draw attention to my return. If I walk behind the stone wall, I can avoid the spotlight shining onto the lawn from the kitchen window. I pick up my case and carefully climb onto the low granite wall—oh, this is fine, easy as anything. I'll just walk along the wall; I have the balance of an Olympic gymnast.

"AHHHHHH!"

I stumble on a lump in the rock, launch forward like a bat without wings, landing splayed across the lawn with a *thunk*. Pain alarms explode in my leg. "FUCKING OW! FUCKITY OW!" I cry. I know I said I don't swear much, but

I think breaking my leg buys me some allowances on the language filter.

As I'm lying there, lamenting that my adult gymnast career is over before it even began, the kitchen door opens, and I see Ted's broad-shouldered silhouette standing in the doorway.

"Laura, what are you doing? Are you all right?" he says, running down the hill and crouching down next to me.

"My leg," I say, trying to sit up, "I think it's broken. Oh jeez, is that my bone sticking out of the bottom? If it is, I'm going to be sick."

I'm not good with gore. When I watched that movie about the guy who got stuck up a mountain and chopped off his own hand, I couldn't look at my hands for a week without gagging.

"That's your suitcase handle beneath your foot," says Ted. "Definitely no bone. Let me get you inside, and I'll take a proper look."

He helps me up, and I let out a wincing *arrrghhhh-eeeehhh* sound, like a fox with its tail stuck in a cat flap. Ted sweeps me up in both arms and carries me back to the house. I murmur protests, but he lifts me so effortlessly that we're inside before I can articulate any sort of proper objection.

In the living room, Ted deposits me gently on the only remaining chair. The furniture that was in here earlier has disappeared; only boxes and piles of objects remain. There are a few lamps on the floor, the side tables they'd once stood on, gone. They emit a warm, low light, giving the room an inviting feel. Ted kneels down to inspect my leg. A thin line of blood trickles down from a gash on my shin.

"I don't think we need to amputate, it's just a cut. You must have fallen on a sharp rock." He fetches a first aid kit, cleans the wound, and carefully applies a large adhesive dressing. "Did you twist your ankle?" He firmly holds my foot in one hand, and then with the other, gently presses the skin. "Does this hurt? Does it hurt?" he asks again, and I realize I haven't answered, distracted by the feeling of his hands on my skin.

"No, it's fine," I say.

Ted carefully packs the first aid case away. He's being all serious and professional; this must be his doctor mode.

"Dare I ask why you were dancing along the wall?"

"I didn't want to disturb you, traipsing across the garden," I say, weakly.

He tilts his face to meet mine.

"If I wasn't disturbed by the car-side flirting and giggling, I don't think I would have been disturbed by you walking through my garden."

Now I wish my leg *was* broken and I was safely on my way to hospital rather than having this brain-meltingly awkward conversation. Clearing my throat, I roll my ankle between my hands to distract from having to respond. Ted picks up the medical bag and his lip twitches with the hint of a smile.

"Do you want me to help you down to the cottage?"

"Could I just have some water?" I ask in an exaggerated hoarse voice. Now that the leg-breaking emergency is over, I feel sheepish about how things were left between us, and I want to apologize before I go anywhere.

He gives me a compassionate look as if to reassure me he's not annoyed or jealous or disapproving or— *Jealous? Why did I think that?* Of course he's not *jealous*. I gulp down the glass of water Ted hands me.

"Ted, I'm so sorry about this evening," I say, putting the empty glass down on the carpet next to me.

"It's fine, I was up anyway."

"No, not now—well, now too—but I meant earlier. You were only trying to look out for me, as any friend would. I was rude to you and I'm sorry."

Ted smiles, a genuine smile that reaches his eyes.

"That's OK. So, did Mr. McGuffin live up to expectations?"

My stomach twists into a knot.

"He's nice," I say, feeling my face getting warm.

"You're blushing. That good, huh?"

I try to temper my smile but feel some accidental smugness radiating out of me.

"And a paid-up member of the Phil Collins fan club?"

I nod, pinching my lips together. "He played 'Against All Odds' on the piano." *Why did I say that?* Ted doesn't need to know that detail.

"Well, I'll expect a mention in the wedding speech," Ted says. "I think it was my detective work on the bee club that cracked the case."

Watching him talk, I can't read his expression, but I haven't heard this unnatural breeziness before. I wave a hand around the room, keen to move the subject on from Jasper.

"What have you been doing in here? Did you keep on packing after the party?"

Ted shifts his gaze to the carpet.

"I couldn't sleep, so I'm trying to be ruthless. I'm taking Dad to his new home tomorrow, then the estate agent wants to take photos of an empty house."

"Do you have to sell it?" I ask, noticing he looks tired, his eyelids heavy.

"I can't afford to keep it, not with Dad's care."

"I thought doctors earn a fortune?" I say, drawing out the word *fortune*.

Ted looks at his hands. "Well, my career is in about as good a state as my marriage at the moment."

"Oh." I feel a jolt of concern. "How come?"

Ted inspects his knuckles then clenches and unclenches his hands.

"It doesn't matter." He glances across at me, almost shyly, then groans. "I'm so bad at this stuff, Laura." For a moment I think he means talking to me, but then I see he's gesturing toward the boxes.

"Let me help you," I offer.

"You don't want to help me sort through my parents' junk at eleven thirty at night," he says, but strangely, I do.

"I'm good at this kind of thing, please, let me help."

Ted's lips move into a grateful smile and he gives a small shrug of acceptance. He disappears upstairs and brings down more boxes, and we quietly unpack the contents. There is old clothes, paperwork, bundles of letters, old bits and pieces collected over a lifetime. His mother's silver-plated hairbrush, dusty watercolors of the English countryside, a calendar from 1995, sticky cookbooks, and half-empty face creams. Endless coat hangers and jars full of pens, boxes of outdated electrical items, a VHS player and an old-fashioned toaster—things no one would ever want or need.

"Gerry didn't want to sort through any of this?"

I can see why Ted has been overwhelmed by the task.

"We started doing it together, but it was upsetting him," he explains. "He tries not to dwell on the past and packing up a house is pretty much a field trip in nostalgia. In the end, he packed up a box of things he wants to keep, the rest he was happy for me to deal with. I figured it's enough of a wrench making him leave this house without forcing him to rake through the ashes of his life too."

"You're not making him leave, you know," I say, hearing the guilt in Ted's voice. "He can't live here on his own anymore. The move isn't down to you."

Ted rubs an eye with his finger. The air is heavy with dust, and my eyes begin to itch too.

"I guess not." He doesn't sound convinced. He picks up a glass paperweight and turns it over in his hands. "I thought I'd just chuck all this stuff, but it feels too—I don't know—disrespectful, not to at least look through it all."

"There was so much of my mum's stuff I didn't know what to do with," I say, looking around. "It's strange, the things it upset me to throw away. Weirdly, her toothbrush really got me. It suddenly felt the saddest thing that she'd never brush her teeth again."

"What happened to your mum?" he asks, cautiously.

"Colon cancer. It was very advanced, happened quickly." I think Ted's the first person I've said that to without crying.

Ted gives me a nod of empathy and understanding, and I feel the depth of compassion in his eyes, none of the pity or embarrassment I usually see when I tell people about my mother.

"Anyway, I suspect it's easier to sort through a stranger's

things," I say, clapping my hands, returning to the task in hand. "We'll make piles. Keep, Bin, Recycle, Sell, that's the way to do it." It's already eleven thirty p.m., but having felt tired at Jasper's house, I now feel a second wind of energy with the prospect of being helpful to Ted.

We work in companionable silence, occasionally holding up things we're unsure of, waiting for the other to point to the pile they think it should go in. I feel useful, filling bin bags and folding clothes for the charity shop.

Picking up a box of videos, I flick through the titles. "*Psycho*, *Strangers on a Train*, *To Catch a Thief*, someone really is a Hitchcock fan then."

Ted leans across to look, then he spreads his legs wide on the floor and pulls the box between them.

"I used to treasure these," he says, picking one out, tapping the label fondly. "These were my teenage years—Hitchcock on a Friday night, Mum baking wonders for my friends in the kitchen." His eyes sparkle as he turns the VHS box over in his hands. "I went to this special screening of *Vertigo* a few years ago. As soon as the film started, I could have sworn I smelled fried dough." He spreads his fingers in front of his face and inhales, as though replicating the experience. "Your mind can play tricks on you like that."

"What's this?" I ask, holding up an old framed photo of Ted dressed as a Boy Scout, with a terrible, crooked bowl haircut. "So, you *were* a Boy Scout. I'm guessing you failed to get the cut-your-own-hair badge," I say with a laugh.

"That is embarrassing," says Ted, his eyes creasing into a

smile as he holds out a hand for it. "That will be first on the bonfire pile."

"No! I like it, you look cute." I pout at the photo. "I almost wouldn't have recognized you without all the facial hair."

In the same box, I find another faded photo of a small boy holding a stick in his mouth, wearing a felt headband with paper ears pinned to it. I start to laugh, "Oh, Ted, this is the most tragic fancy-dress outfit I think I've ever seen."

Ted reaches across for the photo and grins when he sees it.

"This wasn't fancy dress. When I was six, I was so set on getting a pet, I basically became a dog called Leonard for a month until my parents relented and got me a real one."

"Aw, you were the weird dog boy as a child, that's adorable." I make a face of mock pity.

"OK, no more photos for you," he says, taking the box away from me, his hand brushing against mine. "I'm guessing there are no embarrassing photos of you in the world then, Lady Muck?"

"Oh no, there are definitely some bad ones. I had a full-on head brace at one point. I had donkey teeth as a teenager." I stick my teeth out over my bottom lip to illustrate. He shakes his head, rubbing a hand across his lips to hide a smile.

"No, you still look good, even when you do that. No sympathy points for you."

It's interesting to watch someone else ride the emotional seesaw that is excavating the life of a loved one. Ted's mood shifts from fond recollection, like for the videos, to laughing with me over old photos, through to frustration at the sheer volume of junk, back to melancholy over finding his mother's kitchen scales at the bottom of a damp box. I find I already know the nuances of Ted's facial expressions. His brow furrows into two distinct lines between his eyebrows when he's concerned or upset, but when he frowns in jest, only one of those lines appears. So much about him feels familiar to me somehow, even though I've only known him such a short amount of time.

After about an hour, I look at the progress we have made but notice Ted has added nothing to the Keep pile.

"You're not keeping anything?"

"I don't want any of it. It's depressing, that a life boils down to this," he says, waving an arm across the room.

"You have to keep something, surely? How else will you remember?"

Ted rubs his face with both his hands.

"I don't see my mother in these things. I don't see Dad here either. This is just life's detritus, the rubbish we leave behind." His voice becomes sharper. "Mum's gone, and now Dad's going to have to try and sleep in an unfamiliar bed. And for all his bluster, I can see he is terrified, because he knows I am taking him to that place to die—" Ted thrusts both palms into his eye sockets and lets out a low, guttural sob that takes me by surprise.

"Oh, Ted." I shuffle over next to him and put an arm around his shoulder. "I know, it's hard." He leans into me, and we just hold each other for a moment. But then I become aware of the smell of his neck. It feels heady and intimate in a way I hadn't intended, and I pull back, self-conscious. Standing up, I cross the room, to put space between us.

"Now, what is all this?" I say, with forced brightness, as I pick up a large jar full of multicolored sea glass. "Was this your mum's?"

Ted looks at the jar. "Yes, she collected tons of the stuff over the years."

"Right," I say, "and I saw your face when you first told me about sea glass and your mum—that's a happy memory. You should pick a few pieces to keep, and the rest we'll scatter back on the beach tomorrow, let someone else have the fun of finding it."

His mouth nudges into a smile, and I feel pleased that I might have said something helpful.

"My mother's scent," I say, "it's the strongest memory I have of her. I keep a bottle of her perfume by my bed at home."

"Patchouli soap, floury hands, and Elnett hairspray," says Ted, "that's what my mother smelled of." He picks up a small, quilted bag from the pile next to him. "She loved anything and everything patchouli. She even tried to get Dad into patchouli tea at one point, but he was having none of it."

"Patchouli, right," I say, taking the bag from him and making a new pile next to me. Sitting down cross-legged on the floor, I pat the carpet opposite, indicating Ted should sit the same way. "We'll keep that. Now, your dad, close your eyes, what do you think of? What do you want to keep of his?"

Ted's gaze meets mine across the dimly lit room and my stomach contracts. Then he slowly closes his eyes as requested.

"I think of all the things he used to be able to do here: his furniture making, playing the guitar, his love of sailing. I think of my mum, them laughing, this house, our dogs, all the things he loved, all lost to him."

There's a lump in my throat.

"Gerry wouldn't want you to focus on what he's lost. What does he still have?"

Ted pauses, closing his eyes again, humoring me.

"His sense of humor, I don't think he'll ever lose that." Ted bows his head, thinking. "The sky, he never tires of studying the constellations. Gin, not a lot, and never before six, and he does an excellent cheese board."

When Ted opens his eyes, they are swimming with emotion.

"Laughing up at the night sky with a gin in your hand—sounds good to me," I say.

I wonder if Ted feels this intense to everyone. I am now so aware of his physicality, of when he is looking at me. No doubt it is simply the situation, the lateness of the hour, the heightened emotion of what we are doing here.

"Thank you, Laura," he says, his voice almost a whisper. He looks me square in the eyes, and some internal part of me is laid bare beneath his gaze.

When I look away, I try to focus on something solid in front of me, and we get back to work, emptying boxes. Opening a battered shoebox, I find it full to the brim with jewelry.

"Oh, look at all this!" I gasp. "Was all this your mother's?"

Ted comes over to see what I'm looking at.

"More likely my grandmother's," he says. "Dad said you could always hear her coming, she wore so many necklaces and bangles. I doubt it's worth much, just dress-up jewelry."

The box is crammed full of so many beautiful, intriguing objects that my hands don't know what to pick up first: delicate ivory hair slides shaped like leaves, rings full of purple and green stones, a beautiful brooch of a rose on painted porcelain, and a golden bangle lined with tiny silver bees. Vera's Vintage would bite your arm off for such a treasure trove.

"My mum used to repurpose old jewelry. She would have loved this stuff."

I glance up and see Ted watching me, a charmed expression on his face.

"Have it if you want," he says.

"No, I couldn't. These are your family heirlooms—you should keep them."

Ted picks up a long golden necklace with a stone missing. I find myself wondering how easy it would be to replace the stone with sea glass, how great that could look, the contrast between the ornate chain and the simplicity of a piece of weathered glass.

"I don't think any of it is quite my style," says Ted.

"I don't know," I say, holding a necklace up to his beard, "bejeweled beards are all the rage these days."

"Are they now?" he says in a deadpan voice.

I hold up more jewelry to his face and laugh as I attach earrings to his beard and then balance several bracelets on his head. He sits still, allowing me to decorate him like a Christmas tree. It feels strangely intimate, and when my eyes finally settle back on his, we just sit, looking at each other for a moment.

"You should have it," he says. "Anything that makes your face light up like that—my grandmother would want you to have it."

"Can I take a photo of you?" I ask.

"If it's for you, not your followers," he says, keeping his

face still so none of the jewels fall off. Turns out Ted is incredibly photogenic, with his tanned skin and dark, expressive eyes. I scooch around to show him the screen, smiling at the photos, but when I glance up to see his reaction, he is looking at me, not my screen.

The room suddenly feels warm. Putting my phone down, I carefully take all the jewelry off Ted, studiously avoiding his gaze. With the jewelry safely in the box, I pick up a tray full of papers and letters.

"Did they have a good marriage, your parents?" I ask, searching for a thread of conversation to pick up, trusting words more than what is unspoken in the silence.

"The best," he says.

"Can you see yourself ever getting married again?" I pause, then add, "If you do get divorced, of course."

He picks up a cork coaster and spins it in his hands.

"I don't think so." He lowers his eyes. "I can't imagine anything like that right now. Though funnily enough, this weekend has been the first time in a while I've felt fine about her being gone."

"That's great, Ted, that means you're moving on. You can't see yourself with anyone else though?" The question sounds loaded, I don't mean it to be; I'm just curious about him, about how he feels.

Ted's pupils look like heavy weights, rising from a murky sea as he turns to me and says, "I don't think I can be anything to anyone at the moment."

He says it slowly. It feels almost as though he's trying to let me down gently, or warn me off, in case I have misinterpreted his friendliness toward me, or this energy between us. I'm embarrassed that he might be remembering my flirty drunken behavior on the beach.

"Well, when you are ready to meet someone, I can highly recommend airport baggage carousels. Just go and rummage through a few bags until you meet the woman of your dreams." I flash him a silly grin. "It worked for me."

He frowns, with two creases on his forehead rather than one.

"So, letters, keep or bin?" I ask, with a clipped, efficient tone.

"Maybe flick through, check we're not throwing away anything crucial." Ted holds out a hand, and I pass him a stack of papers.

My pile is old gas bills from years ago, letters about Jersey Heritage membership, Scamp's vaccination certificate. Gerry's filing system could definitely use some improving. Then, among the typed letters, I come to a handwritten piece of paper. It looks to be the second page of a letter, though the first page isn't here.

If you need me urgently, you can contact me via the details below.

All my love, Belinda

And then there is an email address and a telephone number.

As I scan the words, my chest contracts; my fingers squeeze the letter, bending the paper where I'm clasping it. Belinda, Ted's wife, she wrote to Gerry; her phone number is right here in my hand. Did Gerry intend to keep this from Ted? I should give it to him, he could call her, find out where she is, finally have some closure. But then I look up at him and see how tired he looks; how emotionally draining this night has been—it's nearly one in the morning, I'm not sure he needs to see this tonight. My mind feels paralyzed by the responsibility.

"What's that?" Ted asks.

"Oh, nothing," I say quickly, shuffling the paper to the bottom of the pile. "Your dad wasn't the best at filing paperwork, was he?"

I didn't even consciously decide to lie, I just heard myself do it.

"That's an understatement," he says.

When Ted goes upstairs to the bathroom, I find the letter again and stuff it into my handbag. I don't have any kind of plan here; I just don't want Ted to have to deal with that right now. I'll keep it safe, give it to him tomorrow in the clear light of day.

I hear his feet on the stairs and look up to see Ted run a hand through his hair as he walks down, tilting his hips to avoid the wooden pillar at the bottom.

"Well, you've made more progress in a few hours than I've made in weeks. You're ruthlessly efficient." He yawns. "Maybe you can get inside my head and do the same sort of clearout."

"Maybe I can," I say. Then he looks at me, and for a moment, it feels like he wants something more from me.

"You need your bed. I'm going to head back to the cottage. Thanks for—" *For what? What am I thanking him for?* "I enjoy talking to you, Ted."

"Me too." Ted ruffles a hand through his hair. "Let me help you to your bed—I mean, to your house," he says, stumbling over his words. "I'll bring a torch, it's dark outside."

I smile at his embarrassment.

"Such a gent."

He picks up my case, then grabs a torch from the kitchen and shines it ahead of me, walking with me to the cottage door.

"Thank you for tonight, Laura," he says, looking down into my eyes. "I'm glad it was my cab you got into yesterday." There's an invisible pull in the air, as though I don't want him to leave, and my mind jumps back to that moment on the beach, when I wanted to nestle my face into his beard. "Sleep well."

"Night, Leonard," I say, feeling on safer ground making a joke. He smiles back and I pat him on the head. "There's a good doggie."

"Night, Lady Muck," he says, and then turns to walk back up the slope.

As I watch him go, I wonder at how different these two men are who I've spent the evening with. Jasper is energetic jazz, whereas Ted is the steady beat of a low drum. Jasper is loose-leaf oolong; Ted is a warm mug of builder's brew. I shake my head as I open my front door, unsure why I even feel the need to compare the two.

ꟹ

LETTER RETURNED TO SENDER

23 September 1991

Dear Annie,
I'm sorry I upset you calling things quits over the phone. Whatever happens, please don't think our summer in Jersey meant any less to me than it did to you. It was a wonderful few months—I think what made this summer so special, though, is that it was always only going to be the summer, Annie.

I'll be in Greece for six months, then who knows where. I go where the work is and I know from experience I'm not cut out for long distance. I didn't make any promises, did I? I never talked about the future; you can't lay that on me.

Please call if you want to talk, I hate to hear you upset. I'd like us to stay friends.

Love Al

PS please send back my grandmother's coin. I will repay you whatever you spent on it.

Chapter 18

My mother and I are sitting in my old bedroom, the one she turned into a jewelry workshop. The floor is piled high with trays; little compartments designed to store Christmas decorations, which Mum uses to stow her magpie finds. She's laying out some treasures on the mottled oak desk: a golden ring with the diamond missing, a collection of hair slides covered in tiny pearls threaded onto delicate silver wire and shaped into flowers.

It's these details that trick me, make me believe the scene is real. How does my brain furnish me with such detailed deceit? The way she tucks an errant strand of hair behind her ear, but twirls it girlishly first, just for a moment. The blouse she's wearing, with coffee stains on the cuff; her nails, always clipped painfully short; the lilt of her voice, "Laura, pass me the thingamee, will you?" And I know exactly what she means.

I have these vivid dreams less frequently now. A painful pleasure, but I would not be without them. They are a chance to see her again, to spend time in her company. On waking, when the deception is realized, I feel the sorrow of losing her all over again, but then my mind scrabbles to collect up the breadcrumbs of detail that will keep her real.

I scribble down in my diary everything I can remember: the coffeed cuff, the thingamee, the hair twirl. These are the details my waking mind forgets, but without them her memory might blur, eventually distilling her to a series of photos and anecdotes like Dad. I must hold off the distillation for as long as possible, so I'm grateful for the dreams.

After writing my notes, I can't get back to sleep. My shin feels sore from last night, and I notice the skin on one side of the dressing is bruised purple. Since it's nearly six, I eventually give up trying to rest, open my laptop, and stare at the screen. Belinda's letter sits accusingly on the bedside table. Why did I take it? I shouldn't be involving myself in Ted's life like this; I've got enough of my own problems to deal with. I stow the page of her letter back in my handbag, resolving to just give it to Ted as soon as I see him this morning.

Between the dream, Belinda's letter, and my evening with Jasper and then Ted, there's too much swirling around my head to be able to focus on work. I skim-read a few chapters of *Tiger Woman*, but it only makes me feel inadequate. I am so un-tiger.

When I hear footsteps outside my door, I sit bolt upright in bed. I assume it might be Ted, also unable to sleep. Opening the front door, I squint into the dim morning light, the amber glow of sunrise still languishing behind the hill beyond Sans Ennui.

"Ted?" I whisper.

"Only me," I hear Gerry's voice. "Sorry, did I wake you with my shuffling feet?"

"Oh. Hi, Gerry. You're up early."

"My last early morning beach walk," he says. "Care to join me?"

Pulling a cardigan around my shoulders, I slip on my flip-flops.

"Can't sleep either?" he asks, and I shake my head.

Gerry leads us down the small path between the fields toward the sea. We walk at a glacial pace, but I don't mind; I'm glad of the opportunity to talk with Gerry.

"Your last night in the house. Was that what kept you awake?"

"Sleep's always a challenge," he says. "My body keeps me awake, not my brain, muscles just can't turn off. Every few hours, if I haven't conked, I have to get up and stretch my legs. It can be less exhausting walking about, giving your limbs a purpose."

"That sounds hard, I'm sorry."

"Is what it is. I don't know where I'll walk at the new place," he mutters, with a note of sadness I haven't heard in his voice before. "I always head to the beach when lying down gets too much. Though Sandy says I shouldn't go out alone anymore, I've had too many falls recently." He lifts his bandaged arm to illustrate. Then he reaches out for my arm and frowns. "Will you promise to push me in the sea if I keep sounding so sorry for myself?"

"Absolutely not," I say, pressing my hand onto his, "or I'd have to go in too and it looks bitingly cold."

We get to the bottom of the footpath and turn left along the sand, heading toward the distant silhouette of La Corbière Lighthouse at the southern end of the bay. The beach is deserted, silent but for the whispering rush of waves and birds pattering about in the incoming tide.

We chat about the party. I apologize for leaving early, but tell him how much I enjoyed talking to all his friends, how honored I felt to be included. As we talk, Gerry stumbles, reaching again for my arm to steady himself.

"Are you all right?" I ask. He nods silently, then turns his face away. Beneath his self-deprecating humor, I glimpse a man ashamed of a body that is failing him.

"So, I was helping Ted clear out some of the things in your house last night," I say, once he's recovered his gait, "and I found something."

"If it was the body under the radiator in the hall, it weren't me, Governor," Gerry says, and I hug his arm affectionately.

"It was a page of a letter Belinda wrote to you, with her contact details." I look across at him for a reaction.

"Oh dear," says Gerry.

"Why wouldn't you have given that to Ted?"

"Hmmm," he says with a guilty sigh. "How did Ted react?"

"I didn't show it to him," I admit. "Not yet."

Gerry lets out a long breath, his arm juddering against mine.

"She sent it, must have been a few months after she left," he explains. "I called her, said it wasn't the way to do things, to just abandon ship like that. I tried to persuade her to speak to him and—" Gerry falters. It's clearly hard for him to talk about. "She was upset, said it wasn't working between them, that they wanted different things, but Ted would never be the one to give it up. She thought he just needed time to get used to her not being there—that she was a bad habit he needed to break, cold turkey. She persuaded me it was for the best, and I agreed I'd give it another month, gave her my word. I put that letter somewhere safe." He closes his eyes briefly. "And then I couldn't think for the life of me where. I was convinced I'd thrown it out with the Christmas cards. My memory must have filed it in an unmarked bin, and I felt too much of an old fool to tell Ted that I'd lost it."

"Oh dear." I sigh. "Were you and she very close?"

"Oh, she's one of life's gems, Belinda is." Gerry grins, a fond memory unlocked, and I feel an illogical stab of jealousy. "No one thinks of their poor parents when they separate, of what we lose." He pulls a silly face, as though it is a joke, but I can see there is truth to it. "In any case, I don't think Belinda is really what Ted is searching for anymore."

I want to ask what he means by that, but I'm drawn back to the question of the letter.

"Should I give it to Ted then? It's addressed to you; you know the situation better than me."

Gerry stops, lets go of my arm, plants his stick in the sand, and then slowly bends down to pick up an empty cider can from the sand. He hands it to me.

"We'll put that in the bin." He lifts his stick up in the air. "This is probably as far as I go these days."

We turn around together, and Gerry slows. It takes him a moment to get momentum in a new direction. I offer him my arm again.

"What went wrong between them? They must have been deeply in love if splitting up was so difficult for them both."

"I come out here most nights, Laura. When I had more steam, I'd go to the end of the beach and then back along the road." He points with his stick to the far end of L'Étacq, where the road curves around behind a long line of houses facing the shore. It sounds like he hasn't heard my question, but I listen patiently. "I always pick up any litter I come across when I'm out. What do you think the young people coming back from the bars think when they see an old man wobbling his way along the road at three in the morning, holding an armful of empty cider cans? What do you think they assume the story is?"

I let out a gentle hum of appreciation.

"People like to fill in the gaps, to paint their own picture, but no one really knows the truth of someone else's story."

"You're very wise, Gerry," I say, as we get back to the footpath that leads up the hill to Sans Ennui. "Have you ever thought about becoming a guru? You could write a book full of all your wisdom."

Gerry lets out a throaty cackle.

"I'd have to call it *Gin and Gibberish*." Gerry taps my arm with his hand then and asks, "What has you up so early then, besides worrying about Ted?"

"I don't know, everything." I sigh. "Work, thinking about my mum and dad, wondering what I'm doing with my life."

"What *are* you doing with your life?" he asks, and his tone is so serious, it catches me off guard.

"Well, that's the million-dollar question, isn't it?" Watching the waves foaming over the rocks, I feel a new clarity as to what's unsettling me. "When I was twenty, if you told me that by twenty-nine I'd be alone in the world, with all my friends moving on, clinging to my job because it's the only solid thing—" I let out a sigh. "I guess that's why I have to believe the universe has a plan for me, because if it doesn't, maybe I'm simply doing everything wrong."

Gerry squeezes my arm tight and taps the end of his stick in the sand.

"Well, Laura, if we consult the book of *Gin and Gibberish*, it would say, the question is only—'What are you doing with your life *today*?' I think I told you my philosophy is not to look too far back, or too far ahead."

"Well then, today I am going on a boat trip with a lovely young man, I am writing my article as best I can, and I am in a breathtakingly beautiful place, having a wonderful walk with you, Gerry."

"Well, that doesn't sound all that bad."

Helping Gerry up the path from the beach, I think he definitely shouldn't be coming down here on his own, he's so unsteady on his feet.

When we near the garden, I ask, "So, what should I do then, about Belinda's letter?"

"I'll leave it up to you. I'll probably have forgotten all about this conversation by tomorrow or fallen over again and knocked it clean out of my head." He makes a funny face by squinting his eyes and pulling his bottom lip up over his top one. I squeeze his arm tighter. For someone whose body is so out of his control, Gerry is astonishingly at ease with the world. It's as though he knows some secret contentment that the rest of us are not privy to; being in his company is enough to make you feel it might rub off on you.

It is strange to think I have known Gerry such a short time and that tomorrow I will go home and not have a chance to know him better. I wonder if this feeling of being stuck, of being left behind, has come from not traveling much these last two years—not stepping out of my own small sphere, not meeting new people, not seeing new places. Every trip I took in my early twenties sent me home with a broader mind and a new perspective on the person I wanted to be. Then again, there's something about this island and the people I have met here. It feels like more than a research trip or a holiday to me; it feels like something I might want to stay connected to when my real life resumes.

Chapter 19

When we get back to the house, Sandy is sitting in her garden with a hot drink and a newspaper.

"Morning! I'm surprised to see you up so bright and early, Laura," she calls over the wall, waving an arm for us to come and join her. I look to Gerry.

"Hold on, I just need a run up," Gerry says, backing up as though he's about to take a flying leap over the garden wall. It must show on my face that, for a moment, I think he's seriously going to attempt such a thing, because Gerry laughs, points at my face, and then rocks forward on his stick to get his balance again.

"Maybe not today," he says. "I'll leave you ladies to it. Sandy, why don't you show Laura round the barn? I think she'd be interested."

"The barn?" I ask.

"My life's work," he says cryptically, then he gives a small bow, turns, and starts slowly making his way up to the house.

"What's the barn?" I ask Sandy as I clamber over the low stone wall.

"Well, Gerry must rate you if he wants you to see the barn," Sandy says. "It's just across the road, we'll have a gander in a bit. How are you feeling?" Her ruddy, round face breaks into a knowing grin.

"I've felt fresher," I say, climbing the slope of her garden. "I blame you entirely for that lethal sangria you kept plying me with last night."

Sandy offers me a croissant from a basket on the table.

"I've put together a box of basics for your kitchen, just some milk, bread, and oatcakes—a few things to keep you going. In the meantime—breakfast."

"This is delightful, thank you, Sandy," I say, helping myself to one.

"So . . ." She raises her eyebrows at me. "Did anything happen last night?"

I frown, unsure how she knows about Jasper.

"Luckily I managed to sober up enough to finally meet Suitcase Man."

Sandy's face falls. "Oh, I thought maybe you and Ted— I saw him take you up to the house?"

"No, no." I shake my head firmly. "He was helping me because I was a little worse for wear—sangria on an empty stomach."

"Oh no!" Sandy puts a hand over her face. Then, peeping her eyes through her fingers, she says, "It's fine, he's a doctor,

I'm sure he's seen worse." She pauses, taking a sip of tea. "So you met this suitcase bloke then."

"I did," I say, and I can't stop myself from grinning.

"I see," Sandy says with a sigh. "Like that, is it? He wasn't a rotter then?"

"Definitely not a rotter. Gerry seemed to enjoy himself last night," I say, changing the subject. I'm not sure I want to tell Sandy more about Jasper; she doesn't feel like a receptive audience on the topic.

"Oh, it was great to see him in such good form. He's had a few low days, so I'm pleased yesterday was a good one for him."

"You're such a good neighbor to him. Ilídio's sister was telling me you're always cooking Gerry meals." I don't even know the names of the people in the flats above and below us in London. I only know their faces to nod to on the stairs; I resolve that when I get home I will go and introduce myself properly.

"Nah. He's the one who's been a great neighbor to me. I'm going to miss him, I like cooking for him." Sandy looks pensive for a moment, frowning down into her mug. "That's one of the challenges with Parkinson's, making sure you eat right, you need to get enough calories. You see how thin he is. That's another reason he needs to go to Acrebrooke, to eat three proper meals a day, no excuses." Sandy blinks back tears, her cheerful front momentarily fractured.

"I'm sure he'll still appreciate your cooking when he comes back to visit," I say gently, as she wipes her eyes with a sleeve.

"Who knows who we'll have moving in. Someone with screaming kids, knowing my luck. Don't get me wrong, I love children, but I get enough of that at work."

Sandy explains she's a swimming teacher. As we finish our

breakfast, she makes me laugh describing some of the little characters she's taught to swim over the years.

"Morning, Laura," says Ilídio, striding out of their house carrying a toolbox. He pauses when he sees Sandy, puts his tools down, squeezes her shoulders, kisses her neck, cracks his knuckles, and then picks up the toolbox again. I love their easy physical affection.

"Hey, hun, would you show Laura the workshop? Gerry suggested it," Sandy says.

"You want to see?" Ilídio asks, tilting his head toward me.

"Sure." I shrug, no clearer on what I'm agreeing to look at.

Ilídio and I follow the path up and across the road, coming to a large one-story barn on the opposite side. He opens the worn wooden door and shows me inside. As I peer into the gloom, my eyes growing accustomed to the dark, I see a room overflowing with woodwork equipment, machinery, and workbenches. There are tree trunks sliced into long planks hanging on every wall, lending the space the feel of a deconstructed forest.

"Wow," I say. Gerry was right. I wouldn't want to have missed seeing this.

"This used to be Gerry's workshop," Ilídio says. "He built the barn himself, took me on as an apprentice eleven years ago. Now I have an apprentice of my own."

"And this is all wood you're going to use to make furniture?" I ask, pointing at the huge slices of tree trunk along every wall.

"Eventually. They can take decades to dry out. Gerry makes things the old-fashioned way, timeless pieces, built to last for generations. Not many people do it like this now—it's too expensive, too time-consuming," Ilídio explains. "Easier to make it cheap, even if it doesn't last."

I walk around the room, admiring the craftsmanship of a bench that sits at the far end. Narrow cylinders of wood bend and curve in the most intriguing way, as though the bench might have grown itself.

"Did the wood come like this?" I ask, stroking the curved panels.

"No." Ilídio shakes his head. "You have to steam-bend it. It's a skilled job to bend wood this thick—Gerry designed his own steamer to do it."

I notice at the far end of the workshop a bench with a soldering iron, just like the one Mum used to use for jewelry making.

"Does Gerry still come in here?" I ask.

"He does. He still has lots of opinions, ideas for how to solve problems. He knows just from smelling the wood how long it's been there." He shakes his head. "It's such a waste. All that knowledge in his head, that can't get out through his hands."

Wandering around the workshop, I find myself reaching out to touch things, feeling the potential of what they might become. Then I'm struck by an idea.

"Ilídio, can I commission you to make something, a present for Ted?"

"Of course, what is it you want?"

"Do you have any paper? I'll need to draw it."

Ilídio finds some graph paper, and I sketch out my idea.

"Can you make it?" I ask when I've finished drawing.

Ilídio taps a pencil on the paper.

"Easy." Then he looks up at me. "He'll like this, Laura. I'll start it now, so you can have it before you leave."

We agree on a price. I know Ilídio is undercharging me, but he is firm on what he's willing to accept. I walk around the workshop as he starts picking out pieces of wood for the project. I want to stay and watch him work, but checking my watch, I realize I need to go and get ready for my date with Jasper.

As I walk back across the garden, I glance up to the kitchen window of Sans Ennui, half hoping I might see Ted, but there's no sign of him. In any case, I need to get dressed, get organized. My chat with Gerry and the tour of the workshop has inspired me. I should stop overthinking things I can't change, focus instead on the potential of the day ahead.

Back at the cottage, I have a shower, then look fondly down at my suitcase on the floor. I have so many options, clothes that actually fit me. I pick out my slim-fit dark capri pants and the fitted blue blouse with the white scalloped cuff and collar. Then I tie a thin blue silk headscarf around my head as a headband. Glancing in the bathroom mirror, I smile, seeing myself again, rather than a ragamuffin.

Picking up my phone, I make the mistake of checking my email and my buoyant mood bursts like a balloon. There are more than fifty new messages in my in-box, on a Saturday morning. At least half of them look to be from Suki and have subjects like: **Feature ideas . . . Teen property developers—how young is too young to start your portfolio?** I skim through, looking for any emails addressed specifically to me.

I find several, sent throughout the night and the early hours of the morning.

Laura,

Disappointed in your social media performance today. Unpolished content and off brand messaging.

S

Laura,

Can you find a *How Did You Meet?* couple who met at a train station? Network Trains want an advertorial. In fact, any train-themed love stories—we could create "Love on the Line" feature?

S

Laura,

We all like your "Then and Now" photos as an angle for the coin story. Keep them coming on social today. Do you have photos of your great-grandparents? Would be good to include images of the original wartime love story.

This is exactly the kind of in-depth, well-researched feature that puts LL above the purely tabloid content. Good work, Laura—confident you can pull something together that has it all; romance, history, and a personal angle.

S

Suki is the queen of this carrot/stick management technique, where she beats you around the head with a large carrot and then compliments you on how good the carrot-shaped bruise looks. I wonder if it is normal to have your anxiety levels so dictated by the mood of your employer. My mind jumps to an image of Ilídio, so calm and at ease on his own in the workshop. What must it be like to be your own master, to not be plagued by a sense of dread every time your phone vibrates?

I have a text from Monica, asking if I'll come over for coffee "with us" tomorrow at ten. I wonder who she means by "us." Has she convinced Bad Granny to meet with me, or does the "us" allude to another one of her kitchen appliances? Either way, I reply saying I'd love to come. Monica is one of the few family members I have left, I would like to get to know her better. Besides, even if she doesn't remember my parents' story correctly, she did say she had photos I could see.

After replying to Monica, I flick through the photos I took on my phone yesterday, pausing on the one of Ted. His eyes shine out from the screen, as sparkling as the jewels in his beard. He really is surprisingly photogenic, considering how little of his face is visible beneath all that hair. I shake my head, flicking the screen closed. Ted's sparkly eyes are not relevant to any of this; I need to focus on what's important.

Looking at all those emails, at how much work I need to do, it feels irresponsible that I've agreed to spend the day with Jasper, on a boat of all places—I'm about as sea smart as a camel. I shall just have to make this trip count—take lots of photos of the Écréhous and pick Jasper's brain for my article on the way. After all, if the universe goes to the trouble of presenting you with your soulmate, you don't tell the universe that you're busy and you have to work. That said, I do quickly reply to a few of Suki's more pressing emails—the hierarchy of authority in my life goes: Suki, the universe, then all other worldly concerns.

When I'm finally ready to go, and I open the cottage door, I hear a voice call down from Sans Ennui. "Laura, morning!"

I turn around to see someone bounding down the slope toward me. It takes me a second to realize who it is: It's Ted, but he looks totally different—he's shaved off his beard.

"Hey, how are you feeling? How's the cut on your leg?" he says, his face dancing with energy.

I stare at him, my mouth agape. *Wow.* It turns out, beneath the *Castaway* beard, Ted is incredibly attractive. I don't mean good-looking, in a "clean-shaven suits him" kind of way; I mean he's the real-life love child of Brad Pitt and James Dean. He has a chiseled jaw, a dimpled smile, and those dark expressive eyes stand out all the more from a cleaner canvas. He's also far younger than I assumed him to be. When I first got in the cab, I thought he must be nearly twice my age, but now, I see he's definitely only late thirties. He's the real-life Benjamin Button, getting younger and younger every time I see him. Perhaps tomorrow he'll be a teenager, heading off to the sea for a surf before school.

"Ted, you— Your—"

My mouth can't find the words, so I finally resort to pointing at his face.

"I thought it was time to de-fuzz," he says, stroking his jaw and then running a hand through his hair, which I swear looks styled somehow. It had been a shapeless mess on Thursday night and now it looks textured, as though he's run some wax through it. Whatever it is, it's hair you want to grab and—*Whoa, what? Where did that thought come from?*

"You look different," I say, biting my lip in case any of the thoughts in my head accidentally fall out of my mouth.

"Different good?" he asks, holding eye contact with me until I have to look away because it feels as though someone is flipping pancakes in my belly. I have a flashback to last night, to the feeling I had as he walked me to my door. His lips look so much more accessible now. Why am I thinking about Ted's lips? Gift from the universe Jasper is going to be here any minute.

"How—how old are you, Ted?" I ask with a frown.

Ted laughs at the question. "Thirty-seven, why?"

"It's just, well, you had a gray beard—it's confusing for people."

"Well, I apologize that the follicles on my face grow a different color to the ones on my head." Ted looks bemused.

With a silent nod, I shift my gaze out to the safety of the sea. My heart seems to be pounding unnecessarily loudly in my chest.

"Thank you for your help last night, Laura. With your system in place, the whole task feels a lot more manageable this morning."

Words come to my throat, but I swallow them before they can emerge as sentences. Beardy McCastaway might have been easier to talk to than Hotty McFace here. *Really? That's the best nickname I can come up with?*

"No problem."

"Listen, I know we hardly got to any of the places you wanted to visit yesterday. How about we head out now, and I can take you to the southern beaches. There's a great spot for brunch, this little café right on the sand where—"

The gravel on the drive crunches, and we both turn around to see Jasper's red sports car drive in.

"I can't today," I say, feeling my face tighten into a wince. "Jasper is taking me to the Écréhous."

Ted pulls a hand through his hair and nods, his brow briefly knitting before ironing out into a smile. His face is so much more expressive now that there is more of it to see—a pulsing muscle in his jaw and these dimpled smile lines around his mouth.

"I see, good." *Good?* "If you have a tour guide sorted, you don't need me."

"It's kind of you to offer, Ted," I say. "It's just Jasper invited me on this boat trip, and—" I glance up at the drive, where Jasper has climbed out of the car and is waving at me. He's dressed in chino shorts with a cricket jumper around his neck; he looks like the Great Gatsby on holiday.

"I'm glad it's all working out as you hoped." Ted nods, turning to walk back up to the house.

The letter, I need to give him the letter! I was going to give it to him as soon as I saw him, but then I got distracted by his new face and— Well, I can't just hand it over now, with Jasper standing there waving; I'd need a moment to explain why I have it.

"Ted—" I begin, not sure what I'm going to say.

He swings around, hands in his pockets, nods his head toward Jasper, and gives me a wink.

"Enjoy yourself, kiddo."

ꩰ

RETURNED TO SENDER

4 November 1991

Annie,
Don't be childish and send my letters back. If you won't take my calls, how am I supposed to get through to you? You can't just say you're pregnant, and then not speak to me about it. Did you think this would change how things stood between us? You can't blame me for not believing you right away.

I will send money whatever you decide, but I want you to consider all the options. We're too young to be parents, Annie! I love my life as it is, you can't ask me to give that up for something we didn't plan. What about your dancing? What about auditioning for shows again, your dance school idea? You can't do any of that if you've got a baby, Annie.

Al

PS I still haven't received the coin. Can you confirm you sent it?

Chapter 20

"There you are," Jasper says with a grin.

He is just as attractive in the light of day, like a lovely box-fresh Ken doll. No! Ken dolls aren't sexy, Ken dolls don't even have genitalia. *Do not* start thinking of Jasper as a Ken doll.

"Who's that then?" Jasper asks, nodding toward Ted.

"My, er—my landlord, Ted. I'm renting his cottage down there. So, tell me more about the place we're going to today," I say, clapping my hands together, keen for us to leave as quickly as possible.

Jasper opens the car door for me. "You are going to love the Écréhous. They are tiny islands between here and France, well, rocks, essentially, that don't get covered by the rising tide. The fishermen's huts there have been handed down through the generations, and made a little less basic over the years. It's like camping at sea, that's the best way I can describe it."

As we drive across the island, Jasper tells me all about his family, about his father's love of fishing. He says being at sea was one of the few times he got to be with his father alone, as none of his sisters were interested in learning how to fish. As he's talking, I sink back into the pages of Jasper's story. I have to remind myself that this is a story I want to be part of, the fairy-tale ending written for me. Ted's new face is not relevant to the plot.

Gran tries to call me while we're driving, but I silence the call and text instead.

Laura: Sorry, Gran, just heading out on a boat trip! Can we speak this afternoon? BTW did you know my surname is pronounced Le Cane, not Ques-ne???

Gran: You are having a busy time of it—keen to have a chat when you have time. Le Cane does ring a bell now you mention it.

Me: ??!??!

Gran: I think all the mums at your school kept pronouncing Ques-ne, and in the end, Annie couldn't be doing with correcting people all the time. You know, I'd quite forgotten it was Le Cane until you said that—how funny!

How funny? How funny? I don't think it's particularly funny that I've been pronouncing my own name wrong my entire life.

"Everything OK?" Jasper asks, as he sees me frown at my phone.

"Fine, just work stuff," I lie, putting my phone away. I don't need another person laughing at my identity crisis.

* * *

Jasper's boat is moored at St. Catherine's Breakwater, a long, man-made promontory stretching half a mile out to sea at the eastern end of the island. Jasper tells me they started building a harbor in the mid-nineteenth century, but the project was abandoned as the bay turned out to be too shallow. The long breakwater wall is now used by fishermen and boats mooring in the sheltered water.

Jasper rows a dinghy out to fetch his motorboat from a mooring, then drives back to pick me up. Once we're out on the open water, I look at Jasper steering the boat, the wind in his hair and the sun on his skin. He looks so at home at the helm. I try to adopt the stance of someone who is comfortable on a vessel this small and unstable.

"Is this cabin we're going to the one you had keys for in your suitcase?"

"Yes," Jasper says, looking over the top of his sunglasses at me.

"I only looked through your things to search for a name or contact number," I quickly add.

"It's fine." He smiles. "I must have taken the keys to London by mistake. Now, be warned, it's incredibly rustic."

"You know, I've always had a bit of a fantasy about remote cabins," I say, moving into the seat next to him, hoping the boat might get steadier the closer you are to the steering wheel.

"Tell me everything," Jasper says huskily, his eyebrows dancing up and down above his sunglasses.

I laugh.

"Not like that." It is like that, but I don't think it would be appropriate to tell him all the graphic details of my Ryan

Gosling/log fire/sheepskin rug fantasy on a first date. "No, I just mean somewhere to get away from it all, off grid—it sounds romantic."

"Well, I hope our little cabin lives up to expectations," he says, taking a hand off the wheel and laying it on my thigh. He seems more confident today, more at home in this boat than he was in his living room. I like this version even more.

It's a twenty-minute boat ride out to the small group of rocky islands. As we get close, I see several houses protruding from the water. It's a bizarre sight, like finding a village in the middle of the sea, each rudimentary cabin, built on inhospitable-looking rocks, jutting out of the water. Jasper says, "Laura, look there," he points to the left of the boat, where two seals are basking on rocks in the sunshine.

"Oh, look at them," I cry. "Look at their funny little faces."

Jasper ties the boat to a buoy, then we get back into the dinghy and row to shore with a cool box and a bag of supplies. On the pebble beach, we leave the dinghy and the bags, and Jasper leads me up into a rabbit warren of huts, all built on top of each other in a little enclave at the far end of the spit. A few other boats are moored nearby, and Jasper waves to a family sitting out on their deck. This place feels like a different planet, a watery moonscape, miles from civilization, and I catch myself wondering how the hell I came to be here. Only a few days ago I was sitting in the airless meeting room at Love Life eating a Pret sandwich.

"Look," Jasper says, stopping to point out a particular cabin. It's the one my mother was standing in front of in one of her photos. He remembered. He helps me replicate the shot, giving instructions for how I should stand, wanting to get it just right. When he's satisfied, I snap a few photos of him pretending to be a model, staring off into the middle distance and giving me his best "blue steel" pose.

Back at the dinghy, Jasper effortlessly lifts the cool box up onto his shoulder, and we walk farther up the pebble-covered spit, where larger cabins stand alone.

"This is us," he says, pointing toward the one at the far end.

The cabin is built on stilts, so we have to climb up stairs to get to the front door. There's a basic wooden balcony overlooking the sea, and a driftwood sign propped against the door that reads: ÉCRÉHOUS RULES: TAKE ONLY PHOTOS, LEAVE ONLY FOOTPRINTS. Jasper shows me around inside; there's one main room with a gas-powered stove and fridge, a small kitchen table, and two green checked sofas around a driftwood coffee table. Upstairs in the eaves are two small bedrooms. There's no log fire, but there is a wood burner. It's rustic and charming, and I fall instantly in love with the place.

"No running water or flushing loos, just a compost toilet around the back," Jasper says.

OK, maybe I'm not *entirely* in love with it. The words "compost" and "toilet" are not optimal first-date words.

"My grandfather built this place from scratch," Jasper explains. "Everything you see had to be brought out on a boat."

"I can see why you love it," I say.

"Worth the effort of getting here then?" he says with a wink.

"Definitely."

Jasper opens the cool box, unpacking all sorts of posh pâtés, sourdough biscuits in a rainbow of rustic hues, and a bottle of rosé. I'm impressed Jasper knows how to put together a decent picnic. I once went on a picnic date in Hyde Park and the guy brought a multipack of Monster Munch crisps and six cans of lager.

Jasper opens a bag of truffle crisps and offers some to me. As I reach my hand in, he pretends to snap the bag shut, like a crocodile. I jump in surprise and then laugh. We look at each other and grin. I feel a glow of contentment. I'm genuinely enjoying myself, and I haven't thought about Ted's newly shaven face for at least five minutes.

I don't even know why I'm thinking about Ted's face at all. I mean, sure, he's superhot now, and he's really lovely, and he isn't fifty as I'd first assumed, but that shouldn't make a difference. He's still too old for me, still technically married, his life sounds immensely complicated, and he doesn't even like Phil Collins. Plus, he made it pretty clear last night that he still loves his wife and he's not in the market for anything like that. Then I have to stop thinking about not thinking about Ted, because it's reminding me of the letter from Belinda sitting guiltily in my handbag. Why am I even having to rationalize this to myself? It's ridiculous; I'm on a date with Jasper, perfect Jasper who ticks all the boxes.

Jasper pulls two sun loungers out onto the cabin deck. Then on a table between us lays out all the food he's brought.

"So, do you bring all your dates out here?" I ask.

"Hardly," Jasper says, wrinkling his nose. "I rarely meet anyone I want to meet for a drink, let alone bring to my favorite place in the whole world."

"Well, aren't I the lucky one," I say, feeling as though I'm reciting lines from some flirtatious play.

"A lot of people our age move away from the island,"

Jasper says. "Of the girls who are left, I went to school with most of them, and the rest I'm related to. Small pond."

"And you're a big fish, are you?" I say, pushing my tongue into my cheek.

Jasper reaches out to take my hand in his.

"Well, I'm not a *small* fish," he says, raising his eyebrows up and down suggestively, and I can't help but laugh. "Right, Laura, are you going to confess what this real cabin fantasy of yours is, or am I going to have to wrestle it out of you?"

ↄℓℓℓↄ

4 November 1991

Alex,

It is over then, is it? Done with. Finished. Everything you said to me this summer, forgotten? I loved you with every particle of my soul, Al, as you did me, and now you try to dismiss it as a short-term fling? Where is the man I loved? He would not be so cavalier with another's heart. Enjoy the Greek islands; I hope your boat sinks.

I am keeping the baby.

Annie

PS I enclose your half of the coin. The other half is mine, I found it and I paid for it. You wouldn't have known this piece still existed if it wasn't for me. It is now as much a part of my family history as it is yours, so I am keeping it for our child. Nice to know you care more about holding on to a piece of metal than a living, breathing human.

Chapter 21

I end up telling Jasper about the Scrabble game and the wood chopping. He's flirting with me, the sun is shining, and the rosé tastes delicious. Somehow sharing my childish fantasy feels part of the script for this ideal date we're on. Jasper claps his hands together, as though accepting the challenge to make my fantasy a reality. There is only pre-chopped wood for the cabin's log burner and no ax, so he ends up trying to hack at pieces of kindling with a bread knife, all whilst shirtless and trying to flex his abs in my direction. His performance makes me cry with laughter, though it is the least erotic thing I've ever seen.

"Right, Scrabble. Unusual, but I like a girl with highbrow sexual interests. I think we have a set somewhere," he says.

With his shirt still unbuttoned, Jasper searches the depths of a dusty games chest, and manages to find an old travel

Scrabble at the bottom. He sets up the board on the driftwood coffee table.

I don't know where I got the idea that playing board games was sexy in any way. In my fantasy, I'd lay down some brilliant word like "quixotic" or "oxyphenbutazone," and the man I'm with would instantly fall in love with my brain as well as my body. In reality, I keep picking out Ps and can't put down anything more impressive than "pop," "pip," or "pap" (which Jasper says is slang, so I can't even have). After the fourth time Jasper asks, "Is this turning you on yet?" I upend the board in faux petulance. He catches my gaze with his, his eyes growing wide, the corner of his mouth twitching into a smirk, and then he leans in toward me.

"Is this OK?" he says in a low whisper, our faces inches apart.

I nod.

Jasper presses his lips to mine, one hand reaching up to cup my face. His lips are warm and soft; it's a good kiss, the right balance of assertive but respectful. Would I have movie sex with Jasper, I wonder? There's something slightly schoolboyish about him: his public-school brand of humor, the brown deck shoes—I'm not sure how wild a man who wears deck shoes would ever be in bed. All of these thoughts run through my mind during our kiss. I cannot believe how well this is all going. He's making me laugh, he's got a great body (that wasn't on my list, but it doesn't hurt), he's got impeccable taste in clothes, wine, and pâtés. That salmon and dill one was delicious; I'm definitely going to look that up when I get home.

"Well, you were right about the Scrabble," Jasper says, finally pulling away. I make a humming laugh noise and berate myself for thinking about salmon and dill pâté for most of the time I was kissing him.

Jasper stands up, then helps me up from the rug and leads me over to a small wooden bookshelf built into a corner of the cabin.

"What I love most about coming out here is no TV, no Wi-Fi. My parents used to ban us from bringing phones. We'd just read and eat and swim. I credit this place with why I've read most of the classics." He pauses. "Tell me again about why you love *To Kill a Mockingbird* so much."

The bookshelf is filled with beautiful worn editions of Penguin Classics. Most of the men I've dated in the last few years didn't read much, or if they did, it was crime novels or nonfiction. I bet Ted reads crime novels. I pause at Jasper's question, unsure how truthful to be, not wanting to upset the fun, flirty tone of the date by talking about anything too serious. But then, I do want to see if there is a deeper side to Jasper; that's a box that needs ticking too.

"My dad died when I was three, and my mum kept a few of his favorite books for me, the ones he reread again and again," I say, running my finger along the spines on the shelf. "Reading the books he loved, the stories he valued enough to hold on to—*Robinson Crusoe*, *The Count of Monte Cristo*, *The Catcher in the Rye*—felt like learning something new about him."

Jasper nods, encouraging me to keep talking.

"Even though I don't remember my dad, Scout and Atticus feel like mutual friends. I know that sounds silly."

"It doesn't at all," says Jasper, pulling a book from the shelf and showing me the cover: P. G. Wodehouse. "I lost my father too, several years ago. He was a lot older than my mother." My mind jumps to Maude. *She is a widow, she's not cheating on anyone; at least that's something off my conscience.* "I remember him reading us Jeeves and Wooster books on car journeys through France. It's my favorite memory of him: his voice, reading those stories. I certainly consider Jeeves and Wooster to be friends of the family."

He looks across at me and our eyes meet, and for the first time I see a glimpse of the more serious, contemplative side of Jasper, beyond the boyish humor.

"I don't want to wait as long as he did to have children. I'd like to be a young dad—to have the energy to kick a ball around with my kids."

He reaches out and starts circling a finger down my back. It tickles slightly, and I arch my spine in response. Then my phone starts ringing, and I immediately look around for my bag.

It's Gran.

"Jasper, do you mind if I get this? I'm sorry, my gran's been trying to get hold of me all weekend, and I just want to check she's OK."

"Of course." He smiles.

I answer the phone and ask Gran to give me a second, pressing the phone to my chest.

"I'll give you some privacy," says Jasper, grabbing a towel from a basket by the door. "I'm going to go for a swim, join me on the beach when you're ready."

He kisses me on the cheek, then I watch as he bounds away down the cabin steps.

"Sorry about that, Gran, I'm here now," I say, putting the phone back to my ear.

"Don't let me interrupt if are you busy, Laurie," Gran says.

"It's nothing that can't wait."

Sitting down on the green checked sofa, I tell Gran where I am, then I explain about my strange meeting with great-aunt Monica yesterday, how confused she was about Mum and Dad's story.

Gran makes quiet hmmmming and ahhhhing sounds as I recount the conversation, then eventually she says with a sigh, "Laura, I'm afraid she's not entirely mad—well, not on this topic anyway. I don't know where the notion about Annie having all these phobias came from, but she's right about the rest." I hear her take a long, deep breath.

"What?" I'd been expecting Gran to laugh, to agree that Monica's bizarre version of events was all nonsense.

"Annie didn't want me to tell you," Gran says, making a tutting sound. "But I suppose it will all come out now you're there, talking to them all. It never sat right with me, you not knowing the truth."

"What truth?" I say, standing up to pace the short length of the cabin.

"Your parents were never married, Laura. They had that summer together, and then you were on the way but"—she pauses—"the relationship didn't last."

I rub my fingers across my eyelids, unable to compute what I'm hearing.

"Everything about that summer is as your mother told you," Gran continues, "but then she came back to Bristol and, well, you being on the way was a bit of a surprise. Alex wasn't quite ready to settle down. He visited when he could, but they didn't make a proper go of it, not together as a family."

"Why would she lie and tell me they got married?"

My voice sounds strange and high-pitched. There's a falling sensation in my stomach, as though the floor has dropped away beneath me.

"Annie didn't want you thinking you'd been . . . an accident." Gran says it cautiously, as though even now, the word might upset me. "She was always an idealist, she wanted you to think the best of him. When we lost him in the accident, well, she didn't see any harm in massaging history a little."

My head feels foggy, so I step out onto the deck for some air. My eyes find Jasper doing a confident front crawl across the water between this rocky island and the next.

"So, he was never around? He ditched us, just like Aunt Monica said?"

"He was around, Laura. He visited you when he could—he loved you the second he set eyes on you."

"Why didn't it last? If they were so in love that summer, why couldn't they make it work?" I bite the inside of my cheek, not wanting Gran to hear me getting upset.

"I don't know, Laurie," she says softly. "Sometimes things aren't meant to last the long term—flashes of lightning rather than slow-burning coals."

My mind races. Mum's story of the proposal in the cave. That wasn't a fudging of the truth or a "massaging of history"—it was a complete fabrication. How many times did I ask Mum to tell me their love story? Did she invent new details with every telling?

"Laura, you must understand, your mother's heart was in the right place," Gran says, her voice pleading.

I let the line go silent, unsure what to say, angry at having been lied to for so long. Looking down at my watch—his watch—I wonder if it is Dad who I should be mad at. What must that have been like for Mum, at twenty-five, deciding to raise me, all on her own?

"Did you even know him?" I ask quietly.

"Yes, I did. Look—even though he wasn't up for being a father straightaway, he came around. The proposal and the wedding and all the stuff he left you might not have been real, but he wanted to be a father to you, Laura. Once you were born, he asked for photos constantly—he loved you, there's no doubt about that. If he hadn't been in that accident, he would have been a part of your life."

It takes me a moment to register what she's just said.

"Wait, what do you mean, the stuff he left me?"

I hear Gran let out a sound, like a tire being deflated.

"What?" My voice sounds angry now. "The watch, the record collection, the books, none of that was his?"

"Oh, Laurie, I'm sorry. I— I shouldn't have said that. I'm not entirely sure." Gran sounds rattled.

"I just want to know what's real, Gran. Will you just tell me what's real?" My vision is getting watery.

There's a long sigh on the line, then Gran says, "When he died, Annie wanted you to have a way to connect with him. You know how much stock she put on objects as conduits for memory. She didn't have anything of his, so she collected a few bits that, well, that could have been his."

"Did he even read *To Kill a Mockingbird?* Did he even like to read?"

"Yes, well, probably—maybe not that specific book, but he did like to read." Gran doesn't sound at all convinced. "Look, you have to understand, when her own father left us, she didn't have anything from him—not one birthday present, not a single memento, nothing to know him by."

"Mum bought the LP collection," I say, and Gran doesn't correct me. "What about the watch, the one I wear every day?"

Gran sighs in resignation. She knows there's no point sugaring what's left of the pill.

"She bought it in a charity shop."

A hand goes to my mouth, but a sob escapes.

"Oh, Laurie, I shouldn't be telling you any of this over the phone. If I'd known you were going there, to rake all this up—" Her voice sounds desperate now. "The coin, you still have the coin, that was certainly real."

"The coin doesn't mean anything if they didn't stay together. Look, Gran, I have to go. I appreciate you telling me all this," I say, tears rolling down my cheeks now. I try to hide the cracks in my voice; I don't want her to worry. "I'm fine, honestly, I-I just need time to get my head around it."

When I've said good-bye, I cover my face with my hot palms. Then, looking around the cabin, I realize I don't want to be here now. My mind jumps to last night, sitting on the floor with Ted, sorting through memories. Of all the places I could be, something inside me yearns to be there, in that cocoon. In that room, with Ted, I didn't feel I had to hide any cracks, perhaps because he was so open with me, sharing the fractures of his own life. I wonder if he is there now, still going through it all without me.

Walking down to the beach, I wave to Jasper. He swims to shore, walking carefully up the pebbles with bare feet. His smile fades when he sees my face, streaked with tears.

"What's wrong? What happened?" he asks. "Is your gran OK?"

"Yes, she's fine, just— Can we go back? Do you mind?"

Suddenly, I can't be on a date, can't handle trying to be fun and flirty and interesting. I can't filter how I'm feeling, and yet I don't feel ready to share any of this with Jasper.

"Of course. We'll go back right away."

Jasper doesn't ask any more questions until we're packed up and back on the boat, steering a course for Jersey.

"Do you want to talk about it?" he asks, once we're out on the open water.

There's something comforting in the sound of the engine and the undulating motion of the boat churning across the sea's swell. I muster a smile.

"My gran just told me something about my family, it's thrown me, I'm so sorry."

Jasper's face is full of concern. He must sense I don't want to elaborate, because he simply puts a hand on my shoulder and says, "Don't be sorry, I understand."

On the journey home, Jasper tries to cheer me up by singing sea shanties—he's an excellent singer and commits wholeheartedly to the delivery, so it does, briefly, distract me. When we reach the still water of St. Catherine's, he turns off the engine. It's so peaceful without the sound of the motor, and my hair whips around my face, buffeted by the wind.

"You know what always cheers my sisters up when they've had upsetting news?" Jasper says, tilting his head to a sympathetic angle and giving me that irresistible dimpled grin. "Shopping. Do you want me to take you to St. Helier—we could engage in some retail therapy?" My face must register disapproval, because his tone shifts, losing confidence. "I know that's— Sorry, that might be a stupid suggestion."

I set my teeth into a smile; none of this is Jasper's fault.

"No, it wasn't at all, but I think I just want to go back to L'Étacq, if that's OK? I just need a little time on my own to think, maybe a lie-down, I didn't sleep well. I'm sorry to ruin today," I say, feeling genuinely bad about all the effort he has gone to.

"Laura, you couldn't ruin anything if you tried."

Wiping my nose on a sleeve, I look up at him gratefully.

"Well, that's definitely not true, but thank you. I really did enjoy today."

Jasper shifts on the seat. "And listen, we're doing a tea for my mother's birthday this afternoon. If you're feeling up to it later, I could come and get you. Whatever the question, I usually find cake and champagne is a pretty good answer."

I squeeze his hand; a maybe. I can't fault Jasper; this was a wonderful date. But I want to be fun, carefree, happy Laura around him, not let him see the morose misery guts lurking beneath the surface. I have to force myself to stop dwelling on the conversation with Gran just to keep myself from crumbling in front of him. Our histories, the stories we've been told, are like static snow globes—we know the patterns of settled snow made by the past. A revelation like this may not seem earth-shattering to anyone else, but for me, it's like someone shaking the globe, burying me in a snowstorm. And I know, when everything settles, nothing will look the same as it did before, and I will never be able to get back the familiar patterns in the snow.

ceeee

RETURNED TO SENDER

12 November 1991

Annie,
Send me the whole coin, or so help me I will come over there and prize it out of your hands. You are angry with me, fine—don't try to use this as currency. You can't give the coin back to my grandmother and then take it away again. She is distraught, Annie. She is an eighty-year-old woman. Don't be cruel.

Al

PS If you keep hanging up my calls, I won't call again. If you send this letter back like the others, I won't write anymore. That will be it, Annie, you'll be on your own with this baby. I mean it.

Chapter 22

Back at L'Étacq, once I've waved Jasper off, I walk straight down the hill, past the fisherman's cottage, toward the sea. The September sun is warm, the clouds are high in the sky, and there is no wind on this side of the island. I just need to sit with my toes in the sand and let my thoughts settle. It's as though someone has stomped through a pond and dredged up all the mud at the bottom, turning the water dark and cloudy.

On my phone, there's a text from Dee asking if I want to talk and three from Suki with various work-related questions. Vanya has also messaged asking, Have you found him yet? Was the universe right? I turn off my phone. As I walk toward the shore, I see the unmistakable outline of Ted, standing at the water's edge. My heartbeat quickens along with my step, as I realize I'd been hoping to see him. The letter; that's why I've been thinking about him—guilt. Before I get to the bottom of the footpath, before he notices me coming, I see Ted draw back his hand and fling something into the sea.

Coming up to stand beside him, I say, "Hey."

He turns to see me, and his eyes shift, as though I've caught him doing something he shouldn't.

"What did you throw in the sea?" I ask. Ted rubs one palm with the other, and I know then what it is. "Your ring."

He sits on the sand, and I drop down next to him.

"Is that not a bit drastic?" I ask softly. His eyes stay firmly on the water. "You could have sold it—it's a waste to throw it in the sea."

He shakes his head. This feels like a symbolic moment for him, some kind of closure, definitely not the time to be presenting him with Belinda's number.

"I wouldn't want anyone else wearing it."

"Did you drop off Gerry at the new place?"

"Yes. He kept making jokes"—Ted drops his head, a smile at the corner of his lips—"about how I was dropping him off at boarding school, and he was entitled to a tuck box." I reach across and squeeze his arm. Ted sighs. "I just don't know what he's going to do there all day. He likes a cold house, and the heating there is full on all year round. The staff are kind, but some residents there are so much worse than him. I'm not sure he'll like being reminded where he's headed."

"He'll be OK," I say. "He's an incredible man, your dad. I'm sorry I didn't say a proper good-bye."

"How was your boat trip?" he asks, eyes still on the breaking waves in front of us.

"I'm glad to have my feet back on solid ground."

He looks across at me and smiles, reaching a hand up to my hair.

"You look all wild and windswept."

I let him smooth it down around my face, then find myself leaning my head into his hand.

"You're back sooner than I thought you would be," he says, in a tone I can't decipher.

His eyes make contact with mine, and he drops his hand almost guiltily from my hair.

"I got a phone call from my gran, it kind of ruined things," I say, my eyes darting to my toes in the sand.

He makes a low hum, an invitation to explain.

"It turns out my parents' love story wasn't quite what I thought it was." I pick up a handful of sand, letting it drain through my fingers. "The way Mum told it, it was this grand romance, an epic proposal, and the perfect relationship until she lost Dad in the accident. Turns out it was only ever a fling. My dad didn't even stick around when he found out I was on the way."

"I'm sorry, Laura. That must have been hard to hear," says Ted, leaning over and nudging his shoulder against mine.

"And, to make it worse, none of the objects I have from my dad were even his. His books, this watch—my mum bought them, so I'd have something to 'remember' him by." I puff out an angry laugh, and take the watch off my wrist, examining it in my hands. "I've worn this watch every day of my adult life. Every time I look at it, I think of him. It's been broken twice, and I paid a fortune to get it mended because it felt like"—I pinch my lips together—"the ticking felt like his heartbeat carrying on somehow." My vision is swimming. It's not even a particularly nice watch now I look at it objectively, the muddy brown color and the hands too thick for the size of the face.

Ted puts an arm around my shoulders, and I want to sink into him. But instead, I fling the watch into the waves as hard as I can.

"It's all just meaningless junk."

Seeing it go, disappearing beneath the waves, I unclip the pendant around my neck and pull my arm back to fling it into the sea too, but Ted stops me, grabbing my arm and gathering me into a tight hug against his warm chest.

"Don't," he says softly. Being folded in his arms feels so good, and I let myself go limp against his body. He talks gently into my hair, and the tone of his voice is like dark amber honey; I want it to ooze into every pore.

"Don't, Laura."

"What, you're allowed to throw things into the sea, but I'm not?" I ask with a half laugh, half sob.

"No, you need to think of your own symbolic gesture, you can't have mine." His words make me laugh, pressing snotty tears into his shoulder. Then he says, in a more serious voice, "These things might not have the meaning you thought, but it doesn't mean they don't have meaning. From what you've told me about your mother, she invested in objects. Perhaps it was hard for her that she had nothing of his to give you." Ted strokes my hair. "Maybe she was trying to give you the father she would have liked you to have."

Ted's arms feel so warm and safe. I feel so known by him; the words he says, the way he touches me like fingers on braille, reading who I am.

"I just hate not being able to ask her about it," I say, my voice calmer now. "I'll never be able to ask her."

"I think when you're young, your parents feel infallible," says Ted, "people who have all the answers. Then gradually you notice a few chinks, and it crosses your mind that occasionally they might be wrong. Then one day, you look at them, and you realize they're just the same as you—cobbling it together, with no real clue."

"Gerry must have more of a clue than most, though."

"I don't know." Ted releases me from his arms and weaves his hands together, looking at the place where his ring used to be. "I think he's just trying to make sense of it all like the rest of us."

Reaching forward beyond his feet, Ted picks something up from the sand, a blue tear-shaped piece of sea glass.

"The blue pieces are rare," he says, examining it and then pressing it into my hand. "This is a good piece. Some people call them mermaid's tears. Do you want to hear the story?" I nod as I inspect the smooth glass in my palm—it looks like a gem, a tear of frosted sapphire. "The story goes that a mermaid watched as a storm threatened to wreck the ship of the man she loved," Ted says. His voice is hypnotic, I love listening to him. I sink my head back onto his shoulder as he speaks and he runs a hand across my hair, my whole body alert to his touch. "She was forbidden by Neptune from intervening in the weather, but she calmed the sea and tamed the waves to save her love from certain death. For her disobedience, she was banished to the ocean floor, never to surface again. Her tears wash up on the shore as glass, a reminder of true love."

I don't know if it's the hair stroking or his perfectly chosen words, but I pull away and look into Ted's face, and then we are kissing. It feels out of my control, the force with which I want to kiss him; I give in to it entirely, planting my lips firmly against his. There's a moment of surprise in his eyes, a flash of startled bemusement, but then it turns into the golden flicker of fire I saw last night on the beach, and in an instant he's kissing me back. His kiss is so passionate, it feels as though the fire in Ted, the years of loss and sadness have suddenly been given an outlet. The energy of it is electrifying.

I climb onto his lap—my thinking mind muted by an animal instinct. Clasping my hands around his face, his beautiful, clean-shaven skin, I run my hands up into his hair, pushing my mouth down onto his. His lips push back with equal force and his tongue delves to explore mine, unlocking some new urgency inside me. The kiss sends a wave of energy down between my legs, and I pull back, startled by the effect his lips are having on the rest of my body. When I pull away, his eyes lock onto mine and I know I should pause, let my thinking brain back in for a moment, but I can't. Perhaps he sees the want in my eyes, because he holds my waist and rolls me over on the sand. Then, lying on top of me, his fingers entwined in mine above our heads. I push my hips up against his, and he lets out a low moan.

Some animal switch has been flicked inside me; I feel feral and wild and completely alive.

This—*this* is kablammo.

Then it ends as quickly as it began. Cold splashes over my feet, and Ted flinches, pulling away. We look down to see the tide has come in, the waves breaking over our legs—we laugh, untwine our limbs, and scramble farther up the beach, away from the water.

We sit next to each other on the sand again, but now the moment has shifted. Where did that even come from?

"I'm sorry," I say, realizing it was me who initiated the kiss out of nowhere. My heart is pounding with exhilaration, mixed with embarrassment at the wildness that just came over me.

"*I'm* sorry. You were upset," Ted says, rubbing his chin with a hand, his eyes closed. "I shouldn't have done that." His words sting—was it a sympathy kiss then? He clasps a hand over mine, and I realize he's holding my pendant in his palm. "Don't throw your precious things in the sea, Laura. You might regret it."

Immediately, I think of his wedding ring. Does he already regret throwing that away? What am I doing? Only an hour ago, I was kissing Jasper. I don't think it's very ladylike to kiss two different men on the same day. Ted is technically still married, looking for his wife, a wife I now know how to find. He lets go of my hand, and I feel goose bumps prickle up the length of my arm. I want to reach out for him again, but I don't.

"Do you want me to see if I can find your watch?" he asks, standing up and making to take off his T-shirt.

"No, Ted." I reach up my hand to stop him. "I have to tell you something." My voice sinks.

"If it's that you're seeing someone else at the moment, well, I kind of know that," he says with an uneven laugh that catches in his throat.

"It's not that, though—well, yes, there is that . . ." I trail off, digging in my handbag for the page of Belinda's letter, my hand shaking. "This was in among your dad's letters; I found it last night. Gerry says he lost it, then forgot about it. He didn't mean to keep it from you."

I pass it to him quickly. He takes it from me, his brow furrowed with two deep lines. I look away, not wanting to see the look on his face as he processes what it is.

When I turn back, hc is pacing in the sand.

"Why didn't you give this to me last night, when you found it?" he asks, his voice hard.

"I'm not sure," I say, closing my eyes, hearing the hurt in his voice. "You had so much else you were dealing with, I thought it might be better seen in the light of day . . ." I trail off, hearing how pathetic my excuse sounds.

"I have to go," Ted says gruffly, folding the letter into his pocket. "I'm sorry, Laura, none of this is a good idea. I can't—"

He lays a hand gently on my shoulder. I touch my hand up to his, giving him permission to go, and it feels what's between us is over before it even began.

And then his hand is gone and so is he. I'm left alone on the beach, perhaps more alone than I've ever been, my head and my heart full of more swirling confusion than they were before.

24 May 1992

Alex,

Laura May Le Quesne, born 22 May, 8:45 a.m.

Photo enclosed. I wanted her to have your name.

You can meet her whenever you want to, just let me know.

Annie

Chapter 23

With soaking-wet capri pants, I walk up the track back to the cottage. The cut on my leg stings from the salt water. I waded into the waves to look for my watch, worried I had littered the sea, but of course I couldn't find it. Ted's cab is gone from the drive. I let myself into the cottage and strip off my wet clothes, lying down on the bed naked.

I turn on my phone and it lights up with messages. There are two photos from Jasper, one he took of us together on the boat and the other a large Victoria sponge cake covered in strawberries.

I'm sorry if I didn't say the right thing earlier. Can I make it up to you with cake? Just let me know, I'll come get you.

His message makes me smile and then feel incredibly guilty. I told him I needed time alone, then used that time to kiss another man. Here is Jasper—perfect, gorgeous Jasper—no games, no "playing it cool" before texting me. He is everything I said I wanted. But now I've gone and confused everything by jumping on Ted. *What was I thinking?* I wasn't thinking.

My phone rings, Dee—she will be able to tell me if I'm a terrible person or not.

"Hey," she says, "you OK? Your gran called me. She told me about your parents. So, your aunt was right? I'm so sorry, are you OK? Are you back tomorrow? Do you want to come straight to mine?"

Dee is one of the few people who knew my mum well, and she's as surprised as I am by this revelation. As we talk about it, I find my anger at being lied to has already mellowed. Instead, I feel sad that Mum felt the need to hide the truth. She was a romantic, and I am sorry that she didn't get the happily ever after she wanted.

Dee is worried about me being out here on my own. I reassure her I am not—that I've spent the morning with Jasper, and then Ted. Then I end up filling her in on everything that's happened since we last spoke on the phone in Jasper's bathroom.

"Right," says Dee, sounding confused. "So Ted is the weirdy beardy old taxi driver, right?"

"No—well, yes, but he's shaved now and he's not weird, or even that old. He's pretty wonderful, in fact."

"Yesterday, you thought Jasper was your soulmate—the one the universe has been leading you to, the person you have everything in common with. And this morning he took you on an amazing day date and you had a lovely time? Am I getting this right?"

I let out a frustrated sigh.

"I did have a lovely time with Jasper." I squeeze my eyes closed. "And Ted kind of ran away after kissing me, and it doesn't even make sense that I like him in that way."

"So, to recap," says Dee, "it's a choice between perfect, compatible, available Jasper, who sounds fully into you and is everything you said you were looking for in a man, *or* hairy old beard guy, who's technically married and runs away after kissing you."

"Well, when you say it like that . . ." I groan.

"Hmmm, sounds like a tough decision," Dee says sarcastically.

"But this kiss, Dee! This kiss!"

"Unsuitable men always kiss better, everyone knows that. Laura, I'm sorry, but it sounds to me like you are looking for reasons to ruin things with Jasper. You were so sure he was the one yesterday. You were sure, even when you only had his luggage to go on, but now he's gorgeous, interested, and single too!"

"I know," I say with a sigh.

"Do you remember Aaron Sargent? Who you dumped because he put the handbrake on at junctions, and Jamie Johnson, who got ditched for buying you a naff teddy bear with 'I'm Yours' written on the front?"

"Look, I don't think this is a 'Laura's being too fussy' situation."

"What about that blind date guy?" Dee goes on. "Vanya's friend, who you discounted because he didn't drink hot drinks?"

"OK, that was bizarre, though. Who doesn't drink hot drinks?"

Dee's tone softens. "You know, sometimes, when people are sad, they don't think they deserve happiness."

"I'm not sad, Dee," I say sharply. "Well, I might be sad about some stuff, but it doesn't mean I'm intrinsically sad—I'm not broken."

"I'm not saying you're broken, I just— This quest for the perfect guy, maybe it's always been about the quest, never the destination. Maybe you don't really want anyone to fill that space in your life." Dee pauses. "And that's fine too, Laura. You are allowed to be enough for yourself. You can be on your own if that's what you want. But at least consider that you kibosh guys before giving them a proper chance."

Anger spikes in my chest. I've had this lecture from Dee before. She just wants everything to be simple, clear-cut, like life has been for her. She's never been on a bad date, never felt lonely or left behind, because she's marrying her first boyfriend. Just because I've been dating for years, waiting for the right person, it doesn't mean there's something wrong with me, does it?

"I don't think that's fair, Dee. Just because I didn't settle for the first guy . . ." I let the sentence trail, instantly regretting my choice of words. "Look, maybe you're right. All the stuff with Mum has got me—"

"You think I settled for Neil?" Dee asks sharply.

"No, I didn't mean to say that."

"Because I didn't. I love Neil, he's amazing."

"I know, of course he is."

"Just because you've never had anything last more than six months—"

"Well, that's not true." I pause. "Aaron was seven."

"Look, I'm going to go before I say something I regret. Just, look after yourself, OK? We'll talk tomorrow."

I close my eyes as Dee hangs up on me.

Sitting at the little oak desk in the cottage, I try to focus my mind on work, replying to the backlog of emails and uploading all the photos I have taken so far. I post online the "Then and Now" pictures of Mum and me at the Écréhous. Then I look at the photo of Jasper and me on the boat, his kind, uncomplicated face smiling back at me. Dee is right. I should steer myself back to Jasper—he is great, and I am acting illogically.

I send the photo of me and Jasper on the boat to Vanya, replying to her question about whether I'd found Hot Suitcase Guy yet. Then I text Jasper, thanking him again for this morning, telling him I'd love to drop in on Maude's party a bit later, but that I can make my own way there. He replies immediately with a big smiley face emoji and I get a GIF back from Vanya of Bugs Bunny with hearts for eyes.

Kissing Ted on the beach was a moment of madness; I was caught up in a flurry of emotions. I need to focus on sensible things—like how I'm going to make this coin story work now. Even if I can flesh out my great-grandparents story, how can I frame my parents' relationship as this perfect love story now? I need a new angle. If I just had a little more time, if I could only extend this trip for another few days . . .

Before I lose my nerve, I tap out a text to Suki.

Laura: Keen to stay in Jersey for a few more days, so much great content to collect! Is it OK if I work remotely, come back on Wednesday?

I've barely pressed send, when the screen lights up with her name. I close my eyes as I answer the call. Suki doesn't like people working remotely. She feels they are more productive in a "competitive environment."

"What? Why? Why is it taking so long?" she snaps. Zero preamble.

"Well, no, it's not, I just—" I stutter, unprepared.

"Because honestly, Laura, we can't afford for you to spend four days of your time on one little article about your parents."

"Well, technically, it's not four working days, since this is still the weekend, and I am working on other content while I'm—"

"Send me what you have. I want to see a draft today."

"The thing is, Suki, um, I'm just trying to rework the angle slightly. New information has come to light—"

"What new information?" she asks, her voice steely.

"Um, well. It's actually quite interesting, because it turns out my parents didn't stay together that long. They never got married, in fact." *Why am I telling her this? This is not going to help.* "And I was thinking, maybe this is an article about love stories that get passed down to the next generation and how they get twisted and embellished into a kind of family mythology. All my romantic expectation may have been built on this story, it's what sparked my interest in other people's love stories—"

As I'm talking, I grow more confident. This is all off the top of my head, but as I'm saying it, I realize it *is* an interesting idea.

There's a grunting sound on the line, then Suki says, "No."

"No?"

"No. You're not Malcolm Gladwell, Laura, I don't want a revisionist history of your family. I want the coin meet-cute, the romantic proposal, the love story to end all love stories that you pitched to me. From what you're telling me now, this whole trip has been a complete waste of time." She sighs heavily. "I want you back in the office on Monday. I think we need to have a serious conversation. I've allowed you a lot of autonomy, and you've shown a real lack of judgment these last few days."

My skin breaks out in beads of sweat, and my stomach starts to cramp. I'm going to get fired. I can't even fathom what shape my life would have without my job. Could I even make the rent if I had to go freelance again? I wouldn't see Vanya every day, she wouldn't be my flatmate or my colleague.

"I-I-I can't leave Jersey yet!"

Suki breathes in, preparing to bark at my insolence.

"I've met someone." I squeeze my eyes closed, not sure where I'm going with this.

"You've met someone?" comes an angry echo down the phone.

"Yes—and it's a great story."

The idea takes shape as I'm talking. I could use my own meet-cute as a story for the site. I tell Suki about Jasper, about the mix-up at the airport, the things I found in his suitcase, and my search around the island to track him down. As she listens, she mellows, her bark becomes an excited yap and by the end of the call, she is cooing with delight.

"You see I can't leave yet, Suki, I only just found him and—"

"No, no, you can't leave," she agrees. "This is perfect—this is wonderful—this is exactly the kind of fated love story people want to read about."

I didn't know Suki was capable of sounding so animated.

"Well, not necessarily a love story yet, it's all so new . . ." I say, in a feeble attempt to temper her enthusiasm. "But a good meet-cute in any case."

"Laura, the greatness of a love story is not determined by the amount of time a couple have spent together—just look at Romeo and Juliet, Rose and Jack, Marius and Cosette—these people barely spend five minutes together before turning their lives upside down for one another. No, this is fate, this is destiny, this is love at first—luggage!"

I'm annoyed she's said that. Now she's going to take credit for that phrase, and I had already thought of the "love at first luggage" tagline.

"Well, I—"

"This could be a good enough hook to land a feature in a broadsheet magazine, great publicity for our brand. It could even go international: 'Love Life's lead journalist, unlucky in love and still carrying the emotional baggage from her mother's death, resigned to a life of writing other people's love stories, unwittingly finds her own . . . in a suitcase!'"

I feel myself frown—I wouldn't have said I was unlucky in love or carrying emotional baggage.

"Leave it with me," Suki says in a singsong voice. "I'll work out how we can maximize coverage—you stay as long as you need to seal the deal with your Suitcase Man. If you pull this off in the way I know you can, we'll have to talk about that promotion again. You know how much I appreciate it when people go above and beyond for a great story."

I'm about to clarify that I wasn't pursuing Jasper for the story, I was pursuing him because I genuinely felt he was the man I was supposed to be with. *Is* the man I am supposed to be with, I mentally correct myself. But before I can say anything, Suki has hung up.

What just happened? It feels like a good thing, in that I avoided getting fired and my boss mentioned the word "promotion," but part of me can't help but feel nervous about tying my work and my personal life so inextricably together.

Suki: Pictures we'll need:

The suitcase

The suitcase contents

You and Suitcase Man kissing

You and Suitcase Man embracing by the luggage carousel, holding your cases in the air, ideally with your leg kicked up in excitement.

What have I started?

Suki: You can look quite pretty when you make an effort—expense a makeover, hair, etc. I don't want any beekeeper bollocks in these shots. If this goes national, we don't need any of your kooky eccentricity.

Kooky eccentricity? Now that's just rude.

Suki: On second thoughts, I'm sending Dionne and Saul out on the first flight on Monday. We need professional, glossy shots for this. Get your man on board for press ASAP.

Dionne and Saul are a stylist and a photographer Suki uses for big product shoots. They're expensive; they style all the minor royals. If Suki's sending them, she's serious about putting this story everywhere. How the hell am I going to sell this to Jasper? He's a lovely guy, but this kind of publicity parade might be enough to put anyone off.

TIGER WOMAN ON QUALIFIERS

When tigers have something to say, do they work on a draft? Do they litter their message with niceties: "yours sincerely," "thank you," "please"? No. They do not. Women constantly undermine themselves with qualifying phrases like, "Sorry," "I'm no expert but . . ." "I just wanted to check," "I might have an idea." Change the words you use, and you will change the way you are seen: I am not sorry, I am an expert, and I'm certainly not "yours," sincerely or otherwise.

Chapter 24

I'm not going to pull Jasper out of his own mother's party just to pick me up, so I order a cab to take me to Maude's house. In the car, I tap out an apology to Dee:

You know I didn't mean it to sound like that. I'm sorry. I'm on my way to see Jasper now. XXX

At my request, the cabdriver stops at one of the honesty boxes by the side of the road, a small stall selling vegetables and flowers. I can't imagine anything like this working in a big city. Checking I have the right change, I pick up a bunch of "modern pinks" for Maude and put the money in the box.

When I arrive, I can hear people out back, so I walk around to the garden. Jasper is chatting away to an elderly lady in a wheelchair while holding a plate of sandwiches and a bottle of champagne. He's laughing kindly at something the woman is saying, and I feel instantly glad that I came.

He looks up and sees me across the garden and his face breaks into a huge smile. I wave, not wanting to interrupt his conversation. He says something to the lady in the wheelchair, and she waves both hands at me in delight. Jasper bounds over and kisses me on both cheeks.

"You came," he says. "How did you know where to come, I forgot to send you the address?"

"Oh, um, Google. I am a journalist." I half laugh, half sigh.

Jasper tilts his head in concern. "And are you feeling better after a lie-down?"

I nod, prickling with guilt as I think about the nature of my "lie-down"—in the sand, with Ted on top of me, his mouth against mine.

"You look flushed, Laura, are you sure you're all right?"

"Yes, fine, thank you, feeling so much better." I pinch my lips together, annoyed at my face for giving me away.

"Let me introduce you to my family. I've already told them all about our suitcase story."

Jasper ushers me over to Maude, who is seated at the patio furniture, talking to Keith and a lady with messy gray curls. At the far end of the table are two women in their thirties who look alarmingly like Jasper but with Kate Middleton's physique and wardrobe. They both have long dark hair, the same dimpled grin, and aristocratic posture. The taller of the two has a long string of pearls around her neck, and the other wears some eye-catching orange earrings.

"Laura, this is my mother, Maude," Jasper says, making introductions, "Keith and his wife, June, then two of my sisters, Jocelyne and Juliette, who are over from the UK for the day."

The sisters both hold up a hand in greeting. Keith eyes me suspiciously, recognizing me from the fete.

"Laura and I met at the fete yesterday," he says, narrowing his eyes. "Glad to see you tracked your man down then."

Keith says it like I'm some kind of sniper out to snare Jasper in my black widow's web, and there he is, sitting between his wife and his mistress in broad daylight, giving me the judgy eyes. I don't often take against people, but I have decided I do not like Bee Man Keith.

"Happy birthday," I say, smiling at Maude and handing her the bunch of flowers. I'm finding it hard not to think a little badly of her too, given the fact that she's invited the wife of the man she's carrying on with to her birthday party. June sits silently, hardly acknowledging my presence. Poor woman, she probably knows what's going on, but Keith's gaslighting her into thinking Maude's "just a friend from bee club." Then again, maybe kissing two different men in the same day precludes me from making moral judgments here.

"Jasper's been talking about you nonstop," says Maude.

"He has," confirms Jocelyne, reaching out to squeeze Jasper's cheek. "He's a smitten kitten."

"Please don't make me sound uncool." Jasper blushes, and I feel a swell of affection for him.

"Well, thank you for letting me gate-crash your party," I say to Maude.

"Jasper's 'suitcase girl' is most welcome. Thank you for these," Maude says, smelling the flowers I have given her.

Jasper buzzes around me, fetching me a drink, introducing

me to his mother's friends. I wonder at how welcoming everyone is. This is the second party I've been invited to join—I can't even think of the last time I went to two parties in the same weekend. The guests here feel more staid than Gerry's. The tone is more cucumber sandwiches and tea from good china than sausage baps in napkins and sangria out of plastic cups.

Jasper leads me over the croquet lawn, up to the far end of the garden to show me the beehive he commissioned Keith to make for Maude.

"There's nothing Keith doesn't know about bees," he explains.

"So, Keith's a friend of your mum's, is he?" I ask, unable to stop myself from prying.

"Yes, they're very close," says Jasper as we walk back toward the group gathered around the patio table outside the house. Then I notice Keith is holding Maude's hand, right in front of June; the man is completely shameless!

"So, what brings you to the island, Laura?" Jocelyne asks, straightening the blue velvet Alice band on her glossy mane of hair.

"Laura's a journalist. She covers love stories, unusual ways people have met," Jasper explains, putting a hand around my waist.

"Ah, a 'cute meet,' I think they call it nowadays, don't they?" says Maude.

"Meet-cute," I correct her with a smile. Everyone at the table then looks at me, clearly waiting for me to expand on exactly what it is I do. "I work for a lifestyle website, we cover all sorts of things, but the love stories are always the most popular. So many people meet online these days, which can feel a little unromantic. I think people still yearn to hear about those magical real-life meetings—to believe that 'the one' might be found in the strangest of places."

"Like meeting through a suitcase," says Maude, one eyebrow arched.

"I met my husband online," says Jocelyne, icily.

"Me too," says Juliette, twirling her string of white pearls around one finger, her top lip curled.

"Ah, well, um, not that the internet can't be romantic too—" I trip over my words. "It's just, er, you know, more, well, it's less—um." No, I can't think of any words to dig myself out of this hole, so I just leave the sentence hanging and take a painfully large gulp of tea.

Jasper offers me a chair and then pulls up a seat beside me, before offering me another platter of cucumber sandwiches. His face is so earnest, so keen to please—a doting Labrador.

"Laura and I have the same favorite book and a shared passion for Phil Collins," he says, wrapping an arm around my shoulders. His easy physical affection makes me self-conscious, worried what all these people will think, when they know we only met yesterday. Perhaps something in my body language gives me away, because when I glance over at Maude, I'm convinced she can see right through me. I reach up to pat Jasper's hand, which is still resting on my shoulder.

"It does feels like someone up there was sending us a sign," I say brightly, giving everyone a beaming smile.

"On dating apps, you can add details like what books you like and your taste in music," says Jocelyne, clearly still annoyed about my earlier comment. "You don't have to rely on careless behavior at the airport to find that."

"Jocey thinks romance is her husband putting the dishwasher on," Jasper says with a smirk, before gently kicking his sister beneath the table.

"Ow! Trust me, when you have three children under six, it is," she says, then turns to me. "Be warned, Jasper wants enough children to make his own cricket team, so you'd have your work cut out."

"Don't listen to her," Jasper says, giving his sister a friendly scowl across the table, "and don't ask Jocey about her children, or she'll tell you each of their birth stories."

"Well, don't ask Jasper about kitchens, or you'll be past childbearing age by the time he's finished talking," says Jocelyne, and then they stick their tongues out at each other.

Looking between Jasper and his sister, I envy this easy teasing between them. I always longed for siblings, to have someone who would always understand where you came from.

"Some love isn't all bells and whistles and fancy stories," says Keith, leaning over to squeeze June's hand. I feel irritated that he is daring to weigh in on the topic of love.

"That is true, dear," says Maude, giving him an affectionate smile.

"Laura, do you plan on writing about Jasper for your website then?" Juliette asks, cocking her head at me.

"Um, maybe. It could be a good story. We'll have to see." I let out a sigh that goes on too long. "June, Keith told me you met through a shared love of maps, is that right?" I ask, keen to steer the conversation away from me and to include June, who is looking left out.

"What's that, dear?" asks June, sounding surprised that

someone is talking to her. Then she laughs a little too loudly and turns to Keith, as though expecting him to answer for her.

"That's right," says Keith, patting June's hand. Maude looks at me, unblinking, narrowing her eyes slightly, as though she knows that I know. She couldn't, could she? Maybe I left fingerprints all over the coat alcove. Maybe there were traces of my perfume on her brown Barbour jacket, and she's just this second sniffed me out. Damn it, I should never have returned to the scene of the crime. That's probably the first rule of crime club.

"Laura's also writing about Jersey," Jasper says, saving June from answering, "a travel article about local dishes and traditions. I thought you could give her a few of your local recipes, Mum."

"I'd be delighted," says Maude, standing up. "Why don't you come inside with me for a moment, Laura? We'll have a root around. I might even have some old snaps of Jasper in his birthday suit you'll find amusing."

"Mum." Jasper rolls his eyes but looks secretly pleased.

Glancing across at June, I'm worried she'll think me rude to leave before she's answered my question, but Keith is now talking to her quietly and her eyes drop to her lap.

Inside, Maude ducks into the kitchen and picks up a large leather book stuffed with loose pages, then she shows me through to the living room and offers me a seat on a blue sofa. I perch uncomfortably on the edge, wondering if Keith's naked body has lain here before me.

"Local recipes, right, let's see what I have," says Maude. As she flicks through the huge book in her lap, I explain my idea for a travel piece told through food.

"It sounds like a wonderful idea. My late husband and I traveled around Europe a great deal, and you know the strongest memories I have of those trips are the meals we shared: a game tortellini in Tuscany, currywurst from the Rhine. You must taste a place to remember it." Maude pauses, smiling to herself. "What is the taste of Jersey then? You've got Jersey wonders, of course, cabbage loaf," she starts ticking off a list on her fingers, "bean crock, apple layer cake, ormer stew, oysters, Jersey Royals done properly, there's an art to that."

I start taking notes on my phone. This is just what I need. Jasper was right about his mother being an excellent resource.

"June used to make a mean apple layer cake," Maude says, pausing to catch my eye. "She has dementia now." She waits a moment for this to sink in, then goes on, "She hasn't a clue who's who. She's in full-time care, but Keith likes to take her out at the weekend. She'll still go with him, despite not knowing his name. There's an acknowledgment that she's somewhere safe, with people who love her."

Her words hit me like a punch to the chest, the strange dynamic between them immediately making sense.

"Oh, how sad," I say, my voice quiet. I feel rebuked, though Maude has been nothing but kind.

"Poor Keith has had a hard time of it," Maude says. "I sometimes think I was luckier to have Frank die on me, than to have endured what Keith has—to see the person he loves fade away in front of his eyes."

A tight ball of shame forms in my stomach; shame at the assumptions I made about people whose lives I knew nothing about. I think of my conversation on the beach with Gerry this morning—about assuming too much.

"Last year, June came here, and she said, 'I'm sorry, I don't remember your name, but I remember I love you.' I cried, and she didn't know why I was crying." Maude blots at her eye with the edge of her hand, and turns to look out of the window. "You know, love is not all about the grand gestures and the cutie meets, Laura." I smile that she still hasn't got the phrase right. "That's the shiny book cover, not the story inside."

She looks back at me with a piercing look. "You want to know what I think is romantic?" Maude asks, standing up and walking over to a dark wooden bureau in the corner of the room. She opens one of the drawers and pulls out a faded blue journal, holding it up and tapping it with the other hand.

"Six years ago, when June was first diagnosed, she came to me and asked for my help with something. She wanted me to write down some memories of her life with Keith—trips they took together, jokes they shared, the bricks of experiences that make up a life together." Maude looks down at the book in her hands. "She wanted to have it all written down, so that when she goes, I can give it to Keith, and the final words he hears of hers will not be the words of a woman who does not know him."

Maude pinches her lips together, her eyes watery, and I have to bite my lip too.

"Why am I telling you this?" Maude asks with a frown, and it sounds like a genuine question, as though she has forgotten. "Ah yes, we were talking about love and romance. Well, to me, this is love. On the day she was given this terrible diagnosis, the first thing June thought to do was to try to make it easier for Keith. And you know, most of the memories written in here, they aren't the grand gestures or expensive holidays; they are hill walking in Wales, memorable meals they shared, taking their son swimming in the sea for the first time, the way Keith always positioned her slippers by the bed so she wouldn't get cold toes in the night."

Maude takes a moment to compose herself before stowing the journal carefully back in the bureau. "I think sometimes your generation gets caught up in the wrapping paper of love." Maude makes a low hum. "This suitcase story you've got Jasper so excited about—he's very trusting. Don't let him get too carried away until you know him a little better."

A heat rises up my neck, like she somehow knows that I was kissing another man less than two hours ago.

"Do you think it's possible to find love again, after you've been married for a long time?" I ask.

Maude gives a small smile.

"The human heart is like a flowerbed, Laura. Once the first blooms die, there's room enough for something else to grow, but it will never be quite the same as that first flower, the initial thrill of seeing what your heart is capable of."

Maude allows me to take pictures of her recipes with my phone. While I have it in my hand, I show her some of the photos of my trip—the pictures I have tried to re-create from my mother's album. She flicks through the photos of me with the cow, the beach at Rozel, the cliff top and Plémont headland, then she pauses, taking my phone and putting on her glasses to look more closely.

"What's this one, dear? Is that my coat alcove?"

"Er . . ."

"There you are," says Jasper, walking in at just the right moment. "Are you ready to cut the cake, Mum?"

* * *

After the party, Jasper offers to drive me home, but his sisters are leaving in a few hours, and they clearly want to spend time with him, so I insist on making my own way back to L'Étacq.

"Thank you for inviting me today. I so enjoyed meeting everyone," I say, as we stand together on Maude's doorstep.

"My sisters can be intense," he says, pulling his mouth into a wide grimace. "But Mrs. Harvey said to me, 'Don't screw this one up, Jasper, she's a beauty.'"

He takes my hand, and I accept the compliment with a smile.

"Are you sure you can't stay?" he asks.

"I'm afraid I must do some work. I'm going to change my flight, stay a few more days."

"Well, that is good news," he says, reaching forward to tuck a strand of hair behind my ear.

"Listen, I have a favor to ask you," I say sweetly, feeling my body tense in anticipation. "I was on the phone to my boss earlier, and I happened to mention you and how we met and, well—"

"She loved it?" Jasper finishes my sentence.

"Yes." I nod guiltily.

"She wants you to write about it?"

"Kind of. I know, it's a bit much—"

"Laura, I get it, it's a great story. Love at first luggage." Jasper moves his hand through the air, as though envisaging the words on a billboard somewhere. *Why does everyone keep using that line?*

"The thing is, my boss got slightly overexcited—she wants to do a photo shoot—" I pause, checking his face isn't reading "horrified." It isn't. "I know it's all a bit nuts, but it would just be a few pictures to go with the article . . ."

"Do they want a shot of me getting down on one knee or something?" he asks. I'm pretty sure he's joking, but I shake my head nervously anyway.

"No, no, nothing like that, just a few photos of the suitcase, of us together—they want to do it on Monday."

I pull my shoulders up around my ears, making what I imagine to be the facial expression of someone who's spent ages twiddling lightbulbs on the Christmas tree to find the one loose connection, and now they're about to turn the power back on, to see if they've done enough to make it work.

Jasper reaches out to put a hand on each of my shoulders.

"Whatever you need, Laura, it's not a problem for me."

"Thank you, Jasper. I wouldn't want you to feel awkward, I can always tell her no if you'd rather not . . ."

"Listen, I'll be honest with you. I've been ready to meet someone for a while now. I've just turned thirty, I've got a great business, a beautiful house that's too big for me, I'm going to need a Mrs. Contessa Kitchens at some point, perhaps some Baby Contessa Kitchens too." He grins, closes his eyes, then when he opens them, he says, "When you knocked on my door— Well, let's just say I wasn't sure I believed in love at first sight until yesterday . . ."

Wow, this is intense. The mention of Baby Contessa Kitchens just made my palms start to sweat. My mouth emits a high-pitched humming sound. But I can hardly berate the guy for getting ahead of himself when I've just asked him to do a *Hello*-style photo shoot with me.

"That is so sweet, Jasper, but, um." I swallow, my mouth

dry, Maude's words of warning heavy on my mind. "We have lots of time to get to know each other better, especially if you come to London sometimes. I wouldn't want to put too much pressure on something that's just beginning."

"Sure, I know. Sorry, I shouldn't have said that."

Jasper's face contorts with boyish embarrassment and he scuffs his shoe against the concrete step. Now I feel terrible that I've made him regret his lovely, romantic words. Isn't this *exactly* what I'd hoped to hear? Wasn't I the one telling everyone yesterday that I thought I'd love him before I'd even met him? Dee's words ring in my ears, about how I sabotage things, so I lean in to kiss him, determined not to let myself ruin this.

He pulls me gently into his arms and kisses me back. His lips are comforting and firm. It's a good kiss, definitely an enjoyable experience, and I try to push all comparisons with Ted's beach kiss from my mind.

When the kiss eventually ends, my mind feels exhausted from the pressure of trying to think the right thoughts, rather than the unhelpful ones.

"So, I was thinking," Jasper says, holding me gently by both shoulders. "Perhaps we could do the photo shoot in one of my kitchens?"

"Oh?" I say, wondering how Suki would feel about that.

"I think the Malala would convey the right atmosphere, don't you?"

TIGER WOMAN ON SELF-RELIANCE

Tigers are solitary creatures; they hunt alone, they sleep alone, they furnish their own needs. Do not look for another animal to make you feel whole. You are not someone's "other half," you are not half of anything; you are perfect, you are entire, you are complete just as you are.

Chapter 25

It is six o'clock by the time I get back to Sans Ennui. All the lights are off in the house, and I walk down toward the cottage wanting nothing but an early night and my laptop. Then I see the outside light on at Sandy's. She's sitting on her patio with Gerry, Scamp snoozing on her lap.

"Laura!" she calls. "Get over here."

I clamber over the wall, pleased to see them despite the siren call of solitude.

"I thought you'd gone this morning, Gerry?"

"I made a break for freedom," he says with a wry smile, but there's a sadness in his eyes.

"He rang me this afternoon, saying he needed to see the sea one last time," says Sandy, shaking her head. "As if he's moved to the flipping Sahara or something rather than ten minutes up the road. You won't get to like it if you don't give it a chance, you old pickle."

"They said I'd have a sea view from my room, but I can't see a speck of water. I won't be able to sleep without the sound of it."

"Didn't Ted make you a CD of sea sounds?" asks Sandy.

"Not the same." Gerry sighs.

"Speaking of Ted, have either of you seen him this afternoon?" I ask, in my best casual-inquiry voice. Sandy gives me a knowing look. "I see his car's not back?"

"Probably picking up fares—it's where he goes when he doesn't know what to do with himself," says Sandy, raising both eyebrows and slowly nodding.

"I gave him the letter," I tell Gerry.

"Ah," Gerry says, and bows forward in his chair.

"What letter?" Sandy asks, eyes darting between us.

Gerry and I explain about Belinda's letter.

"And now I've given it to him, and he's gone," I say mournfully.

"He won't have gone far," says Sandy, reaching out to squeeze my arm. "He'll call her. He'll want to get the divorce rolling now. I don't know what planet Belinda was on, thinking she could just dance off into her hippie-dippie sunset and ignore all the gritty details of a separation." Sandy sounds angry.

"He's going to think I hid that letter from him," says Gerry, pressing his palms against the sides of his head.

"Yeah, he's definitely not going to pay up for that sea view now," Sandy says, and then she and Gerry start giggling like children.

"Hey, this is serious," I say, looking between them. "Who knows where he's gone?"

Sandy narrows her eyes at me.

"How was your day with Mr. Suitcase Man? I saw the red sports car this morning—very fancy."

Ted was right about living on a small island, no keeping secrets.

"Fine," I say, flustered. "I'm just worried about Ted, as a friend."

"We all are," says Sandy.

We sit in silence for a moment, all looking out to sea, and I breathe in the quiet.

"That watery horizon is a spirit level for the soul," says Gerry. "When you look at it for long enough, it puts life straight again."

In that moment, I know exactly what he means, and I don't know how I've stayed in the city so long, where there's no chance for recalibration, no clean horizon to level you. Even with all the emotion this trip has thrown up, there's something about watching the ocean that puts everything into perspective. Maybe Jersey is rubbing off on me. I don't think I've even checked my phone for the last— *Hang on, where is my phone?* I pat down my pocket and search through my bag.

"Oh no. I think I've lost my phone."

"Did you leave it at Mr. Sports Car's house?" asks Sandy, tapping a finger against her chin.

"Probably." I sigh. "This is a disaster."

"Maybe it is, maybe it isn't," says Gerry, tipping his head backward and looking up at the sky.

"Well, it is. If my boss can't get hold of me—"

"Oh, I meant to tell you, the internet's down," says Sandy. "There's some glitch across the whole of St. Ouen's, should be back on in an hour or two."

"What?" I cry, horrified. "I can't be offline." As I say it, I hear how pathetic I sound. I'm not a doctor on call or a politician running the country. Then I think of my argument with Dee, the need to amend my flight, the fact that Dionne and Saul are coming here on Monday—the constant nagging feeling that I have a thousand phone calls I should be making.

"You can use my mobile, if there's anything urgent?" Sandy offers.

"Do you know what happens when you don't have your phone?" Gerry asks. I look at him, waiting for an answer. "Life."

"All right, Yoda," says Sandy.

"Yes, 'live for today' is all very well until I lose my job and can't pay the rent," I tell him.

"Someone sparky like you?" Gerry gives me a wink. "You'd find a way." Then he bows his head and presses his papery-skinned hands together in prayer. "There is an old proverb: He who fears to suffer, suffers from fear."

"Oh no," Sandy says, covering her eyes, "you've unleashed the proverbial Gerry."

"Man who waits for roast duck to fly into his mouth must wait very, very long time," says Gerry.

"He'll just keep spouting proverbs at you until you beg him to stop," says Sandy. "He has proverbs for every occasion, mainly from cheap Christmas crackers by the sound of them."

"Fear blows wind into your sails—"

"OK, she gets it," Sandy says, standing up and putting both

hands gently around Gerry's neck, pretending to throttle him. This makes Gerry stop his guru impression and wrinkle his nose into a silent laugh. I smile at them, cheered up by their jokes, but the conversation does make me pause to think—Would it be *so* terrible if I lost my job? If I didn't have the familiar routine? But then the thought makes me feel a bit sick and panicky, so I ask Sandy if I can bring my laptop over and hotspot off her mobile, just to get through my most urgent tasks.

Sandy goes to make a pot of herbal tea, and she and Gerry carry on chatting as I sit beside them tapping away on my keyboard and making calls from Sandy's mobile. I change my flight, email work with an update, giving them Sandy's phone number and the address at Sans Ennui in case of emergencies. I call Maude from Sandy's phone, asking if she's seen my mobile at her house; she hasn't but gives me Jasper's home number. I call him and it goes to answering machine, so I leave a message explaining the situation, asking if we can meet for lunch at his place tomorrow.

Having been subjected to hearing all my logistical arrangements, Gerry and Sandy both pretend to yawn at how boring I'm being.

"It's a wonder the human race survived as long as it did without mobile telephones, isn't it?" Gerry says, pushing his neck back against his collar.

"You are king of the Luddites, Gerry," says Sandy. Then she turns to me and says, "He was opposed to the wheel when that came in too."

"Terrible, newfangled round things," says Gerry in mock disgust.

Taking the hint, I shut my laptop, return Sandy's phone, and give them both my full attention. I know they are only teasing me, but now I feel rude to have disturbed their peaceful evening. As we drink tea, they share stories about the island and its history, what happened here during the war. Gerry tells me about the Occupation, how the Nazis used forced labor to build most of the tunnels and sea defenses still visible around the island. A few of these prisoners escaped and were sheltered by local families who risked their lives to help them. He tells me his mother and grandmother hid a starving Ukrainian in the eaves of Sans Ennui for more than a month. "He was called Avel and he loved birds; he left scratched drawings of starlings and seagulls in the beams of the loft, and you can just about make them out if you crawl up into the rafters."

"Oh, you must tell that story to whoever buys your house," I say, "otherwise it will be lost and no one will even know the drawings are there—that's a part of history."

"A lot of history gets lost," Gerry says somberly.

We move on to talk of cheerier things, and I absorb their words and stories like warmth from a campfire. Sandy kindly suggests I can borrow her bike over the next few days if I want to get around independently. Eventually she stands up and says, "Right, Gerry, I should be getting you back or they won't let me take you out again. Strict curfew, they said."

"Rules are there to be broken," Gerry replies.

"Not by me." She holds out an arm to help Gerry to his feet.

"Do you think Ted's OK then?" I can't help asking for a final time. I wonder if he's tried to call me.

"He'll be back, Laura," says Sandy.

"What makes you so sure?"

"Because he shaved that beard off, didn't he?" she says with a wink. "I know what that means, even if you don't."

Before I can ask her what she thinks it means, she's helping Gerry over to her car, and Ilídio appears from across the road, wiping his hands on a rag. He must have been in the workshop.

"You boomeranged back here already, Gerry?" he says.

"Yes, and I'll be back in a few days to check you're doing your cabinet joints the way I taught you, young man," Gerry says, waving a finger at Ilídio, his face contorting into a pretend scowl. Ilídio laughs.

Once Sandy and Gerry have driven away, I ask Ilídio, "How's my commission coming along?"

"Come and see," he says, beckoning me to follow him back across the road to the workshop.

He shows me the bare bones of what he has made, and I feel excited about how it's going to look, how much I hope Ted will like it.

Looking over at the window, I wander across to the workbench where the soldering iron stands, running my hand across the pockmarked wood covered in scratches and imprints from tools. How many things must have been created here over the years. The creations of Mum's I loved the most were the necklaces she made from soldering together solitary earrings that had been bereft of their other halves. This gnarled workbench makes me think of her—of the hours she committed to breathing new life into lonely old stones.

Then I think of the Ukrainian man's bird carvings in the rafters of Sans Ennui. How wrong it feels that whoever buys the house might not know they are there, that the only remaining physical evidence of the man's story could be lost. On impulse, I ask Ilídio, "Could I use this workbench?"

"Of course," he says, "keep me company."

"Do you have any silver wire?" I ask.

"I have everything," says Ilídio, walking over to a tall chest of drawers. I follow him and watch as he searches through a cabinet full of tools, buttons, hinges, and cardboard boxes. He pulls out some brown paper bags and inside one finds a coil of silver wire. "I keep all sorts. You never know what you might need. Use whatever you like."

"I can pay for whatever I use."

He shakes his head as he gives me the wire.

"Comes with the commission."

The porch door of Sans Ennui is open. Ted told me they rarely lock the house, which feels so alien to me, a Londoner with two security bolts on my front door. Inside, I call out his name, though I know he's not there because the drive is still empty. I pick up the shoebox, which is sitting on a window ledge, waiting for me to take it. Then, on a whim, I pick up the jar of sea glass too. My veins pulse with a long-forgotten feeling, the anticipation of what I might create.

Back at the workshop, I show Ilídio the box of jewelry.

"What will you do with it?" he asks.

"I don't know yet," I say. "Do you ever feel like you just need to channel your energy into making something with your hands?"

Ilídio smiles and cracks his knuckles. "Every day, Laura. Every damn day."

Until now, anything related to jewelry making has felt almost macabre to me, too steeped in loss. Picking up tools would have felt like wearing Mum's clothes or sleeping in her unwashed sheets. But now, something new bubbles its way to the surface, as though these feelings have been brewed and distilled into something else entirely. The watch and the book and the music, I clung to them as though they were physical totems of love, but here in my hands, I have something real that Mum gave me: her love of making things. She taught me how to find the quality beneath the tarnish, how to bend and melt and thread and polish and pick things apart. I might never be as good at it as she was, but not doing it at all would be like nailing up the attic on those birds.

Ilídio and I set to work in companionable silence, he at his workbench and me at mine. As I unpack the treasure trove from the shoebox in front of me, feeling the textures of metal and stone in my hands, the familiar clinking of tangled chains, I feel a flush of energy, the creative part of myself waking up. It's lain dormant for a long time, too tired from work, too busy online or scrolling on my phone, too tinged with the sadness of association. Yet here, now, it holds no sadness.

I wrap green sea glass in silver wire, then solder each droplet of glass to a vintage chain bracelet. From Ted's box, I take a simple necklace of silver mesh, mend it, and then weave a layer of sea glass through it. It takes on a life of its own once I've started, like a wave of silver, with all the secrets of the sea caught in its motion. Dee has always encouraged me to create things again. I cannot wait to show her this necklace—once she is talking to me again.

Time disappears into the place it goes when you are in

creative flow. When I next look up through the workshop window, I realize it is dark outside. I must have been sitting here for hours. Ilídio has gone. A coffee cup is on the bench behind me with a Post-it note stuck to it: *Didn't want to disturb you, stay as long as you like. Put key under pot.* He must have crept away to bed. I must go myself. Before I leave, I lay out my creations on the bench, put the sea glass bracelet around my wrist, and feel something I haven't felt in years: pride.

"Thanks, Mum," I say softly.

She led me here, to what I needed.

6 July 1992

Dear Alex,
She is wonderful, isn't she? I knew you would love her the second you laid eyes on her. You can visit her any time you like. I printed out the photos of you holding her—copies enclosed. She has your chin, don't you think? And your huge feet—she will be a giant!

I'm sorry, Al, but I still feel the same way about the coin. Finding the coin is what led me to you, to Laura, and I want a piece of it for her. You don't experience objects the way I do—I feel all the memories it holds when I have it in my hand, visceral to me. If your family would promise to leave both pieces to Laura once your grandmother passes, then I would return my half until then, but I'd want it in writing. I agree, better for the pieces to stay together.

Love,
Annie

Chapter 26

That night I dream I'm in a pitch meeting with Suki—a standard anxiety dream for me. Usually I'm naked or mute in these dreams, but this time, I am a tiger, towering over her, roaring at the room. That's what comes of reading *Tiger Woman* before bed. The tone of the book, with all its grandiose affirmations, is a bit much for me. But beyond the metaphors, perhaps the message of tuning back into your instincts is a valid one; I don't think it was logic that led me to that workbench last night.

I wake feeling surprisingly well rested. Looking out of the window, there's still no sign of Ted's car in the driveway. Where did he sleep? Has he left the island to go and find her? How worried about him should I be?

I need to check my emails now the Wi-Fi is back on, but I

left my laptop at Sandy's, and when I climb over the wall, no one is home and the house is shut up. This would have been enough to send me into a panic yesterday, but this morning I feel uncharacteristically calm. It is Sunday; surely I can afford to be disconnected for one morning of the weekend. So instead of fretting, I decide to go for a sea swim.

Stepping into the garden with my towel wrapped around my bikini, I close my eyes, and turn my face to the sky. The sun feels brighter here somehow, though the September air is still cool beneath the cloudless sky. Running barefoot down the path to the sea, I throw off my towel as I hit the sand and plunge headfirst into the waves, not giving myself a chance to wimp out. The icy water winds me, stripping me back to something elemental. Then, once I've caught my breath, I look out to the watery horizon; Gerry's spirit level, leveling me.

In the sea, I can't help thinking back over the conversation I had with Dee, before she got upset with me. Her theory that my search for the impossibly perfect guy could be a distraction, because I don't believe I deserve to be happy. She's wrong—I do think I deserve happiness, and honestly, I don't think my subconscious is that clever. But maybe I need to rethink where that happiness is going to come from. The feeling of contentment in the workshop last night—it gave me a glimpse of a different kind of happiness, the one you can only find from within.

Even if I do have some soul-searching to do, there's no denying I had a great time with Jasper yesterday. I laughed, I felt fun; there is such levity and brightness to him. But then Ted feels like this anchor point, drawing me in. And in the map of my mind, all roads lead back to that kiss. He made it clear enough that it was a mistake; I need to forget what happened on the sand. I hope he is OK, though. I would like to know that he is OK.

After warming up in a scalding shower, I get dressed in coral shorts, a white V-neck T-shirt, and vintage gold flats. Still no car on the drive. I decide to take up Sandy on her offer to lend me her bike. It's a beautiful day, only a few miles to Monica's house, and I could use the exercise.

It turns out the road is a lot more uphill than I remember from the car journey, and I'm glowing by the time I knock on the hedgehog-shaped door knocker.

"Ah, Laura, you came, fabulous!" Aunt Monica cries as she opens the door. "Now, I must apologize—I had my facts muddled when I saw you on Friday. It was my nephew Oliver who nearly married a woman who had all those phobias, not Alexander. She was called Annie too, which is where the confusion came from."

"Don't worry," I say as I take off my jacket. "I thought it might be something like that."

"Now, there's someone here who'd like to meet you, and a chocolate log, made fresh today. Kitty, more work for you, dear!"

She leads me through to the chintz-laden sitting room, where another woman is sitting in one of the mustard-colored armchairs, holding a cup and saucer in her hands. I guess her to be in her eighties; her body is of a sturdier physique than Monica's, and she has white hair set into a bob. She is dressed in green corduroy trousers, a neat checked shirt, and a sweater vest with a green enamel peacock brooch pinned to it. Her eyes are gray and glazed; the look of someone who might be blind or partially sighted.

"Laura, this is Sue, your grandmother," says Aunt Monica.

"My grandmother," I say, reaching a hand to my pendant, suddenly, inexplicably nervous to meet Bad Granny.

Sue carefully reaches out a hand to feel for the coffee table next to her, so she can put down her cup and saucer. Then she reaches her empty hands out to me, so I walk toward her and offer up my hands for her to squeeze.

"Laura," she says, as though it is a foreign word. "I met you once, you know, a long time ago."

"You must have been knee-high to a hedgehog," chips in Monica from the kitchen.

Looking at my grandmother's face, there's something so familiar about her. Then I realize what it is: She has my nose, the same narrow bridge and pert tip.

"I have the same nose as you," I blurt out.

She peers at me, squinting her eyes.

"May I see, with my hands?" she asks. "My eyes aren't so good."

I nod, guiding her hand to my face. She runs a finger down the bridge and then gently pinches each side. The last person to touch my nose was probably my mother. Whenever I asked questions about her love life, she'd pinch it gently and say, "All right, Nosy Nora." My grandmother's touch unlocks the memory; I'd forgotten all about Nosy Nora.

"That's certainly a Blampied nose," she says with a nod. "A very fine nose it is too."

"Mum used to say that," I say, softly.

Sue invites me to sit down. She asks how I'm enjoying my first trip to Jersey, which parts of the island I have seen. Her voice is clipped, reminding me of my old headmistress from school. I tell Sue about my mother's album, about me retracing her steps, while Monica listens in from the kitchen, where she is dusting her chocolate log with icing sugar. I explain I came here to write about the coin but confess that the version of the story I was told might not have been accurate. Sue pauses for a moment, reaching out a hand for mine.

"I'm glad you didn't know what really went on. It was all so silly, Laura." Sue sighs. "I'm afraid your mother and I didn't see eye to eye on a few things and, well, time marches relentlessly on without anyone noticing."

"What did you fall out about?" I ask. "Was it money, Dad's will?"

"It wasn't money," Sue says, shaking her head, "well, not any old money. It was that wretched coin—the ha'penny."

Monica comes through from the kitchen with cups of tea for us both.

"When our mother, Margorie, passed away, she wanted her husband's coin buried with her," Monica explains. "But your mother had it and she wouldn't give it back, certainly didn't want it buried in the ground. We were all so raw after Alex's accident . . ." Monica trails off.

"It felt like another thing Annie had taken from us." Sue speaks slowly, but her voice has a resonance to it, as though she is used to having an audience.

"Another thing?" I ask, feeling myself frown.

Sue's face creases into a wince.

"All these years later, it won't hold up to logic. I was a grieving mother and reason gets sent to the back of the queue behind pain and anger. This extra work he took on, the well-paid job in Morocco; he did it all so he could contribute, so he could help Annie. Would he have rushed off otherwise, so soon after the summer season? I'm not sure." Sue shakes her head, and I feel my jaw tense at the implication. "Perhaps that was unfair," she adds quickly, "but I'm just explaining how it was we lost touch. I did write to Annie once, you know, an olive branch of sorts, but she didn't reply. I'm only glad Monica kept the door open all these years, giving you the chance to eventually walk back through."

I kneel down at my grandmother's feet, reaching a hand to my pendant, which now feels like a lead weight around my neck. Everything I thought it represented was wrong. It was the source of more conflict than love, and I don't want it if it wasn't meant for me. I unclip the two pieces of metal from the necklace and press them into my grandmother's hand.

"I'm sorry if my mother took these from you. You should have them back."

Sue feels the pieces between her fingers and starts to cry, a silent trickle glistening between the creases of her pale, papery cheek.

"I can't even see them." Her mouth falls open, and she holds her head in her hand as her face crumples. "I missed knowing my granddaughter over two pieces of silver. I am a foolish Judas."

"Now, now." Monica strides over and puts an arm around her sister's shoulder. "She's here now, no point regretting what's past."

"Yes, I'm here now," I say, reaching out to squeeze my grandmother's hand. "I'm only sorry I didn't ask Mum more questions about you all. I didn't know any of this."

Sue presses the coins back into my palm.

"You must keep them. I have learned my lesson not to put trinkets over flesh and blood."

Her words make me think of my mother, the magpie. She chose the coin for me, over my Jersey family. Have I, like her, been too intent on trying to keep hold of a history, a story, by having something tangible to lock it in? Then again, without the coin, I wouldn't even be here.

Monica brings us all a slice of chocolate log to go with our tea, and the mood shifts to cheerier terrain. Both women want to hear all about my life, about growing up in Bristol, my work, my interests. I end up telling them all about the jewelry Mum and I used to make together, the fairs we'd go to every weekend, hunting out shiny things.

"Perhaps that is the Blampied in you," Sue says fondly, "my father's jeweler streak."

"Well, I think I have a long way to go before I'd be considered a proper Jersey bean," I say. "I've been calling myself Le Ques-ne all my life, I only learned it was pronounced Le Cane this weekend."

Sue finds this so funny that she chokes on her piece of cake, and it takes a good few minutes for her to regain her composure.

After tea, Monica sits down next to me with a photo album she's picked out.

"I've spent the last few years writing people's names on the back of all these old photos. Once we've gone, no one will remember who anyone is otherwise."

She takes me through pages of photos; there are several of William Blampied, who started it all, dressed in his army uniform before he left for the war. There is a picture of William and Margorie's wedding day, at a Jersey church in 1936. Pictures of Sue, Monica, and their brother, Graham, as children on holidays in Greece and France. Finally, we get to pictures of my dad as a child; I've only ever seen a handful of photos of him, and I stare in wonder at eyes so similar to my own, looking back at me from a faded photograph.

"Do shout if this is dull, dear," says Monica.

"It's not dull at all. I know so little about Dad's family. Does your brother, Graham, have children? Do I have cousins?"

"Oh yes, Deidre, Oliver, and James, and they all have children of their own. I'm sure they'll want to meet you."

I have cousins. I have family beyond Gran. The thought brings a lump to my throat.

"Oh, would you mind fetching the box from your car, Monica?" Sue asks, and Monica waves a finger in the air as though remembering it herself.

"I kept a box of your father's things. I suppose I thought you might come for it one day," Sue says.

Monica returns from the car with a battered cardboard box in her arms, and I jump up to help her with it.

"It's probably not much worth keeping, just things I couldn't throw away at the time," Sue explains.

Monica and I open it together. Inside are a few well-thumbed books, mainly thrillers and murder mysteries. School certificates, a journal of handwritten recipes, and a small tin of baby teeth, which makes Monica and me both grimace and then laugh.

"Why do people keep these?" I ask, shaking my head.

"What's that?" asks Sue.

"Teeth," says Monica wrinkling her nose. "Hedgehogs have flat teeth like humans, you know. Some people think they have sharp teeth like rodents, but they don't. They're just like us."

I bite my lip to stop myself from smiling, imagining Monica with tins full of hedgehog teeth hidden all around her house.

This box feels like the remnants of a room thrown hastily together. Beneath the paperback books is a plastic file with an "A" written on the front. It is full of letters, some typed, some handwritten. There are clippings from the *Jersey Evening News*, articles about the coin that I have seen before, and then, unmistakably, my mother's handwriting. Monica pats my shoulder.

"We'll leave Laura in peace to have a looksee, shall we, Sue?" she says, taking her sister by the arm and guiding her through the sliding door, out into the garden. "Birds need feeding in any case."

In the file I find letters my mother sent my father, the bones of their breakup drawn in ink, clipped neatly together. Why would Dad have kept these? There are also letters from him, which she returned unread. He kept everything. The words I read fill the holes in the narrative that no one would explicitly say: Dad did not want me.

As I read, I feel a weight settle on my shoulders. Now I truly understand why Mum lied, why she wanted to paint me a prettier picture, why she didn't stay in touch with his family.

Not only was I not wanted, but the coin I wear, the symbol of their "fairy tale," is in fact what tore the family apart. But if they fought so bitterly over it, how did I end up with both halves?

I fold the letters away. I've read enough. I stretch my arms above my head and look out into the garden, where Sue and Monica are still refilling a bird feeder, one seed at a time.

"Anything of interest?" Monica asks as I walk out to join them.

"They hated each other."

"They didn't," says Sue, as Monica puts an arm around me.

"That summer—I've never seen two people more in love. It might not have lasted, but there was certainly love there," says Monica.

I rub my palms over my eyes, feeling them prickle with emotion.

"I'm sorry, it's just, I thought I was coming to Jersey to write an epic love story. Instead I've found—I don't know—some fantasy my mum invented."

"Right, I think we might need something a bit stronger than tea for this," says Monica, patting me on the back, then she calls toward the kitchen. "Sorry, Kitty, you haven't done the trick this time."

I laugh and wipe my eyes. Aunt Monica helps Sue back inside and then strides through to the kitchen and pulls three glasses from the cupboard. She decants a slosh of dark brown liquid into all three and then tops them up with a splash of ginger beer from the fridge. Trotting through to the living room, she hands one to me and the other to her sister.

"Now, take it from two women with over a dozen decades of experience between us, there's no such thing as a 'happily ever after.' Maybe a 'happy for now,' if you're lucky."

Sue nods in agreement.

"People fight, people break up. It doesn't mean it wasn't

real and it doesn't mean it wasn't worth having, Laura. All these films where people walk off into the sunset at the end and you're led to believe all their problems are over . . ."

"I quite agree," says Sue. "It's a dangerous myth to peddle."

"I prefer action and adventure films myself. Have you seen *Lethal Weapon*? Oh, I do like that series. If you're going to sit down and watch a lot of unrealistic hogwash, it might as well have explosions in it, that's what I always say. Wasn't Mel Gibson such a dish in his day? I was so upset when he died—I lined up all my ornamental pricklers, and we had a Mel movie marathon to mark his passing."

"I don't think he's dead, Monica," says Sue.

"Isn't he? Who am I thinking of then?"

"How am I to know what goes on in your head?" Sue tuts.

I find myself smiling at the sisterly patter between them; it makes me miss Dee.

"Are you married, Laura? Seeing anyone special?" Sue asks.

"No, I'm not. I haven't had much luck with dating recently." I find myself trying to hide a smile. "Though funnily enough, I've met two men since being here."

"*Two?*" both women say in unison, which makes me laugh.

"An island this size, that must be a record," says Sue.

"Well, well, spill the beans, girl," says Monica.

I bite my lip, trying to think what to say.

"Well, one is perfect for me; we've got everything in common, and he seems to like me too—"

"And the other?" asks Monica.

I pause for a moment before answering.

"The other one is more complicated, less suitable, and I don't know if he likes me or not."

"But?"

"But I can't stop thinking about him."

The truth of these words startles me, as I admit to myself how much I am thinking of Ted.

"Well, there's your answer," says Sue, tapping her forehead. "Men are like woodworm. Once they've wheedled their way in, they're almost impossible to get rid of. Even when you've had the wood treated, the holes are there to stay."

I'm not sure this is the most romantic analogy I've ever heard.

"Ah, it's been a while since I've had any woodwormy wood," says Monica wistfully, causing me to splutter on my damson gin.

Declining another round of drinks, I say regretfully that I must go. I need to retrieve my computer, track down my phone, and finalize the photo shoot tomorrow.

"How long are you here for? You will stay in touch, won't you?" says my grandmother. "You should meet Graham's children, your second cousins. You're a Jersey girl at heart, Laura Le Quesne," and she pronounces it *Ques-ne* with a wink.

"I'm not flying back until Wednesday now," I say, squeezing her hand, "and I would love to stay in touch."

"We could talk to Graham about having a meal with his brood, before you go."

Sue turns her head toward Monica, who says, "We'll do some plotting and let you know what we can organize."

The idea alone plants a glow inside me. I always longed for more family, to be part of one of those scenes in Christmas movies when the extended family gets together—everyone brings a different dish and people tease each other, the way Jasper and his sisters do.

"And you will take your father's box?" Sue asks.

I feel like saying I don't want it, that I don't want anything that belonged to my dad now, real or imagined.

"I'm afraid I wouldn't have room to take it on the plane. Plus, I came here on a bike."

But Monica has already picked up the box from the floor and is walking toward the front door with it.

"I'll nip you back in the car, we'll sling your bike in the boot. You'll have a proper look through, see what you want to keep, and throw the rest away. It will all just get put on the pyre when we pop our clogs otherwise. Sue, come on, polish off that piece of cake, and I'll drop you back to yours en route."

My heart sinks at the responsibility of throwing away the last vestiges of a man's life. But then I look up at Sue and Monica, feel the warmth these women have shown me, and think of the family I am yet to meet. Something Ted said comes back to me—about love being a chain letter through the generations. Perhaps Dad and the coin caused a link to break, but now I am here, and I can pick up the pieces of the chain once more.

Chapter 27

We drop Sue off at her house in St. Ouen's village. I untangle myself from the bicycle handlebars to say good-bye and she promises to be in touch. As we pull into Ted's driveway, Monica leans over from the driver's seat and attaches an enamel pin to my jacket. It has a picture of a hedgehog on it, and beneath are the words "I just needle little love."

"There, that's better, isn't it?" she says. "Stay in touch, chickadee. It's nice to know I have more family left out there in the world who don't have prickles, ha-ha!"

"There's one thing I don't understand, Monica," I say before getting out. "How did I come to have both pieces of the coin? In Dad's letters, he didn't want Mum to have it."

"I don't know," she says. "Annie claimed he sent it to her

before the accident, but I'm afraid Sue was never convinced she didn't get it by deceit."

Monica sees my face fall and reaches out to pat my hand. "Don't let the ending ruin their story. They still met through the coin, fell in love, had you, loved you—both of them. The rest? Well"—Monica sighs—"maybe life's more about carving out happy chapters than finding a single happy ending."

She is right, it can't all be about where it ends, and as I look across the car at her, I decide Aunt Monica isn't the least bit mad.

Once I've taken Sandy's bike back to her place, I stow the box of Dad's things in the cottage. I want to change before going out to meet Jasper, but just as I've taken my clothes off, I hear another car on the gravel. Throwing on my dressing gown, I rush over to the window to see who it is. I hope it might be Ted, but it's a black cab, and I squint to see who is inside.

A red-brogued foot stretches out of one door—a perfect made-to-measure camel-colored petite trouser suit, huge sunglasses, the neat black chignon—Suki!

I dart away from the cottage window. I don't know why I'm trying to hide—clearly, she's here to see me. What in the name of Beelzebub is she doing here? Then I remember my lost phone, my unchecked emails. I dare another peek through the window. Suki is sniffing the air as though trying to pick up my scent.

"Suki?" I sidestep away from the window and into the open doorway.

She lifts her sunglasses and squints down at me, then says something to the cabdriver and he turns off the engine.

"Wh-what are you doing here?" I ask, suddenly very aware it's twelve noon and I'm currently wearing a dressing gown.

"Looking for you, Little Miss Missing in Action. I'm glad you at least emailed with your new"—she gestures toward the cottage—"whereabouts."

"That's sweet of you to worry, Suki," I say, folding my arms across my chest. "I lost my phone, but I'm not missing."

"Well, there's been a change of plan, darling—we have a huge suitcase brand that wants to sponsor this story. Travella luggage came on board last night," says Suki, holding up a smart leather holdall. "Love Life US loves it too. They want to use the story for their launch next week, but they want it ASAP, so we need photos today, then we'll send them the whole package with copy on Monday. This is bigger than simply our little family now, Laura. With you going off grid, I thought I needed to come and take control—steer this rudderless ship."

I usher Suki over to the patio furniture outside Ted's place. I'm not going to invite her into the cottage and make her sit on my unmade bed. She brushes off a chair with the back of her hand before sitting down.

"So, is he on board, this chap of yours?" Suki asks. "I was worried for a moment, when you went MIA, that he might have murdered you."

I'm genuinely touched.

"Ah, right, no, definitely alive. I've literally been offline for about"—I look for my watch, but it's not there—"well, less than eighteen hours. But in answer to your question, yes, Jasper is on board."

"Good, though a murder piece might have got us some clicks too, hey?" She tries to grin, at least I think it's a grin; it looks like a hiccup got stuck in her nostrils. "I jest, Laura; I'm immensely pleased you haven't been murdered."

I laugh politely, nervously knitting my fingers in my lap. I can't believe Suki is here, in Jersey, for *my* suitcase story.

"The most important thing now is the photo shoot. I want to be in and out of this wilderness by tomorrow afternoon." Suki gives the sea a distasteful look, brushing down her jacket, as though worried the air here might damage the fabric.

"Dionne and Saul flew out with me; they went straight to scout locations as we weren't sure what you'd lined up. Oh, and my man at the *Mail* has already said they'll run it alongside a feature on our US launch." Suki claps her hands. "You couldn't have timed this thing better if I'm honest, Laura. So, what have you organized?"

I can't admit that I haven't planned anything yet because I spent yesterday discovering my parents' love story was a lie, kissing two different men, attempting to live out a cabin-themed date fantasy, attending a sixty-fifth birthday party, and then making whimsical jewelry late into the night.

"I'm sorry, Suki. I— What with persuading Jasper, and getting to know him, then losing my phone, I'm afraid the details of the shoot haven't been locked in yet—I thought the team wouldn't be arriving until tomorrow."

Suki nods toward the cottage with a smirk.

"He's in there, is he?"

"Oh no, no!" I shake my head. Oh great, she thinks I'm in my dressing gown because I've just been lounging around having sex all morning. "He's not here. I was just changing my clothes because I've been out exercising."

Suki looks suspicious.

"Well, I'm glad you've been having some delicious 'exercise' time with your new beau. Maybe you'll be less of a Moping Morag around the office now you've got yourself a ticket back to orgasm town."

I make a pained mumbling noise. I really don't need to talk to my employer about thc status of my travel arrangements to orgasm town.

"Well, anyway, I must get on," Suki says, getting to her feet, "cab's waiting. You take an hour for this," she waves a hand at my face. "Get yourself . . . presentable. Here's my spare phone," she says, taking a smartphone from her bag, "so we can stay in comms and you can bring your beau up to speed."

"Jasper was keen to do the shoot at his house," I say, feeling nervous to suggest it. "He sells kitchens."

"Laura, this isn't an opportunity to *sell* things. This is a story of true love, of two people brought together by destiny!" Suki throws up her hands.

"A little reciprocal PR would make sure he's definitely on board, and tagging more brands would gain us more cross-post content." I give her a hopeful grin.

Suki sighs. "Fine, give me the address. We'll recon at his house at fourteen hundred hours, style you there, do some nicely lit couple photos, then head to the airport and beaches for coverage shots. Don't you worry, Laura, we'll keep your boy sweet."

As soon as Suki's gone, I pick up the phone she left me and download my contacts from the cloud. There are so many people I need to call. First, I ring Jasper and update him on the new plan for this afternoon; he sounds delighted, then says he must hurry off to "prepare the space." Then I text Dee and Vanya to let them know I lost my phone and am staying in

Jersey a few more days. I hover over Ted's number. After changing my mind several times, I eventually send him a text saying simply: Are you OK? x Laura. Finally, I call Gran, just in case she's been worrying about me, which of course she has. I reassure her I'm fine and then fill her in on my meeting with Bad Granny this morning.

"Gran, there's one thing I don't understand: How did I come to have both halves of the coin?" I ask her.

"Oh, that blasted coin!" she says. "They argued about it for years, a lawyer even came knocking once—it was all deeply unpleasant."

"Why did she care so much, when it ended like it did?" I ask.

"She felt the coin was a part of your story as much as it was Margorie's. She believed she must have found it for a reason—she didn't want to let it go." Gran sighs, and I hear the sound of her Sudoku pencil tapping against the handset. "Before he left for Morocco, out of the blue, Alex sent her the other half, saying he wanted it to be yours, that the pieces should stay together."

My eyes begin to itch. He'd wanted me to have it.

"I'm sorry I didn't tell you any of this sooner, Laurie. Sometimes it feels better not to look backward, to let the past stay in the past. When are you coming home?"

"I'm going to stay a few more days actually, Gran, I-I've kind of met someone."

"Have you now," Gran says, instantly sounding more cheerful. "There must be something in the water on that island, I tell you. What's his name then?"

And for a moment, I pause, because I don't know which name I want to say.

TIGER WOMAN ON OBLIGATION

As women, we spend so much of our lives feeling obliged. Obliged to show up when we say we will, obliged to turn up with a smile, obliged to tell everyone, "I am fine." But obligated is just another word for oppressed. The only person you are obligated to is yourself.

Chapter 28

I'm rapidly running out of clothes. The legs of my capri pants are now dry, and they're probably the smartest trousers I have with me. If I wear them with my backless gray silk blouse, Suki will hopefully deem me smart enough. Changed and made up, I'm about to leave the cottage when Ilídio comes over holding something large and square in his arms.

"I just finished it," he said, holding it out for me to see. "Is this how you imagined it?"

I press all my fingers to my lips. It is perfect. He's made a memory cabinet to hang on the wall: a wooden frame, full of tiny drawers and shelves to stow trinkets and mementos in. I've read about them but have never seen one in real life, so I just drew how I thought it should look. They are a way to keep memories of a person or a place, a distillation of details, which can be displayed almost as a piece of art.

"It's beautiful, just how I imagined it. This must have taken you hours."

"It did, but when you said it was for Ted, well— It's a great idea." Ilídio glances across at me. "He's lucky to have someone like you come into his life."

Sans Ennui is still empty, but I leave the cabinet just inside the porch with a note:

Ted, something to hold the best memories of this house in. Thank you for everything, Laura

I'm waiting in the driveway for the cab I've ordered to take me to Jasper's when Ted's car pulls in. I freeze when I see him, every inch of my body remembering our last encounter. He gets out of the driver's side and walks purposefully toward me. He looks a mess, as though he's slept in his car.

"Hi," I say, my voice coming out as a croak.

"Hey," he says, resting one hand awkwardly on his hip; the other briefly massages between his brows. He does not meet my gaze. It's ridiculous—he has been gone less than twenty-four hours, I have only known him a few days, but I realize I have missed him, missed his face.

"I'm sorry I left yesterday—after the beach."

"It's fine," I say, waving a hand as though to brush it off as nothing.

"I tried to call you—"

He called me.

"I lost my phone," I explain. "I'm sorry I didn't give you the letter straightaway. It was none of my business." He doesn't correct me, but when he finally looks up and meets my gaze—it's all still there, the kablammo that makes my entire body fizz. "Did you call Belinda?"

"Yes," he says. A wave of disappointment washes over me—but of course he did.

A taxi pulls in behind Ted's car. He turns toward it.

"You're going," he says, more statement than question.

"I have this work thing, a photo shoot."

"With Jasper." He shifts his gaze to the ground. He looks so tired. We stand in silence for a moment, and I stare at his forehead, willing him to look up and say the right thing, but I don't even know what it is that I want to hear. What could he possibly say that would make any of this simple?

"You still think he's the man the universe sent you?" he asks, eyes finally coming back to meet mine.

"I don't know," I say, honestly, "but the way we met is a good story. My boss has flown out here this morning and wants to feature us on the website, and I—" I want to say, *"in the absence of anything else,"* but worry that wouldn't make me sound great, like I'm a monkey, swinging from vine to vine, just looking for someone to hold on to.

"A messed-up old cabdriver isn't as good a story," says Ted, scuffing the gravel with his shoe.

"Ted, I wasn't under the impression the messed-up old cabdriver was even an option. We kissed, and then you disappeared to call your wife, who you're still clearly in love with. It's nothing to do with the 'better story,' I'm not that shallow. Anyway, you're not even a real cabdriver, or especially old."

His mouth twitches into a smile.

"I'm not in love with her anymore, Laura. She just left frayed ends that we needed to discuss." He pauses, rubbing his palm against his neck. "I'm sorry I disappeared; I didn't know how to react to what happened." He lets out a heavy sigh as though he's waiting for me to speak. When I don't, he says, "Laura, my life is a mess. Did you know I haven't been to the hospital where I work for four months? I'm on a leave of absence."

My face must register surprise, because he gives me a rueful nod, "My hand started shaking, I didn't feel safe in an operating theater. My mind went straight to what Dad has, and if it was that, I didn't want to know. The whole career I had planned would be over before it even began. So, I didn't tell anyone why I needed time off. I finally saw a doctor a few weeks ago—she told me the shaking was down to stress. I'd worked myself up so much about what it might have been, I'd only made it worse."

"Oh Ted, I'm so sorry you've been dealing with that." I take a step toward him, to give him a hug, but he holds up a palm, as though to tell me to wait, he hasn't finished.

"I've got to sort out a divorce, I need to sell this house quickly to pay for Dad's care . . ." He exhales a long, slow breath and closes his eyes. "I can't be saddled with the expectation of being someone's romantic hero too. I met you three days ago, what promises can I possibly make you?"

The words hit me like a punch to my chest.

"Of course not." I feel my cheeks burn. "It was just a kiss, Ted, I don't expect anything from you."

I make to walk up the grass to the waiting cab, not wanting my face to betray my disappointment. As I pass him, Ted reaches for my hand and pulls me around to face him.

"It wasn't just a kiss to me," he says firmly, his voice low. Searching his eyes, I see something I never want to let go of. Then his gaze drops to my arm, and he notices the bracelet I'm wearing.

"What's this?" he asks, gently lifting my arm toward him so he can see.

"I made it last night, from the jewelry you gave me."

"You put the sea glass into it."

I nod. He turns the bracelet around on my wrist and, where his thumb touches my skin, I burn with a need for him to touch me again.

"You did all this wiring yourself?" he asks, running a finger around the silver wire.

I nod again.

"It's beautiful," he says, but he's not looking at the bracelet anymore; he's looking at me.

"What do you want me to do, Ted?" I ask quietly, my heart pounding against my chest. There's a glimmer of hope in his eyes, but then it vanishes.

"Do you want me to ask you not to go, to give up your great suitcase story?" he says, his voice hoarse. "I can't offer you anything concrete, Laura. All I know is that I like spending time with you. I'd like to get to know you better. You're the first person who I've wanted to kiss in ages, and that's a big deal for me." Ted slides his hand down my arm to hold my hand again. "I guess with me you get a different type of baggage—and it won't look so great on the cover of a magazine."

I close my eyes, my fingers weave between his. The feel of his skin, like a warm sea that I want to cover every part of me.

"My boss is in Jersey, Ted. It's all set up. I can't let them all down at the last minute."

He drops my hand, and my skin goes cold.

"You're right. It isn't worth losing your job over."

His words sting.

"If I hadn't met you, Jasper and I would work," I say, almost angrily. "We have everything in common, he's my age, he's single—he's . . ." I groan in frustration, not sure what I'm saying, or why I feel angry.

"I get it. You don't need to explain. I shouldn't have made things more complicated for you."

The cabdriver beeps his horn.

"Look, Ted"—I close my eyes, trying to think—"just let me get this shoot out the way. It's not like I'm marrying the guy—it's a few photos. There's nothing to stop you and I getting to know each other better after that. We could meet up in London when you're back."

"You'd be telling the world that this is the man you've fallen for," says Ted. "You really want to do that, if it's not true?"

Before I can reply, he brushes a hand through his hair and glances back up the hill to my waiting cab. Then he kicks the grass, turns, and walks toward the house. I'm left watching his broad back retreat from my reach. The judgment implicit in his words fuels my anger.

"Maybe some girls need more than a 'hey, let's hang out,' Ted!" I call after him in frustration. "I can't risk my whole future on a 'maybe.'"

Ted turns at the top of the garden, his jaw clenched. "You want me to turn up here in a horse-drawn carriage with a dozen roses? Maybe some fireworks in the sky spelling out how I feel? Laura, I like you and I think you like me. I'd hoped that would be enough for now."

He turns to go into the house, not even waiting for me to respond. I clench my fists and run to the waiting cab. Of course I don't need fireworks and roses, what an arsehole thing to say. But he's expecting me to let everyone down, stand up poor Jasper—who's been nothing but kind to me—all for a "I kind of like you," like we're seven years old or something? Plus, Ted's life *is* a complete mess. I bite my lip so hard it hurts. I do feel terrible for him about his work situation, the stress he must be under, and I wish I could just go back and give him a hug—make sure he's OK.

I dial Dee's number on the phone Suki lent me. I need to make things right with her, and talking will distract me from fretting about Ted.

"Hey, it's Laura," I say.

"Oh, hi." Her voice is cool.

"So, um, I was just calling because I wanted to ask your opinion on the partisan nature of the way Supreme Court judges are appointed in the US. Do you think the system should be reviewed, especially when a nomination comes up during an election year?"

"You did not call to ask me that." I can hear Dee smiling over the phone.

"I did! I read an article about it and it's fascinating, especially when you compare it to our own judicial system in the UK. I thought we could thrash out a solution between us, you know, two intelligent women, not talking about men."

"I would love to talk to you about that, and I know that's your version of an apology."

"Oh, Dee, don't be angry. I'm sorry for what I said about Neil—of course I don't think you settled. I love Neil—the way he talks about you with such pride, how he bought you a laminator for Christmas and you thought it was the best present ever. You are perfect for each other; I'm the relationship screwup here."

Dee sighs. "I'm sorry if I overreacted. Look, I love Neil, but sometimes it's hard not to be jealous of all the excitement you get to have being single. I haven't had half the drama in my lifetime that you've had on this one weekend away."

"Dee, I'd swap all this drama for a good man who loves me any day of the week."

"So, how's it all going to end? This episode of *Laura Land*," Dee's voice has softened. "I hope there is a happily ever after in there somewhere?"

"Well, Suki is here in Jersey. Would you believe it? She flew out this morning. I think plot-wise I could use a tornado, a house to land on her, and then some red slippers to get me home."

"Or a minor alien invasion? Ooh, a body swap comedy where you *become* Suki? Now that I'd watch."

"I think I'd rather have the alien invasion—anyway I should go, wish me luck, love you."

"Love you too."

After saying good-bye to Dee, I see I have a message from Vanya, warning me Suki is on her way to Jersey. I reply:

She already found me—I'm going to meet her now. Fear I've found myself in a bit of a Katniss/Gale/Peeta situation . . .

She'll know what that means, Vanya loves The Hunger Games books.

Vanya: Which one is Suki? Peeta?

This makes me laugh.

Laura: No, Suki's not a part of it. Well, maybe she's Snow.

Vanya: I'm Team Gale all the way. On a date right now, but will call to hear all when he leaves. The fish miss you, as do I. X

At Jasper's place, I find the rest of the team already there. Dionne and Saul have set up a lighting rig in the Malala kitchen. Suki is chatting away to Jasper as if they are old friends. I overhear them having a conversation about the advantages of polymer resin work surfaces. Jasper is wearing a fitted black T-shirt with ContessaKitchens.com written across the front in pink writing. As I walk over to them, Suki picks up the picture of Henry Cavill on the stag do, which is next to her on the side.

"See, Laura, not so hard to find, is it?"

"I'm not sure I can let you have that, though, Suki. I would need to ask the chaps if it's OK," Jasper says, shifting his weight.

"Oh, Jasper, don't be such an old prude," Suki says, pouting at him and then prodding his chest with a finger.

Jasper actually blushes and then says quietly to me, "She's hard to say no to, isn't she?"

I don't have time to respond, as Dionne pulls me into a chair and starts tugging at my hair.

"Makeover time!" cries Saul. "This is like the part of the movie where Dionne turns you from Plain Jane into Hot Hilary, and you *finally* get the guy." He winks.

"I don't think anyone would describe Laura as a Plain

Jane," Dionne says, and I see her roll her eyes at Saul in the reflection of the portable makeup mirror she's set up. "I've been looking forward to seeing what you look like with a full face of decent slap, though."

"Don't go too Kardashian, will you?" I ask, feeling myself frown.

"Sacrilege," Dionne hisses at me, but then she pulls out a makeup palette the size of a Ping-Pong table.

Jasper comes over and hands me a coffee, then goes for a kiss on the lips but misses slightly, and it's a half cheek, half lip smack. Saul cocks his head and hugs himself, as though swooning at how cute we are.

"I'm sorry about this circus, Jasper," I say quietly.

"It's fine, I enjoy a circus," he says, then he leans over and picks up three apples from a perfectly styled fruit bowl and starts juggling with them while pretending to walk an imaginary tight rope. "I was born for the circus!"

Saul laughs, Dionne claps, and even Suki smiles in approval. I can tell they all like him; he's very easy to like. I think of all the *How Did You Meet?* couples I've interviewed this year, and wonder if any of them ever had doubts they didn't vocalize at the time. I wonder how many of those couples are still together.

Twenty minutes later, my hair has been styled to within an inch of its life. I'm wearing what feels like a cement mixer's worth of makeup, highlighter, contouring cream, and who knows what else. Looking in the mirror, I think, *Well, at least no one will recognize me.*

"Right." Suki claps her hands. "New plan. Laura, we're

going to broadcast a little interview live from the website, to trail the full write-up to come. The Travella marketing team loved the idea of a live *How Did You Meet?* with you both. So, we'll knock that off first, then move on to the stills shots. Oh, and when you're telling the story about the bag, you must make sure you mention the brand name—Travella. There are a few other brand partnerships I've added in there too—if you could say how much you love the smell of Colton Rouge products, Jasper's preferred toiletry brand, plus socks from Greeves—"*Where the discerning gentleman buys his footwear.*"

She's throwing this on me at the last minute, so I don't have time to object that my genuine *How Did You Meet?* story is being turned into some kind of shopping channel infomercial. She pushes the case full of products in front of us, and then starts counting down to live while Saul mans the camera phone on a tripod.

Jasper whispers in my ear, "You look gorgeous by the way."

"Good afternoon to all you romantics out there." Suki beams to the camera. "Now, our regular viewers will be used to hearing Laura Le Quesne's voice hosting these interviews—she's tracked down some of the most romantic meet-cutes out there. But today's live broadcast is a little different—because this time, Laura finds herself on the other side of the camera. Laura, Jasper, tell us"—Suki leaves a dramatic pause—"how did you meet?"

Before I can speak, Jasper jumps in.

"Well, it all started when our eyes met across a crowded concourse at Gatwick Airport. I saw this beautiful creature, and I just knew."

I frown, then try to stop frowning, aware of the camera

picking up every expression I make. Jasper's not telling it right. The whole reason it's a great story is because I found the suitcase first, that the contents led me to him, not that our "eyes met across a crowded concourse."

"Of course, being British, I didn't know how to ask her out at the time, but destiny wasn't going to let my reserve get the better of us." Jasper shoots a smoldering look to the camera and smooths down his T-shirt to make sure the lettering of his website is fully visible.

"Right, yes, but really the story began when I picked up the wrong suitcase at the airport," I say, attempting to get the narrative back on track. "I only realized it wasn't mine when I got to my hotel room. At first, I was annoyed I didn't have my case. But then I found all these things in the bag, these possessions that spoke to me. I thought it had to be a sign."

Why did I agree to this? I thought it was going to be a few photos; speaking to a camera feels like much more of a commitment.

"What was in the Travella case, Laura?" asks Suki, wide-eyed, willing me to keep performing.

"Well, there was a book of piano music—Phil Collins, I've always loved Phil—and—"

Jasper starts singing "In the Air Tonight." Out of frame, Suki flaps her hands at him angrily but says lightly, "Ha-ha, I don't think we have clearance for song lyrics, Jasper. What else was in the case, Laura, tell us about the Colton Rouge?"

Saul is making a face at me from behind the camera, as though he's watching his favorite cashmere jumper get tumble-dried. Dionne is leaning against the wall, watching Jasper as though he's a box full of newborn puppies.

"Oh right." My heart sinks down into a puddle inside of me, where it finds my soul squatting like a miserably deflated balloon animal. "I just love the smell of Colton Rouge, and I knew any man who had such great taste in toiletries had to be the man for me."

Now I sound like a complete wally. Who goes for a guy based on their discerning taste in fragrances? Then I remember my checklist, all the things I thought were so important, like being well dressed, musical, having the same tastes as me. Jasper gives my arm a squeeze, as though he senses I've lost enthusiasm for the sales pitch and is nudging me to keep the energy up.

"I've also got great socks," cuts in Jasper with a click of his fingers.

Suki is shooting daggers at me, probably because I've stopped smiling.

My hands ball into fists, a bead of sweat trickles down my back, my breathing grows shallow. All these years I've defended my job, focused on the positive elements and ignored the parts that made me uncomfortable. Suki says we're all one big happy family, but now I see her scowling across at me, I know she doesn't have a single motherly feeling toward me. Any loyalty I felt going through with this shoot for her sake was entirely misplaced.

To keep my hands still, I thrust them into the pockets of my trousers. My fingers find the blue sea glass, the mermaid's tear Ted gave me on the beach. I rub the surface of the stone between my fingers.

"The moment Laura and I met to exchange our bags, right here, in this gorgeous Contessa Kitchen, with all these bespoke fixtures and fittings, I saw straightaway how much we had in common." Jasper grins at me.

He really is lovely, and sweet and incredibly good-looking, in a Christian Bale, Ken doll sort of way.

But he is not Ted.

And "I like you" from Ted *is* enough.

Never mind the fact that Ted can't promise me anything beyond today. I'd rather have one day with him, even if it leads nowhere, than spend my time with anyone else. And maybe I'll lose my job, and I have no idea what to do next, but as the proverbial Gerry said—maybe that's OK.

Suki coughs.

"What have you got there, Laura, what are you fiddling with?" Suki says in a trying-not-to-sound-furious-because-we're-live-but-clearly-bloody-furious voice.

Everything is suddenly so clear to me, but how am I going to get out of this without hurting Jasper? He has gone along with all this; I cannot walk out or admit my doubts live on air. If anyone is going to be embarrassed here, it should be me, not him. So, I say the one thing I know will kill the interview dead, that will make Suki cut the live feed immediately.

"I'm sorry, I can't in good conscience go along with this deceit. It isn't true, it isn't real," I say, taking a deep breath. "Neither of us had Travella bags—they were John Lewis's own label."

TIGER WOMAN ON INSTINCT

Half of the battle is knowing what you want. When you know what you want, you can pounce on it with four paws. If you don't know: Stop. Breathe. Look. Smell. Tiger Women have senses, instincts. Use them.

Chapter 29

"Agghhh!" Suki screams. "Cut, cut, cut!" She leaps from her chair, launching herself at Saul, knocking the camera phone and tripod to the floor, where she and Saul then scrabble around to end the transmission.

"What?" Jasper looks at me with confusion.

"I'm so, so sorry, Jasper, but I can't do this. I've just realized I have feelings for someone else. I can't be a part of this interview."

"Laura Le Quesne, what the hell are you playing at?" Suki fumes, picking herself back up off the floor and dusting down her trouser suit with both hands. "Are you having a seizure? What am I witnessing here?"

"I'm sorry, Suki, I don't want to lie anymore," I say,

looking at her through unblinking tiger eyes. Though I have only skim-read it, and it's not a book I would have chosen myself, some of Tiger Woman's philosophy must have resonated because suddenly I don't want to feel obliged; I don't want to be polite; I don't care if I end up alone; I just want to listen to my gut and be the version of myself I am when I'm with Ted—raw and unfiltered.

"Who? Who do you have feelings for?" Jasper asks, a look of bewilderment on his face. "I thought this was all going so well. We have so much in common."

"I know, it was and we do. You've been so lovely and kind and I really have enjoyed spending time with you, but I think sometimes the heart doesn't make any sense at all."

"Right," says Suki, striding toward me. "We'll blame the interview outage on some kind of interference. Let's start it again, we won't do it live, we'll salvage it in the edit."

"No," I say, squeezing Jasper's hand and then walking past Suki, away from the lights.

"No?" she says in angry bemusement.

"I won't do this interview. I'm sorry, Suki."

"Laura, don't be childish. If we don't deliver this, you'll be letting down the whole Love Life family, not just me. Think of your colleagues, of *their* jobs." Suki's face looks as though it's trying to make a conciliatory expression, but her eyes are shooting arrows at me.

"I'm sorry, Suki, but no, you can't control this one." I shrug. "I want to write real stories again, I want to write things that are true, not just 'brandable content,' and if that means leaving Love Life, well, then so be it."

Dionne is staring at me, unblinking in disbelief. Saul is fanning himself briskly with a hand, as though all this drama is causing him to overheat.

"After all I've done for you!" Suki snarls. "Well, don't come crying to me when no one wants to read your 'truth,' Laura. The truth is boring. People want to buy a dream, not be reminded of reality."

"You're wrong—I think all any of us want in this world is something real."

Picking up my handbag, I head for the door. I have nothing more to say. My legs are shaking, and I need to focus on putting one foot in front of the other, to walk in a straight line.

Once I'm in the hall, I hear Jasper calling after me.

"Laura, I don't understand. What happened in there? I was going to name a kitchen after you," he says, with wounded eyes.

"That's so sweet of you, but you know, I don't think I'm kitchen material, Jasper. I'm really more of a living room girl."

Jasper is still looking at me like a puppy, and I do owe him more of an explanation. I close my eyes, searching for the words, and when I open them, I say, "You know you told me how all your family wanted you to stay in law, that being a lawyer was the right fit for you, a sensible career. But you just had this feeling—about kitchens, this calling." Jasper frowns, trying to follow what I'm saying. "This guy, Ted, I've just realized, he's kitchens for me."

Jasper rubs his chin with his hand, his eyes darting left to right as he processes what I'm saying.

"And I'm law?"

I nod, giving him an apologetic smile.

He puts a hand on my shoulder, looks me in the eyes and

says, with all sincerity, "Well, you go get your kitchens then," and then he raises his fist in the air, as though he's an American football coach, sending me out to the field.

I don't know how I'm going to get back to L'Étacq without waiting here for a cab. I run out into the road, flagging down a car as I go, hoping the island's hospitality stretches to hitchhikers. The first car around the bend pulls in, and I run to get into a purple Ford Fiesta, driven by a woman in her thirties with curly red hair and a gray whippet on the backseat.

In my haste to get across the road, I'm nearly hit by a car coming the other way. It screeches to a halt, and I thump both my hands on the bonnet, shouting with fear and fury, "Hey, watch it!" at the driver. Then I see who is driving—Ted. He jumps out, leaving the driver door open, the engine still running.

"What are you doing here?" I ask, my breath quickening, my heart pounding against my chest.

"I've come to make a grand gesture," he says, running around to the front of the car to meet me. "The cabinet you left me— Laura, I love it, it's the nicest present anyone has ever given me." He runs a hand through his hair, his eyes earnest. "I was being a coward. I know I've only known you three days, and I know I'm a mess, but—pick me, let me be the one who tries to make you happy. Am I too late?" Ted grins, a sheepish grin. "I'm ready to burst in there and challenge your Suitcase Man to a duel if need be."

"I don't need to be dueled over, thank you, and you're too late anyway," I say. "I walked out."

"You walked out? What about your job?"

"I'll find another one, one that doesn't involve selling my soul or being with the wrong person." I shrug.

Almost before I've finished speaking, Ted takes me in his arms and kisses me, and every particle of my body melts into joyful jelly. After an irresponsible amount of time spent kissing in the path of oncoming traffic, I apologize to the red-haired woman for holding her up, and Ted and I climb into his cab, grinning at each other.

"I need to shower when we get home, I must look ridiculous with so much makeup and all this hairspray," I say, reaching up to scrunch the bouffant blond helmet of hair.

"Home?" Ted says, a grin stretching from ear to ear.

"Well, you know, the fisherman's cottage—home for now."

Ted pulls the car into gear and starts driving up the hill, away from St. Ouen's.

"Where are we going?" I ask, turning to look at the road behind us.

"I thought you wanted a grand gesture?" says Ted.

"I thought storming into the interview was going to be the grand gesture?"

He shakes he head and reaches out a hand to hold mine.

"Nope."

Ted drives us back to Plémont, to the place where the hotel used to be, where my parents spent that first summer falling in love.

"Ted, what are we doing here?" I ask, looking at the deserted headland.

He runs around and gets a box from the trunk and then, with his hands full, beckons me with a sideways nod of the head.

"OK, I don't have a lot of experience with grand gestures, so I might have got this completely wrong," he says. "Will you just close your eyes while I set something up?"

I smile at how nervous he is. I'm not sure the grandest of romantic gestures start with someone being told to close their eyes so close to a cliff edge, but I go with it. If he asks me to walk anywhere with my eyes closed, I might have to voice my safety concerns.

Then music starts to play from a sound system—"One More Night" by Phil Collins.

I open my eyes, and Ted is holding out an arm, beckoning me over. He takes my hand, and we walk up the path together. My face aches from smiling.

"I thought you hated Phil Collins."

"I do," he says. "But if you love him, I'll allow my ears to be assaulted once in a while."

On the flat plateau of grass, he's marked a large rectangle out on the ground with silver tape.

"This is where the old dance hall used to be; I looked up the plans."

"You didn't!"

Then he draws me into his arms, and we dance cheek to cheek on the cliff top to one of my favorite songs, and the air is pure magic. How did I not realize earlier—that it was Ted all along?

"So how did I do?" he says quietly in my ear. "Grand enough?"

"Perfect," I reply. "Just the right amount of effort, without being over the top."

"A live band would have been too much then?"

"Yeah, that would have been too much," I say, tilting my face to look up into his eyes.

"Do you think your own kids will be on this cliff top in thirty years' time, dancing to Phil Collins, trying to replicate the most romantic night of *their* mother's life?"

"You're backing yourself then, if you think this is the most romantic night of my life," I say, pressing my tongue into my cheek.

"Damn, I knew I should have gone for the band," he says, and I swallow a laugh as I lean my head against his shoulder.

"Seriously, though, I think I've learned not to hold on to other people's love stories too tightly," I say. "That it's not the story that's important."

Ted holds me tighter, an electric charge coursing between us, and I tilt my head, allowing my lips to find his.

Back at L'Étacq, Ted's house is empty, so we walk down to the fisherman's cottage. Ted has brought food to cook us, Jersey Royals and lobster from the fishery at the north end of the bay. Scamp bounds across the wall and jumps up at Ted.

"Hey, Scamp," Ted says, picking him up and nuzzling his face into the top of the dog's head.

"You made it then?" Sandy calls over the wall, a delighted grin on her ruddy round face.

"He did," I say, but we can't stop for small talk now. Ted puts Scamp down, and I pull him inside, the bag of food left on the side, then drag him over to the bed.

"We're going to do this now, are we? I'm not going to wine and dine you first?" he asks, his voice low, his firm hands clasped around my waist.

"Oh, I think the Phil Collins cliff-top move is all the wining and dining you'll ever need to do, Ted Palmerston," and then I let out an involuntary squeal as I feel his hand caress the skin on my back.

"Do you want me to stop?" he asks, his face creasing with concern.

"No, no, I definitely don't want you to stop—that was a good squeal, sorry."

He slowly unbuttons my blouse and we lie on the bed, his hands gently stroking my waist. I reach up to pull off his shirt, desperate to feel his bare body against mine. He leans forward and I feel the thrust of him beneath his jeans. A shiver of anticipation arcs through me. I want to be in control, so I roll over, straddling him, rolling my hips against his, pressing his hands above his head.

"Where did you come from?" he says, his voice heavy, his eyes following mine, as though marveling at me. I bend down to kiss his chest, wanting to lay claim to every inch of him. "I haven't—I haven't done this in a while," he says, sounding as though he is desperately trying to stay in control.

"I'm sure you'll remember what to do," I say with a breathy laugh as I start unbuttoning his jeans. *Wow, Ted is definitely no Ken doll.*

He reaches both his arms beneath mine and pulls me up to his eye level.

"I want to see your face—" he murmurs, as his body presses against mine, removing any air between us.

Then, even though there aren't any cameras, we have *the movie sex*. You know that bit where you see a close-up of a man kissing a woman's neck, and it's all low lighting and dewy skin;

that happens. The shot of the man's rippling back muscles tensing as the woman's hands clasp around his whole body with her fingers spread wide; that happens. The part where the woman's toes stretch out and curl in orgasmic bliss; that happens, three times. We even move to the shower and do that scene where you see a hand press against the glass and then it swipes down the steam, because, you know, the shower is steamy but so is what's happening inside. If I died this second, I'd want my gravestone to read: *Died happy having the movie sex.*

Afterward, as we lie there entangled in each other's arms, glowing with perspiration, I say, "That was pretty awesome, right? It's not just me?"

Ted laughs and kisses my head. "That was, indeed, awesome."

"Is that how you usually do it?" I ask.

"What do you mean?"

"I mean, are you always that good?"

Ted takes his hand from behind my head and sits up; his forehead furrows into single line. "I don't know, Laura, it's not a competition."

"No, I didn't mean for you to compare, I just meant—maybe you're just really good at sex, and I'm the one who's been doing it wrong all these years."

Ted gives me a friendly scowl and reaches out to lay his hand on top of mine. "I don't think that's possible." Then he turns onto his side, leans over and lays a trail of hot kisses up my neck before whispering in my ear, "You are spectacular. You have woken me up, and I never want to be asleep again."

Chapter 30

I think he was talking metaphorically, because he does sleep—spooned against my back, while I struggle to drift off. I could never sleep with someone spooning me, but I don't want to let go of him, so I just lie there, awake, a giant grin plastered on my face, wondering how long I have to wait before I can wake him up by kissing his neck. In the morning, after we've indulged in another extremely satisfying movie marathon, showered, and dressed, Ted cooks up the meal he bought us last night. I'm not convinced I'm going to fancy lobster for breakfast, but when he presents it on toast with eggs on the side, it turns out I'm ravenous.

Ted points out the fisheries on the headland, visible from the house, a converted bunker built for war but now the site of fresh fish barbecues and rosé by the sea. I think of the history that bunker has seen, and I feel briefly disappointed that I won't be writing my foodie mini-break article for Love Life now. Food is clearly taken seriously here, and so much history seasons every plate.

Ted and I sit at the patio table and between mouthfuls just gaze at each other as though if we blink, the other person might disappear.

I glance over to the next-door garden.

"This is where Sandy comes out and says 'Morning!' in that voice she does," I say.

He nods. "The number of times I've had Sandy give me that knowing 'Morning,' I should put up a higher wall."

"You've cooked lobster breakfasts for a lot of lady friends, have you?" I ask, raising an eyebrow at him.

"I doubt there would have been a cooked breakfast when we were teenagers," he says. "My culinary skills are pretty limited now, let alone back then."

"Your parents were fine with you having girls sleep over? Growing up, Mum never let me have a guy in my room with the door closed, even when I brought boyfriends home from university."

Mentioning my mum instantly puts her face in my mind, and I think how much she would have liked Ted—his easy demeanor, his complete lack of pretension, how thoughtful he is. It seems wrong that she went to her grave thinking Aaron is who I ended up with; Aaron, who put the handbrake on at junctions. Then again, perhaps she knew me better than I knew myself and sensed that he would not be a long chapter.

"I think when we were teenagers, it was more about sleeping out in the dunes than bringing people home," Ted says, shifting in his chair. "So, what would you like to do today? I'll take you anywhere."

"I'm going to help you clean the house, get it finished."

"That doesn't sound like a great way to spend the day—there's so much of the island I haven't shown you yet."

He reaches out to cover my hand with his, and I don't think I've ever felt this contented in my entire life. How can everything change, in a weekend? Then we hear a voice from across the wall.

"Morning!" Sandy says, standing right there, hand on hip, a clownish smile of satisfaction that her matchmaking ambitions have come to fruition.

"Do you want to join us?" Ted asks, leaning back in his chair. I catch a glimpse of his chest beneath his linen shirt, and a flash of what we were doing earlier this morning sends a tingle of heat across my skin.

"I wouldn't think to intrude," she says, making wide, embarrassing eyes at us both.

"Sandy, I assume the incredible cabinet Laura gave me is Ilídio's work?" Ted asks.

"He told me Laura had a big hand in the design," she says.

"It's now my favorite object in the entire house," Ted says, turning back to look at me with a twinkle in his eyes.

"It's pretty much the only object in the house," I say, following his eyes with mine. I love that I can just stare at him now. I don't have to look away; I can just shamelessly stare at his ludicrously attractive face.

After breakfast, we set to work clearing the house, and I help Ted pull out a few of the small objects he wants to keep, things that will fit in the little drawers and windows of the memory cabinet.

"I thought this compartment could be for one of your mother's patchouli bags," I suggest, "and this one could hold a few pieces of her sea glass collection—"

"I think I prefer seeing the sea glass on you," he says, pulling me into his arms.

"Come, on, we'll never get this finished if you keep distracting me," I say, nudging him away with my head. "These little shelves here," I say, pointing to two of the rectangular openings at the bottom of the cabinet, my head feeling giddy as he starts kissing up behind my ear. "You could put little photos in, one of Gerry and your mum, and then something of yours here."

"Can I put you in the memory cabinet?" he murmurs, his breath hot against my ear. Then I admit defeat and give up all pretense of trying to keep the house clear-out PG-rated.

It takes us a while, but we finally do get the house empty, the carpet vacuumed, and the last bits and pieces into boxes for either the charity shop or the skip. All that remains to keep, Ted has packed in cases, to either store or drive back to England on the ferry.

"Will you take this back to London with you?" I ask, nodding toward the memory cabinet.

"I guess so," Ted says, a heavy look returning.

The bubble of pleasure we have found in each other has distracted us from the realities of both our situations. The real world was always going to creep back in sooner or later. I have not opened any of the angry emails from work nor answered the work phone. What will I do now—dust off my old contacts from when I was a freelancer, or temp for a while until I can work out a better plan? I don't know what Ted is thinking. He told me he has a review meeting with the hospital in a few weeks, about going back to work. If he doesn't return straightaway, will he even want to be in London? I guess if he stays here for a bit, it's a short flight for me to visit. Do *I* want to be in London now that Vanya is moving out of our flat? If I'm not working at Love Life, do I even need to be there? As my mind dances down all these avenues, I try to rein it in—focus on today. Whatever happens, it won't be impossible for us to keep seeing each other.

"I will keep it with me wherever I am," Ted says with forced jollity. "The perfect way to remember this house, to remember all the life lived here."

Then I think of the story Gerry told me—the birds.

"Can I see the carvings in the beams of the attic?" I ask. Ted looks surprised that I know about this. "Your dad told me about the Ukrainian man who was hidden here during the war."

Ted takes me up to the loft, hands me a torch, and says I need to lie on my back and shuffle backward through to the narrow space behind the water heater. It takes me a while to locate the drawings on the beams, and when I find them, at first, I'm not sure what I'm looking at, but then I make out wings, scratches for feathers, the distinct angle of a beak. Though they are rough, there is a real sense of motion in these drawings—the person who made these longed to take flight.

"Do you know if he survived the war, if he ever got home?" I ask Ted through the wall.

"I'm not sure. I think he survived but I don't know what happened to him. It was my great-grandmother who knew all the details. We should have written it all down while she was alive."

I crawl back out of the small space and sit next to Ted at the top of the stairs.

"You must write down everything you do know about him being here and give the story to whoever buys the house. Some things are too important to be forgotten." I wipe my eyes, which are swimming, suddenly inexplicably emotional about the idea that these birds, and what they meant, might be lost.

"You're right," Ted says somberly, "we must be guardians of stories more significant than our own."

He puts an arm around me. The sound of a car crunching on the gravel rouses us from our moment of reflection. We look at each other—wondering who that could that be. Walking downstairs and through to the porch, we see a cabdriver, the one who brought me back from Maude's party yesterday. He waves my phone out of the driver window.

"I assume this must be yours, love," he calls. "I've been retracing my steps from yesterday to see who might be missing it."

I'd forgotten all about my phone.

"Oh, thank you so much!" I say, running over to retrieve it. I'm amazed any cabdriver would go out of his way like this—perhaps it's only possible when you live on a small island. "That is so kind of you—I must give you some money, let me get my wallet." I start to head to the cottage to find my bag, but he waves me away.

"Just pay it forward," he calls, then clocks my tear-stained face and says with a wink and a wave, "and cheer up, eh, now you've got something to smile about." Then he reverses far too fast back up the drive. Ted and I catch each other's eye and start to laugh, the kind of laugh that once you've started, it's hard to stop. It isn't even that funny, but it might be our first "in joke," and those are the most delicious kind.

Back inside the house, once we've composed ourselves, I plug in my phone.

"Can I take you to my favorite beach now?" Ted asks, but I'm distracted by my phone lighting up with messages. I realize I've enjoyed being out of contact for a while, and I'm not sure I'm quite ready to let the outside world back in.

There are messages from Suki, from other people at work, all trying to track me down yesterday. Then messages from today that Suki has sent to both my phones. We need to talk Laura. Call me ASAP.

"What is it?" Ted asks. "All OK?"

"Everything's fine. I think I might leave the phones here today."

Ted doesn't say anything, but he raises both eyebrows and then reaches to rubs the space beneath his chin, his hand searching for the beard that is no longer there.

Ted and I pack a bag of beach things, and he drives me to Portelet, a cove on the southwest of the island. There are so many beaches here I have yet to explore. Flying in, the island looked so small from the window of the plane, an accidental rock protruding from the endless sea, but now, the more I explore, Jersey's size feels deceptive, like a Tardis.

We walk down some steep steps to get to the beach. A tiny

island, with an old fortification on top, sits in the middle of the picture-perfect bay. Ted tells me it's a Martello tower called Janvrin's tomb.

"Janvrin was a sea captain returning from France in the early eighteenth century," Ted says, as we walk down the last of the steep steps. "He fell ill, then because of plague quarantine restrictions, he wasn't allowed to land in Jersey or see his family. He had to stay out on his ship, where he died a few days later. He was buried on this islet right here—his wife had a tomb erected as a monument of her love and to preserve his memory."

"What a sad story," I say, looking out at the tower.

"It served its purpose, though," Ted says, taking my hand as we walk across the sand, "because I'm telling you the story now, three hundred years on."

"Do you think anyone will remember us in a hundred years, let alone three?" I ask wistfully.

"If you are saying you want me to build you a Martello tower, Laura, I'm not sure I have the skill set," Ted says, leaning in to kiss my shoulder.

"It's never too late to learn a new skill," I reply, leaning my head into his.

We walk down to the water's edge and swim around the islet of Janvrin's tomb, the sun glistening off the dark blue water. Ted's a far stronger swimmer than me, and I claim to need a lift for the last bit, so I can wrap my wet limbs around his warm, broad back. We have pizza on the beach at Portelet Bay Café, a gentle breeze drying our wet hair, and we talk animatedly about nothing of consequence. We don't discuss what this is between us, or our plans for next week or even tomorrow; we just tell silly stories and get lost in the pleasure of each other's company.

"I've missed being this person," says Ted, squeezing my hand as we walk back up the steps toward the car park at the top of the hill.

"What do you mean?" I ask. He stops walking, and we turn to look at the view one last time, the tower on the island, sleek sailing boats edging toward the horizon, a scattering of people on the pebbled shore.

"Some people bring out the parts of yourself you like the most," he says. "I like the version of myself I am when I'm with you."

"I know what you mean. I feel the same, like I don't have to filter myself around you. I'm not sure if this raw version of me even existed before."

"She was always there," says Ted. "You just hadn't met her yet."

When we finally get back to L'Étacq, my hair feels full of salt, my skin is slightly sun-kissed, and my face glows with the feeling of being the version of myself I love the most.

We get out of the car and hold hands as we walk down to the cottage together. I imagine we'll have a shower, then indulge in an afternoon in bed—I think I would be happy if could just relive this day over and over again forever; my own delicious *Groundhog Day*.

Then I notice someone sitting at the patio furniture in the garden. A slim woman with long dark hair and a feline yoga body. She's wearing a floating turquoise dress and has a floral print scarf tied around her hair. She has that effortless, serene beauty about her, as though she meditates every day and never eats chocolate, or if she does, it's only dark chocolate, and then only one square at a time. She's looks up at Ted with familiar eyes.

"Who's this?" I ask quietly, but when I turn to look at him, his face has drained of color, his eyes unblinking.

"Belinda."

Chapter 31

Belinda. Oh no, I thought this was all going a bit too well. It's like those movies where it's all wrapping up nicely, but there's still fifteen minutes to go; you know the bad guy they conked over the head with a saucepan is going to stand up and stab someone at the last minute.

"Hi," says Belinda, giving us both a wave. "Well, aren't you looking well, Ted? Now I can see why." She nods toward me.

"What are you doing here?" Ted asks, still standing motionless in the middle of the lawn.

Belinda gives a delicate shrug, and I notice she has the most amazing shoulder bones. I don't think I've ever even noticed someone's shoulder bones before, but hers are exquisite.

"After what you said on the phone, I wanted to come and

see Gerry. Plus, I figured I could bring the divorce papers in person. Is Gerry not here?" She walks around the patio table, her hips moving in this sultry, hypnotic way.

"He's already gone to Acrebrooke."

"He'll hate it there," says Belinda. "I can't imagine him in a home."

I feel a twinge of jealousy that she knows Ted's family so much better than I do, that she knows what Gerry might or might not like. Ted is still standing frozen, staring at Belinda as though she might be an apparition. She walks over to him and kisses him on each cheek, then extends her hand to me.

"I'm Belinda, you must be the new girl." She smirks knowingly, and I feel myself bristle. She says it as though I'm the new shopgirl, wanting to remind me: *He's known you five minutes, but he loved me for almost a decade.*

"You should have called first," says Ted, clearing his throat.

"I tried. The landline has been cut off." She looks down at her feet, eyelids fluttering. "And I'm afraid I had to erase your mobile number when I left, in case I called in a moment of weakness, Teddy."

Teddy? Ted is not a Teddy. I look at Ted; his eyes are closed. When he opens them, he glances across at me and, maybe I'm imagining it, but I can tell he doesn't want me here for this.

"Shall I be mother and make tea?" Belinda offers, biting her impossibly bee-stung lower lip.

"I should leave you to it," I say, waving a hand between them.

"No," Ted says firmly, "there'll be nothing said you can't hear. I thought we said everything on the phone, Bell?"

He calls her Bell. A whole history no one else will ever

share. Belinda turns her attention to me and gives me a wicked smile.

"She's very young." I feel my skin grow hot and my eyes drop to the ground. She laughs. "I taught him everything he knows, so you can thank me later."

"Bell, stop it." Ted growls.

"Sorry." Belinda sighs and smiles. "You know I'm only teasing." Then she rolls her eyes.

It's too much. I can't be here any longer; I'll cry, and that will make me look like a pathetic little girl next to this confident, formidable woman.

"I'm going to go," I say, turning to walk up the hill.

"Don't," Ted says, his eyes full of pain, but I know me being here will just make this more difficult for him.

"Honestly, it's fine, I need to make some calls anyway. I'll catch up with you later." I attempt my best nonchalant smile, like I find myself in this kind of love triangle every day of the week. Now I come to think of it, I guess I was sort of in a love triangle with Jasper and Ted . . . *Maybe I do find myself in a lot of love triangles*. Despite feeling conflicted, I definitely preferred being the one in the middle. Better to be the one choosing than the person someone chooses between, especially when the competition looks like a combination of Audrey Hepburn and Angelina Jolie.

I pick up both my phones from just inside the porch and then try to stop myself from glancing back at the lawn, but I can't. They're in the middle of the garden hugging; Ted's shoulders are rising and falling as though he might be crying. I shouldn't have turned around; now I feel like my feet have been whisked from beneath me by an undercurrent, and I'm being pulled, powerless, out to sea, away from my Ted-shaped shore. My heart breaks a little for Ted too—he was so lost, not knowing where she'd gone, and now here she is, in his garden, two days after he finally took off his ring.

As soon as I'm far enough away from the house, I furiously blink my eyes, determined not to cry. The light is on in the workshop. As I knock gently on the open door, Ilídio turns off the electric sander he is working with.

"Laura, what's wrong?" he asks, his face full of concern.

"Nothing," I say, shaking my head firmly. "Can I just sit in here for a bit?"

"Of course," he says, putting down his tools and cracking his knuckles. There's something strangely reassuring about the sound. "I'll put the kettle on."

The comfort of a kettle. And then I start thinking that maybe it's quite nice to give your kettle a nickname, especially if you live alone, and maybe Aunt Monica is on to something. I might name my own kettle—Kevin, perhaps. Then I sit, and I make jewelry, and I try not to think about the man of my dreams talking to the woman he loved, only a few hundred yards away.

I'd like to say the jewelry distracts me, that I get into perfect flow again, but I don't; I burn my hand on the soldering iron, and I can't stop staring at my phone, hoping for him to call me, to tell me she has gone.

My phone is full of texts:

Suki: Laura, I want the work phone back. Take a few days of personal time to get your head together, but I will expect you back in the office next Monday. I don't want to lose a perfectly good employee over this nonsense.

Vanya: WHOA, what happened in that interview? Everyone's saying you quit. You are on fire, girl!! Though maybe you absorbed Tiger Woman's roar mantra a little too literally? Hope you're OK, call if I can help. X

Vanya: PS Thought Jasper looked HOT. Is he your Gale or your Peeta?

Jasper: I got two kitchen enquiries off the back of our broadcast! Plus, Suki wants to include Contessa Kitchens in an interiors feature next month. Thank you for the intro. Sorry you didn't think our floorplans were in alignment, all the best. x J

As I'm replying to Vanya, telling her I'm fine, it's complicated, and I'll call her tonight, a text from Ted flashes up,

Ted: Where did you go? I'm taking Bell to see Dad. Back soon, please don't go anywhere.

No kiss. *Don't go anywhere.* Maybe he wants to let me down gently, in person—Ted would be courteous like that. Part of me thinks I should just leave now. Fly home and forget this whole weekend of madness. Except I'm never going to be able to forget Ted, am I? I'm certainly never going to forget last night. Maybe Ted's ruined sex for me now. Like showing someone a film in surround sound from the comfort of a luxurious private cinema, and then telling them they have to watch all future films on their phone, at the back of a bus, with crappy broken headphones.

Maybe I should move back to Bristol, be closer to Gran. Perhaps I should grovel my apologies to Suki and simply go back to work next week. Though I don't think I want to do that. The idea of being freelance again, which terrified me before, now feels strangely exciting. I could still write things I wanted to write for Love Life, but I could also write other, more serious things, for other publications. I could be my own boss again and work from anywhere.

Something needs to change, I know that. At the very least, this weekend has given me a taste for the restorative power of the sea, my need to see the horizon occasionally. I promise myself I will try to get out of the city more at weekends. Maybe Brighton would be a nice place to live?

As my mind races with possibilities, I feel a creeping anxiety about all the new decisions I'm going to have to make once I get home. I turn to the workbench and see a coin on the table. *Maybe I should let fate decide*. Heads, I walk out of here right now, pack up and go home. Tails, I stay. I spin the coin on the work surface, waiting for it to fall, but it comes to a stop on its side; even fate thinks I'm a lost cause.

When Ted eventually returns, I'm sitting on the bed in the cottage.

"You're here," he says, standing in the doorway.

"Did you think I wouldn't be?" I ask, mustering a sad smile.

"Please don't look like that." He comes over to sit beside me and puts an arm around me, pulling my head to his broad shoulder.

"How do I look?"

"Like a sad puppy." Ted presses a palm against my cheek.

"Your wife coming back kind of rained on my parade," I admit, leaning into his hand.

"She's not 'back,' Laura, and she's no longer my wife, she hasn't been for a long time. She only came to serve me with divorce papers and to see Gerry."

"Do you want to divorce her?"

"Laura, trust me, I do."

I turn to look at him and feel a flicker of hope. "Where is she now?" I ask.

"I left her with Dad. She was upset to see he's got so frail."

Reaching up for Ted's hand, I'm unsure of what to say. Ted takes it, his fingers entwining in mine, and with the other, he slowly rubs my back.

"I know we haven't known each other long, Ted, but"—I sigh—"well, someone like Belinda casts an intimidating shadow. She was the love of your life, your dad adores her, she's so beautiful and—"

"And she broke my heart," Ted cuts in. "She left me, without allowing me the chance to even discuss it." He takes my hand in his and pulls it onto his lap. "Besides, I don't believe you only get one chance at love in a lifetime, I hope not anyway."

He pulls my face up to meet his and kisses me tenderly, and I feel how much he wants me to believe him.

"Look, things weren't right in our marriage for a long time before she left. We both changed a lot in our thirties; we both hit this life junction, and we went different ways. When she left, I felt I'd failed her, failed us—but when we spoke on the phone on Saturday"—he pauses, thoughtful for a moment—"I realized I'd been clinging on to an idea, to two people who don't even exist anymore."

"That makes sense," I say quietly, trying to sound mature and understanding.

"But still the sad face," he says, needling his chin into my shoulder.

"I'm just—I've never felt like this before and I'm jealous that you have."

"I've never felt like this either," says Ted, turning to hold me by both shoulders. "How could it be the same? Laura, from the moment you got into my cab and shouted at me, I've done nothing but think about you." I cringe at the memory, but smile despite myself. "Like it or not, you do make the world a prettier place for me, and when we started talking in the car, well—it was kablammo central for me."

I smile up at him because he's saying all the right things.

"I think for me, it was when I saw you coming out of the sea in your wet clothes."

"Oh, so you're just after my body rather than my sparkling conversation, are you?"

"Am I allowed to say I enjoy both?"

And then he kisses me again and I don't have any more doubts.

Chapter 32

The next morning, I wake to find an empty space in the bed next to me. I walk up to the main house, wearing one of Ted's shirts as a nightgown, hugging it around myself against the cool wind coming up from the sea. I assume Ted must be doing a last bit of cleaning in the house. The skip is being collected this morning, and then he's handing the keys over to the estate agents this afternoon.

There's a smell of fresh coffee coming from the kitchen, and I find Ted in the living room, looking at the memory cabinet, which he's hung on the wall. I move to stand next to him, and he puts an arm around me, then notices I'm wearing his shirt.

"Do you ever wear your own clothes, Laura?" he asks, a teasing smile on his lips.

"Not if I can help it," I say, resting my head on his shoulder. "You hung it up."

"I wanted to see what it looked like. It fits perfectly here." He points out what he's put into each compartment: his mother's scent bag, the hair slide Gerry picked out as one of the memories he had of his own mother, a piece of sea glass, a snuffbox his grandfather James brought back from the war, and even an old collar tag with Scamp's predecessor's name on it.

"I didn't know what to put in for Dad. I thought maybe his old guitar pick—something to symbolize all the things he used to take joy in under this roof." He opens one of the small doors in the cabinet, and there's a miniature gin bottle inside.

I look sideways at Ted and realize he's Benjamin Buttoned on me again; I swear with his bright eyes and his bed-ruffled hair, he's verging on early thirties now. Just looking at him makes my stomach drop. My body feels like a sunflower, drawn toward the sun.

"Perfect. I'm glad you like it," I say, wrapping an arm around his waist.

"Knock knock," comes a voice from behind us, and we turn to see Belinda standing in the porch, her hair cascading over her ridiculously attractive shoulders. She's wearing a silk tiger-print kaftan over jeans so skinny they could be chopstick holders. My balloon of happiness instantly turns into a bowling ball and hits the ground with a thud.

"I thought you'd left?" I find myself saying, trying to pull Ted's shirt down to cover my luminous white thighs.

"Grrrr," says Belinda, making cat paws with her hands, "you're jealous, that's good, it means you like him."

I have never felt such a strong desire to wrestle another woman to the floor and strangle her with her own ridiculously expensive-looking kaftan.

"Bell, don't," Ted says, taking a step toward her.

"It's OK, I'm on my way to the airport, I've done what I needed to do here." Belinda looks serious for a moment. "I'm pleased I got to see Gerry, and I'm sorry I didn't come sooner. I won't leave it so long next time."

What, she's coming back? She disappears for years, not a trace, and now she's planning her next visit like some tanned, toned specter. She's going to be like that scary girl in *The Ring*, showing up whenever I'm half naked, just to show me how much browner her legs are than mine. The disappointment must show on my face, because Belinda turns to me with a sharp smile.

"Don't worry, little bear, I won't be getting in your way."

"Why are you calling me little bear?" I ask, giving her my best Paddington Bear stare.

Belinda gives me a cryptic smile. "It's your inner animal."

"My what?" I ask. She sounds as though she's quoting *Tiger Woman.*

"Laura, don't engage with this—" Ted starts to say, but I bat him away with a wave of my hand.

"No, I want to know."

"Well," says Belinda, inviting herself in and pacing around the empty room, "I am a tiger, Ted here is a bear, as are you, so you see you two are far better suited; your auras match. You'll enjoy doing beary things together."

"I'm not a bear," I say, through narrowed eyes. "If it's my

'inner animal,' I get to choose, and I don't want to be a bear. I've read *Tiger Woman* too, you know."

"You've read it?" Belinda looks pleased and steps toward me, peering into my eyes as though trying to find something inside. "Well, don't go changing, Ted doesn't need another tiger in his life."

"I am not a bloody bear, OK," I explode. Something about her tone has pressed all my buttons, her territorial pacing around the room, as though she's about to spray the house with her musk. "You don't get to say what animal I am."

"Whoa," says Ted, stepping between us. "OK, let's just take the animal aura conversation down a notch. Belinda, what did you want to say—before you go." He pauses, looking at her pleadingly. "And I do think you need to go."

Belinda waves a hand between us.

"I like that she has fire in her belly." Belinda gives me a smug smile. "And that she's read my book."

"Wait. Your book?" I say after a beat. "You wrote *Tiger Woman*?"

"What's *Tiger Woman*?" Ted asks, looking between us in confusion.

"Only the bestselling self-help book of the year," I say, unable to hide my amazement.

"We don't use the term 'self-help,'" says Belinda, wincing, "but thank you. We'd describe it as a memoir, of a woman throwing off the reins of the patriarchy, of societal oppression and expectation. It's about reclaiming your base nature, finding your inner Tigress."

Ted's face is screwed into a knot of confusion.

"What?" he says.

"You're a bear, you wouldn't understand. Anyway, the long and short of it is, until all this paperwork is filed, we're still married." She pulls a wad of papers from her bag. "So technically some of my tiger riches will come to you."

"I don't understand," Ted says, looking between us both.

"This book has sold like a billion copies," I explain to Ted, feeling my eyes bulging from their sockets.

"I have two more book deals in the pipeline: *Tiger Woman Eats* and *Tiger Woman Sleeps*." Belinda gives a little yawn, then turns to Ted with a more serious expression. "I would like to pay for Gerry's care. He is family to me." She pauses, serious for a moment, talking only to Ted. "Look, I know I hurt you, and I'm sorry. I'll never forget what we once were to each other, but my path is now a solo one. I didn't know how to extract myself from us, except by cutting the thread." She looks guilty for a moment, her gaze dropping to the floor. "I was selfish—thinking what would be easiest for me."

"I was worried when you disappeared," Ted says, his voice firm and controlled. "But I don't need you to come in and fix anything. I can look after my own father."

"I know, and I know I have amends to make, but— He's so upset about you selling this house because of him, Ted. Please let me help."

Ted sighs, and Belinda goes on, "Just have my half of the London house, if you'd rather do it that way; you put down the initial deposit, so it's only fair. However we work it out, don't sell Sans Ennui, please."

"Fine, I'll keep the house." Ted gives a short, sharp nod. "Congratulations on your book success." He smiles briefly at Belinda then turns back to me.

Belinda claps her hands. “I think this is a group hug moment,” she says, reaching out her arms to me. I definitely do not think this a group hug moment—I’m skeptical of group hugs at the best of times—but before I can stop her, she embraces me with her long, lean, tigery arms.

Chapter 33

Dad's box sits unopened on the floor of the cottage for several days. I don't get to it because I am too busy exploring the island, spending time with Ted, and meeting the rest of my Jersey family. My great-uncle Graham and his children are warm and welcoming, and interested in me—everything I could have hoped they would be.

It is not until Thursday morning, when I am due to leave that afternoon, that I finally get round to opening the box. I owe it to my dad to at least look through some of the paltry remains of his life on this earth. Helping Ted with the house, sorting through my mother's things, it's made me wonder what I want the world to remember me by. It might be morbid to think about death, but losing both my parents has made me conscious of how short life can be; it's made me think about what kind of legacy I'd like to leave.

Then again, maybe Gerry is right; there's no point worrying what the future holds or looking back on the past. Today I am happy. Today I feel lucky. Today the world is a good place to be. Maybe the only real legacy any of us can hope to leave is to be a link in the chain that keeps love flowing through the generations.

I take a photo of everything in the box. I'll hold on to the letters Mum wrote, but there is nothing else here I want to keep. At the very bottom of the box, I find a padded envelope hidden between two crime novels. Inside the envelope are two cassettes. They are mixtapes, identical, and written on the spine of each tape case, in Dad's handwriting, is "The Soundtrack to Your Life." There are some great song choices, and even two Phil Collins tracks. I smile—maybe Dad really did love Phil Collins after all.

Underneath the tapes is a card.

Dear Laura,

Welcome to the Soundtrack to Your Life! I'm going to record a mixtape for every one of your birthdays from now on. I'll send one to your mum for you to listen to and keep a copy, so you'll have a complete collection when you're eighteen. When you're old enough to appreciate it, you can sit back and listen to your life as I heard it. I might not see you as much as I'd like, little one, but I'll be damned if you grow up having shit taste in music. This is the first tape—twenty of the best songs from around the time you were born. Songs that make me think of you, songs me and your mum listened to the summer we met. Can't wait to see you when I'm back from Morocco, precious girl.

All my love, Dad

He never sent it. He made the tapes, wrote the letter, but he hadn't addressed the envelope. I know I shouldn't need this proof. I know now that love can't be measured in objects or shared tastes, but, reading his words addressed to me, seeing the songs he chose—"Another Day in Paradise," "That's Just the Way It Is"—it's like he knew exactly what I needed to hear: the epilogue to my parents' story. I hug the tapes to my chest.

Sandy is hosting a goodbye lunch for me in her garden before Ted takes me to the airport. I've been in Jersey a whole week now, yet it feels as though I've been here for months. Perhaps Jersey is like Narnia in *The Lion, the Witch and the Wardrobe* and I've been here for years, but in London time, only a few minutes have passed.

Ted has brought Gerry to join us for lunch, and he's full of stories about some of the other residents in his assisted living community.

"There are a group of women who call themselves the Miss Marple Club," he says, shaking his head. "They watch murder mysteries together every Tuesday, stopping them before the end, and then placing bets on who they think the murderer is. They've all seen the episodes a hundred times, but they forget who did it, so the game never gets old." Gerry lets out a cackle.

"So, you're making friends then?" says Ted, hugging a cup of tea between his hands. He's let his stubble grow back over the last few days, and truth be told, I sometimes miss the beard.

"It's like the first day at school again, except no one can remember anyone's name, least of all their own," Gerry says.

"Oh, Gerry, stop—he's exaggerating," says Sandy, rolling her eyes.

"You wouldn't rather have a carer at home then, now that money's not so tight?" Ted asks.

"No," Gerry says, picking up a mug and moving it, shakily, toward his lips. "I'm happy enough where I am; the food is great and I like having people around me again. Plus, it's nice to see this house full of you young people." Gerry looks across at me. "I hope you'll be back, Laura, that we haven't scared you off with our island ways."

"Oh, she'll be back," says Ted, reaching across to put a hand on my arm.

In the last few days, we haven't really talked about the future, and I haven't wanted to ask. Ted took the house off the market; I spent time in the workshop making jewelry. We swam in the sea, and I explored more of the island. I even made a bean crock for Ted, Ilídio, and Sandy following Maude's recipe.

Ted is taking the ferry back to England next week. He has a meeting with the hospital about resuming work. He also got a call about an offer on the house in London; he's closing books, opening new ones. I don't know where our story goes from here, but I know that even if we only had this one week, I would not do anything differently.

"What about you, Laura?" Sandy asks. "What are you

going to do when you get back to London? Are you tempted to make peace with your boss?"

I shake my head. I've already spoken to Suki. She was remarkably open-minded about discussing my role going forward. Something about her feels different, but I couldn't put my finger on what.

"I've said I want to go freelance, choose the articles I feel passionate about, maybe free up some time for jewelry making. I know I don't want to do the *How Did You Meet?* segment anymore. I've had enough of chasing other people's love stories."

Ted squeezes my shoulder.

"I'm sure you'll find a way to find passion in your work again," says Ilídio, giving me a wink.

As we're talking, a green car covered in hedgehog stickers pulls into the drive at Sans Ennui.

"We caught you—you haven't left yet!" Monica calls, as she climbs out of the driver's side. I see Sue sitting in the passenger seat and I jump over the wall to meet them.

"You didn't need to come and see me off," I say.

Sue opens the passenger door, and I help her out.

"Have you got it?" Sue asks Monica, who hurries around the car holding a small wooden box. She hands it to Sue, who presses it into my hands.

"We wanted you to have this," she says, nodding her head toward the box. "Our father's tools—his engraving kit. When you said you made jewelry, well, we thought it would be nice for them to be used again. They've sat unloved in this box for eighty years."

I open the lid to find a set of wooden and steel tools: pushers, burnishers, and gravers, all perfectly preserved.

"Are you sure?" I ask. "They look too precious to use."

"They're tools, they were made to be used."

"Thank you, thank you both," I say, wrapping an arm around each of them. Then I pull back, remembering I have something to tell them: "I found something, in Dad's box—a letter he wrote to me, a mixtape he made. He was planning to make me one every year."

"That sounds like him," says Sue, nodding slowly.

"And the coin," I say. "He did mean for me to have it. Gran said he sent his half to me. He wanted both parts to stay together."

Sue reaches out to find my hands. I take them, and she squeezes my fingers gently. It's as though she's telling me she doesn't need to be convinced.

"It is your coin, Laura." Then she pauses, closing her eyes. "But don't hold on to these things too tightly. Objects only hold the meanings we give them."

There is a pained look on Sue's face—regret, remorse? I move our hands gently up and down together, an acknowledgment that I know what she is trying to say.

At the airport, Ted parks the cab and walks me into Departures. He's not taking the boat back for a few more days.

"So, I'll see you in London then," he says, pulling me into a tight hug.

"I hope so," I say, taking a last inhale, savoring the smell and feel of his neck.

Pulling back to look at each other, we both grin. I don't want to leave yet, to walk into the cold—anywhere without the warmth of his gaze.

"I didn't pay you," I say with a gasp, remembering the fare we agreed last week.

Ted laughs.

"I think I can let it slide."

"No, I want to pay you," I say, feeling it as a point of principle.

"You can buy me dinner in London," he says, reaching out to take my fingers in his.

"What about your tip?" I watch his face, trying to memorize every inch of it. "I always tip my cabdrivers."

He raises his eyebrows, a mischievous smile playing on his lips. Then, I remember my grandmother's words—*don't hold on too tight*—and before I can overthink it, I take the coin from around my neck, unclip half from the pendant, and give one piece of the shiny ha'penny to Ted. He takes it but looks at me with eyes that say *I can't, it's too much.*

I close his hand around it.

"You can give it back to me when I see you; just hold on to it, for now, keep it safe." Before he can object, I kiss him on the cheek, then turn and head toward security.

"Laura!" he calls after me, and I swing back around. "Don't go picking up another man's luggage anytime soon, will you?"

"I'll try not to," I say, with a wink, and then, swinging my hair as though I'm in a shampoo commercial, I stride off toward the departure gate. Reaching a hand up to my pendant, I feel the empty space; where once there was a whole, there is now only a crescent of coin. I am leaving the island lighter than I came, in so many ways.

LAURA LE QUESNE'S GUIDE TO JERSEY BEACHES AND BAYS

1. Best Bay to kick off your shoes—Bouley
2. Best Bay to hunt for sea glass—Rozel
3. Best Beach to dance beneath the stars—Plémont
4. Best Beach to spot Henry Cavill naked—Grève de Lecq
5. Best Beach to drink too much sangria or eat lobster by the shore—L'Étacq
6. Best Bay to see the beautiful bioluminescence—La Rocque Harbor
7. Best Beach to have a paddle-boarding date—St. Brelade's
8. Best Beach you'll only know about if you're local—Beauport
9. Best Beach for pizza and PDAs on the sand—Portelet
10. Best Beach for gazing at the horizon and resetting your soul—St. Ouen's

Epilogue

FIFTEEN MONTHS LATER

"Thank you so much for agreeing to do this, Laura," says Suki. "It only seemed fitting that it would be you who interviews us. You were always best at these things."

She squeezes Jasper's arm and looks up at him like a wide-eyed schoolgirl.

"Well, what's one more for old times' sake?" I say with a smile. "It's good to see you both. How is your family, Jasper?"

"They're so excited about the wedding. We're having the reception at my mother's house," says Jasper. "My sisters are all terrified of Suki, which is just the way I like it. None of them dare boss me about when she's around, ha-ha."

He leans down to kiss her, and she sinks into his arms—I

still can't get my head around the change in Suki this last year; it's as though Jasper's adoration has smoothed away some of her hard edges. I have to avert my gaze as the kiss carries on an awkward amount of time.

"And how's Ted?" Jasper asks, finally freeing his lips to talk. "Suki said you were moving to Jersey full-time? Do you need a new kitchen in that old house you're going to live in?"

"I think we're good for kitchens. But yes, Ted finally got a job at the Jersey hospital, and since I can work anywhere, we'll be living there permanently now."

"Are you still writing?" Suki asks. "I haven't had a pitch from you in a while. You'd better not be offering your ideas elsewhere before coming to me first?" I hear the familiar edge in her voice.

"Well, I'm writing less and less these days," I explain. "The jewelry design is taking up so much of my time."

"We looked at your website! I'm so impressed, Laura," says Jasper.

"I saw that Bee Bee Graceful wore one of your quaint necklaces to the book launch where she revealed her true identity. I'm sure that didn't do you any harm PR-wise," Suki says, her eyes challenging me for a reaction. "Not that your designs aren't charming, but I'm sure it helps to have a global influencer on your side."

"Well, yes, that certainly helped raise my profile." Suki still hasn't forgiven me for leaving. She pretends to play nice, especially since she credits me for introducing her to Jasper, but a little backhanded insult can usually be found in there somewhere. "Right, shall we get this on tape then?"

Jasper and Suki take seats on the red studio sofa. Avril, the camerawoman, has the lighting and the sound all set up. I perch on a stool out of shot and notice how strange it feels to be doing one of these interviews again, with these two, of all people.

"So," I say in my best presenter voice, "Suki and Jasper, tell our Love Life subscribers, how did you meet?"

"Well, it all began when one of my best journalists, who shall remain nameless, ha-ha, went to Jersey to research a story, and she picked up the wrong suitcase at the airport . . ." Suki begins.

The interview goes well. Suki does ninety percent of the talking, but it is clear how besotted Jasper is, he can't take his eyes off her.

When he is finally allowed a chance to speak, he says, "The funny thing is, Suki is not my usual type at all. I usually go for blondes, and she's got black hair; she's city, I'm country; she hates boats, I live on them; I'm a foodie, and she doesn't seem to eat anything. She can't abide the kind of music I like, but well, something about it just works—all I want to do is make her happy. Love works in mysterious ways sometimes, doesn't it?"

"It does. Congratulations on your engagement," I say. "Can you tell us about the proposal?"

"Well, Jasper sent me a text, asking if I could get him a drink from the fridge in the Emmeline kitchen—which you can see if you swipe up from this interview. It's one of his best sellers; anyway, I trot along and open the door, and Jasper has taken all the shelves out and is sitting in there with a ring."

I can't help laughing at this. They hadn't told me that detail when they asked me to do this interview.

"Of course, I fainted clean away. It was so terrifying finding a body in the fridge, so he only got to propose properly once the paramedics arrived and I was sufficiently conscious."

"It was a bit of a botched job, I'll admit," says Jasper, "Though it does go to show how exceptionally spacious Furlong Fridges are—I put them in all the Contessa Kitchens. Luckily, despite scaring her half to death, Suki still said yes. We'll have to split our time between London and Jersey, but we'll make it work." Jasper leans over to kiss Suki's head, then rolls up his sleeve to reveal a small "Suki" tattoo written in italic on his forearm. "I never thought I'd be the type of person to get a tattoo."

"I've got one too," says Suki, "but I won't show you where."

And then they start tickling each other, giggling and whispering in a way that makes Avril and me feel we'd both like freakishly large fridges to climb into.

Once we've wrapped filming, I have to run; I'm meeting Ted for dinner after his shift at the hospital.

"Laura, are you sure I can't persuade you and Ted to do an interview for us?" Suki asks. "Your story is *almost* as good as ours, and it's always good to have friends of the Love Life family doing their bit to support the brand."

"No, I don't think so, Suki. We're—" I try to think of a tactful way to say that we don't want to share our story with anyone else. "We're trying to keep things low-key."

"Fine." Suki sighs. "Well, I'll give you the nod at our wedding to make sure you catch the bouquet. Oh, and Henry Cavill is coming too, so if you want an upgrade on Ted, let me know and I'll sort out the seating plan."

We say our good-byes, and I run to the train to take me down to Chelsea and Westminster.

The Fulham Road is damp from an earlier rain shower, the pavement busy—people queue for buses, pull their coats around them, and hurry off to wherever they are going. The streetlights have just come on in the early evening light, and there is an amber glow in the air. After waiting outside the front of the hospital for five minutes, I see Ted come out through the doors, looking left and right a few times before he clocks me. I don't call out to him. Sometimes, I love just watching the way he is in the world; I savor this stolen moment to take him in before he sees me. He's grown his beard back, at my request, but it's short now, well groomed, and I love it, my Beardy McCastaway.

He sees me and tilts his head, shrugging as though to ask why I didn't call out his name.

"All right, Lady Muck?" he says.

"How was it? Your last day."

But he doesn't answer, he just picks me up off the ground, folds me in his arms, and kisses me as though it were the first time. It's his I-don't-care-who's-watching kiss, and it floors me every time.

"What was I saying?" I ask, light-headed, when he finally puts me down.

"You asked about my day." He smiles. "It was fine, emotional, but I'll stay in touch with everyone, I hope. How did the interview go with Suki and Jasper?"

"Bizarre," I say. "I still can't get my head around those two together. Nothing about them as a couple makes any sense, but then you see the way they look at each other and—"

"Kablammo?"

"Well, yes. Vanya says Suki's completely changed; she even lets people work remotely now, mainly because she's in Jersey half the time herself. Oh, before I forget—Dee rang. She, Neil, and baby Isaac are all going to come and stay next weekend, Vanya too, so they'll all be there for the exhibition launch. We might put Vanya in the house and the others in the cottage—apparently Isaac's a terrible sleeper and is up half the night with colic."

"If we ever have a baby, Laura, you do know we won't be able to relegate it to sleeping in the cottage?"

"Yes, I know, but we'll cross that sleep-deprived bridge when we come to it, shall we? Dee won't mind, she loves it there; it's cozy."

~~Jasper~~ Ted pauses, unzipping his backpack to retrieve his copper bracelet from an inner pocket, then he fastens it back onto his wrist. He's not allowed to wear jewelry on shift, but otherwise, he wears it all the time. I made it for him; it's a plain copper band with his half of the coin embedded in the front.

"I've got so much to organize before the jewelry exhibition next weekend. It might have been ambitious to think we could move everything out of my flat, get all our things over on the ferry, and plan the launch of my first official collection, all in the same week," I say, hugging his arm tight into mine as we walk along the damp pavement.

"Well, Ilídio's made all the display cabinets already, and Sandy's invited half the island to the opening. It will be fine, don't worry," says Ted.

"Do you think Gerry will be able to make it?" I ask,

turning to see Ted's face in the streetlight. He pulls my hand up to his lips and kisses it.

"He'll be there, Laura. We'll all be there for you."

And I know, as I have for a while now, that this man will be there for me, as long as I want him to be, as I will be there for him.

I have no illusions about happily ever afters—I know life will bring its challenges and nothing is forever—but I hope we might be happy today, and for as many todays as we are lucky enough to have.

Acknowledgments

Do you read the acknowledgments at the end of a book? You do? Yay, me too. I know, some people like to get a little glimpse of what goes on beneath the bonnet of a book, so here is a little peek into the people and places who helped get Laura's story on the road.

Firstly, the person who always points me in the right direction, my steering wheel, my agent and friend, Clare Wallace. Thank you for your sound advice and your patient ear. Secondly, the wheels of the book, without whom this story wouldn't have gone anywhere—the fabulous teams at Arrow and Putnam—Sonny Marr, Kate Dresser, and Tricja Okuniewska, who all helped craft various drafts of this story. Amelia Evans, who took the rights to the US. I have included a list of publishing credits over the page so I can thank every single member of US Team *Just Haven't Met You Yet*.

My husband, Tim, I'm going to say you're the heated seat in this car analogy, supporting me all the way. Thank you for always filling our car with petrol, literally and metaphorically—you are a hero. Traci O'Dea, my friend and fellow writer, I think you were my GPS system on this one. I always value your perceptive and intelligent criticism. If you are interested in poetry, look Traci up, she's enormously talented.

The body of the car—the story itself—was born from so many things, but for his part, I must thank Andrew Garton, who talked to me about his experience of living with Parkinson's. Gerry is not Andrew, but I would never have written a character like Gerry if I had not met Andrew—I'm not sure I would have believed such sanguine wisdom existed. Andrew is a cabinet maker, and I wrote this element into the story after being lucky enough to see inside his workshop. Andrew, I hope I have managed to convey a little of your life philosophy in these pages.

Also making up the body of the car; the island of Jersey. I moved here seven years ago and have fallen in love with the history, the beaches, and the people who I now call my friends. It feels such a responsibility to set a book in the place where you live, to do a place justice, which of course, my words cannot, but I hope Islanders will see the Jersey they know in these pages. If you didn't know much about the Channel Islands before, I hope this story might inspire you to learn more or even come and visit.

My friends and family, my in-car entertainment—keeping me sane and singing as I drive along. I miss seeing you all more often. My invaluable support network of writer friends, Debut20, 2020Debuts, and The Savvy's.

Finally, and most important, you, my readers, my passengers in the car. I hope you enjoyed going on this journey. Writing this, I often worried who on earth was going to appreciate my weird sense of humor, who would want to read a book about flying tampons, Phil Collins, and coat alcoves, all washed down with the serious themes of memory and loss. Hopefully, if you've read this far, you might be that person. If you did enjoy this, please do consider leaving a review online. It makes such a huge difference to authors and helps others to discover my books, which in turn helps me write more books! A special shout out to my biggest US fan, Doris Biddix, who I think recommended *This Time Next Year* to everyone in North Carolina. Thanks for the support, Doris!

I *love* hearing from readers on social media, so do get in touch:

Instagram: @sophie_cousens

Twitter: @sophiecous

Facebook: @sophiecousensauthor

If you would like to stay up to date with my latest news, find out what I'm reading, access bonus content, and see photos of some of the *real* locations featured in this book, you can also check out my website and subscribe to my newsletter at www.sophiecousens.com.

I will sign off hoping that you, dear reader, have a spirit level for your soul—be it a person, a place, or simply a cup of tea and a good book.

Publishing Credits

PUTNAM/US TEAM

Kate Dresser—Editor
Nishtha Patel—Marketer
Kristen Bianco—Publicist
Tricja Okuniewska—Assistant editor
Sydney Cohen—Associate publicist
Sanny Chiu—Jacket designer
Monica Cordova—Art director
Sally Kim—Publisher
Ashley McClay—Marketing director
Alexis Welby—Publicity director
Meredith Dros—Managing editor
Maija Baldauf—Associate managing editor
Hannah Dragone—Production manager
Erica Rose—Production editor
Tiffany Estreicher—Interior designer

Just Haven't Met You Yet

SOPHIE COUSENS

Discussion Questions

Jersey Wonders Recipe

PUTNAM
— EST. 1838 —

Discussion Questions

1. The heroine of *Just Haven't Met You Yet*, Laura, is a journalist specializing in all things love. What do we know about her love life? How does her job inform her outlook on life?

2. We learn early on that Laura is very attached to her parents' epic romance. How did her parents meet, and how does their love story dictate what Laura wants in her own life? Why does she decide to write an article about them?

3. When Laura accidentally picks up the wrong suitcase at Jersey airport, she is convinced that she has found her soulmate. What would you do with the suitcase if you were in Laura's shoes? What items would convince you you'd found your soulmate?

4. Though Laura enjoys certain elements of her job as a journalist, she doesn't find real fulfillment in it. What is her true calling, and how does she come to realize that?

5. Ted, the cabdriver who ferries Laura around Jersey for her article, has a complicated romantic past himself. What were your first impressions of Ted, and what do we come to learn about his gruff demeanor?

6. The majority of *Just Haven't Met You Yet* takes place in Jersey, which is part of the Channel Islands in the UK. Why is it a special place for Laura, and what were your first impressions of it? How does the sense of community play into the story?

7. This novel is full of wonderful and vivid secondary characters, including Laura's family, friends, and the residents of Jersey. Who were some of your favorites, and why?

8. There are excerpts of *Tiger Woman* and the *Jersey Evening News* interspersed throughout the novel. How did these elements play into your understanding of the story? What did you make of the ways in which these texts came together, and what surprised you?

9. Discuss the differences between Jasper and Ted. How does Laura grapple with those differences throughout the book? Why does she make the choice she does?

10. How important is the theme of memory in the novel? Laura's mother believes objects can be conduits for memory. Does Laura believe this too? How does her emotional investment in objects change as the story goes on?

11. What do you think is in store for Laura and the life she pursues at the end of the book?

Jersey Wonders (Des Mèrvelles)

Makes: 40 wonders

Preparation time: 2 hours 45 minutes
(including 2 hours resting time)

6 cups self-rising flour

1 stick (4 oz.) cold, unsalted butter, cut into 8 pieces

1 cup superfine sugar

A pinch of nutmeg (optional)

6 medium eggs

Vegetable oil, for frying

Sift the flour into a large bowl and rub in the butter until the mixture resembles bread crumbs. Add the sugar (and nutmeg if you are including it).

Whisk the eggs and add to the mixture. Begin stirring with a wooden spoon, but as it comes together, use your hands to form a light dough.

Turn the dough onto a floured surface and briefly knead until smooth; this will take less than 5 minutes.

Lightly dust a tray with flour. Using floured hands, form the dough into golf ball–sized shapes. Place these on the tray, cover with a damp cloth, and let rest for 2 hours.

Roll each of the balls into a 2 by 4-inch oblong. With a sharp knife, slit the center of each oblong and twist the top end through the slit. (You can google "Mèrvelles, Jersey wonders" to see some examples of how they should look. There is debate from parish to parish on how to tie these "knots" of dough, and the technique varies across the island.)

Jersey wonders are deep-fried. Fill a deep frying pan with enough oil (at least 2 inches) to cover the dough. Heat the oil over a high heat (375F/190C). You'll know the oil is hot enough when a cube of bread dropped into the oil turns golden brown within 10 seconds.

Line a baking sheet with kitchen paper or paper towels. Working in batches, drop four to six wonders at a time into the oil. Cook for 2 minutes, then, using a metal spoon or fry ladle, carefully turn the wonders and fry for an additional 2 minutes, until golden brown.

Transfer the wonders to the baking sheet to drain. Let cool for several minutes so you don't burn your tongue! Share with friends and family.

Leftovers can be stored in an airtight container for up to 2 weeks.

NOTES

Traditionally, Jersey households would cook the wonders as the tide went out—because, so the story goes, cooking them on an incoming tide would result in fat overflowing from the pan. You can check the tides near you at www.tide-forecast.com.

As a rule, wonders should be served plain and never be eaten with icing sugar or dipped in jam or custard. But then again, rules are there to be broken!

About the Author

Photo by Max Burnett

Sophie Cousens worked as a TV producer in London for more than twelve years and now lives with her family on the island of Jersey, one of the Channel Islands, located off the north coast of France. She balances her writing career with taking care of her two small children, and longs for the day when she might have a dachshund and a writing shed. She is also the author of *This Time Next Year*, which was an instant *New York Times* bestseller.

VISIT SOPHIE COUSENS ONLINE

SophieCous
sophie_cousens
sophiecousensauthor
Sophiecousens.com